SISTER STEW

Fiction and Poetry by Women

Edited by Juliet S. Kono and Cathy Song

Bamboo Ridge Press

1991

This is a special double issue of Bamboo Ridge, The Hawaii Writers' Quarterly, No. 50 and 51, Spring and Summer 1991, ISSN 0733-0308.
ISBN 0-910043-22-1.
Copyright 1991 Bamboo Ridge Press
Indexed in the American Humanities Index
Indexed in the American Index of Periodical Verse
Published by Bamboo Ridge Press
Cover Art: "Meanwhile" by Mary Mitsuda   (Acrylic on paper. 40″ H x 60″ W)
Book Design: Suzanne Yuu
Typesetting: Gail N. Harada
"The Olomatua" by Epi Fuaau was first printed in *Pacific Island Voices*, No. 2, Summer 1990.
Grateful acknowledgement is made to Leona Yamada for the title "Sister Stew."

Bamboo Ridge, The Hawaii Writers' Quarterly is supported in part by grants from the State Foundation on Culture and the Arts (SFCA). The SFCA is funded by appropriations from the Hawaii State Legislature and by grants from the National Endowment for the Arts. This issue is also supported in part by a grant from the National Endowment for the Arts (NEA), a federal agency.
Bamboo Ridge Press is a member of the Coordinating Council of Literary Publishers.

Bamboo Ridge Press
P.O. Box 61781
Honolulu, Hawaii 96839-1781

Library of Congress Cataloging-in-Publication Data

Sister Stew: fiction and poetry by women / [edited by] Cathy Song and Juliet S. Kono.
    p. cm.
    ISBN 0-910043-22-1
    1. American Literature—Hawaii.   2. Women—Hawaii—Literary collections.   3. American literature—Women authors.   4. American literature—20th Century.   I. Song, Cathy, 1955- • II. Kono, Juliet S., 1943- •
PS571.H3B4   1991
810.9'9287—dc20   91-11471
                                                                   CIP

2   3   4   5   6   7   8   9   10
1992   1993   1994   1995   1996

CONTENTS

7	INTRODUCTION	
8	MARIE HARA	*You in There*
15	MAHEALANI KAMAUU	*What I Wanted to Say to My Mother*
		Little Runaway
18	DIANE KAHANU	*When I Was Young on an Island*
20	FAYE KICKNOSWAY	*Mother*
		Untitled
26	LOIS-ANN YAMANAKA	*Parts*
34	T. M. GOTO	*Bone White Moon*
		Miranda Cries, Father's Raping Me and
		Blaming It on Caliban
36	MIYOKO SUGANO	*Otosan*
38	JOAN PERKINS	*Bros*
39	CHERYLENE LEE	*The Hardest Move*
50	LYNN KUHNS	*It's Over on the Back Porch*
52	AUDREY FORCIER	*Dreamsong*
53	PRISCILLA ATKINS	*The Amish Girl*
54	FUKU YOKOYAMA TSUKIYAMA	*A Cup of Flan*
63	M. SUZUKI	*Childhood*
		To Move Your Organs
		Connections
		Who She Was
68	HOLLY YAMADA	*B-League Playoff*
76	TAMARA WONG-MORRISON	*Middle Road*
78	NORMA WUNDERLICH GORST	*Christmas Eve, Hawaii*
		White Ducks
		Point of Entry
		Warner Avenue Shop
		6190 Grayton Road
		Lute Player
87	STELLA JENG GUILLORY	*Father Assumes His Squatting Position*
		In the Hotel Room in Hong Kong
91	LISA ERB	*At the Grave of My Mother's Mother*
		White Eclipse
93	CHIN YUNG	*Citrus*

95	LORNA HERSHINOW	*Letting Go*
105	NELL ALTIZER	*Pearl*
		Pantoum
		Runes for the Stepmother
		The Churching of Women
112	MARY LOMBARD	*Breakfast Time*
119	SUSAN BARNETT	*Mary's Special Child*
		Pagoda
121	JUDITH VATES	*Two Seasons and a Japanese Lover In New York City*
123	ADRIENNE TIEN	*Mo Gui Body*
131	AMY UYEMATSU	*lexicon*
		Deliberate
134	JESSICA HAGEDORN	*Nostalgia for the Mud*
137	SUSAN LEE ST. JOHN	*Angie and the Cessna*
144	JILL WIDNER	*In Transit*
		Glassing the Horizon
		Geographers
158	LYN WALTERS BUCKLEY	*The Wooden Studio*
183	SUE COWING	*Barbara*
		A Letter from Worpswede
		Young Girl with Flower Vases
		To Clara Rilke-Westhoff
		My Breathing
194	GLORIA OLCHOWY ROZEBOOM	*Whiteness Visible*
210	MAVIS HARA	*Carnival Queen*
225	CRISTINA BACCHILEGA	*Bonsai*
226	SUE LIN CHONG	*Small Endearments*
242	DARLAINE MAHEALANI MUILAN DUDOIT	*Silk Dragons*
		A Portrait of Willy
245	H. MCMANIMIE	*Bituen*
247	MARJORIE SINCLAIR	*Lava Watch*
255	LORETTA PETRIE	*Cross-stitched*
256	EPI ENARI FUAAU	*The 'Olomatua*

264	LEONA YAMADA	*Chicken Feet, Sister Stew*
		Mall
269	PERLE BESSERMAN	*The Last Good Witch in New York*
288	MARI KUBO	*Winter 1989*
		The Cross
296	SHEILA GARDINER	*Changes of Being*
		Play It with Pathos, Ruby
299	SUSAN NUNES	*The Science of Symmetry–A Love Story*
309	LEE KYSELKA	*Secrets*
		His Eye Is on the Sparrow
		A Wailing Wall
315	MEREDITH CARSON	*Light*
		Dusting Books
318	KATHY PHILLIPS	*Speaking to Kuan Yin*
		Kuan Yin, Inventor
322	CONTRIBUTORS	

For Atsuko Asayama
– J.S.K.

For Karin, Andrea, and Janice
– C.S.

These writings are our voices. They range from the operatic to the sensible, to the hidden and discreet, to the plaintive, even to the disembodied. They are the voices we grew up with. They are the moments of our mothers, our daughters, the intimate voices with which we speak when we speak to a loved one: voices to heal, to ward off evil, to call to compassion, the sounds we make when we grieve. The voices tell of the moments when we listened, watched, and understood, as if life, like a piece of music, could be apprehended in all its strangeness.

Here is the voice we heard at the kitchen window when we were peeling potatoes, waiting for life to happen, our bodies lithe and leaning toward that moment when we would awaken in our own beds, mistresses of something unnamed, but yearned for. Its rhythm is found in the rocking chair on the porch, in the swaying hammock between the trees where we discovered the book that led us away and into ourselves on summer afternoons of sun, leaves, and hours. Here is the voice that chased us across the fields, calling ourselves home. It's the voice of a mother telling a young child to wash her hands, her face, say her prayers, be good. It's the voice at the grave. It's the voice of our devotion—waiting for children, for husbands, counting the hours into beads. It's the voice dying, the voice giving birth. It's the moment of pure singing, the voice we sang with when we were all alone. It is many hued like our anger, what we wanted to say to our fathers, our lovers, the first cry of pleasure. It is the voice of a sister, of the letters we write to brothers and never send, the voice of our breathing made visible, the advice of a maiden aunt telling us how to make stew. It's the voice of artifice—our invention, the work we do, the dream in which we imagine carp rising.

Juliet S. Kono
Cathy Song

YOU IN THERE

You lie there as if you were already dead. Your eyes don't focus on mine. They don't open up big to let the irises take in my image. So far today the only sign you give that you recognize my presence comes just briefly with the slight pressure of your grip in mine. But the rest of you works along with the respirator, which is breathing for you, because you can't.

They did a tracheostomy to help you breathe. The emphysema is fairly widespread, the doctor said. He compared your trying to breathe to a person drowning, because the lungs no longer process the air.

You have no voice. The deep resonance of your talking is in my imagination now, but I hear it as what I think you are thinking. You have shriveled. Always the biggest person in any room, the one who generated all the energy and noise and laughter in a given space, you suck on the air you take in and diminish in size by the hour.

The spooky feeling we used to laugh about when we visited this hospital remains in this place. Fears circle me. This is going to be your last room if you don't hurry to protest the way this feels. It's not like you to keep so still. You need me to bolster you, to talk you up and out of here. You need to connect to my energy. But first you must come back from wherever you are floating.

The soap opera on the overhead television screen is the last one that will play during your lunch, but you don't care to follow the plot that you have talked about for years. You don't watch or listen. You don't care what's on or who's in here with you.

Something about you now is out of focus. You look fuzzy at your edges. I hang on to your fingers, stroking the smooth hand, shaping the oval fingernails, hoping for some kind of response to my being here. I no longer notice the difference in the color of our hands side by side; what I care about is that you are not there in feeling, that the balance between our natures, your being so heavy and my being so light, is not reflected right in this place we occupy now.

The room where you are is pastel green mostly, with yellow and orange flowered vinyl wallpaper on only one wall, the one behind your head. Looks like they tried to erase the institutional look with that one bright touch. It's the kind of hospital room that you worked in for years, and the ward outside is warm and busy with soft-spoken nurses bustling around. If you would pay attention, you would enjoy talking with them the way you always question people about their work. The techniques are different, and they're using new, time-saving machines as they go around from patient to patient.

You don't care about the computerized thermometer the nurse tries to tell you she's going to put into your mouth. You don't say "Ahh . . ." or make any face at all. Your being passive is so unlike you that I look at you again.

But later when you seem to be more awake, you are nervous. You avoid looking at the doctor, the occasional nurses, the visitors who deposit flower arrangements, get-well money, a *bento* plate on the bedside table. Your eyes don't stay on anything very long. You don't want to look at me.

Everyone who enters the room is prepared to do something for you. Everyone wants a response or some kind of sign from you. Some try to say upbeat, encouraging things to you. One old lady says, too loudly, "Bumbye come betta, *ki-o tsukete!*" You would have said that heartily to any one of your friends before. You make no sign of hearing. The people who come in here go out carefully.

Your oldest living sister arrives before anyone else in the family. The nurses laugh about her later. "You rememba da one yesterday? She wen ask at the section desk for Mrs. Duffland," they report to me confidentially.

"When she came inside hea, she look and look at your mother. She call her name, 'Kikuko! Katie!', and then run outside, back to the duty nurses. She says, 'It's not my sister!' J'like that. Screaming at us. We had to go check the patient i.d.

number, l'dat. She cannot believe her own eyes, and she's scolding us j'like we did something to yo' mother. Maybe we hiding her. Something else, yeah?"

Auntie Ritsi would be able to find something wrong with the hospital staff, that's her way. She's the one who always takes care of herself and keeps up with all the latest diets and health trends. She rarely goes out of her way to see you and always corrects your English. She speaks only standard English herself. It must have scared "the pee out of her"— your words—to see you so sick. Everybody calls Ritsi Minami the extra tight one. You used to call her Mrs. Mina-Mina, remember? Since a gift was placed on the counter by your glasses, a pair of fuzzy blue, airlines stretch booties, she must have believed finally that it was her sister in there.

Lono and Ellen come in to see you and talk in whispers. Ellen places your crystal bead rosary in your hand and says she'll call the temple priest to pray for you. Lono strokes your forehead and says, "Auntie? Auntie, come home, okay? I like you get well and cook for me, alright?"

The other family members telephone each other, but it's the neighborhood who comes to see you. They bring kids. One ties a red heart balloon to the foot of your electronic bed.

Betty brings you an orchid plant. "Too bad she cannot see good, yeah? Wait until she's better. *Kawai-sona.*" Betty blows her nose. Your eyes are open but not in focus.

The owner of the Arirang Bar hands me a bottle of homemade *kim ch'i* for when you get better.

They ask me who found you after your collapse. One lady keeps asking, "Is that so? Really?" Her husband says "Yeah?" to everything. They are curious about details. They keep looking shocked.

They listen patiently to the story of how many times you had tried to quit smoking before they told you it was emphysema. I explain again how, luckily, Betty came over extra early with the morning newspaper and found you slumped over the kitchen table, how the ambulance took so long but was packed with all the equipment you needed to keep breathing once they got you onto the stretcher, how we were so relieved that you're okay even though you're not yourself yet. You look peaceful while we stare at your face and continue to talk about you softly.

The early evening is the best time for them to visit. The hospital corridors are filled and noisy with people, who look for their patient's room. Except for family, nobody stays very long, though. Maybe it's the way the rooms are like dark cocoons with only a flicker of ongoing TV light, a slow motion aquarium illumination, and the flooring tile everywhere holding on to an undefinable, persistent smell. Or how bursts of sound from people talking seem to get very loud and animated then fade in quick spurts into all the other regular noises, which flow on when the talkers decide to quiet themselves and whisper again.

Nobody minds when you don't recognize them. They greet each other, as if that were all they needed to maintain a pleasant, working face. The landlord of the next-door apartment building is surprised when you decide to smile at him. I am, too. We both try to talk with you, but you aren't really interested.

I talk about medication and therapy with your doctors. You would be very interested in what they say. They will get a psychiatrist to you, they promise to encourage your will to fight. They warn me not to have false expectations as they talk above your blanketed form. Not even when Dr. Kaneshiro takes your pulse—you always judged doctors by how they did it—do you pay attention.

You don't care at all about anything like that. When we are alone, I talk and talk to you. You show no sign of hearing. You groan and make small ah ah sounds that frighten me, and then you subside into breathing.

You jerk suddenly as if in an animated dream, and the rosary falls to the floor breaking the string and scattering the shiny beads. Groping on my hands and knees, I search all over the floor and under the bed to find each one in order to string them up later. I pray for you with each bead I find. "Let her live. Let her live." I alternate it, out of breath but hopeful, with "*Namandabutsu-Namandabutsu-Namandabutsu.*" I am too superstitious. It's not really an omen, I say to myself.

You stir and act alert, as if you are yourself again after an afternoon nap. I quickly take the opportunity. Because your eyes are yours again, I can talk to you.

"You can't just give up now, because only you remember O-Baban so well—maybe five or six people now living knew her at all—but no one as close as you, Mama, and if you go, all the true memories will go with you. All the important things about what she did and how she was will fade away from all of us." I add firmly, "You're not ready to join her yet," in answer to the thought I know you have just had when I mentioned your mother.

"And anyway, how do you know if there really is any life afterwards?" I go on, knowing I have you thinking.

Then you give me the sullen, mean-eye look. It's how you answer my comment. In that way you remind me that you will have me remember you do believe that dead people can communicate from that time after they pass on. I don't argue. I am so happy that you are yourself again.

I try for another run. What do I have to lose?

"O-Baban lived to 95. You are so young yet." You close your eyes.

I stand by the window and look down at the back of the hospital where an old wooden building is all that's left of the former hospital plant. I remember to remind you how long ago we once took O-Baban there to visit an old man, who was dying in the care-home wing.

"Funny, yeah, how when we got to him, he said he knew that we would be there before he died?" That story doesn't register for you. But it's the kind of story you loved to tell.

Outside, down there, the sunlight is intense and very different from the fluorescent light in the room. I tell you about how Baban liked to peer out of the windows of the old Kohala house to look at the garden. You nod. Or is it an uncontrolled quiver. No matter, I am so happy I am tempted to open the glass door to the small lanai outside to let in some real air.

But I should stick close to your bedside and hold your hand or wait for some word that you might want to write on the pad of paper waiting on the swivel table top. I am afraid you will write D-I-E again like the first time we tried to get you to communicate when they moved you in here.

I yelled, "No, no, no," to you, but you pretended not to hear me. You were sly in your denial. I took the pencil and put it away.

You are much better now, I tell you again. I should brush the false teeth in the plastic container marked with your name so that they will be ready to wear when you feel up to it. I should tell you encouraging things about how you will get better and be able to sit out on the little concrete lanai in the sunshine, just like being on the porch at home.

You don't talk with your body or your eyes. I don't talk. Like you, I make no sign when nurses come in and out to do things and make cheerful comments. You face has no expression no matter what is said, whoever says it. You take in liquids and food and medicine by gurgling tubes. The places on your arms and neck and side where the tubes are inserted look like reddened, irritating entrances into your pain. The white-wrapped cut in the center of your neck is mysterious in the way its tube dangles, inactive.

I get afraid and squeeze your hand, hoping to find the safety of your telling me what you want me to do. And harder. I try to fix your attention on me, the most comfortable way to be with you. But you can't respond from where you are. Your hand wants only to pull away from any more pain, that's all. You drift in and out of sleep.

On the third day, you are up very early like a regular day. You look ready. You search my face, and I know what you are thinking.

"Now why is she here?"

I don't know why either.

When you die, you seem very relaxed at first. You have let me know with a hand squeeze that you understand me as I tell you that I love you so, and I want you to live. You tell me a clear No with your half-closed eyes and your shaking head. You ignore my anger. You sleep a while. Then you do open your eyes and slowly take me all in, and that does make me happy. But you crumple back inward by degrees, and I want you to rest. Your breathing sounds good.

An hour later I sit in your tiny bathroom preparing lots more of the Yes reasons. I practice how to say them: You have to go on a "once in a lifetime trip"—your words—with me to Las Vegas and San Francisco and Tokyo, and you have to wear a big white orchid to my wedding, which will be someday very soon, and you have to stay alive to see your future grandchildren and you have to come home and sit on the porch and tell everybody what happened in the hospital . . . and you just have to. Because. That's the only way it can be.

When I go back to hold your hand, you are gone.

WHAT I WANTED TO SAY TO MY MOTHER

Mother in your arms
I was baptized in fire:
In through the soft fontanel
I breathed your blue flame, it
Seared my swollen raised skin
Turning it black as burnished leather
And on that pyre of maternal love
I bled until desiccated,
My heart and entrails
So much powder
For a Chinese apothecary.
All that funereal time
What was left of me—
A ghost in blue bottles.

LITTLE RUNAWAY

It came to pass
A sworded angel
Forbade the garden.
My father never made it back
(Fed up with the roiling banshee angel—)
And I journeyed shortly thereafter.

I stole quietly away—
Got my shit together
My blue party dress
My shiny red earrings
Nobody saw me
Not the whispering ti.

That star-filled night
Kua Road was quite illumined,
Mahina so gentle:
    The gate held its creak—
    The dogs barely noticed.

Goodbye lantana! and
Farewell mountain apple!
I will miss you, sweet mango
and even you, practical pear.
Dearest Zinnia
I am a stranger now—
An angel holds the answer to
The blue dress
The plastic earrings
The shhshhshhshh of eucalyptus
The goat man's house
Maunaloa lunar blossoms.

Maybe you can guess
What happened next—
The angel sent her messenger
And
Scared shitless—
I went back
I paid homage to the angel—
The ti is still sighing.

DIANE KAHANU

WHEN I WAS YOUNG ON AN ISLAND

When I was young on an island
my brother caught gray baby sharks
on his bamboo fishing pole.
When he'd catch a shark,
he'd call the other kids and
we'd come running with clubs
of driftwood to beat the shark
to death.

When I was young on an island
my brother made moray eel traps
of silver pineapple juice cans
and a can opener, the kind that
makes triangle holes. When he'd
catch an eel, he'd give it to the
neighbor cat and we'd all watch
the tiger-striped cat
take the eel out of the can
and eat it.

When we were young on Paikō Drive
in Kuli'ou'ou and we played war,
my brother invented the battle charge.
He'd wait for a hard wind to pick
up the sand and just when the wind
was strongest, he'd yell, "Charge,"
and we'd run, head down, into a zillion
tiny bullets of stinging sand
hurled by the wind's hand.

When we were young on an island
my brother invented the jellyfish

test. He was an Apache Indian that day.
Tortured, he would not cry out.
We caught see-through jellyfish
in our hands and held them
while they stung us. Whoever
cried out first or dropped their
jellyfish lost. I remember sinking
to my knees with pain and finally
laying down in the cool, shallow water.
Only my burning jellyfish hand
held out.

MOTHER

1.
The gesture at the end of your fingers
prevents the air
from entering or leaving
the vacuum cleaner
in the building to the left
of where Mother once stood,
dreaming she was Shirley Temple
and whole
and wonderful.

2.
Her lips are bullets
She digs in my mouth with a wooden spoon
says dead people talk through my pillow
the sign of the cross cures warts
Her eyes are in a glass on the night stand
They stare through the walls all night
while she sleeps

3.
She carries her children in her pocket
with kleenex and lint—faces,
anger suffocated off: her
children.

She has tales for each: televisions,
garages, new linoleum. So good, such
perfect children.
Laminated, glossy, wallet-
sized.

4.
Mother, O
Mother, I have you
under my fingernails.
You are the worm
in my intestines.
And I love
you.

5.
Lilac is another way to say
"Mother."
And the horse called "Bobsie"
in the barn.
It was so many years ago.
She was young, then.
The barn and Bobsie.
The lilac and Mother.

6.
Is she the beast of the field?
Does she creep about?
What does she want?
Her bones ruin the soup.
How she lies; even her touch
is wicked.

7.
Gnats fly in
and if you have the newspaper spread for them
they light down on it
and in their wings
and on their legs

is a yellow powder
not like the pollen bees carry
but thicker
almost wet–like
and if you watch
you see them bring it
how it gathers
there on the paper

UNTITLED

1.
Can there be another I, another wall, snow,
fence, straw, wet
in the line the eye

travels entering and leaving
morning,
then afternoon,
then hills, later small hallways

where music forgets its purpose,
its memory? Which tree, swallowing
clear voices held
between teeth long enough, accompanies
forgetfulness? I have been

I and later, there was sound.
Hope and refusal were observers,
trembling

by a bridge, yes, wide as a knife,
visible in clouds. I am care-

ful here, continuing; it is difficult
to do this,
talk as accompaniment, music
feathering the small hairs
on the ridge of my ear.

There is a sink, how speak it,
near the room's corner, small,
evocative, a shadow
curving near it.

There was I, hand, knuckle, no more,
perhaps, than distant

figures crossing landscape
from photograph to
photograph, the perfect wind
drowsing above them.

2.
The eyes' slow
movement conjoins objects
in the shifting light
of their randomness.

Why nervous here? It is all
so quietly observed. A weakness

in her hand, its shadow, from the
light so directly above
where she holds it out

above the small white table, confuses
shapes, awkwardly
releasing each

from how
it is known. Breath
exhaled, her eyes' glance, its
silence, presses into
practical outline. The heart

is sack–like, is it not? surrounding
the air tears leave.

Before tenderness,
before memory, the weight in each
disguised, hands assumed, in air,

a forgetfulness which now,
as landscape, as recognized objects

suspended in the eyes; search.
disappear. Night, which to her

is rough-hewn, appropriate, climbs down
the small, hard buildings
she imagines conceal,

however badly, the body's appetite
which is, after all, fragile.

PARTS

I. PAIN IN PARTS

The Brain

My head
is fuckin sore.
Don't anybody
talk.
Don't anybody
ask me questions.
Don't any one
of you kids
move in this
living room.
First one
who breathe
going get
one good whack
with the flyswatter.
You. Cook the rice.
You. Fry some spam.
Open one can corn.
Everybody
shut the fuck up.
I work all day long,
I come home
and all you doing
is watching tv.
Sit down.
Shut up.
I gotta rest.

The Face

Stop muttering
under your breath
before I pound
your face.
Want me
to punch
your face in?
You cannot run away
from me.
Try.
I catch you
and give you
double lickens.
Now get
your ass
in your room
and fold
all the laundry.
Then I'm gonna
teach you
how to iron
your father's shirts.
Go. The laundry
is on your bed.
Hurry up.

The Eye

I
found this letter
in your panty drawer.
Did you write
all these evil things?

Looks like your
handwriting.
Like me read this
to Joy and her mother?

Like me call them up
come over for lunch
right now?
What you mean,
no, wait?
So you did
write it.
            I
cannot believe
that so much evil
can live
in one person.
You are a evil child.
You are filthy.
You are a hypocrite.
Stay in your room.
Forever.

II. BLAME IN PARTS

The Nostril

What I told you about digging your nose?
Who taught you that?
You going get two slaps
I ever see you doing that in public again.
Good for you your nose bleed
and I hope you get sore stomach too
for eating that shit.

And your uncle, next time I see him,
he going get two slaps too
for teaching you damn kids
to eat your hanabata.
Gunfunnit.

The Foot

Who the hell'n use my rubber slippers?
Gotta be somebody with toe jams.
You? You? You? Then who, gunfunnit?
The fuckin ghost? Gotta be one of you clowns
'cause I no more toe jams
and I was like that since I was small.
Here, smell this shoes.
No more stink, eh?
Here. You. Wash this with clorax
and hang um on the clothesline
in the sun.
Maybe the smell go 'way.
And if I catch the asshole
who using my rubber slippers
and making me catch their toe jams,
I going broke their fuckin ass.

The Mouth

Whoever ate all the meat
from this stew is asking for it.
Who the fuck took all the meat
and left the vegetables and soup?
Gunfunnit. I put three trays meat
and all gone. Let me see your plate.
You. Let me see. YOU.
YOU the one. You damn pig.

Why no leave some meat
for the rest of us, asshole?
Next time, I going put three trays meat
and chop up your fuckin dog too
so get meat for everybody.
You like me do that?
Then no get greedy.
You guys piss me off to the max.

III. GIRL IN PARTS

The Ass

Who you slutting around with?
You better not be a whore
or you going find your ass
passed around from one Joe
to the next. *She give, you know.*
They all going know
how fuckin easy you are
and you going think they love you
and you going think you popular
but all they thinking is you spread fast.
They going say, *I love you I love you c'mon
let's do it.* And what you going say?
Girl, you better say no,
you going wait until you married.

The Crack - One

What are you fuckin trying to do?
You no more shame
always sitting in dark corners
with Felicia's brother?
Felicia my friend, you know,

and you, you goddamn fuckin 12 year old slut
sitting in dark corners
with that 19 year old brother of hers.
What he was trying for grab
from between your legs?
Think I wasn't looking, eh? Gunfunnit.
No tell me the deck cards.
Why you put the fuckin deck of cards
between your legs
when you know he wanted um?
You wanted him for touch your crack?
Answer me.
Answer me.

The Crack - Two

Why you had to tell me this?
Don't look at me.
Yeah, you better hang your head.
Don't you ever talk about this again.
Don't tell nobody.
Nobody. You fuckin hear me?
Don't ever tell your father.
What you expected?
I told you about being a cock teaser.
This is what you get.
You deserve it.
He a 19 year old man
and you bending over
right in front his face.
What the hell did you expect?
Where he took you?
Why-did-you-follow-him-there?
What did I say
about going into a man's room?

You liked it?
Felt good?
Say it louder.   Sore?
Good for you.
Now you a HO-A.
You not a virgin.
Nobody going love you.
Nobody going marry you.
Everybody going use you.
Once you know what it
feels like, you going want it
everytime.
You never
going be able
to stop
yourself.
Dirty girl.
Dirty
girl.

IV. WHAT THE HANDS DO ABOUT
ALL OF THESE PARTS

Advice from a 14-Year-Old Friend

Take the needle. Take it.
Cut your arm. Cut.
See. You feel no pain
'cause you already sore inside.
Keep going. Make plenty lines,
as much as you can take.
Feel good, yeah? Feel icy, yeah,
when the needle break your flesh?
Push um deep, the needle,
till you see the white part

of your meat. Spread um—
spread the cut you just made
before the blood get hard.
Look inside. Trippy, yeah,
the small blood drops?
How your head?
Feeling white?
Kind of gray, yeah the feeling?
Going away, the pain inside,
'cause you getting numb.
You whole body not throbbing yet?
I remember the first time
I did this. Felt so good
when my whole body was going
and the blood started dripping
on my leg and my friend
wen' tell me taste um,
'cause that's me spilling out
of myself. Tasted like rust.
And I wen' forget about all
the shit that was happening to me.
My father took me emergency
that day. That was the first time
I seen him cry.
No. No need towel.
Lie down. Let the blood
drip on the sidewalk.
Then we write yo madda's name
with the blood and when dry,
she going know
you was here
and she going know
how much you love her.

BONE WHITE MOON

Sky off the wing purple with love, halfmoon–guarded flight
circling discontentedly, dinner already served and eaten,
drinks twice, movie over they want to shower travel grime.

Thrill of aviation, their throats air–condition chilled,
they look on halfmoon–bathed velvet night and remember
folds of skin and fat and muscle, family and friends.

You, reader, may know this state in which the lover becomes
a portion of moon, seas, and flying. Notwithstanding
varicoses, it is a way to navigate the truth of purple.

Trying to make out waves window–seaters lurch on order into
flotation seat cushions. Passengers belt in
for descent to love and the grimacing island shorelights.

MIRANDA CRIES, FATHER'S RAPING ME
AND BLAMING IT ON CALIBAN

Stop the canoe—I'm getting ready to vomit. Don't be
stupid—there's land.
Watch out, an iceberg! What? Shut up stupid.
Boom.
Dad says my mom is dead and Caliban's mom was a witch.
Witches were burnt: to procure and disseminate birth control
is still criminal.
A patriarchal fiction? Yes, they still believe
a god impregnated Mary with Jesus and stupidity Rosemary's
Baby. Who me?
I'm only a woman.
Come impregnate me—isn't that why you've made up the lie
that nobody was ever gassed and cremated in Nazi Germany—
no, not at Dachau, not there so clean and German and Father.

OTOSAN

When the moon is full
and the rabbit pounds *mochi*,
I remember you, Otosan, lifting me up to the sky:
"Don't be afraid of the dark," you said, "See that moon?
We'll just pour shoyu on it and eat it."

When my brothers and sister were bad,
you called them one by one into the parlor,
sat them down on the straight back chairs
and lit the *yaeto*, a moxa wafer, on their backs—
to drive the mischief maker out,
I think you said.
I opened the door a crack and peeked,
glad it wasn't me.

When I was bad, into the closet you put me,
my hands tied loosely behind my back,
locked in among the futons, cushioning
my bounces round and round and up and down
until you let me out.

One night you locked me
out of the house,
but the top of the back steps
served as a stage. I sang,
leaning against the kitchen door
to the rabbit in the moon pounding *mochi*
until you let me in.

When I ate the forbidden green mangoes,
but refused to admit it,
I kneeled on the grass, head bent, receiving
the steady, restrained beat

of the broomstick handle.
You held the stick
and tradition rained its blows on my head.

We played it out, you and I,
until Okasan's sobbing
"Tell him, yes! Tell him!"
reached me. She knelt beside me,
peering into my face, pleading.
With my "yes," you sighed
and flung the stick away.

When the moon is full as it is now,
I remember you, Otosan, lifting me up to the sky—
the warmth of darkness
and the rabbit in the moon forever pounding *mochi*.

BROS

Early every morning they were off,
in beat-up Keds, jeans bagging at the knee.
Nix on the Wheaties; down the slope and gone
light on their bikes and wild as migrant birds—

out where the cosmos shifts with riveting speed
and life rips by on slick and vibrant rails,
to posted places, magic with prohibition
where young boys learn the smell and force of fear.

At dusk, half-anxious; up that grueling hill
a gleam of returning T-shirts, riding hard
still locked in the same unconscious tight formation,
Ken's pedals an inch from Chuck's rotating spokes.

Midnight, and the two of them still talked.
Across the hall I'd hear through half-shaped dreams
soft and assured, words of perfect love:
Ken, you dildo. Chuck, you peckerhead.

At family dinners now they stiffly sit
polite as wives, and neither of them speaks.
Eyes, in endless, seemingly random moves
compass the crowded room, and don't meet once.

I wonder: doesn't either of them hear
still so insistent, through this scripted chat
a sound of treble voices, hard and pure:
You jerk-off, Kenneth. Chas, you shit-for-brains.

THE HARDEST MOVE

After the eyes, the second string is the hardest one to move. The one attached to the hand: the spate of wooden flesh so expressive in its curve of grain: facing downward, a negative, a show of indifference, of casualness, of forgetting: and equally demonstrative facing up, askance, as if vulnerable, as if ready to receive, as if begging for an answer.

I know all the gestures of the palm: how to turn it away from the body or bring it close to the face, or bring it close to another's face, quickly, as in a slap, or slowly, with great tenderness. I know what can be done with the palm, the pleasure and pain it metes out. I have studied all the angles, measured all the reactions it draws. I have made a simple hand movement contain libraries of feeling. I am a repository of emotional precision, I am a manipulator of souls. I have all that—in my palm.

I am puppeteer. Or I was. Or I will be. Maybe it was another lifetime. Or maybe it was this lifetime. Before I awoke one day to find myself strapped down and corseted, confined by leather straps with yards of plastic tubing hanging from my flesh. I lose track of time.

A nurse enters, brisk, efficient, a woman calm of face regardless of the emergency—blood spurting onto sheets, screams of agony, the stench of cleaning up uncontrollable bowels.

"How are we today?"

There is no answer of course. She doesn't expect one. How can I answer with a tube stuck down my throat, forcing me to breathe to a rhythm I don't really like; placed in a bed like an abandoned marionette, tubes dangling from every hole except my ears? These hollow strings were not meant to be pulled. If tugged, they do not raise an arm, a leg; do not breathe any movement into inert appendages. They precipitate no action. The strings and straps attached to all my extremities, invading every orifice, are used only to maintain. These keep me immobile while fluids drip in and out, a reversible flow of streams, unnatural, yet still conducting the precious tide of life: digestion and excretion, circulation and respiration. Even my hands are tied down, the better to keep me from moving. My hands, giver of motion.

I try to move my left hand, gesture. The nurse does not see. She is busy checking my blood pressure, the only thing that moves in my body of its own accord. And maybe I am wrong at that. For the drugs dripping into my veins pull my blood this way and that, controlling my very heartbeat the way I once controlled a puppet's palm.

"Time for another blood sample." The nurse talks, but not to me. She talks to the air above the bed, to herself, to the breathing machine, which emanates a wheezy mooing sound. The nurse does not look at my face. I am not a man to her. I am bed number 26, ICU, Code Blue, the one to watch for abnormal vital signs, the one whose blood must be thinned and thickened, the one who, at any moment, may cease to need such exacting care. She balances a tray filled with vials and needles on the flat of my stomach. She wraps a tourniquet around my arm and proceeds to draw blood from her table.

I want the nurse to look at me, look into my eyes. Then she would have to notice. What is behind the eyes, I know I can still control. The movement of the eyes, the most difficult trick to learn, I know I can still execute. It was always my trademark. I could make my audience weep, all with the use of the eyes.

"What do you want?"
"You know what I want."
As easy as that. A look, a glance exchanged, but deep, riveting, as though the entire world could be promised. The words didn't really matter.

It was all in the eyes: amazing for their simplicity; transparent lenses tinged with color, imperceptible movements, a reticulate net expanding or diminishing, the range of positions, half-closed, cast down, then opening as if a shade had been drawn up letting in sudden sunlight. Such miracles of subtlety: a complete ballet performed for another within the span of a blink.

It was all a matter of training, skill, timing the blink, positioning the light to make the eyes glow, the ability to use a glassy substance to mirror what someone else wants.

"When I look into your eyes, I forget myself."

Nonsense. It wasn't a moment of forgetting, but one of recognition. It was all in making the eyes reflective. Then it was easy to make someone fall in love. They fell in love with their own imagination: an irresistible force. And once that happened of course, the person became a puppet. A person in love will do anything. I learned that very young.

"Mommy got you something special for your birthday. Go on, open it."

I opened a box stuffed with white tissue and lifted out a clown. But it wasn't just an ordinary clown. It was a heavy clown half my size, dressed in blue satin with a huge red ruffle at its neck. It had strings attached to its arms and legs and wooden bars attached to the strings.

"This is your very own puppet, Lincoln. And his name is Lester. Can you say his name?"

I shook my head, realizing in an instant where my mother was heading.

"Come on, say it for Mommy, Lester. Don't you like him?" I nodded.

"Then say it for me, baby. Come on. His name is Lester. Lester."

"... es ... es."

"I'm going to take him away if you don't say his name properly."

"NO." I could say that word well.

"Lester can move his arms and legs. See?" Mother pulled at the strings and made the clown move. I was amazed. I grabbed at the clown, knowing by instinct what the strings were for. I made the clown move the way my mother had. It was her turn to be amazed.

"Lincoln, you're such a clever boy. I've never seen anything like it. And only five years old. You really like Lester, don't you?"

I nodded.

"And you want to keep him, don't you?"

I nodded again. And this time Lester nodded too.

"Well if you can make him move like that, then you can say his name, Lester. Come on. Say it for Mommy."

I made Lester wave his arm.

"His name, Lincoln. Say Lester. LES . . . TER." She spoke with loud emphasis.

I made Lester wave his arm furiously.

"You can say it, I know you can. You're just not trying. You're being stubborn."

Lester was now doing deep knee bends.

"Lincoln, how will people ever know how smart you are if you don't learn to talk?"

Lester was spinning on his toes.

"Lincoln, look at me. I know you're a very smart boy. All the doctors say so. You're going to do great things. That's why I named you Lincoln. Now if you love your mother, you'll say it, won't you? Say it."

I didn't say it. I couldn't say it. I couldn't pronounce any words beginning with the letter "L"—including my own name. But I was able to keep Lester. That was the beginning.

She won't look at me. The nurse busies herself with checking the tubes, the numbers, the flash of information recorded in all the machines. She prefers to look at inanimate numbers rather than at my face. Maybe she sees no difference. She refuses to meet my eyes. She avoids them the way Mother avoided looking into cats' eyes. She hated cats, found them unnerving. She didn't like their eyes she said because they looked "too blank."

An orderly comes in. He is tall, big-boned, lumbering in a good-natured way. He has a booming voice.

"I have to wash him down. A visitor's coming. Daughter, I think. Can you help me turn him?"

Impossible. I want to shout. I don't have a daughter. I have no children. My puppets are my children. Who is coming to visit me? I don't want anyone to see me like this. But I cannot say anything with the breathing tube down my throat.

The orderly and nurse turn me. He undoes the tie of my gown at the back. He wedges me between pillows and the rail of the hospital bed so I can't slip onto my back again.

I feel a warm damp cloth being rubbed down my back. He isn't gentle, but firm making crescent-shaped curves with the cloth. My skin feels slightly chilled. He washes my back, my buttocks, my legs: careful with the tubes that jut from my anus, the vein in my thigh, the blood pressure monitoring wire stuck to the tip of my big toe. I have a bed sore on the right buttock. He smooths Vaseline on it. When he is done, he and the nurse turn me onto my back. The lights on the ceiling seem to bobble. I can't focus on them, they seem to be slipping down, sliding along the ceiling, which curves into semi-darkness.

"I think you should wait before continuing," the nurse says.

"His heartbeat just jumped to 160. Let him rest."

My heartbeat jumped? How can this be? I didn't make it jump. I try to focus my eyes. Get that gleam back into them that I know is so effective. Focus on the lights, let them reflect in my eyes. But the lights on the ceiling keep sliding. I want them to stop. I want my heartbeat to go back to normal. I don't want to be tethered to this bed. I want my hands' freedom. How can I tell them? What gesture? Nothing moves but the overhead lights, which continue to slide down the ceiling. The nurse fiddles with the ventilator, the machine connected to my lungs through a tube that hangs from my mouth like an overextended tongue.

Puppets don't have tongues. They don't speak to be noticed. Tongues don't have to be used for talking. I learned that when I was six.

"Lincoln likes leftovers. Now you say it."

I shook my head.

"Lincoln likes leftovers. Come on, I know you can do it. There's nothing wrong with you. Everything is normal, you're a very healthy boy."

"In . . . In . . . In."

"Try putting your tongue to the back of your teeth. Curl

it, like you're going to fling something off it and blow out at the same time. See?"

I watched the speech therapist's mouth, her tongue stuck to the back of her upper teeth, a massive column of pink. How did she manage to breathe like that? She made noises that sounded like laughter.

I tried to follow her example. I felt like I was gagging.

"No, not the bottom teeth, push the tongue to the top."

My tongue felt like a huge pink brick.

"Open your mouth wider and relax."

She put her fingers in my mouth and tried to move my tongue.

"Relax. I'm just going to move your tongue so you know where it's supposed to go, what it feels like. Okay? Like that. Now remember that feeling."

I did remember the feeling, but not the one she thought. I didn't know where she placed my tongue, but I remembered the foreignness of something in my mouth: the firmness of her thick fingers, slightly salty, the rawness of having my tongue curled around something warm and moving, the wonder of feeling both wet and dry.

"Now breathe. Blow through your mouth. No, don't suck in, blow."

I closed my eyes and felt her flesh pressing against my curled tongue. I flattened my tongue against her fingers and drew my lips down around them, sucking as hard as I could. My very first blow job.

A doctor enters the room. I cannot see her with the room darkening, the ceiling lights on my horizon. But I hear her voice.

"Is he responding to the digoxin?"

"No. His blood pressure is dropping. Heartbeat at 140. Right now he seems to be stabilizing, but I don't think it will last. When will his daughter get here?"

"Soon. She's been alerted. Has he been cleaned up?" What are they talking about? I don't have a daughter. A man would remember if he had a daughter, though I admit to being bad at names. I don't remember names. I don't remember faces. I don't remember any relatives—only puppets. The ones that do what I want. Who is coming? Not a daughter, some imposter surely. I want the doctor to look at me, look into my eyes.

"Too bad she has to see him like this. Any response to pain?" The doctor pinches my hand. That hurts. It hurts a lot. I try to show her how much.

"What's the morphine drip?"

"One cc every four hours."

"Not enough to knock him out. She'll have to make a decision."

What decision? Who is the doctor talking about? I'll make my own decisions, thank you. I've always made my own decisions. I hate not being directly addressed, ignored as if invisible. Why is it, if you can't talk, people assume you can't hear? I can hear, I can think, I can feel. Maybe the vision is blurry now, but I can still control the movement behind the eyes. That's what counts. The most difficult part to control. Ask any puppeteer. The hardest to make life-like. Just ask me. I'll show them.

I hear a tray crash in the room. I'm sure I flinch at the sound, but no one seems to notice.

I learned to talk without L-words. I didn't have to talk that often. I learned other ways to communicate—with my hands, my puppets, my pliant tongue. People were drawn to my quietness: the way I could make puppets express things through movement, the way I could excite feeling, the way I learned to kiss.

I ran away from home at sixteen, tired of my mother's manipulation, her recrimination of words. I didn't need to be reminded of my impediment. I changed my name to Bismark, the better to introduce myself. It was an unusual, memorable name. It caught people by surprise.

My puppets changed as well. Through the years I stopped working with puppets the size of wooden dolls, but worked instead on manipulating puppets nearly human-sized. I developed complicated sets of pulleys and rods to add smoothness to their movements. I could work puppets in unison. I watched actors, dancers, performing artists. I studied European marionettes, Indonesian shadow puppets, Japanese Bunraku puppets. I watched "The Ed Sullivan Show." I decided to make my puppets dance, not just jump up and down, but do actual choreography. They performed ballet, tap, flamenco, jazz, modern, and belly dances. They did cancans, tangos, rain dances, polkas, tarantellas, hulas, and yes, strip teases. I was arrested three times for exposing wood-shaven pubic hair. The outrage made me famous.

My puppets were asked to perform in major cities. I traveled around the world. The amazing thing with my puppets was how people saw themselves. In every country—a classical ballet in Ghana, a steamy tango in Bangkok, a subtle performance of Tai Chi in Barcelona—the audience read their own stories into the puppets I moved. Each gesture held meaning for them, regardless of the culture. People saw what they wanted to see. I became a master at giving them what they wanted.

My silence diminished as my reputation increased. I learned to replace any words beginning with the letter L. A person was not "lazy," but idle. I did not "labor," I worked. I did not order "lasagne," I ate cannelloni instead. I was never "late," but tardy. I did not "linger," I tarried. I did not buy "lingerie," I bought negligees, camisoles, teddies. I did not "love," I was fond.

"You are the strangest man, I ever met."

"Because I work with puppets?"

"You know what I mean. How can you go through life being so unconnected?"

"Everyone is unconnected. I know people, many people. I have to, it's part of my work."

"Being alive is more than that. Don't you have any feelings?"

"Of course."

"Like what?"

"We've gone over this many times."

"I've worked hard for you. All those costumes, the sets."

"I'm grateful."

"I've done everything you wanted."

"You wanted to."

"I've tried very hard to please you."

"You have."

"And yet you still can't say it, can you?"

I know that stage, I've come to it countless times. I take this young man over to a light. I look into his eyes and let him look into mine. He sees himself reflected in my eyes. I touch my palm to his cheek and whisper, "What do you want?"

Eventually he leaves because he doubts what he sees in my eyes. Doubt is never enough. But I was not "lonely." I was unaccompanied.

"I'm sorry that it's come to this. It's very difficult for families, I know." The doctor is speaking in soothing tones.

"I've been here before." A young woman's voice, broken, quiet. Who is she? I want to run my head toward her, though there is only blackness in the room. I can only hear voices and they come from a distance. I want her to speak up. I do not recognize the voice.

"We've reached a point where we need to know the family's wishes."

What is the doctor talking about? What family? Whose wishes?

"I'll be frank. Your father's condition continues to deteriorate. His organs are failing one by one. First his heart weakened, but surgically we corrected that. Then his spleen and prostate failed, his kidneys and liver began to go, and now we think the gall bladder may also be involved."

Involved? She makes it sound like a love affair, not like some kind of prognosis. The doctor is describing a cutting of strings, one by one, casting each organ adrift. The voice keeps drifting farther away. I have to concentrate carefully.

"Is there any hope of recovery?" The young woman sounds like she is crying. I want her to stop crying so I can hear her better. I can't place her voice. She is a stranger posing as my daughter. Why didn't they ask her for proof?

"Recovery would require at least four more major surgical procedures. We don't think his heart could survive. He is on life support as it is. But if the family elected, we could undertake the risks. However, I must warn you, his heart has already sustained extensive damage. Even if he could survive surgery, he would have to be on life support for the rest of his life."

My god, they are going to take the word of a hysterical young woman to cut me open? How can I get them to look at me? This farce has got to stop.

"Has he suffered brain damage?"

"We don't know. We did have to apply shock to his heart when it went into arrhythmia. His brain could have had less oxygen then. We've had to put restraints on him because of his involuntary movements."

Involuntary movements? The idea is absurd. I have always controlled every nuance. They must be talking about someone else.

"Do you think he's in any pain?"

"He is not comatose, but he doesn't respond."

Of course I can't respond. I'm tied down to this damn bed. I have a tube stuck down my throat. I can't speak, can't gesture, and they've refused to look into my eyes. What is left? All my tools have been taken.

"We have your father's Living Will on file, which he sign-ed three years ago. Are you aware of its conditions?"

"Yes. When my mother had cancer, they both made their decision."

I don't remember signing any Living Will. I don't re-member any cancerous wife. There must be some mistake here: a terrible mistake. They've somehow got the wrong bed, mixed up the patients. Mistakes can be made. In ICU, every-one looks the same—sheets, tubes, breathing machines.

"My parents didn't want life-support: they didn't want to be human vegetables."

I am not a vegetable. I am a puppeteer. I can still control the movement behind the eyes. That skill never leaves a person after he's mastered the trick. It's an important gift. You either get it or you don't. A small but essential art, the one that creates entire worlds.

"Doctor, are you telling me he's only being kept alive now through artificial means?"

The woman's voice is faint. I don't hear the doctor's reply.

"I'm sorry, but I think the time has come . . ."

I hear muffled sobbing like far-off thunder.

"I'd like some time alone with . . ."

"Of course, whatever . . ."

I don't want to be left alone with her, this stranger, this sobbing woman. She obviously doesn't know me at all. I don't know her. She is touching me now, stroking my hand, my arm. Her skin feels like warm silk. She smells of flowers like funeral parlors. She mumbles, her voice low. Only a few words reach me.

". . . don't know . . . dad . . . love . . ."

She hums on, becoming fainter and fainter until I imagine her silence. I am aware of her fingers on my cheek. I smell roses. I feel her palm. That spate of flesh. The gesture not words. Plain for anyone to see. A matter of faster, slower, up and down. Yes, I know that string. The second most difficult move.

And finally, someone is looking at me. I feel her searching my face. She must see what is in my eyes now. She must see what I've learned, created. It no longer matters that she is a stranger. I know she is staring into my eyes. She'll read their message. This is my chance.

Her hands feel indistinct to me now. No longer discrete fingers and palm, but only a pressure, almost weightless, touching me like a brush. The brush moves on my forehead, gliding down without heat. It stops above my eyes. I imagine her eyes, brown spidery nets protecting a pit, contracting in wonder, squeezing tears down her cheeks. Look deep into my eyes, they say, tell me what you want. I wait. The brush closes my lids.

IT'S OVER ON THE BACK PORCH

I used the back porch. Unlike the front porch, pearled with sunlit-scrubbed milk bottles and appliqued with wipe-your-feet-first carpets, the back porch was dim and smelly, jelly-smudged and sometimes more.

The back hallway tunneled catacomb-like past sturdy brown cases of long-necked bottles of Blatz beer. The cases of "empties" were stacked there too, but their bee-alluring sweetness tattled that they were not. Sometimes the sugary musk of old beer was nearly overpowered by the heady yellow fumes of Dad's aged Liederkrantz. He ripened his foil-wrapped cheese in the window-focused afternoon sun. Then I'd give in and use the front porch. But never if a turtle was back there.

Down the hall from the cheese window, there was a partition between the stairs leading up to the attic and those descending outdoors and to the basement. Less often than I surrendered to the cheese, I was caught by the sight of a three-penny nail pounded into that partition. Tied to the nail was a length of cotton clothesline. Secured in the noose of that line was the scaly conical tail of a headless snapping turtle. Then the back porch party smells faded.

Snapping turtles are archaic creatures; relics from the primordial swamps where death was just sluggish acquiescence to the timeless dictates of evolution. A snapping turtle, even on my suburban back porch, even as I clutched my crackling cellophane package of Oreos, even as I hummed Annette's harmonies, even as I bent beneath him to tighten my tennies (laced top-to-bottom), took long time to die. That's why he had to hang inverted, anonymous.

Without the head and its hooded beak and slitty sheathed eyes, that hanging thing was still obviously a snapper. The octagonal peaked shell was fenced with gnarled ridges, sectioned off like some prehistoric scorecard etched with tallies of victories longstanding. A haze of green and drying moss was all that accented his boulder-like body. He had no color of his own, just as wharf rats and English sparrows have no color: "survivors" don't brag.

From under that massive drab somber sarcophagus fortress, four stumpy legs ringed with cross-hatched wrinkles splayed to five toes, each hooded with a yellow horny nail. Some nails were coated with his own blood, some with mud, none with moss. Gentle and persistent sounds scratched from the painted partition as the rough, shingled legs reached out over the jelly smudges through the damp, beery, back hall air. He took a long time to run out of mud to shove aside, to finish tearing up his last victim, to give up his final swim.

Mom said it was all reflexes, nothing supernatural or heroic. Nothing to feel sorry for. But the back porch swim went on for so long. The massive roof of a shell and its relentless occupant were too easily held back by that tassel of clothesline. Head or no head, that snapper should find its way back to mud and water and prey and, maybe, life. Reflexes, huh. Sure took a long time. Sooner or later, though, the soft scratching stopped. The back porch was silent except for bees buzzing at the window. On the other side of the back door, there was soup on the table and beer in the refer. Dad would eat his stinky cheese as always: late at night and alone.

DREAMSONG

All summer and late into the fall
tibouchia arranging and rearranging
itself outside my bedroom window.
An electric rhapsody of slender brown stem
and soft pink bud bursting
into a staccato of purple bloom.

"Murasaki" you would say,
marveling at its particular hue.
I see you in the yard
gathering the fallen flowers
and you are calling me.
My childhood name comes songlike
as I fly to the door.
The wind comes up
and suddenly you are gone.
I walk the yard and all around
petals are falling soft as snow.

My eyes open, the dream ends, and
the morning sun on the tibouchia
plays a fugue full of forgiveness.
I sense those moments between the notes.
They are full of bones snapping, muscles tearing.
Those particular silences are bright colors
between thin black lines.

THE AMISH GIRL

An overabundance of celery in an Amish garden
is a sign of an engagement.

She was there first,
then they saw her.
Two girls, riding their bicycles
south of town, chasing down green aisles
of soybeans and corn under the wide lid of a midwestern sky.
She was rarer than a pheasant
up close at the fence like that.
They slowed, then stopped
at the edge of her vision, stilled
by her translucence.

This could be a painting.
Dust from the garden
smoking the hem of her burgundy dress.
Hair, light as corn thread, pulled tight
beneath a porcelain cap.
And her clear eyes staring off across the field
where men and horses ploughed the black soil.

When she saw the girls, her hands
fluttered to her face like flushed birds.
And she turned and ran through rows of celery,
her long dress rippling the garden
into green waves.
And envy ran through them like the desire
they were too young to name.
She was as simple as a blue summer
with young men in broad-rimmed hats working the fields
and rows of celery waiting to be picked.

FUKU YOKOYAMA TSUKIYAMA

A CUP OF FLAN

There used to be a relatively peaceful time called "Before the War" or "Before Evacuation" in the small, quiet country town of Santa Lucia, which sat unobtrusively on the highway of the king a few miles inland from the Pacific Ocean. Long ago, the Spanish padres called the road El Camino Real as they walked between the missions and rested for short periods at Santa Lucia before they resumed their journey to San Francisco.

Years later, some young Japanese families settled in the valley and raised abundant crops of superb vegetables, berries, and lively children. As the former were trucked to bustling markets, the latter walked long distances to the elementary school, crossing busy El Camino Real twice each day without mishap.

Except one day.

I remember nothing about the accident, not even going home from school with the other older children that afternoon, so all of my life I have had to rely on the stories others told me. There were different versions. Some said I was running as fast I could, which wasn't very fast, to try to catch up with them, while others claimed I was dawdling, fidgeting with my metal lunchbox or flinging my sweater around. Still others claimed the speeding car simply did not see me because I was so small, and did not brake in time.

Strangely, I do recall, even thirty years later, that I was wearing my favorite chartreuse skirt with its matching jersey pullover top that had three dark green stripes running across the front. The outfit was still quite new, but someone in white was cutting it off my body with large scissors, clucking her tongue saying, "Oh my gosh, look at all this blood, poor thing."

I kept hearing all kinds of voices, mostly white women's

voices, asking me over and over, "What's your name, little girl, where do you live, what's your father's name, how old are you? Can't you understand English?"

Then someone said, "Go and get Benny from the kitchen. He's from her country, I'm sure, and he can talk to her." Although I kept answering their questions, they didn't seem to hear, and my heart was pounding extra loud, and beating all over inside my head and body.

"She couldn't be any more than four-years-old, and look, she's as light as a feather," the white figure was saying as the others wrapped my head, and the streets came weaving back and forth at me and turned into monstrous snakes again and again. But in between I thought I heard a vaguely familiar voice that sounded like one of my father's Filipino workers from the ranch.

Far in the distance I thought I heard my mother's voice calling me. "Tama, Tama, can you hear me?" Another strange white voice was saying, "Mrs. Tokita, all she's been murmuring for the past three days is something that sounds like 'ee-tie, ee-tie.' What does that mean?"

My mother's usually cheerful loud voice was soft and subdued, and I was sure that I had died, for the Italian neighbor's kids who were my friends told me that at their Catholic Church the nun said everybody whispered or talked quietly in heaven. No noises like on Earth.

Mother's voice was closer now, and I could smell her familiar Mama-smell of carnations and rice and sweet *shoyu*. She put her warm, plump hands on mine, and through half-closed eyes I could see that she was wearing her best blue silk dress with the white bamboo leaves printed upside down. "In Japanese, it means 'hurt,'" she explained to the woman dressed in white who stood by my bed.

"Since she's finally come to, why don't you go home and get some rest now," the nurse, who had been introduced as Miss Anderson, told my mother. "She's been here most of the time since you were brought in," she said to me.

In Japanese my mother told me I had been run over by a car, and that my left leg was broken in two places. My head was bandaged up because there was a bad bump on the back, but that the doctor had said I would be all right. Then the streets began to come at me again, weaving back and forth, turning into huge snakes, and the cementlike cast on my leg squeezed more pain into both legs that were securely hung from the ceiling in traction.

"I am your special nurse," Miss Anderson said, as she ran a warm wash cloth over my face and neck. "Can you speak English? You haven't said anything in days now, but I know you're not unconscious."

I peered out at her from half-closed eyes, for I was having a very difficult time opening them normally. She was a big lady, with very white eyebrows, and short yellowish white hair that curled under over her ears. It looked soft, like rabbit fur. She had a long, thin nose, and from where I lay, I could see not round nostrils, but thin, long slits, and I wondered if she had a hard time breathing. She looked old, but then she didn't seem that old. There were no wrinkles on her cheeks, just two wavy lines on her white forehead. She wore very light pink lipstick, and no rings on her fingers. There was a large round watch on her wrist with big numbers, and she looked at it closely when she counted my heartbeats to see if I were alive or not. She smelled like my mother's freshly starched clothes, and lavender soap.

Miss Anderson was extremely efficient and performed by the rules. When my father thanked her for being kind and caring toward his daughter, she remarked crisply, "According to the Florence Nightingale oath, nurses must be personally impersonal, and we must not let our emotions interfere, you know."

News got around quickly in the small Japanese community of Santa Lucia, and even as I emerged from unconsciousness, I could smell the fresh green of ferns and fresh cut flowers of all kinds. There were potted azaleas and hyacinths, daffodils and tulips. The dresser top was stacked with boxes of chocolates. Miss Anderson opened my favorite, the white box with a picture of a pleasant old lady on it. There also were boxes of Hershey's kisses.

"Oh, these Japanese bring too many gifts to the hospital. And there are entirely too many visitors every day," she complained. "And what are all these cans?"

"Canned peaches and fruit cocktail," I informed her, for when the small group of friends rallied to support each other in times of illness or the birth of new babies or recovery from such, they gave each other useful gifts that the whole family could enjoy. I could tell by the shapes of the white store paper-wrapped gifts that some had six cans, the rounded triangular ones had nine, and the larger flat ones had an even dozen. "I hope some of them are pineapples," I said, "because my sister and I love them."

Among the regular visitors were four of my mother's close friends who always told me, "You listen to us because we have known you even before you were born," indicating they had my best interests at heart, and that went for all the other offspring of their circle. They laughed, criticized, agreed, gossiped, disagreed, and even my hospital room, which had become smaller for all the gifts and their presence, was not spared. Whether awake or asleep, whether they were there or not, I could hear their murmured conversations.

. . . poor thing, she will never walk again . . . oh no, she will, but it will take a long time, years maybe . . . and one leg will be shorter than the other . . . she will limp . . . she will be a cripple . . . nobody will want to marry her . . . you can't say that, you said you wanted her for your son's wife ten or twelve years from now . . . not anymore . . . you want someone healthy so she can take care of you in your old age . . . laughter . . . so selfish . . . the Tokitas should have taken her to a big hospital in the city . . . instead they had that butcher operate on her . . . she'll have big ugly scars . . . with that concussion, she will never be quite right . . . remember the Nakamura's boy . . . the car accident five years ago . . . he is funny kind . . . shh, Tama can hear . . . but she can't understand much Japanese . . . but she can understand just enough . . . no need worry, she's only six . . . she's the Tanaka girl's friend . . . oh you mean the third one . . . you know she is not Tanaka-san's daughter . . . laughter . . . too pretty for

Japanese . . . Filipino father . . . better looking . . . laughter . . . but tell your daughters marry only your own kind . . . let's go, here comes the Christian woman, the one from Nagasaki . . . acts like a white woman . . .

Whenever the Christian lady came to see me, I felt as if I were preparing to die the next day. She came in the evening, said long prayers to Kiristo, and even made Miss Anderson kneel down to pray. My nurse soon excused herself, saying, "Mrs. Nogi, just five minutes. Please." Mrs. Nogi was different from the other Japanese ladies, for she spoke perfect English and gentle Japanese, and had unusual greenish eyes, and the other women said she was *hapa*. With her "now I lay me down to sleep . . ." ringing softly in my ears, I would try with all my might to keep my eyes open, and watch the pattern on my ceiling made by car lights as they sped down the street outside. I kept awake by reciting the pretty Spanish town names, "San Diego, Santa Monica, Santa Barbara, Santa Paula, Santa Maria, Santa Clara, San Anselmo, Santa Papala." Miss Anderson always said, "There's no such place as Santa Papala."

"Yes there is," I'd retort, "because I have an auntie that lives there in a big white house with a lacy front porch." But the thing that really bothered me was what the ladies were saying about my friend Aiko Tanaka. How could her father be Filipino; Mr. Tanaka was Japanese.

"You just aren't eating," Miss Anderson scolded me again. "It's been almost a month, and your body is getting thinner. I'm responsible for you, so I've got to fatten you up. I'll talk to Benny to make a lot of good things for you to eat."

"Who is Benny?" I asked, for I had heard his name several times already. The nurse brought in the meal trays three times a day, and I sometimes heard her say "Thanks, Benny," at the door, and I thought I saw a brown face peek in from time to time.

"Oh, he's the Filipino boy who cooks in the kitchen," she said, not elaborating further. "Now eat this soup," she said, putting a spoonful up to my mouth. "It's good."

"It tastes tired," I said.

"Tired? What a funny little girl you are. Food never tastes tired. It's either tasty or not tasty. You've got to learn more English words," she reprimanded, as usual.

"I want *omusubi* with *ume* inside," I told her.

"What is that?"

"A rice ball, except it's a triangle, with a sour red pickled plum in the middle. And black seaweed wrapped around on the outside," I explained.

"Seaweed? Black?" Miss Anderson exclaimed. "My word, such strange things you've been eating. No wonder you're so scrawny. If you want rice, I'll get plenty of rice for you. I love rice myself, with lots of cream and sugar on it, and raisins and dates mixed in sometimes."

Soon after, some new, more substantial foods began appearing on my food trays. The tall man with the brown face put his head in the door more often as he handed Miss Anderson the trays.

"Hello, Tama," he said, "feeling better?"

"Is that Benny?" I asked my nurse.

"Yes, that's Benny. Thank him for the good food he's been cooking for you," she told me as though she were my mother.

She waved him away as I obediently said, "Thank you."

I was happier now, for there was a new, delicious custard with a brown sugar, penuche-like layer on the bottom of the cup. And my mother brought small *omusubi* with *ume* often.

Dr. Reed came almost every day or so to check on my left leg, and put his fat fingers under the cast to see that it wasn't too tight, and pulled both legs together "to make sure they would grow straight together. Wouldn't want one shorter than the other now, my little Jap girl?" He would adjust the pulleys and weights, give the cast a slap, and leave me wincing. Every day I would carefully match up both legs together so that neither he nor the visiting ladies made nasty remarks about one getting shorter than the other. More than the gossip of the ladies, something about Dr. Reed bothered me.

It wasn't his red hair, or his carrot-colored beard, or his large rough hands, or his roaring voice. It was what he called me.

"I don't like Dr. Reed," I told Miss Anderson finally.

"Why, what a thing to say," she said aghast. "He is one of the most respected men in the community. His family has been here for generations!"

"I don't care," I said, covering my face with the bed clothes. Whenever I feared facing adults, that's what I did. In my other life, I might have been a turtle, I was convinced. Miss Anderson pulled down the sheets with a questioning look on her face.

"He called me a Ja—Ja—a Jap." I felt the dreaded word squeezing itself out of my tight throat.

"Oh my dear, it's just short for 'Japanese,'" she explained lightly.

"No, it isn't. It's a bad word. It is not nice to call us that," I cried, pulling the sheets up over my nose and fixing Miss Anderson with the most hateful look I could give anyone.

"There, there," she said. "Oh, look at those round almond eyes, so tired. Now take your nap like a good little girl."

Miss Anderson was gone on a short errand one early afternoon, and I had dozed off, having spent most of the morning stretching my toes in their mid-air position. I thought I heard someone coming into my room. My eyes closed a lot, but my nose and ears hardly ever slept, and so I could hear and smell various people who came and left my room. There was a vague scent of pomade in the air, like the kind I smelled in the emergency room when I first was brought in. Soon the door opened again, and the tall man with the brown face that peeked in before came in. His black shiny hair was combed back neatly and smelled of the hair dressing as he approached my bedside table.

"Hello, Tama," he said, as if he'd known me a long time. He had a wide, friendly smile and a broad nose. "You do not like the plan?" he said, pointing to the dark green custard cup on the table.

"Plan?" I asked, in a small voice, puzzled.

"Oh, I am sorry. I forgot," he said carefully. "I must pronounce it 'flan' because that is the correct name for it." He rolled his *rs* which had a familiar ring to them, for I had heard similar, musical voices in my father's fields during lettuce harvesting and at my friend Alice's father's pool hall and restaurant in Chinatown. "I make it special just for you."

"I like it. Thank you," I said, "but I can't reach it."

"You look better than when I first saw you in the emergency room when the car ran over you. The nurses told me to come and talk to the little Filipino girl. They said you did not understand English. But you did not understand me either. I told them you were Japanese, not Filipino, but they said, oh you are all the same," he laughed. "Your father is an educated man," Benny added.

"Oh, do you know him?"

"Yes, I see him every morning when I bring the breakfast tray. He was reading the paper yesterday when he was waiting for you to wake up." Dad fed me every morning.

Since I had memorized all the first-grade books, my father brought lots of other stories for me to learn to read. Miss Anderson was surprised that I could read at all but most astounded when she first heard me speak. I told Benny that, and we had a good laugh. After Benny fed me, spoonful by spoonful, and wiped the excess flan off my mouth, I asked if he had any little girls like me.

"No, I am not married. Too busy working. I go to night school to learn more English, reading and writing. No time for a wife. But I have four little sisters in the Philippines. The baby one is just like you," he said.

As he reached over to pick up the spoon and empty cup, his cheek brushed lightly against mine. It had a nice, warm brown feeling.

Just then, my door flew open, and in came Miss Anderson, apologizing for being late. When she saw Benny, her face tightened up and became very red. She rushed at him and shouted, "What are you doing? How dare you interfere with my patient! Get out of here right this minute!"

Benny quickly walked out without saying anything. I pulled the sheets up over my nose as my heart beat faster, and looked intently at Miss Anderson. She had scolded Benny, who was a little taller than she, as if he were a small boy.

"Did he hurt you?" she yelled at me. "Did he touch you?"

"No, he only fed me the flan because nobody else was here. I couldn't reach it," I answered in a small voice.

After she calmed down a bit, she pursed her lips together and said, "I'll have him fired. He had no business being in this room. The very idea. He doesn't know his place."

The empty cup of flan had fallen to the floor and broken into two uneven pieces.

I never did see Benny again after that incident. He had been my friend, for after I'd survived the initial crisis, my parent's friends stopped visiting as regularly as they had before, and, since children under twelve were not allowed to come in, I was beginning to feel lonely. I guess Benny was lonely too, and seeing a small brown girl who reminded him of his little sister, had begun to bake me extra sugar cookies and other goodies, and dropped in for short visits.

I missed hearing the Filipino folk song he used to sing to his sisters about "planting rice is not so fun." The song had a lively rhythm to it. I would hear him singing the song up and down the hallway, in and out of my room as he went about his work. I wanted to learn the whole song but he always had to hurry back to the kitchen saying, "Next time."

But there was no "next time." I wondered if Miss Anderson had had him fired. Why had she been so livid with rage: had he been a threat to her care of me? Why didn't she want him to be my friend?

After caring for me so efficiently for two months, Miss Anderson was satisfied that I was healing magnificently, and laden with all gifts from my mother and father, left me to minister to a more unfortunate child. In another few weeks, I received a new pair of crutches so I could go home and learn to walk again.

The pain had long since left my legs, but a twinge somehow had transferred itself to the memory of Benny. I was puzzled about the way of grownups, the doctor, the nurse, my mother's "Greek chorus" of commentators and others who inflicted as much pain as the speeding car that hit me.

Over the years I have thought of Benny and wondered if he still made that wonderful flan.

CHILDHOOD

Up in the attic
I cringe
When I accidently kick
An old Roach Motel
And it sounds like someone just shook
A half-full box of Raisinets.

In the corner,
The perforated surface
Of the air hockey table
Is coated with a layer of dust
Like the Barbie "Airliner"
Next to it—
A vinyl, miniature section of airplane,
Complete with carrying handle
And tiny stewardess supplies.

I remember playing dolls
With my brother,
Throwing the plane
From the swing set
Like in sequels of *Airport*.
GI Joe, Barbie,
And Kojak
(Ken with his hair shaved)
Were the repeated victims
Scattered in the yard from impact.
Although GI Joe
Had kung fu grip,
He always lost his arms
Since they were easily plucked
From his sockets,
While the others,

Found in the worn, dirt groove
Beneath the swing
Or on the slant of the doghouse roof
Were fortunate
Just to be unconscious.

TO MOVE YOUR ORGANS

Saturday night
Drinking almond tea
You explained your sister's theory
About energy accumulation
Cats jump over shoes
Because they sense energy
Channeled through the feet of the wearer
And steps retraced
From the paths of strangers
Cats and all animals retain energy
Like shoes
So eating meat is a problem
The violence of slaughter
Leaves negative vibrations in the body
And meditation becomes difficult
Bad energy can be released
By psychic healers like Ananda
Who come every other Tuesday
To move your organs
You ask if I would like to meet her
Obviously knowing that I don't buy this
Or maybe think you're just fucking weird
But I have to love you
Because you don't care
It gives me a strange sense of courage

CONNECTIONS

She got on
At Chinatown
And pulled at her hair
Near the back of the bus.
Dark strands
Fell
Across her white-skirted lap
And she connected the curved black lines
To each other
With the fine point
Of a sharpened pencil—
Its metal band
Clamped flat by molars
To squeeze out the last bit of eraser.

The passenger behind
Grasped the back of her chair
To brace himself at a stop.
A glimpse over her shoulder
Told him
That she was even stranger
Than the old man from yesterday
Whose briefcase was filled
With sliced white bread.

All she wanted
Was prolonged touch—
The confirming pressure
Of being drawn to another.
Wondering how it would feel
To be held forever.
She closed her eyes   thinking
It might be warm.

WHO SHE WAS

She was not surprised
That my obsession was to hide
And wished for a large cape
To throw over us like a tent.
She was trying to help me
Because she never felt like hiding.
She wasn't sure who she was
But enjoyed watching that person
In anything reflective—
Windows,
Christmas ornaments,
Restaurant spoons,
Her dog's eye.

She preferred metal to mirrors
Because it didn't stare
When it watched her back.
The white spots from the lights
Followed her when she moved her head
Or walked around the room
Like the eyes of portrait paintings
And she was obscured into dark lines
That shifted and skewed
Whenever she waved her arms.

B-LEAGUE PLAYOFF

November 1969

K sat frozen on the hood of her father's Chevy, afraid to look at them. She had watched them come reeling out the door and stumble towards her; but then she had to look away. She felt the flattened beer can bounce off her knee. *They were throwing things.* She couldn't look at them. The filthy packed snow ricochetted off the windshield and splattered on her shoulder. "Squaw meat." *Squaw meat?* She couldn't look at them; but still she had seen their faces. *I'll stop wearing my hair in braids.*

Then she thought maybe it was funny. Drunk boys. Stupid boys. She thought about going inside to the dance. Her friend Lilly stood in the doorway, facing inside, knee-dipping to the live sounds of Earl and Earl. Boom chuck. Boom chuck.

Lilly didn't look ready to leave yet and K felt conspicuous just sitting there. She traced her finger around a small chili stain on her white Levis. She tried to think of it as blood in the snow but the stain wasn't red enough. Then she decided that it was rust and her leg was rotting metal. Her body—steel, rusting. She slid off the car and motioned to Lilly still knee-dipping in the doorway.

"Isn't this great," said Lilly. "I mean the whole town comes out for these things, even if they weren't invited to the wedding. Even if they don't like the bride and groom. Isn't this hilarious?"

The wedding dance was everything Lilly promised it would be. Lots of drunk friendly folk, mostly farmers—all full of sloppy piss and vinegar, ready to rabble rouse the night away, not paying too much mind to the bride and groom who were dancing so slow that it was much more like hugging and leaning, no matter if the song was for foot stomping.

They had driven in a straight flat line across the South

Dakota plain, nearly an hour out of Rapid Falls, to Lilly's old hometown of 900 people just for the occasion. Lilly's nephew, who was ten years older than she was, was getting hitched, and Lilly told her it'd be a good time and endless food for all.

"Yeah, so, when do you think we should get going?" K didn't want to sound overly anxious so she nodded her head to the music.

"I wanna get me a dance with a sweet old cowboy first. One more for the road," said Lilly, talking straight out through her nose.

"Yeah, okay. Maybe I'll just sit right out here. I'll be okay," she said, her eyes on the three stupid boys, their voices fading. They were tossing empties at each other now.

Lilly wasn't listening and went inside.

When they got back into town, they decided to shoot the loop a couple of times before going home. They swung by the Spur and saw Quigley's Ford pickup. Quigley and Chester stood up in the back of the truck bed and waved frantically. K pulled into The Spur parking lot and rolled down the window.

"Howdy, China girl."

"Hi Chester, so what's up?" she said, inching off the brake.

"She's not Chinese, Chester," said Lilly. "So you look like official Spur rejects—86ed again?" She shouted this over the top of the idling Chevy, standing from inside the car, her head and torso out the window.

"Nah, we didn't get kicked out," said Chester. "We haven't even tried to go in yet."

K fingered her braids and stopped at a stray hair, tucking it, unsuccessfully, into the proper row. Lilly would want to stay. Another night in The Spur parking lot. Maybe getting kicked out, maybe not. K looked hard at her friend and wished she could be more like her. They spent these countless nights sitting around in Quigley's truck, or getting 86ed from the only three-two beer bar in town, or driving endlessly around Oglala Avenue and up and down Highway 2, but Lilly made it seem as though they were on an adventure or a mission. She liked to shake up the regular Spur patrons—

Spurheads she called them—mostly truckers, underage foosball fiends, and the other tenacious minors who could stand for hours in the icy South Dakota air, hopping from car to truck to car, and, finally feeling the cold, trying again to go inside The Spur; sometimes victorious, sometimes not. Lilly always said they got kicked out for being so outrageous, never mind that none of them would be the legal 18-year-old drinking age for at least a year.

Nobody would miss the Chevy. Her father was in Minneapolis for the weekend and her mother knocked out early these days, but she used her midnight car curfew as an excuse to go home.

"So ditch the car at your house; Quigley and Chester can follow you. Besides, this might be the night we get the Quig to talk." Lilly winked, perfectly scrunching half her face, so that with each side of her profile she looked like two different people.

"God, Lilly."

Going back to The Spur in Quigley's truck suddenly seemed like a good idea. She could talk to Lilly alone on the way to her house. Tell her that they threw things at her. Tell her that she didn't care because they were stupid and drunk, and besides, it was funny how stupid they were.

"Those boys. . ." K said, taking the long way home.

"What, Quig and Chet?"

"No, at the dance. The ones outside. There were three of them."

"Burl and Tommy. Burl's my cousin's stepbrother." Why was everyone somehow related in that town? The life of her own small family never touched, even in passing, some second cousin, some nephew, some cousin's stepbrother. She wondered if Lilly was as unattached to her boundless family members as she appeared.

"Yeah so, he hates Indians, I guess."

"I wouldn't worry about it. He hates everybody."

"But it was weird. They thought I was Indian. I mean, I couldn't say 'no I'm not' because I'd be like saying it's a bad thing to be or something. Anyway, I felt proud. Isn't that dumb? And I felt good because they were so stupid."

Lilly thought it was great. She was eager to take credit for masterminding this serendipitous deception. But K wasn't sure if this was what she wanted to hear from her. She took precarious comfort in Lilly's approval. Lilly assured her that deception was a most powerful skill, and besides, wasn't it such fun? Perhaps it was. Yes, she would try to think of it like that. Fun. Trickery. So, she wouldn't tell Lilly about the fear. Not that she thought they would actually hurt her, but the paralysis from *not knowing how to think of this* filled her with a numbing sense of suspended panic. Still, this was not the first time. But they had never thrown things.

When she pulled in the driveway she was pleased to see only the porch light on. Her mother would be sleeping and it made sneaking out the back door easier.

The cold came crashing in. "Why can't you just roll down the window when you gotta spit, Chester?" K knew why, but when Chester opened the door she felt herself being sucked out, bulleting forever across the South Dakota plain (so beautiful in its uncompromising stinginess, brutal in its monotony) ripping up the skies and never banging into hills or trees or buildings; and at sunset folks would sit on their porches and point to the streaks in the sky. And on Rosebud they would say she was Never One of Us and they'd call her Her Too Many Wings. And one day there would be a postage stamp and a commemorative coin.

"I don't wanna dribble on Quigley's door."

"He's polite. Aren't you, Chester?" Lilly patted his knee.

It would not be until the last night of the 1970 B league basketball playoffs that she would indeed be sucked out of Quigley's pickup and find she had too few wings and land on the gravelly side of the road in her own vomit, the nervous retch stock-piled in her stomach—a delayed reaction to a playoff only she and two others would witness.

And Quigley, his Ford being a benevolent appendage, always had a sixth sense about when to slow down so his passengers might have a windless moment to light cigarettes and, on special occasions, cherry cigars; and he had a feel for windows and doors and spitting and throwing up, so he would have already slowed to first when she opened the door to let it out and went out with it; and he would have already stopped and backed up by the time she started to cry.

March 1970

Hick traffic all night long. The Bs were in town for the big event of the season. Such a welcome invasion that Quigley had a new shirt and everyone helped clean the Ford.

It was the one time out of the year the town of Rapid Falls could feel smugly worldly, for with the flood of small towners, this isolated place of fifty-some thousand seemed a metropolitan playground.

K ironed her newly bleached bell bottoms then sat softly next to her father on the lumpy sofa. She squinted, blurring his silent profile, then focused on the face that appeared on the black and white Motorola. This face, so angry. The grumbling of Pine Ridge. He wears a headband and he is facing the un-seen reporter; the words, so angry. This face and the one next to her—he could Never Be One of Them. Her father tucked a pillow under his head. And then the commercial about assimilating . . . what? Nutrients to build strong bodies 12 ways. Assimilating. Wondrous bread.

Her father, looking collegiate in his baggy cords and letter sweater with no letters, was starting to snore, a familiar routine in front of the TV during the news. Her mother came in from the hallway and gently pinched his nose till he sputtered some and opened his eyes. "He stops breathing sometimes," she said. "This is very dangerous."

"I need a ride to Quigley's, Mom. Everybody's meeting there before the game."

It was decided her father would drop her off at Quigley's. Her mother pinched his nose once more for he had loudly stopped breathing again.

There was a yellow Volkswagen and the face inside made her heart tighten. Was that the one? Well of course he would be in town: wasn't everybody? "Dad, I'm not sure this is the way we should take to Quigley's." She risked a look in the rearview mirror. *It was turning around. It was following her.*

Her father said nothing and gave her an unreadable glance, but she knew it meant he knew where he was going and how he was going to get there. She wanted to turn around. The back of her head was burning. She took off her stocking cap and her scalp felt squirmy.

They were passing her father now. She tried to look and not be seen at the same time. Wadding her cap in her fist, she slid down and leaned forward, trying to focus through the smeary driver's side window. So now *they* were following the yellow Volkswagen, but soon it sped up, leaving them behind, and leaving her wondering how she could be so moronic.

But there it was, everywhere, all night. One more time before they reached Quigley's. In the parking lot at the game. One lane over when they were all packed in the pickup driving down Oglala Avenue. At The Spur. And even, as she came around the silo and to the west side of the tool shed, there it was. Still, she couldn't be sure about the face.

She was glad she had already peed before she saw it sitting there, abandoned—temporarily, she guessed, for the passenger door was open and tinny car-radio music hit the dead air. But by then it almost annoyed her, for she had finally peed and could finally relax and allow the waves of fatigue to wash over her. But now she felt the tightening in her heart. Still she thought, well, why not? Let's get this over with. Scalp me.

Well, it was too late to be sorry she hadn't gone right home after the game. But why didn't she just stay closer to the truck with the others? Always wandering off to pee. Well, it was too late. Come out then. Show me his face.

The old Beckner place still smelled like a farm even though the main house had burned down the summer before. The fire had taken everything except the foundation, the hand-crank pump, the silo, and the tool shed. The smell. So strong, even in the snow. How is it that the cow chips survived? She picked up one in her mitten and skipped it. Well come on then. Where is your face?

The fatigue again. How long did they drive up and down and around Oglala Avenue and finally in a straight flat line down Highway 2, listening to Quigley's broken 8-track Buffalo Springfield tape? And in the middle of "Broken Arrow," when it starts to warble, and leaks from the other tracks start seeping through, Chester pulls out the tape and Lilly keeps on singing in her best nasal-twang-quasi-falsetto Neil Young voice, and nobody seems to notice the difference because she sure can sound a lot like him. These nights always seemed to culminate in a disjunction at the Beckner's place: everyone separating from the captive Ford, checking out the unmarred snow and then marring it, and then coming back together to lounge around the pickup before getting back inside for the tight squeeze home.

The snow crunches behind her. She looks not over her shoulder but down at the boots and then the face. Yes, it is him. The voice behind him is saying, "Damn, Burl, I'm freezing my ass off. Let's get on home." This other, from behind, notices her now. "Lord, what's some girl doing out here? You must be freezing." Not an unkind voice.

Burl is slow and says, "Well, you need a ride somewhere or something?"

She is stunned at that moment. Maybe her mouth opens a little. There is no fatigue: her thinking only he *doesn't even remember*. Well why should he? It was a small and careless thing. Still she can not speak.

"Shit, what's wrong with you, Pocahontas? Hey, maybe you're Chink or Cong or something? No Speakee English?" Burl is moving toward her now and she is inching closer to what remains of the corral fence, three leaning posts, the wood shredded and sagging in the middle.

"Come on Burl, leave her alone." The kind voice.

"Is that it? You're Cong or something? Hey, maybe you know kung fu and you could chop me in two, huh?"

"Burl. Let's travel, come on." But the kind voice is in the car now.

"Yeah maybe I could."

This stops him. He studies her. Her face gives him nothing; she is as dead and cold as the air between them.

"Yeah, well, maybe you could." He takes a swipe at her head and misses but her cap falls off when she jerks back.

She is trying to think of a movie or perhaps a TV show where they fight by leaping in the air and kicking, and where they use their hands, not wadded up in a fist but straight and flat with bare edges. But she can only think of fist fights and shoot-outs at the O.K. Corral. Well it was true, she had only seen one, maybe two scenes, where their straight flat hands were weapons. But Burl's sudden lunge makes her remember and invent something that stupefies them both, and sends him in retreat to the yellow Volkswagen.

She slams the edge of her mittened hand in a straight flat line into the decrepit fence beside her, splitting the top frayed rail, which, from the weight of the splinters and powdery sawdust, disintegrates the feeble second rung too. She is startled to hear the wordless sound that comes out of her; a sound meaning only that a heartfelt war whoop could never be a bluff.

TAMARA WONG-MORRISON

MIDDLE ROAD

Wear slippers when walking over that sand
It can cook your feet
Out Polihale way,
the white coral wears shark's teeth.

Almost Halloween and she washes clothes,
Costumes, customs painted in acrylic,
Recycled sheets for the street monster.
Today he twirls the white mouse around by its tail,
This Christmas he'll be King Herod in his pre-school play.
"Bring me the Christ child, for I want to worship him too,"
    he'll say.

This baby's first birthday luau is an E-minor chord.
All the usual dendrobium orchids, paper lanterns,
And steel-guitar for the videotape.
Still, things are out-of-tune:
The aged artist dances of "going back to her little grass
    shack,"
Her oldest daughter desires to be a man
And blown away by it all is bleached blonde George.

Soccer game—win or lose—they are taught to cheat.
Screaming coach wipes his cocaine-nose on his sleeve,
Slack-breasted mothers shout at their kids, "Stupid
    sonofabitches."
The clean-team wins—one long kick from centerfield.
The sole goal.

Beer bellies and baseball caps,
They call themselves "Johnny's Angels."
Johnny Angel has a crooked halo
And a devil's forked tail:
A cherub smile every mother loves.

He is the center mark from where
All others stray,
Cut their hair, pretend—
Hang rubber snakes upside down.

Some children here are grown
Still trying to be kids,
Correcting other people's verses in another language
As if it mattered.
Well, what matters?
The center-line on the road,
The yellow marker that says, "No pass or go,"
The rock answer that balances the scales?

He has "it," the metronome tick,
The ability to sway to extremes
And return
Home base.

CHRISTMAS EVE, HAWAII

Lonely and sleepless at 3 a.m.,
I come to the moonlit garden
where the dark rustles
and a plover's fleet whistle
cuts the air—
sounds telling of other awakenings,
other lives, the ones we never touch
except through sounds, or words
read in a newspaper
and then forgotten as I will forget
the thin drone of a plane
just now dragging its lights
behind a cloud.

Yesterday, I read about a man
camping with his family,
who was dragged sleeping from his tent,
held spread-eagle by wrists and feet,
and thwacked against a tree.

Some scars we bear for life.
When the final bandage
falls away, what will be visible—
the tree bark's imprint over his eye?
The wire in his jaw bone?
What of his screams
still reverberating in his blood
in time to the slow heave
of his body as he remembers it
flying forward and back
graceful as a child
on a swing?

Now we must sing
"O Come All Ye Faithful."
The wavering candles
remind me of this morning's
watery moon. I wonder
why I can't remember the words,
or the plover's cry,
or the feel of your blue–white wrist.

WHITE DUCKS

Silenced by the light
entangled in dark water,
by the soft *qua, qua* of white ducks,
and the steady lap of eddies
against a hollow hull,
a woman and a girl
listen to their hearts
palpable as the sound of their voices
dying just now into the enisling air.
From the girl's face—
contours indefinite as down
blown by the wind—
flows a longing that fingers
the curves of the mother's face,
memorizing what changes,
draws farther away
with each silent departing second.
And the woman,
staring past the ducks
into the dark lake,
feels the longing—a brand
against her breast—
looks deeper into what flows
beneath them,
torn as the water tears
with each stroke of webbed feet,
her separateness
sinking to the lake's bed
beneath circles that repeat, and repeat.

POINT OF ENTRY

Sensing the promise
pledged by a first cut
into the wood, he pauses,
all past and future choices
gathered into the hand holding the plane.
On the bench of his daily devotions
lies a maple slab, split and joined
so the grain chevrons, the inverted Vs
enigmatic pointers he salutes
with a nod. The wood,
gray with attic age, already old
when shelved, waits,
an unread book on green cloth,
pages possessing cell-on-cell
the heart of a tree felled by the ax,
the original wedge.
Cool morning light
spills over the templates, chisels,
knives, the rows of bottle varnish—
ochre, russet, red wine—behind him,
the photographs of Amatis and Strads,
and the ones of Heifitz, Kreisler, Menuhin.
He hears the rattle of dishes,
the oven closing, his wife
singing *Du, du, liegst mir im Herzen*,
feels again the stirring,
the tug of an unflawed opus,
grasps the plane tighter
and begins.

WARREN AVENUE SHOP

Disturbed by the shifting tensions
of his mood at the bench,
she pauses over her ledger, listens
to the shop's singing silence
like the sound of two swift spindles
playing out their lives
into this room, this refuge
of work and hope, the two-ply cord
of their marriage
uncut for forty years.
She glances at his stooped back,
the straining shoulders
bearing down on the chisel
cutting the violin's wood, giving birth.
She almost calls to him to rest,
but waits, the numbers
on the ledger pages reminding her
of her own unfinished task.
They curl down the page
in a graceful script
more suited to the hand of a princess
than to the rough, cuticle—
ragged fingers that hold the pen
as lightly as the girl in Leipzig
held a book while posing for her photo
forty-three years before,
the one she signed "Your guardian
spirit in a foreign land,"
and gave him as a talisman
before he sailed for New York. She
doesn't notice (never notices)
the pain of her hands
nor her aching bunioned feet

in the sudden blur
of the month's gains (and losses),
as she brushes away tears
for him, for their work,
for the sausage and apples they
will share after grace, here,
in their shop, on Warren Avenue,
Detroit, Michigan, U.S.A.

6190 GRAYTON ROAD

Her hand drops the lace curtain
across the leaded window
and falls quiet,
except for the pick of forefinger
on thumb, tics
like a clock telling
her need for him.
In the gathering dusk
lit by the street light's
gleam off new snow,
she listens to the house—
a heater's warm sputter,
the scrape of the boy's chair,
the girl's book page turning.
The black phone, hooking
what ifs from the dining room air,
overlooks the table set for four.
China and silver glitter
in the growing dark.

★   ★   ★   ★

Forty years later, setting a place
for one in the kitchen,
she knows he is safe,
would come if he could
to tell her of the fine violin
he repaired, of the stories
shared with Emil, of Mr. Little
whom he again
misnamed Small—
and she would listen and laugh
like a young girl,

full of pride in him,
for her part in him.
She is not lonely.

Upstairs, in the maple chest,
lies his letter,
sent to Germany
before they married,
the yellowing sheets whisper
thin against the wood—
"To love someone and see the sun
setting . . . I want to be with you
day and night, so that no harm
may befall you and no stone
may make you stumble . . ."

LUTE PLAYER

"Papa, I love you," she wants to say.
Each day the singular moment passes.
The words, unsounded, flood her heart
before the portrait on the pale blue wall.
Hals' troubadour, slyly glancing,
plucks the strings no one hears,
deep tremors she feels in topaz silence,
as if fingers stroked away her song, her cares.
His smile—knowing Mona Lisa's thought—
belies her own, defies her to fathom
notes both false and true sliding
from past to future as lightly as Papa's
when he lifts down his lute with its satin band,
strikes the chords' silver, and sings.

FATHER ASSUMES HIS SQUATTING POSITION

When Father assumed his squatting position,
he rested his weight
with both heels flat on the ground
and balanced himself by putting his elbows
on his slanting lap—
a posture which I associate with
peasants and peddlers,
not refined as the scholarly tradition
of sitting at the desk, studying calligraphy
and reciting a classical poem.

In our one-room dwelling,
Father prepared tea while squatting
at the edge of a low table.
First he drenched the tiny cups and tea pot
in a large bowl with boiling water.
Packing the tiny teapot
with tea leaves to the brim,
Father poured scalding water
to quickly strip the imperfection
from the rugged dark green leaves.
He extracted the essence of the tea
into the brew the way
the alley night air brewed the dew.
Serving tea in small cups
required steady hands;
repeating the ritual
demanded devotion.

Squatting, Father added charcoal to the stove
which warmed up a corner of the room.
Around the fire, he and his friends
sat on low bamboo stools,

their cheeks glistening, voices rising,
dark hair not yet gray.
They would go on
scheming how to market beef jerky
procured according to their old way
or compiling four-thousand years of history
into a scroll presentation.
They dreamed of making a name for themselves.

IN THE HOTEL ROOM IN HONG KONG

I took out my white skirt
and found on it a dark stain.
I thought about you, the afternoon
you led us to your garden
in the middle of a rice field.
Digging up taro, you told me to watch out for the plant;
the sap stains badly.
Standing on the narrow mud border,
you carried a hoe, hung from it a basket of taro,
huge leaves and stems sprouting like umbrellas.
You planted your feet, not wavering.

I hear the stream calling me.

You grew up in this valley surrounded by hills
and the Zi Jin mountain.
In the stream you cleaned vegetables,
washed clothes, bathed your children,
took the water buffalo for a cool dip.
Now you share a well with your neighbors;
your grandchildren come to fetch drinking water.
I watched them carry two heavy pails of water
hung from a bamboo pole on their shoulders,
body slender and strong,
small feet lightly tapping the dirt road
without spilling a drop.

You are always in the kitchen.
You keep the stove going day and night.
There is a presence of carbon monoxide
in the room. You have become so used to it
I am convinced it flows in your blood.
One evening you sat next to me

in the yintai, the shadowy balcony,
across from where your son-in-law and daughter
dried their grain before storage.
You dozed off while talking about the harvesting time.
The space is closing in within this land.
Here the darkness cannot be broken,
lamps in China are too dim.
Have you ever wanted to leave this valley?
You asked me to send you letters,
even though you can't read.
I want to hear from you,
even though you can't write.

LISA ERB

AT THE GRAVE OF MY MOTHER'S MOTHER

I had thought we could love only that
which has form. Like the 'apapane's bill curving

a million years to the desperate lobelia.

After, another flower arriving
at the bird's very red,
is form. Like the termites who dashed themselves

at the lamp before mating,
dropping messy wings in my hair. I didn't mind.

Women, too, who one responded unfailingly
to the moon, the first time they tuck a man inside,

are beautiful. The blood holds—
is held, but the milk may rush to the nipples
at a single cry,

even the cry of an animal, and spill.
After the abortion, I thought I had eyes
a person couldn't be born with. More color.

Like those blond sailors with their Portuguese
lovers, like you. Giving up everything and staying.

WHITE ECLIPSE

The white flowers below my window
resemble naupaka, but are not.
At night, ghosts, but not. When your envelope
arrived with missing hands and sealed
mouth, I thought another woman.
You must have shown her the naupaka—
one half stranded in the sand,
the other on the mountain.
It's always the same story with flowers.

CHIN YUNG

CITRUS

1.
My youngest boy and I watch as Spring,
our two-week old kitten,
scrambles across
the slick yellow oak floor
and splays glove-like—
an insignificant bundle of bones,
wrapped in wisps of white.

I gaze into her open fragility,
one green, one blue eye . . .
I wonder at how she has managed
to cleave a niche in my heart,
I want to watch her grow old.

2.
We carried a small, clear plastic tube,
like the ones cake frosters use,
filled with a pink, murky liquid,
to a spot shaded by large banana leaves.

We carefully dug a small hole,
with an ordinary gardening tool,
and watched the rich brown soil
supplant the thin, green grass.

We placed the tube,
filled with the remains of
our aborted fetus, lovingly,
within the roots of a baby orange tree.

We shifted soil from the shores
surrounding the slender sapling,

over the dreams of an unborn
girl-child.

3.
Spring, tiny kitten, lies listless,
her fur moist and disheveled, staring
with one green, one blue eye . . .

We cradle a small bundle of bones,
and bury her next to our daughter.
A tidal wave shakes my body.
The scent of citrus is nine years old.
The wind shifts through the dry banana leaves,
and mourns a heavenward sigh.

LETTING GO

Last summer—in South Africa's winter—I walked down the corridor of Fairmount Primary School, trying not to show I was sniffing the air to take in the odor of my past. All I was conscious of smelling, though, was my nervous perspiration.

The past fifteen minutes had been rather comic as well as embarrassing. I was relieved to be out of the principal's office. He'd been courteous, all right, though obviously puzzled by a visiting alumna who spoke in a British accent of teaching workshops in Hawai'i. And I had to concede it was a bit outlandish to come back to Fairmount hoping for any real contact between my middle-aged teacher self and that happy elementary school student who had questioned very little.

I wondered if the Afrikaans head of the school had suspected that my oh-so-American talk of creative—and critical-thinking skills workshops was mostly a polite ruse to get me past the vestibule and the curious school secretaries and into the inside corridor. I should have realized there would now be a tight security system for the school—along with all those wrought-iron gates barring the entry to walled-in Johannesburg houses. I had naively thought I could simply walk in to wander the school halls—looking like somebody who had a right to be there. Instead I'd had to press bells and speak into grids and pretend that I had pedagogical business with the school. Blah blah about the whole language movement in American schools, and how I'd be glad to help; blah about writing across the curriculum. The fellow had been pleasant enough, though. Young for a principal. My heart went out to him. He'd seemed genuinely sorry when he spoke of how many Jewish students in his increasingly wealthy area now were transferring to private schools in order to study Hebrew, and how much of a loss that was to Fairmount, which was already shrinking as the neighborhood got older. He had a real problem in not knowing which African language to make available to his students—who from the coming term would be black as well as white. At least there was no longer the old problem of only white kids learning only English and Afrikaans.

Feeling awkward at how my footsteps pounded down the hall, I passed the grade one and two classrooms and struggled to remember sitting up at the front, facing the others, reading aloud to them as the teacher graded at her desk. This corner of the building didn't house strong interest for me though, and I doubled back past the principal's office and headed for the more senior classrooms. What I would now most easily call grade seven, the final academic grade level of the school, was called standard five. Only the little ones were in grades, at six and seven. At the important age of eight we were promoted to standard one, and were never to be in grade school again. Mr. Blumberg had led the top standard five class at Fairmount. I remembered our nervousness at having a man for a teacher, but nothing that he taught me. I could at once recall the ginger of his moustache and his freckled, beaky aspect. Of the grade-teachers who had deployed my reading skills, time had eroded all memory.

"Lorna!" My head shot around. The voice was less familiar than the accent, but I knew it. The woman facing me was in her early forties—stocky, a grizzled look to her mop of tight curls. It took me long seconds of direct staring before a small and sassy girl peeked at me from her square form.

"Hello. You're Colleen's sister, right?" I was surprised at how easily Colleen Feldman's name swam into attachment to this puffed up version of her rambunctious little sister. What was her name—Shirley?

"Lorna *Josephson!*" This woman spoke loudly and was obviously pleased to have two names to hold up when I was sinking without anything more certain than a family connection. A bamboo cane switched in her hand—a pointer for boardwork, I hoped, and not any sign that brutalizing children was still in vogue in Johannesburg primary schools. The older sister had been what our close Johannesburg community called "wild." Fishing for any evidence of real wrongdoing, I could dredge up only one incident, in form one of our neighborhood high school, when Colleen had high-stepped into my shocked attention. She had begun her menstrual period during the school day, and had fitted herself out quickly with the regulation pad available at the office. She had been so pleased to be wearing a livid badge of her new maturity that she did a can-can kick for the group of girls standing around during break in their grey school uniforms.

Shirley stayed long enough to speak of her sister's divorce and remarriage—and laugh loudly at her having two kids under four at the age of forty-four—and then turned into a noisy classroom, her voice raised to a brassy roar. She seemed an unlikely teacher.

I hurried outside the school building, and stood uncertainly on the pavement, looking over the square recess park across the road. The July day was cold enough to make my shins ache a bit. It was always a shock, after years of acclimatized living in Hawai'i, to exchange summer for dead winter—and I was suffering from early arthritis. The park was entirely deserted, though the babble of childish voices behind me made it easy to remember years of precious school breaks spent out here. Just before we left the school, my close friend Jenny had stood under that tree and pressed a hand tightly on each flat breast: 'They HURT.' At the time, I'd been hideously embarrassed that my friend would touch her chest like that in public—right on the playground.

Thoughtfully, I crossed the road and took the diagonal path that divided the school park. With a sudden vividness, I recalled taking this very track the day the school bus had brought us standard fives back from a week at the Kruger Game Reserve.

The trip had, after all, been my first away from home. My dad's emergency pharmacy had always been busiest over the holidays, and with my mother employed as the shop manager, there had been no chance of family vacations. Most of the popular kids had jeered at the idea of a holiday for the top school class—though at twelve they were intrigued at the idea of a coeducational week under only intermittent scrutiny by a couple of teachers. And the Game Reserve was available to us now because, months past the popular dry winter season, the veld grew high and the animals had much more cover from sightseers driving on the sandy tracks. With water everywhere, the game had no incentive to roam to the deep water holes. I had not known just how high bush cover could grow, being a city girl, nor how loudly a whole class of children in a bus could talk, driving all game deep into the veld. I'd been excited at the prospect of spotting lion and leopard, and seeing impala leap gracefully over the road like they did in bronze at my favorite downtown park, and had argued that I deserved the chance to travel. My hardworking parents had finally agreed.

Unused to a bathroom shared with anyone but my sister Gail, and after a lifetime of public lavatories separated by gender as well as race, I had been appalled at the toilet on the bus—one scratched aluminum job with a chute or broad funnel leading down to the red African soil a foot below it. Boys on the broad back seat would eye any luckless girl handing her way to the ill-smelling cubicle at the rear, and then twist ostentatiously around, staring at the dusty road in the wake of the bus and howling and pointing at wet traces left behind. Wasn't it Maureen who'd had to go when the bus was stationary, and whose rush of urine had been greeted with tribal ululations of delight by boys and most of the girls? I could still see the broad fixity of her smile as she came shakily down the bus steps afterwards, when we were all standing around waiting to board again after spending two hours at the water hole and its viewing platform—and even then seeing no game at all because of the racket we made. Seven years later, I remembered the school trip vividly enough to sit through a Johannesburg- New York flight without one trip to the toilet. I was ready to leave home for a year as an American Field Service exchange student, but not to be seen leaving a toilet cubicle that men could be waiting for.

Sharing a camp bungalow with several girls had not been too embarrassing because Ruth and Jen had, as usual, taken up a position on either side of me. My bed was under a window, and on the first day Mr. Blumberg had appeared framed in it, his Adam's apple and freckled nose hooking at the air, and had brought his face all the way to the glass, so that his spectacles nearly hit the window. I'd felt sorry for how awkward he looked, and how short-sighted he must be, and had smiled at him and waved. He checked on us often, too, both day and night—far more than the woman teacher did. And he kept on singing the same song. Whenever I saw him, he would trill out, in ginger notes, "Lorna's busting out all O-over!" and hum the rest of the spring ditty: "Lala lah lalah la la la lah!" I had wondered over his cheerfulness. Usually, in the classroom, his note was asperity—nothing like these high spirits.

My own spirits were fairly crushed during the long days of sighting not a single free-moving wild animal—the boys at the back of the bus apart—and by the edict against allowing us school kids into the Pretoriuskop Rest Camp dining room at night. I would have loved the chance to eat in a restaurant, a rare treat, and to see my food. The school group sat at two long trestle tables out on the red stoop or verandah, under high bare bulbs that were shaded by dark green metallic cones. Hard-carapaced beetles, fuzzy moths, and fat-bodied termites would hurl themselves against the lights, ping off the green shades, and drop softly into the plates below, where the kids sat in relative darkness, joking loudly over the poor fare.

"How's the baboon and beetle soup?"

"Man, this hippo flank is overcooked."

"The boy says that we get croc stew tomorrow, hey!"

I ate less heartily than usual from small portions, and nervously drank very much less water than was normal for me. It was some comfort to be able to cinch in my school uniform belt to a new hole late in the week.

October weather wasn't hot enough for swimming, but Ruth and Jenny and I and some of the other girls often sat around in the late afternoon on the banks of the kidney-shaped pool, and sometimes Terry, wielding his comb, would come up, his sleeves pushed back in just the right way. Errol was always with him, smiling his big easy smile. Roy would be there also, steel-straight, his hard body tense in the presence of the girls. Twice Blumberg sat around behind us for what seemed like hours, and when we finally got annoyed with his policing and left, by loud arrangement, for a walk around the perimeter of the camp, he passed by me very closely and sang his usual song with what seemed like a particular pointedness. I couldn't work out why he'd changed the words from "Spring is busting out all over," and I didn't see why he wouldn't leave our crowd alone. I knew how to behave, after all, and there was no reason to think I was wild or might break out when Colleen and her lot were off giggling in a corner and using make-up when Mrs. Gordon could no longer notice—once the high camp lights went on and the fast African dusk gave way to a night sky far blacker than anything I'd see in Johannesburg.

Apart from how our noise had prevented every possible animal sighting, and the singing on and off the bloody bus, and the reek of the bus toilet, I could salvage only my idiot incomprehension of Blumberg's sexual interest and the joy of eating sweetened condensed milk, spooned down at night in a blur of thick girlish pleasure now gone forever. Most sharply, I remembered the day I came home. Funny, that. My first holiday had collapsed into lots of uninvited insects, the distant barks of animals unseen, and the lonely singing of a wretched teacher. The clearest picture is of coming back—my first ever return home.

The bus had raised a cheer, in and out, when it swung up Fairmount Street and parked in front of the office. Parents were waiting, their cars (noticeably free of red African dust) parked up and down the city road. A very few nannies were there to walk the unlucky home. They would carry the suitcase and ask about a Game Park reserved for whites only. After a week away from their boys and girls, even the most committed tennis- and bridge-playing moms had worked the homecoming hour into their social calendars and had waved the bus in. They were hugging their kids and moving off swiftly to their cars. I had of course expected no mother on a busy work afternoon—and my father had, so far as I knew, never been to my school. They knew me better than to have our Johanna waiting, as if I were a kid when in fact only months stood between me and high school. Home was little more than a mile away. I picked up my suitcase, proudly independent, and cut through the playground in the direction of Sydenham Street. Some turns, and shifts of the suitcase from hand to hand, and I was moving steadily up Elray Street, very close to the shops that fronted my house. It was exciting to come through the alley and see 12 Sydenham Street before me, looking ordinary in the afternoon sun. The week, though hardly as terrific as I had hoped, had left me smug at how flat and everyday the place looked. Nothing changed *here*.

Setting my scuffed case down, I unlatched the front gate and then grabbed up my baggage for one last haul up the path. Only when I climbed the verandah steps did I recognize that my week away had not left things exactly as they had been before.

My aviary to the left of the front door was quieter than it had ever been. No deserted game reserve had ever held the field of silence as that floor with its litter of blue and green budgerigars. Each bird was on its hard back, angled this way and that, dry claws extended up into the careless air. Very clearly, no one had fed or watered the birds for a week. No one had even noticed the effects of fatal neglect. Standing alone on that school ground thirty years later, I remembered holding still on the verandah a long time, taking in the meaning of the soundless, motionless cage.

Back again in Hawai'i—and able to say home again in Kaneohe—I find myself trying to work out why I can't remember feeling angry that afternoon, long years before. I remember the shock, the dismay, the sense of loss, my weeping over how light the bodies were. I can see where I buried them in the back garden, all nine lifeless birds, that afternoon, before my mom would be upset by the pitiful sight of them. My nose ran as I dug their graves. I'd been hungry and thirsty that week, for the first time I could remember. Even though I had tilted tins of condensed milk down my throat and eaten chocolate bars, I had missed our cook Thomas's two-course, insect-free dinners and had experienced gnawing pangs. How horrible to fail of strength, to flutter off a perch, and no one caring. But I can't report waves of anger or blame. It didn't occur to me to remonstrate with my parents. They worked all day and my dad worked all night, and I had chosen to leave my birds to a busy household. My sister disliked animals and never went near my bird cage. Our maid Johanna came in at six in the morning and left the house for her servant's quarters at the back at nine at night. Seventeen years before, she had found her informally adopted daughter (understandably called Lucky) squalling for her life in a rubbish can, inside a stained brown paper bag. And by then Lucky already had her own baby, and Johanna's son Michael was unemployed again. My birds and their hunger were not her business, finally. No, as a kid I knew that my life was easier than my parents' and lots easier than the servants' lives, and different from my older sister's, and that the birds depended on me, whose word clearly did not have much weight with the others. And I stoically bore my sad homecoming and learned that there are consequences of going away.

What taught me to feel for the birds *and* for several members of the household? In parallel circumstances, wouldn't my American-born-and-raised son David have made his servant-less, hardworking parents suffer accusations of slow murder, of animal torture, and large-scale massacre?

I have for years spoken against the corrupting influences of being raised in South Africa's Johannesburg suburbs. For decades I have been proud to have chosen freedom—at the pain of emigrating twice, and making my children strangers to their grandparents. But what if I have made them strangers to everybody? What if patience, and compassion, and kindness, and self-control come from the hard soil of a childhood like my own—outside democracy?

In South Africa, as a child, I knew inequity of power and that my opinion wasn't sought, and that many people suffered horribly even though they worked very hard to help their families. And I knew harsh reality from the many books I read to entertain myself. Poverty and struggle and transience were conditions of the earth. Dickens had taught me a lot about privation, and courage, and the necessity of effort. I knew next to nothing about sex, which was proper for my age, but a lot about heart-wringing injustice, both witnessed and in literature, and I didn't see how raising my voice about neglect of my pets would raise my spirits or the dead birds.

I must admit that I have become an American mom. I live in a complacent and powerful country, I can buy more for my children than my parents could, and I've the education that gives me the power to teach them more than my parents could teach me. And yet I am powerfully aware that my son, whose pets I help feed, and whose opinions I seek, and whose muscular body I sometimes drive to the local school, is slow to put himself in others' shoes and walk around in them, and quick to shout. I see him breaking things I would never have hoped to own, and walking past books I would have begged and bartered from my sister, and I believe that he hasn't felt a pang of hunger in his eight years. How will he learn to make himself count, and how very hard he must try to change the way things are?

I am not saying that South African white children nowadays are more empathetic than American children, for the young relatives I met in Johannesburg this past summer are as soft as David is. I guess I am moving to a new sense of how an insensitive world can teach sensitivity. My dad was always at work, and was a distant, dignified figure. My mother never told me what she felt. Our family servants could never trust us to understand them and were startling evidence to me to how all people did not speak English and eat Jewish cooking and share the same world view. They believed in the evil little one, Tokoloshe, and built their bed up high with bricks, to rest out of danger, and yet worked out their days in a world crammed with hazards, including my own father and mother. In such a hard and puzzling world, I had to think hard. I had to make out things by reaching imaginatively for some interpretive frame that would accommodate them. I had to work out why it was wrong of my mother, a lady so deeply kind I never heard her say a cutting word, to give soap and deodorant to our servants as their Christmas presents. I learned to swallow back judgment and to lament inwardly over how wrong my father was about black people being wholly different from white.

Now I am becoming more and more quick to speak impetuously and loudly. I used to bury my words along with my hurts. America has taught me some complacence and the relief of complaint, but also a sense of being heard, and of my right to question. I read less and less and say more and more. I am beginning to tell people what they should have done, and to feel confident I have the power to improve things.

The part of me that is still orthodox in its suffering Jewishness and guilty white South Africanness tells me it is only when I know how hard it is to make a difference that I remember to work mightily for that end, knowing that I speak from only one unimportant place in a largely indifferent world. Like my optimistic country of adoption, this side of me warns, I am gaining a false sense of power. I must learn to curb my tongue, again. I must say less and write less to my students and stop overfeeding them and spoiling them as developing writers. And as a mother, I must let David struggle alone into connection with others.

And the American Lorna hoots and jeers. She insists I was so angry with my parents and my sister and our maid Johanna for forgetting their promise to feed my birds that I went numb and didn't even know my anger. She tells me that too much is much better than too little, whether in pleasures or words or emotions. When David voices loud consternation or indignation, his South African mother purses her lips and wonders who he thinks he is; his American mother cheers and closes in for a vocal contention of wills.

It is the American Lorna who has learned to value expression over stoicism. I have stopped hiding my feelings so noticeably that even in America I am seen as over-emotional, too intense. But openness teaches me to listen, too, to what a lot of people say, in addition to my own children. And as a result I have lots more feelings to talk about. There's little left that is stiff, or buried, or silent. For long years, I used to run the cold water tap when using the toilet, and shake my head over American friends who took their conversations into the bathroom. Now I let everyone know when I'm pissed off. And if my feelings can flow unashamed and strong in these next years, I shall send out my stream upon the sands, and welcome all faces at the window.

PEARL

Fivewide we're round the table and the leftover
ham, cornbread, potliquored green beans, yams,
Mary and Martha, Beatrice—*puella osculis
dilectissima*, my father calls her—and, back
for a visit in the kitchen, "now that I've laid
my burden down," our Pearl. She has buried the
seventh of her thirteen children, her hands sore
with the weeping and the digging, washed,
    wiped over her eyes.
Under this zinc table where we sit,
speaking in soft lullabies of lost children, I cried
once, "I am white!" "And God is white," I cried
furthermore, the thunderclap of my punishment
lowering. "God took his great big brush,"
then Pearl said, "dipped it into the root
brown soil, swiped some, licked up the yellow
sun with it, splashed some, lowered it into the
volcano, swabbed some a fine burnt sienna, and those
bristles were still hot when he brung that brush
hard up against the bitter water of the Mother of
Chocolate tree and painted me, and out of the
blue of His own good reasons, He be skipping,
He be skipping some folks, *girl*. Skipped you."

PANTOUM

The two chairs we photographed last Spring
at the Kuilima in rain light
are emptied of everything except the air beside
the sea wall braced for the spray.

At the Kuilima in rain light
when I climbed a wet plumeria tree,
the sea wall braced for the spray
that stung your eyes to tears, but you blinked

when I climbed the wet plumeria tree
blurring the print more than sea water. The hurt
that stung your eyes to tears (but you blinked,
dumb-struck, reeling!) is the past all out of focus

blurring the print. More than sea water the hurt
rocks salt in the wounds we begin with,
dumb-struck, reeling. Is the past all out of focus
then, at the breakwater, the light cry?

Rocks, salt—in the wounds we begin with
minerals, weed, kelp, climb in the dark.
Then, at the breakwater, the light cry
waking our skin up to the loss of everything:

minerals, weed, kelp, climb. In the dark
the shutter, the other's loving eye, is wide:
waking, our skin up to the loss of everything,
we close the photograph album, open

the shutters. The other's loving eye is wide
on the reef shadows, blue-green at the horizon.
We close the photograph album, open
whatever distances we need to see

on the reef. Shadows, blue-green at the horizon,
are emptied of everything except the air beside
whatever distances we need to see
the two chairs we photographed last Spring.

RUNES FOR THE STEPMOTHER

THE FATHER'S

See how the pitfall of your voice
breaks down the ground of my children.
You are not what I'm used to,
not what I've lived:
this story in the middle of the woods,
my dribbled crumbs and finger bone
gnawed to the nail.

Yes, yes, you haul me with the willows,
yellow and afternoon,
into the flanking
holler of the earth's bruise,
body becoming in the lightning swipe only
my own where I howl.
What does the wolf hold against me?

You are not young, you are not beautiful.
You are no wife.
I enter your broom
house and its switches—mine, not mine—
with my axe. Your trees are my lumber,
wet with my wax.
How to make the challah rise you will
learn from my daughter whose hair
hangs in hay lanks over the table
and whose voice
is attended in doors and not yours
and not yours.

Yet she comes to you, sweet, other syllable,
honey and myrrh, mother, mother.

The deer eye at the brake
with its corner of dust is all amber
broken and level as bread, the must
shot in the woods.

I tell you there are barrels with spikes
that roll down cobbled streets
women like you.

Read the children these legends,
I tell you.

Eat their steaming hearts.

THE SON'S

My sister and I walk hand over
hand along the water where the old
shoes of dolphins flag their tongues, air, air!
and the fishermen scrape
from the scales of rain
blows a mermaid's earsplitting half notes.

I hold the rock's marina in my eye,
my birth the right
harbor all the sails head for.

Behind me your shadow reels a second thicket,
and I keep a second watch, the fly
catcher's worm and feather in my wrist,
ticking.

Brother and sister, we walk the long enchantment.
Her palm, zebra, dove,
and docks of fingers when I need
them leaves like your shedding
glance the green disgrace of dragonflies.

I am the changing and the changed.
Over my head the trunk of love
grows while I walk in the wilderness
leather as animal, each longing inch.

You call when the woods are burning
the deer out of me
that lays row after row of candles
at my sister's feet.
And I run, and I come, a great buck,
out of her bridal into the brake
where the velvet
antlers fall before my eyes.

Sand under sand on the beach crumbles,
the crab shuttle and back
bone of your hand burn me,
heir to the realm, into a goat
boy and voice of grass,
puling the corn silk (love!) out of my throat like straw,
out of my straw like ocean into gold.

THE CHURCHING OF WOMEN

We talk about abortion. We lie down
with such a word. *O Lord, I found*
trouble and heaviness, this weight.
He smoked a cigarette. He paid for
half of it. He graded papers. He
tried to rape me on the way to the woman
who swipes speculums from Kaiser, wipes
them clean, says, softly, *baybee,* as she
pries my legs apart. This is a dream,
it's not, O wake us up! Make babies
out of day and hang their crazies
into clay we can spit clean, rub rosy,
work their orange into pots. My tits,
I can't believe they were so fat!
I baptized all the pieces in the toilet
water. And the black orderly who sang,
Swing low, sweet chariot. Comin for to
carry me home. After they rolled me back,
I ate a hotdog, I was empty. There
is a kitchen table in New Jersey,
shakers, mustard, but they cleared it.
Can't remember, did it hurt? *Daily*
increase this woman in wisdom and stature,
be thou to her a strong tower in the face
of her enemy. Will we be damned,
burn forever, the babies in Limbo? Mother,
where's that? Mother of God! Hormones
carved out make you grieve like that.
And when I try to tell him he can't get it up.
O sweet Jerusalem, high as a woman on this bed,
this wrack, tie me to you, shred to the shard,
mother to daughter, lover to lover.

BREAKFAST TIME

Song Li Nguyen Stevens pushes the metal latch in with her finger and waits, her ear pressed to the darkness, her eye on the patch of moonlight at the end of the hall. Slowly, she guides the bedroom door closed. Trailing her hand along the wall at her right, she makes sure the two other bedroom doors are closed. She veers around the laundry pile next to the bathroom. She slides forward, careful to shift her weight evenly from one bare foot to the next, to avoid hurry and excitement, to remain a shadow, a wisp. She is careful not to make a sound.

She crosses the living room. Outside, a truck shifts gears as it turns onto King Street. The reflection of its headlights flashes around the walls of the small kitchen. Then it's quiet enough to hear the tinny strains of music from the radio in the apartment next door.

She turns on the wall lamp above the kitchen table. Taking care not to scrape the stool against the floor, she moves it next to the cupboard, stands on it to reach the top shelf, and pulls out a long, fat box with the word "material" printed in crayon in large, red letters on the side. The letters overlap the sketches of birds and flowers and the Oriental characters scrawled on the cover. She puts the box on the table and opens it.

Inside, there are various sewing implements laid out on top of some shiny black material. She places scissors, thimble, tape measure, several spools of black thread, and a package of needles on the table and pulls the material partway out of the box. The lamp does not provide much light, so she bends into it to search for the place she left off the night before. She takes her time selecting just the right needle, a small-eyed one, difficult to thread. Then she begins to sew.

She sews quickly, her hand following a rhythm. Not a single tiny stitch shows on the silky black stuff. Occasionally, she stops to turn the material, to rethread her needle. When her hair drops forward, she loops it behind an ear and sews on, hardly missing a stitch. From the radio, the songs come and go, and, except for a little tuneless humming now and then, she pays little attention. In the daytime, she might listen to the words and practice them. Songs were more interesting to her than spoken language. She felt closer to English listening to them, but she is now so absorbed in her task that nothing seems to exist but her weaving thread and the fluid movement of her hands. Only once, while someone sings "I wanna get you on a slow boat to China," does she stop what she's doing. Her eyes turn dark; her hands limp: a moment only, a pause. Then she's sewing again, faster than ever, her head bobbing with the effort.

Finally, she cuts the thread. She puts the needle in its packet and leans back against the wall. Her heart is thumping. She looks at the stove clock. It's 4:35 a.m. She's finished. Not a single machine stitch. She had started with an idea that moved around, changing in her mind's eye, and some shelf paper, and nothing else. That was two years ago. She didn't think she could do it, but she did: she's finished. She's made the dress.

She sits motionless. All this time, she has thought only of the doing, never of the ending, and now it's over. The scheming, the saving, the excitement, the fatigue, the excuses, the long secret hours—all of it, over. Tucks will be needed, of course, here and there. Darts and adjustments. Ironing. But the making of it is over. She must try it on now, study it before a mirror. To see it whole, to see if her purpose is true, her vision real. To mark its completion, like a statue unveiled.

But how can she? How can she bear to look? What if it's not right? But there it is: she wants it just so, and, if it's to be just so, exactly so, she'll have to try it on, and if she does that, she won't be able to stop her eyes from looking at what she has made. How can she not look?

She glances at the clock: 4:35. It's too late. Everyone will be up soon: it's almost breakfast time. Quickly, she moves to the stove. She takes the coffee pot, removes the filter, and fills the pot with water. Out of a can from the counter, she measures coffee, puts the filter into the pot, the pot on the stove. She takes a can of guava juice from the freezer, leaves it in the sink, makes sure the toaster is plugged in, the bread ready, margarine, eggs and sausage out of the refrigerator, cups, plates and forks on the table. She thinks about the dress she's made and flies about the kitchen. If anyone should wander into the kitchen this early, they'd find her busy, breakfast begun.

She looks at the clock. George will be up at 5:00, his mother and the boys at 5:30. There's no time, no time to iron it, and she can't look at it until she's ironed it. That would be out of the question, but still, she can't go to work without looking at it. Just one look, very brief; she'll hurry: she has the time, after all; she'll make the time.

Or maybe she could stay home today, call in sick. Yes, his mother won't be home today, so nothing would come in her way; she would have the whole day. A whole day in the house alone! She feels giddy thinking of it. But no. The new order for the outer islands. She knows as they all do that the new order would keep them working; that it was important to get this order out on time. These were hard days for the company. The company was growing at this time; it was very busy, and she was the best seamstress. She had to go to work. She had to save her sick days for the boys.

She closes her eyes. If the company finds out pink gives her a headache, they'll give her chartreuse to work on, and that won't help since it's the intensity of color that bothers her. This means she must go on working, trying to block out the stiff feel of 40 percent factory cotton: the hot, chemical smell of it, the flat, non-wrinkle, neon sight of it, a whole world of it spread out on her cutting table. No, somehow, pink is not for today. She can't touch it or think of it; she can't go to work today. Because today is the day of the dress. It is the middle of the third week of the month, the third month of the year, a day not of beginning or of ending, but a day of going somewhere, a good day.

But tomorrow: tomorrow the weekend starts: the busy time. She would never have a chance to see the black dress on the weekend with someone always in the house. This means she would have to wait until Monday morning.

Monday morning!

It is now 4:42. She looks at the black silk shimmering in the light, certain she can see a rainbow in it. She has twenty minutes. But since it takes her husband at least ten minutes to get out of bed, she really has almost half an hour. "I cannot not try this dress today," she whispers, "I cannot wait. Quick! Oh, quick!"

Immediately, she turns, whips off her tee-shirt and holds the dress up to her front. In the dim light, her thin arms look golden, her neck delicate. But she is bony. Her shoulder blades stick out like the wings of a small bird. Her back is heavily ridged with scar tissue. Handling the dress with care, she slips it over her head. When a hook catches in her hair, she does not yank or pull, but works at the problem with her nimble fingers until it comes free. She pulls the dress all the way on, fastens the hidden snaps, and arranges the folds. Then picking up one of the kitchen stools, she glides with it into the living room.

A noise. A door slamming. She stops in the center of the room, frozen to the spot in her black dress, holding the stool in mid-air. There is just enough light from the kitchen to make out a jumble of furniture crowded together in the small room: a couch covered with a patterned sheet, one overstuffed and two folding chairs, a TV set, a coffee table stacked with Popular Mechanics and Sears catalogues, shelves made of plywood and cement blocks containing at least a dozen ceramic shepherds and shepherdesses facing in various directions. Her mother-in-law's collection.

The noise has come from the apartment next door. Mr. Mendo is home from guard shift. He's turned the radio off; the Mendos are going to bed. She knows this but can't help trembling. The silence is sudden. She can hear herself breathing. It will be light soon. Slowly, she glides across the room.

Carefully, she closes the bathroom door before she turns on the light. Her face looks pale in the harsh fluorescent glare. Her black hair glistens. Her hand shakes when she reaches up to close the door of the medicine cabinet. Placing the stool before the mirror, she gathers the dress above her knees and climbs up.

The mirror is small, the space cramped; the light flickers. She can see only part of the dress, the bottom part, but not the hem. She rises on her toes, but still cannot see the hem. She frowns, twists her head, turns from side to side, stares over her shoulder. Then she steps down, places the stool upside down on the toilet seat, and stands again before the mirror; this time to see the top half.

The dress is simple. The sleeves are short and drop delicately over her shoulders. The neckline curves gracefully and modestly to a point between her breasts, and there is no line at the waist. The folds hang rich and heavy in the skirt. But the dress is not merely black and well-made. It rustles; it catches the light; it dazzles. At the slightest move, colors leap in the sheeny black. She turns, one sleeve flares and parts, revealing her bare shoulder, and small slashes of red appear. She turns again, abruptly this time, and the hidden scarlet blazes forth, a beacon in the night. She lifts an arm and the living red flashes out before it disappears again.

She backs up as far as she can to get as much of the dress as possible in the mirror. She leans forward to examine this or that button or seam and turns it up to see it under brighter light. She runs her hand here and there, searching for rough places. She fingers the appliqué running from her neck almost to her waist. This shows only when she turns slightly to the side. The thread she used is near but not quite the same color as the black dress, the design one that she worked out on the box: peach blossoms framing a large bird just lifting its wings in flight. She is proud of her appliqué; the women in her village are famous for this kind of work; she knows what she's doing here. She runs her hands down her hips and stands still in her black dress. And then she smiles. She lifts her chin and her dark eyes glow. She hugs herself. The thought flashes into her mind that she's done it; the dress is beautiful.

"OK. I did it," she whispers.

She has finished the dress. She is pleased with what she's made.

But now she has to hurry. She turns out the light, grabs the stool and runs for the kitchen as the alarm goes off. She no longer worries about making noise. They expect her to be up and moving about the kitchen, making lunches while the sausage cooks slowly. They know she often rises early to do some extra sewing for a few neighbors. They don't know, of course, that she spends time and money following her own visions. Today this makes her laugh, and she flies about the kitchen full of energy. She hits the button on the stove to start the coffee, draws off the dress, and in one quick motion pulls on her tee-shirt wrong side out. She sweeps black scraps from the table and crawls on the floor to get every thread. Then, quickly, she packs the dress in the box, returns the box to the shelf, and makes sure its label "material" plainly shows. Yes, the dress goes back into the box and on the shelf where it belongs.

She smiles. She has not made the dress to wear. There is no occasion in her life for such a dress, and she doesn't like to attract attention. She's too shy. Much too shy to wear such a dress. It's for a beautiful woman, a model, to wear; or perhaps it's for a special event, for someone to wear to Washington, to the White House, for someone to wear while shaking hands with the President of the United States.

It's 5:15. She whirls around smiling when she smells soap and shaving cream. George stands in his underwear yawning in the kitchen doorway. He flicks on the ceiling light and slumps down on a stool with his elbows on the table. The kitchen looks small in the glaring light.

"The coffee, Song. It's boiling over again."

"Oh, oh, oh!"

"Honey, I don't like to wake up and find you not in bed." He takes Song Li in his arms. "You look so happy. You're so little, so warm. Too bad we can't both stay home today." His grin is huge.

"Oh, I like that. Just once, OK? When we finish our new order."

"When we finish the renovation."

"When the sun is shining."

"Or the rain pouring down."

"Or the boys graduating."

"Or Mom off visiting. Hey, Hon. You finish your project?"

"What?"

"My jeans. You mend'em?"

"Oh!" She turns away to stir the sausage. "This weekend, OK?"

Her heart is beating fast. The room is so warm. She didn't mend the jeans. The thought flusters her; she doesn't know why. Something is welling up; she feels a tear rising. She won't even look at the box on the shelf now.

The kitchen fills with the cozy smell of sausage; it's still dark outside, but the tiny kitchen is daylight bright. George is yawning. One small son wanders in and attaches himself to Song Li's leg. His warm little body won't be separated from the leg until his breakfast is ready. Song Li ruffles his hair, and the lump in her throat goes away. There will be more days after today, of course. And many mornings. She leans over her son to put the plate of sausage on the table. Right now, it's breakfast time.

MARY'S SPECIAL CHILD

When all the other kids were in school,
you used to sprawl
on the sidewalk out in front,
stretched the full width of the stairs,
and draw with chalk,
your unspeakable rage
in ever widening circles . . .
sounds of traffic going by so loud,
you couldn't hear your mother calling

Even in winter, wearing just a sweater,
sleeves pushed up to elbows, you drew.
Sometimes, in a frenzy of inspiration,
you raised the chalk to your lips,
bit down hard,
and tasted what it was like
to be lonely

PAGODA

Early morning, India,
we met behind the huge white family house,
alone for the first time.
The vast green lawn, wet with sapphire dew,
sparkled like a jeweled blanket
beneath my bare feet,
as I tiptoed towards you

You waited, silent in that hushed hour,
sheltered in the pagoda.
Mourning doves chanted lilting songs like mantras,
lulling us to meditations

I heard nothing but my heart,
beating in my ears;
nothing but the snapped twig explode
beneath your father's window

At last,
merged in the musk
of long grass and ginger,
I heard the koyel sing

JUDITH VATES

TWO SEASONS AND A JAPANESE LOVER IN NEW YORK CITY

for Toyo

1.
In August
Under a tar roof
We sipped green tea
And admired flaming orange geraniums
Sweltering in a window box
Above Third Avenue.

He did not consider
A hand fan too effeminate.
The lines of his slight but muscular body
Were enveloped in a cotton sleeping kimono
Bound at the waist
By a lilac colored cummerbund.
His hair was long and dark.
It glistened like the strands of seaweed
Which he fished out of a steaming soup bowl
With a pair of enamelled mother-of-pearl chopsticks.

2.
In mid-December,
Under a confederate gray Manhattan sky,
Silver skyscrapers were powerless
To refuse an ermine collar.
The wind whipped in gusts
Hurling powder and flakes
From one deserted corner to the next,
Which we dodged
By playing a game of frozen hopscotch
At 3 a.m.
Unable to sleep

Like excitable children.

He wore blue jeans and cowboy boots.
Playfully, he opened a large bamboo umbrella
Under which we strolled,
Heads bent in opposition to the storm,
Reminiscent of a Hiroshige print.

When we spoke, our frosty breath
Emphasized the sentiments
As if in quotation marks.
We huddled, laughing at our silliness
Beneath the red lacquered parasol
Which bled onto the bleached snow,
Causing the concierge, the next morning
To suspect foul play.

MO GUI BODY

At one time, Jin and I were united against the world, the only Chinese students at a remote university studying film and video production. We weathered nights without sleep, passionately bringing to conclusion our many joint projects. We struggled together—editing my amorphous documentary into a thing with a beginning, middle, and end. Once, in a single day, we etched out over two hundred drawings, animating to shaky life Jin's fantasy of temple statues leaving the altar to dance. Our biggest project, a dramatic film, was finished one crystalline morning just as the sun was coming up. We drove to the park in back of my house and drank vodka straight from the bottle and decided to get married someday soon. Those were the glorious student days before we entered the real world and began to live together.

We came down to the big city, and Jin, with the aid of his Taiwanese contacts, immediately landed a job in a fledgling production company. Within a month, he moved up and I took his place. I never thought that I would need Jin's help to find employment in America. And who would have imagined, least of all me, that I would be jealous of Jin's job! Shouldn't I be grateful? He'd given me his old position. Even if I was stuck in the office dealing with invoices, at least I could boast I was in a video production company. But now I'd been the office assistant for more than six months, while he was out with the director, among the crew, hanging curtains and lighting shows.

"Did you have dinner out?" I asked, always the first to break the ice when he came home.

"Yeah, we did—you should've come."

I raised my eyebrows doubtfully.

"I called up the office on our way back, but you'd already left."

He was sincere; I softened a little. This wasn't the first time

I'd been the only one in the company to miss a dinner. It happened a lot, the crew went out to work and on their way back would end up having a good meal together.

"Where did you go?" I asked. "Was Director Chen there?" I couldn't help it, I just had to know who was there, especially Chen. If he was there, who knows what company business I might be missing. Who goes where and who knows what is very important for getting ahead in business.

"Director Chen wanted to go—he wanted to see the waitress with the *mo gui* body."

"*Mo gui* body, what do you mean?"

My Chinese language isn't what it should be, but it's not bad considering I'm American-born. I knew the word, but I wanted to be sure I understood this perfectly.

"She supposedly has a fantastic figure."

"But what does *mo gui* mean?"

"*Mo gui!*" Devil or demon . . . something out of this world."

"Well," I said, surprised by how excited I suddenly felt. And I imagined the crew in the restaurant ogling as she took their order and then brought their bowls of noodles to the table. I saw her moving serpent-like past the tables, her head turning hypnotically, eyes blinking, conjuring before men's eyes image upon image of a silky, twisting female body.

"I didn't think it was anything," Jin said and ripped the brown paper cover off the latest issue of his computer magazine.

"But what did the others say?" I stared at Jin hunched into his magazine like he was hiding from a rain storm. "What did Director Chen think?"

"He looked her over—he thinks it's fantastic."

"And, *okay* was all you thought?"

"It was okay—but I didn't think it was so great."

"Was Dojo there? What did he think?"

"Dojo was the one who knew about her . . . when he was at another company they all used to go have a look at her when they had lunch."

"I want to see her."

"Why not." Jin seemed bored. He put his head deeper

into his computer magazine.

About a week later, the crew finished up early, and I was still in the office taking care of some invoices when I saw Jin getting ready to leave.

"Hey Jin," I said, "don't go home—let's have dinner out."

He agreed and we walked down to the corner. Jin opened the door of a restaurant called "Plum Branch." I'd passed it many times, but I'd never thought of going in. Its large, flat, fish tank-like windows are so greasy, you could cut sticks of lard off them. Fortunately, the table and chairs were clean. We sat down. The only other customer in the restaurant was an old man sitting with his back against the wall taking his time with his tea. A waiter brought his pad and looked at me with a sour expression. I let Jin order while I surveyed the room. There were boxes of Tsing Tao beer, an import from the People's Republic of China, by a closed door and not far away, plastered on the wall was a Republic of China flag. I was thinking about this when Jin touched my arm.

"There she is . . . the waitress with the *mo gui* body?"

I didn't have a chance to turn around; the waiter was suddenly back at our table with my steaming bowl of soup and noodles. He set it down and put a plate of sliced braised chicken in front of Jin. When he was out of the way, I turned around. I scanned the take-out counter, seeing only a young man, an old woman, and a teenage girl.

"Come on, eat." Jin was gobbling his food.

"Where is she?"

"You missed her."

"You didn't mention this was the place!" I pursed my lips and frowned. "Tell me when you see her again."

I thought of changing seats with Jin so I could watch the counter, but that would really look ridiculous and Jin would think I was crazy. I ate my noodles and turned my head occasionally.

"You really think her body is just okay," I said.

"Well, I guess it's pretty good. I can't tell. Maybe in spring, when she puts on different clothes, we'll really see."

I ate in silence for a while.

"What's so great about it? Curves or what? Does she

have big breasts?"

Jin gave me a strange look. "Nothing compared to some American women. I guess by Chinese standards, they're big."

Feeling annoyed, I sipped my soup and let Jin finish all the chicken. Was he thinking that a nice girl from Taiwan would never talk the way I did?

About a month later, I was in the kitchen making some dinner when Jin showed up unexpectedly early.

"I thought you were doing a show."

"They could do it without me. I'm not feeling well."

"Too bad." I went back to my cooking. I heard him sit down in the living room. "Jin," I yelled. "You want some of this?"

It used to be we always shared our meals. If we didn't cook together, we cooked for each other. But that was before Jin got so busy and his hours got crazy and I got stuck in the office with the invoices. He wasn't the type to say anything though. He really believed in letting everyone live their own lives. Sometimes, I admired his expansive attitude, but lately, I thought of it as selfish. He just didn't want to bother with anyone but himself. He knew I wasn't happy and told me to quit my job—"just do it," he'd say. But maybe he just didn't want to have to see me everyday, sitting there . . . maybe he wanted me to move away. After all, he was having a time of it, going to fashion shows and turning lights on the city's most beautiful women. There I was always home early and sulking. "Be patient" was another line. He thought I might get on crew, but I had my doubts. I was too good as the girl in the office.

"Where did you eat lunch?" I said when a commercial came on the television.

Jin gave me a look like he was really mad and then, to my surprise, instead of bursting out with anger he swallowed and told me the dish was better than I'd ever made before. Then he said, "We ate at the 'Plum Branch.'"

"Oh," I said, "did you see her?"

"See her?"

"The waitress with the *mo gui* body?"

"She was there."

"And what did you think this time?"

"What I thought before. If you're so damn curious, why don't you eat there and see her for yourself."

Why was it that I never got to see her? There they were, the whole crew, seeing her almost everyday, lapping up her curves with their eyes. Going from head to toe, checking every nuance of her *mo gui* body. There I was in the office, filling out the invoices—keeping track of the money so they knew whether or not there was any left to spend on lunch! I told Jin later that night that it wasn't fair. I was part of the company too! Shouldn't I go to some of these dinners too!

Jin must have said something to Director Chen. I felt so embarrassed. It was around three-thirty when he came in to grab his coat. He said he was driving the van over to pick up the crew. They had just finished packing up after a luncheon show. Did I want to come? They were going to have lunch on the way back.

"Sure, I was just going to eat." That was a lie, I'd eaten at noon.

At lunch, I got so nervous, my stomach turned into a ball of jute. I wasn't used to being around everybody and acting buddies with Director Chen. I was disappointed too. He'd gotten out of the van near the "Plum Branch," and I heard Lee say something like "let's have a look," but Director Chen shook his head and we went to a place a block away. Probably, because of me.

Everyday for almost a week I went to have my lunch at the "Plum Branch." It was usually crowded and I couldn't always get a seat facing the take-out counter, but I tried. And I tried to figure out who she was, but I couldn't. There was an old lady, a young guy, and then two, sometimes a third, young woman who worked the counter. I just didn't think any of them could qualify. Their dark baggy clothes certainly didn't suggest much of anything. The one that sometimes wore a T-shirt was flatter than a postage stamp. None of them had *mo gui* faces, for sure. There was one, tall, sullen looking with some meat on her bones, but—*mo gui* body? I tried following the eyes of the single men who came in, but their gaze only led to the scrawl of characters announcing the specials.

The week ended and I felt dismal. Maybe Jin would come home at a decent hour and we could go to a movie. I should have mentioned it before. At eight that evening, he still wasn't home. Where the hell was he? Was he out with the *mo gui* waitress? I saw them dancing cheek to cheek. Lights flashing across her face, Jin's hand reaching for her hip. I went out to the grocery and bought a pack of cigarettes. I hadn't smoked in over five years. Jin was a smoker. He'd been saying he was going to stop ever since we met. Hah! I walked around the block three times and then headed back to the apartment. I was putting the key in the lock when I heard the last ring of the telephone. I stormed into the room expecting to see Jin watching TV. The place was just as I had left it.

At quarter to eleven a ferocious anger rose out of my gut. How come I'd never seen the waitress with the *mo gui* body! How come the one time I'd been with him to the "Plum Branch," she'd appeared then disappeared? What kind of joke was this? I pulled open the closet that the two of us shared. I grabbed Jin's best dress shirt and tried to rip it in half. The seams held as firm as Jin's thickly muscled forearms. Cursing, I opened the window and dropped it out. The arms spread like seagull wings; it seemed to feel the air and then floated down, and, just as it was about to reach the pavement, I saw a figure standing on the sidewalk. The shirt fell right at Jin's feet.

He picked it up and looked up, and I quickly drew my head inside. What a fool! How was I going to explain it? In a flash, Jin was in the apartment, red flames of anger dancing around his eyes. "Why did you throw my shirt out the window! HOW COME?"

"I didn't throw your shirt out the window! I dropped it by accident! And where the hell have you been all night! You could at least let me know once in a while if you're not going to be back until midnight!"

"I tried to call you—but you weren't here!"

"Sure! I go out for half a second and that's when you try to call. Is it so hard to try again?"

"I was working! Dammit! Didn't Director Chen tell you

at lunch that we got an unexpected job?"

"Director Chen doesn't even know that I exist! I'm just the girl in the office."

"Give me a break!"

"You give me a break! I'm sick and tired of missing everything. You guys go out all the time—"

"We're working!"

"Oh, I guess I don't work."

"What is wrong with you?"

"You've been covering up! You were probably at a porno movie tonight. Did she go? Or did she star in it?"

Jin grabbed my arms and pushed me down on the couch. 'You are making no sense at all. What do you mean 'she'? You nut!"

"The waitress . . . the *mo gui* body waitress!"

Jin let go of me and began to laugh. I've never seen him laugh so hard. I thought my crystal vase, the one with the old withered flower in it, the only one Jin ever gave me, was going to fall off the shelf and break.

"Stop it!"

"You are such a fool!" He was still laughing. "Call a taxi!"

"You call your own taxi!"

"Come on, put on your coat." Jin looked at his watch. "Hurry up."

Jin dragged me by the arm. We got in a cab and Jin directed it to the "Plum Branch." We went inside and he ordered two small snacks.

"Now turn your head. There she is."

It was the sullen woman. She wasn't beautiful, she wasn't ugly. She had on the baggy clothes she always wore.

"Well, what do you think?" Jin said.

"I don't see it. That's her?"

"Director Chen thinks she's got a great body."

"But you can't really see it—"

"So, I said, wait until Spring."

"Then you do think—"

"I already told you a dozen times—she's okay."

"You're right, she's okay, but *mo gui*?"

Jin reached across the table, took both my hands and

shook them, "You're the only *mo gui* I know."

We went home on the subway. We made love, warm and sweet. Afterwards, Jin fell asleep but I was still awake—thinking . . . Director Chen and Dojo, both bachelors, what do they know about women? And Jin, what did he really think? He said I was a *mo gui*, not that I had a *mo gui* body . . . something's not quite right . . . is it me . . . or him . . . or something else?

An invoice like a feather, barely there, floated through my mind just before I fell asleep.

lexicon

try not to be insulted
when they call us oriental.
let exotic be a compliment.
even the most educated among them
will ask how long we've been here,
be genuinely surprised we speak English so well.
don't expect other wrongnamed people to be any better.
immigrants from Guatemala and Mexico
will keep calling us Chino,
even when we explain we were born here.
'you know what we mean,' they'll say,
and we'll tell them our parents were born here too.
'you know what we mean,' they'll insist,
so we'll tell them our grandparents came from Japan.
they'll nod their heads,
still calling us Chino when they talk among themselves.
don't let these daily misunderstandings get to you.

learn how to differentiate.
slanted eyes is o.k.
but not you slanteyes, tighteyes, sliteyes, zipperheads.
to most of them Jap, Chink, or Gook all mean the same.
don't let them tell us that 'kill
the fuckin Gook,' spoken in combat,
is separate from 'too many Chinks moving in'
to Anaheim, California, or Biloxi, Mississippi.
watch the mouth and eyes carefully as they say the words.
maybe our closest friends can call us crazy Japs,
but be cautious when their talk turns
to those sneaky Japs who attacked Pearl Harbor,
who deserved to be put away in camps,
bombed at Hiroshima and Nagasaki.

pay close attention to headlines
which warn about 'influx,' 'imbalance,' 'invasion.'
don't consider any place safe anymore.
watch what they hide in their hands.
in Raleigh, North Carolina, Ming Hai Loo
was gunned down by two brothers
who hated Vietnamese. Loo was Chinese.
and it didn't matter if Vincent Chin
was clubbed to death
by two Detroit autoworkers
who mistook him for Japanese.

don't expect them to ask us our real names.
don't even try.

DELIBERATE

So by sixteen we move in packs
learn to strut and slide
in deliberate lowdown rhythm
talk in a syn/co/pa/ted beat
because we want so bad
to be cool, never to be mistaken
for white, even when we leave
these rowdier L.A. streets—
remember how we paint our eyes
like gangsters
flash our legs in nylons
sassy black high heels
or two inch zippered boots
stack them by the door at night
next to Daddy's muddy gardening shoes.

NOSTALGIA FOR THE MUD

Here's what I want to say. Right before I gave up music, I was full of myself. The happiest I've ever been. Terrifying and permanently etched in my mind, those final concerts will always seem bigger than life. You slinking through the audience, decked out in emerald green lipstick and embroidered Turkish fez. Waving goodbye to us at the airport, as the band boards the jet that takes us on . . . a dream. Our first and last international tour. Straight to hell. My band as opening act for Sister Mercy's No Bullshit Satin Soul Revue. She is a living legend —a survivor of the chitlin' circuit—authentic, gritty, magnificent, temperamental. She calls her classic songs "ugly music," she calls herself "Godmother to James Brown." Hers is a fourteen-piece orchestra, complete with Sammy Davis, Jr. lookalike emcee and topless backup singers who call themselves "The Hoodoos." She only talks to the men in my band and marches past me as if I am invisible. I eat shit, I grovel like a white boy—I am so grateful to be on the same bill with her.

This tour is so nasty, you have to pay your own way. 120 degree heat and humidity. No shade. Parasites in the water. Boiled English food the only thing available. Where are we? I cry everyday I'm there. "B. Goode! How could you be so bad?" Elvis and the boys needle our manager Brian mercilessly, in the last-ditch effort to keep our spirits up. I want to kill B. Goode, who responds by giving us daily pep talks on the importance of working, on work as an end in itself, and the prestige of opening for the legendary Sister Mercy, rumored to be the protégé and only female ex-lover of Little Richard. "Think of what you'll learn! Think of the riffs you can steal from the horn section!" Brian is hysterical and dehydrated, his pale face swollen with insect bites.

"Brian, what kind of shit have you got us into?" I wail in disgust. "They got bugs here so vicious they can bite your dick off!"

"Sister Mercy just as bad," Jamal says. Brian shrugs, helpless. We try to stay high enough so nothing matters. Ray shows up late for everything. Sometimes he doesn't show up at all. Elvis wanders off into the bush, looking for Ray. And you

in the dream, slinking down the Nile in your papyrus canoe. Walking a tightrope in your embroidered fez and gauze veil, the lipstick slash across your mouth a deliberately nasty, supernatural green. "I'll save you," you promise me, perfectly balanced and confident on your perch above the ravine. Nasty nasty nasty neon green.

And the only boa I ever wear is a constrictor around my neck, while Jamal whispers in panic, "Does the Congo still exist?" And Elvis responds with a sneer, "I can't keep up with history."

I am pregnant. I moonwalk and shuffle across the creaking, makeshift stage of the outdoor jungle arena. Searchlights blind my eyes. My mother suddenly appears, pushing my father onstage in his wheelchair. His hands are clasped in prayer, his tongue hanging out, ready for Holy Communion. We are in the Africa or Asia of my imagination; I'm ashamed I can't tell the difference. The foliage is familiar, it's easy to be fooled. My band is a flop. The natives are simply not interested in colored rock n'roll. A powerless concept to most of them.

They clamor for Madonna. They invoke Billy Idol. Something exotic, without gravity. They throw overripe bananas at me, and screeching spider monkeys at Sister Mercy, who stops in the middle of her fabulous rendition of "It's a Man's World" and stomps offstage. She returns a few seconds later, brandishing an Uzi. We aren't sure if it's a toy or for real, but no one wants to find out. You don't fuck with Sister Mercy; even this tough audience gets the message and simmers down.

I am pregnant. I wear a black Maidenform corset, gasping for breath. A lace boa constrictor is wrapped around my neck. To appease the restless crowd, sleazy B. Goode introduces me, with apparent desperation, as Madonna Demivida. "Straight from Motor City! You remember Motor City, don't you?" He's delirious with malaria, drunk from too much quinine. I stumble out, my hair hidden by a cheap blond wig from 14th Street. The booing begins all over again. Where are you? Where is Sister Mercy? Sister Mercy isn't there to protect me. She's backstage, fuming in the shadows. She wants no part of my sorry show. The mob curses us in English, threatening to throw us into the crocodile-infested river then laughing because it is all a joke. A village matriarch leaps up in my face. "You are not worth killing," she announces. She cracks a perfect brown egg on my forehead in a gesture of . . . blessing? Contempt? Again I am not sure. Government troops are forced to intervene. We are tried without a jury, dismissed and deported as SECOND-RATE WESTERN IMPERIALIST SO-CALLED ARTISTS before being shoved into a Russian army plane along with members of Sister Mercy's Satin Soul Revue.

We are flown out of the jungle in the middle of the night, back to the safety of Motown memory.

ANGIE AND THE CESSNA

Angie awoke with the idea of going to the country fair. She lay beside me in her big platform bed. I was still up in the sky, flying in my hard silver armor.

"Star," Angie touched my thigh with her cool foot, "it's a new day."

Angie was my mother, and she had been blue for the past few weeks because her boyfriend Paul had cut his hair and left the commune, and she hadn't had her period for a month and a half. I slept on Paul's side of the bed to keep Angie company. I buried my face into her pillow; the worn cotton smelled of his thick dark hair.

Driving to the fair would be an extravagance Angie didn't often allow. She didn't believe in cars, telephones, vacuum cleaners, or electricity. They upset the harmony of nature, she said. I, on the other hand, loved machines and their noise. When I was four, Angie overheard me telling a friend of hers that I wanted to be an airplane when I grew up.

"But darling," Angie had said, as she watched me running in circles, my arms outstretched, humming through my teeth, "you're human."

"You could be a pilot," Angie's friend had said. "Or a stewardess on a big passenger plane. A 747."

Passenger planes, with their cumbersome lounges and spiral staircases, didn't appeal to me much. I saw myself as a light plane, a single-engine Cessna, beating the air with my small propeller, exhilarated by the fight to stay aloft.

I hardly talk about it anymore, now that I'm eleven, but at night I still dream of flying. I'm tough and cool and strong as I lift above the commune, pulling my wheels into my body. I can't nod or otherwise acknowledge Angie and her friends as they wave up to me, but I lower my eyes and watch them get smaller and smaller, shrinking into black dots.

Angie was beating a rhythm on my back. "There's a drum

workshop at the fair today," she said. "Hurry and get up."

I was still heavy with sleep. When I opened my eyes, Angie had rolled onto her back. She stared at the ceiling and absently ran a hand up and down her stomach.

"There's nothing in there," I said. Angie falls in and out of love a lot, and when she's in love she takes chances, but she never gets pregnant.

"Are you sure, Star?" Angie said, turning to me. "Maybe I'm sterile?"

"Are we going to the fair today?" I asked.

"Yes!" Angie sat up suddenly and threw back the covers. She stretched from side to side, her pink breasts bobbing. "Isn't that a wonderful idea? When I woke up this morning, I thought: the fair. The fair is the answer to all our troubles. It'll take our minds off our worries." She pulled on one of Paul's old undershirts and wrapped a batik skirt around her waist.

I changed my clothes under the covers, worming out of yesterday's underwear and then pulling on the panties I left at the foot of the bed the night before. Angie never wore underpants or brassieres. Personally, I preferred them. I liked the feel of the clean-textured cotton against my skin.

Angie was in the mood to cook. She whipped up a batch of blueberry muffins and blueberry-banana pancakes. She put the muffins on a white doily and poured syrup over the stack of golden pancakes. The syrup dripped over the sides of the cakes like icing. I cut myself a fat wedge.

Angie was eating in dainty bites and drinking tea like a duchess, her little finger stuck out. She had brewed a pot of tea from bark and sticks and pennyroyal herbs that was supposed to make her abort. The tea was bitter and black, but Angie sipped at it, rolling it on her tongue as if it were chocolate mint.

From the kitchen window, I could see Islene picking her way to our dome. Islene was a bony woman about my height. She was wearing only a straight turquoise skirt and had left her top bare and brown. A wide woven strap crossed her chest; a small drum hung at her hip. Islene looked pretty much the same naked as she did dressed: she was all hair and bone and teeth and eyes, large, liquid eyes that stared right through you.

Islene's eyes irritated Angie. "She's like a ghost," Angie would say. "Slipping around, trying to dominate you with that hypnotic stare." Then she'd cup her face in her palms, just like Islene, and stare into my eyes until I couldn't stand it anymore and cracked up.

"Are you driving to the fair?" Islene stood in our doorway, tiny beads of sweat on her nose and upper lip.

"Oh hello, Islene!" Angie pulled out a chair with a flourish. "Come and dine with us."

Islene glided to the table. She ran a hand over my head and tucked a strand of hair behind my ear. She pulled the strap over her head before she sat down and held the drum in her lap.

"We're taking Arnold," I said. Arnold was the '69 red Chevy truck that belonged to the commune.

"I see." Islene smiled slightly, propped her elbow on the table and looked into my face. Angie stood behind Islene's back and rolled her eyes to the ceiling. "Tabu, a Nigerian drummer, is giving a workshop at noon," Islene said.

Angie picked up a newspaper tabloid from the kitchen counter. "Noon, above the Creativity Pavilion," Angie read. "Discover the natural rhythm within you."

The Creativity Pavilion was a big, flat roof resting on log poles. A narrow stairway led to the top of the pavilion. Ten or twelve people stood in the grass below, milling around, posing with their congas and tablas or wood tong drums. They all looked washed out, with stringy hair and pale complexions from the long Oregon rains. Angie walked right into the middle of them, swishing her long batik skirt. She held her hand out for me.

"Come on, darling," she said, "don't be a speed bump." She planted herself next to a solemn man with sad eyes and a beard and hair like Jesus.

Islene stood off to the side, her ceramic drum strung over her shoulder and across her breast. The only other kid in the group, a girl a few years younger than me, sat a few feet away with a cherry wood drum and two rubber mallets.

"Everyone else here has a drum," I said to Angie.

"Anything can be a drum, sweetheart," she said. "You can clap, or stamp your feet, or maybe someone would share with us." Angie reached over toward Jesus and thumped the skin of his drum. "What a lovely tone."

I looked up to the sky, hoping for jet contrails.

"Can't you just see it, Star," Angie was saying, "these hot summer nights, you and I outside our dome, bare-breasted, drumming among the crickets? We have to get a drum."

My head was still tilted back, searching the pure blue sky. "Everyone would hate us for disturbing their meditations." My voice came out of the back of my mouth.

"We'd help their meditations," Angie said emphatically. "Our drumming would clear their minds, take them back to a primordial state."

A stout black man strode into the group. He was shorter than Angie, but built wide and sturdy. His hair was matted into dreadlocks, and he wore a purple beret, a striped vest of heavy cotton and leather huaraches. He walked up to a girl leaning against the stairs' handrail. She had long blond hair and pale eyelashes. She held a tambourine at her side, limp, like it was an old sack of sandwiches.

"Let me see that," the black man said, holding his hand out for the tambourine. His voice was smoker hoarse and raspy.

He planted his feet far apart and rocked back and forth, jerking whenever he hit the tambourine. "Yeah," he moaned. "Yeah."

He handed the tambourine back to the girl, and clapped in time as she beat it with a stiff arm. She tried to match her timid pecks to his big, broad claps.

He jumped around in the circle of drummers, clapping, beating on the drums, teaching rhythm, grunting and shaking his head like a lion. The ground shook. I closed my eyes and flew into the tangle of an African jungle, flashing my red night signals, listening to monkey caws and wild laughter fade beneath the talk of village drums.

Angie pinched my cheek and I opened my eyes. The black man stood in the center of the drummers, rocking side to side, his eyes closed. He hummed between clamped lips and out of his soul.

The drummers gazed at him. They were concentrating hard, counting, their eyes fixed. Only their hands moved. Islene edged back and forth in a short space by the pathway. Every now and then she'd tap her ceramic drum and nod her head.

Angie once told me that Islene used to teach "Religions of the World" at the university. I tried to imagine her standing in front of an overhead projector in sensible shoes and beige blazer, comparing Buddhists and Unitarians. I looked around at the circle of dull faces. Their eyes were numb with a kind of polite interest.

The black man started to sing. "Black earth mother of America!"

Angie turned to me, shimmying her shoulders. "Isn't he wonderful? He could read my rap poem about American capitalism."

The black man was shaking, streaks of sweat running down his tight face.

"Rise and take your due! Shake off the white demons! The demons who exploit you, who kill your children, who steal the food from your mouth."

He snapped his head forward and looked straight at Jesus. "Hey, man. This ain't sorry, wrong number. You got it!" He shoved his hand straight out in front of him. "I'm black Africa, the mark of Cain. I'm running yellow, pus from a sore. My balls are burnt Post Toasties and I'm screaming black, and blue blood."

Everyone kept drumming. I edged over to the girl with the rubber mallets. She stopped and looked me over.

I bent close to her ear. "What's he doing?" I asked.

"I don't know," she said, "but he's not Tabu the Nigerian."

"He's not?"

"I saw Tabu at Bumbershoot Festival in Seattle. He's tall and skinny with short hair."

The black man stood tensed, glaring at Jesus. "Lies! Lies! Thieves! Murderers!" He spit out every word in a big spray. Sweat dripped down his nose, around the corners of his mouth, off his chin. He took a step toward Jesus and paused. "You—" He thrust his fist in the air, "deny it! You—deny my dignity! You—deny my life!" He kept taking steps toward Jesus until he was about a foot away, glaring down into those sad, pious eyes. Jesus stopped drumming and rested his fingers on the edge of the conga drum.

Angie, who was still sitting next to Jesus, was bobbing her head back and forth, clapping her hands and shimmying her shoulders. Her eyes darted around the circle. She caught me looking at her and winked.

"Slaveholders!" He bent from the waist like he was in pain. "False teachers! Landlords!"

Islene had walked around the back of the circle and came up behind us. "I think he has too much negative energy," she said in her low, soothing voice. "I want to start an om chant, to diffuse him."

"Die! Die! Die!"

I shrugged. "Well, O.K. If you think it'll help."

Islene lingered a bit, her hand on my shoulder, then walk-ed over toward Angie.

The girl with the mallets gave me a look. "That's a ridiculous idea," she said. "Are you going to do it?"

I shrugged again. "Maybe not. It might irritate him."

"Maybe the drumming is making him angry," she said.

The drummers kept staring ahead, kept drumming obe-diently. Their faces were blank, motionless, except for Angie's. She was grinning up a storm, while her eyes shifted between Jesus and the black man. She stood and stomped her feet with her legs spread out wide, half-squatting. She pulled off her T-shirt, then clasped her hands over her head. Her nipples looked pink and raw in the bright sun.

"Gross." The girl watched Angie with her arms crossed, the fluorescent green mallets sticking out from her armpits. "That's disgusting."

Angie danced, turning her head from side to side. The black man was screaming in a hoarse strained voice, and stand-ing so close to Jesus he dripped sweat on his conga. Islene came up behind Angie and put her hand on her shoulder. Angie stopped dancing and turned to Islene. Then she looked down at her feet and pulled her batik skirt up slow, above her thighs, up to her belly. Blood was dripping down the inside of her legs. Angie smeared the blood with her palms, painting her thighs tannic red. The girl with the mallets mumbled something, her face closed tight against the hot sun. The drummers kept banging on and on.

I rose above the drummers, my head whirring, until they shrank into a tiny circle of figures. The sound of the drums grew thin and mechanical. Strings of bright-colored flags flapped beneath me. I watched the circle, then the fairgrounds, then the whole wilderness of Oregon, turn slow on an axis, and grow smaller and smaller. I rose into cold air, where there was nothing but the white hush and mist, where there was nothing to smell—it was so clean. It was so cold, my eyes froze open. But I saw nothing. There was nothing to see.

IN TRANSIT

Two sisters, dressed in wool, sat under stars on a concrete bench in the orange-yellow light of two gas torches. The trade winds were blowing, and a low drone was coming from the jet engines idling out on the runway. It wasn't easy to separate the diesel smell of exhaust from the smell of plumeria in the air, although occasionally Annie, the younger of the two, inhaled loudly, trying to.

Kate was the one who had insisted they wear wool. She'd told Annie they wouldn't be in transit for more than a few hours and it wouldn't be hot in Honolulu at midnight anyway. But it was, and Annie could tell her sister was just as uncomfortable as she was by the way she kept pulling her collar away from her throat. Annie looked at the floor. Kate's feet were neatly crossed at the ankle; hers were shoved out in front of her, half in and half out of her shoes. Kate wore navy blue stockings and strappy leather heels; her feet were bare, shoved into caramel-colored leather clogs, which had a row of miniature star-shaped rivets along the seams. Kate's navy blue tunic was belted and cut to the thigh of matching wool knit trousers like a conservative mini dress. It was from Saks; Annie had seen the tag. Everything of Kate's was, even her hair, which was dark and straight and shone red in the light, cut neat in a cuff to her collar. Annie's sunbleached hair rippled in tight shiny waves over the shoulders of an undyed, lanolin-smelling wool turtleneck. Because the hem just reached the belt loops of her narrow-legged corduroys, if she lifted her arm even slightly, her bare waist showed.

Annie slipped her feet out of her shoes and ran her soles across the concrete floor, tilting her head back to breathe and look at the stars. A few white blossoms had fallen from the plumeria trees behind her. She pulled one of them with her toes across the floor toward the bench. "Will you worry about John while you're away?" she asked, twirling the white flower she'd picked up from the floor down her arm like a pinwheel.

Kate looked up from the book she was reading.

"I mean, do you ever wonder if he sees other women?"

"Annie, I'm only going to be gone three weeks."

"Dad already has you set up with that geologist in his office—Peter—with the yellow Fiat. Did you tell John about that?"

"Well, no. I probably won't even go out with him. And if I did, it wouldn't mean—. Why are you asking me this, Annie? Are you starting to worry about Thompson?"

"I don't care if Thompson sees other women, but he won't. If he can't sleep at night, he'll just make a pot of tea and have a conversation with me. I bet I'll even wake up. Or at least I'll get that itching in my ear or ringing or whatever it is you're supposed to get when someone's thinking about you."

"You only feel that way because you haven't slept with Thompson. That's when everything changes."

"We've slept together."

Pulling her hair away from her ear, Kate's fingers caught in one of the large silver loops she was wearing. "What?"

Annie smirked up into the dark heavy leaves hanging down from the branches over her head and leaned back lower into the bench. Kate was so easy to shock it almost wasn't a pleasure.

"Annie. You said you would talk to me when—"

"We haven't *slept* together," Annie explained. "We've spent the night together. I've fallen asleep next to him. What's the difference?" she asked, not really wanting Kate to answer. "I'm going to go look for a candy machine. How much longer do we have to wait?"

"About an hour. Get me some Dentyne, will you?"

"What if there is no Dentyne?" Annie asked, already walking away, already knowing the answer would be Double-mint. She hated gum.

On the other side of a pair of glass doors at the end of a corridor, there was a cigarette machine next to a candy machine. A young man wearing a white polyester long-sleeved shirt, dark, tight acrylic slacks, and black leather cowboy boots was crouched in front of it pulling all of the knobs in succession. If he'd been older she could have ignored him. But he wasn't old and the sight of him annoyed her. No one wore clothes like that. No one wore their hair that short. Thompson wore Levis and flannel shirts, he wore wire-rimmed glasses and a beard, he drank peppermint tea, he didn't smoke, and he was a sculptor. He'd gone to Choinard for a year and would have finished art school if the FBI hadn't taken him away for playing hooky from one lousy weekend of National Guard duty. They'd locked him up in the Presidio for six months, given him a certificate of dishonorable discharge; then about three years ago he'd moved to Santa Cruz where he'd rented the barn behind her sister's boyfriend's house. Annie had spent the summer modeling for him in a brown velvet chair he'd bought at the Goodwill and set on top of a table. She liked the way he seemed to think she was something worth studying. She liked to wonder what he thought about when he looked at her so closely, but he got mad if she tried to talk. Now the summer was over and she had to go back to Kuala Lumpur where her parents lived for one more year at the K. L. American School.

"Come on," he hissed. "Come on. Work."

He was crouched in front of the cigarette machine reaching his hand up above the silver trough into which the pack should have fallen. He seemed to be fingering the inner wall of the machine and hadn't realized Annie was watching. Annie ignored the way she was almost attracted to the way his feet looked in the boots. She stood back from the candy machine, arms folded over her breasts, her right hip cocked to the side, her right foot turned in. She hoped she was outside his peripheral view because she didn't want him to turn around; she just wanted him to give up and go away. She could see his BVDs hiked up above his belt through his shirt. She hated that kind of underwear. Thompson didn't wear underwear. He turned his head around with a jerk and the first thing she noticed was the way he grabbed hold of his camera case which was slung over his shoulder. How paranoid, she thought.

"Hi," he said, transformed when he saw her. She wanted

to throw up. Even if he'd been dressed differently she wouldn't have liked him. He was too polite, too interested; besides, she didn't like young men. Thompson was thirty-one. "Machine's broken, I guess," he said to her. "Where y'all goin' tonight?"

"Y'all?" Annie repeated.

"I saw y'all girls over there underneath them flower trees. You sisters?"

She shouldn't have answered. She shouldn't have said anything. And he had blue eyes. She didn't like blue eyes. "I don't see anything I want," she said, deciding to forget Kate's gum. She turned to walk away, but her foot came out of her clog and, as it came down, her arch hit the edge of the wooden platform. She hopped on one foot, wincing, then finally bent down, her arms folded in, her head bowed over her knees, fully conscious of the way her Peruvian poncho draped to the floor all around her. She imagined she looked to him like some kind of dramatic angular bird and she wished she were. She wished she could fly into his face, then away, leaving a dark scattering of feathers at his feet for him to be dumbfounded about.

"Are you all right?" he wanted to know, hugging his camera case to his side with the inside of his elbow. "Hey—are you?" he asked, trying to give her his hand. When he saw she wasn't going to take it, he looked up the passageway toward the garden where he had seen her earlier. "Do you want me to get your sister? I mean, if she is your sister. You didn't break anything, didja?"

Annie stood up and limped on her bare foot to her clog lying on its side on the sidewalk. She hadn't noticed how shiny the smooth-worn floor was. Torch reflections were waving like flags at her feet. "No thanks," she said, sliding her foot back into the clog.

"Hey. I didn't mean to . . . God, why are you just walkin' away? I wanted to talk for a minute. Can'tcha just . . ."

Annie pretended she hadn't heard him.

Kate looked up from her book when she heard the slow uneven hammer of Annie's arrival. "Why are you limping, Annie? Do you have my gum?"

"No, I don't have your gum." Annie had stuffed her poncho through the strap of her purse so that the beige hairy llamas were bunched together unattractively and the fringe was dragging on the floor. Kate pulled it through so that it hung evenly as Annie explained to her what had happened.

"Evenin', ladies." Annie thought there was something obscene about the way his camera case dangled down the front of his shirt, open but somehow still snapped onto the camera he was holding. "How're y'all this evenin'? Sure is a helluva time a night to be waitin' on a plane," he said, looking at his watch. "What time are y'all leavin'?"

"One fifteen, if it's on time," Kate said. "We've been waiting since 10:30 for a connection to Singapore. My daughter . . ."

For about the hundredth time that summer Annie noticed how easily Kate adjusted to small talk. She didn't want to listen. Kate was safe. Now that she'd told him she had a daughter, he was going to assume she was married, then he'd start thinking Annie was the one he should be talking to after all. "I'm going to the bathroom," she announced.

"Uh, Miss? Uh, before you go, wouldja mind if I took a picture of you two sittin' there under this flower tree? It won't take but a minute."

Annie looked at Kate. Her fingernails dug into the concrete surface of the bench. If Kate would only look at her, she'd see her eyes telling her to say no. Say no, goddamnit, Annie screamed, but she was only screaming on the inside. On the outside, she heard Kate saying, "I'd love to have my photograph taken. Where would you like us to stand?"

"Oh, right where y' are's fine. I don't mind."

"Let's go stand in front of the carp pond—on the bridge," Kate said.

"Okay. Maybe I'll even catch the back of one of those oversized goldfish glimmerin' in the background."

Kate stood up, lifting her leather carry-on bag over her shoulder. "Come on, Annie," she said laughing with him.

"I don't want to."

"It won't take but a minute," Kate said in a lowered voice, mimicking his accent. "It will make him happy, then he'll go away. C'mon."

"No, you two go ahead. I told you, I have to go to the bathroom."

"Well, if it's all right, I'll just take them right here. I don't mind this ol' bench. Besides, I can still see those white flowers hangin' over y'all's heads if I stand back far enough." He moved back and had snapped two, three, maybe five shots before Annie had the chance to move. The white light of the flash continued to explode under her eyelids for a long time. She hated what Kate was doing. Rubbing her eyes, she tripped slightly over her shoes stepping into them.

"Where are you going tonight?" Kate asked him. She was only twenty-four, but she acted like she was everybody's mother.

"Saigon, Ma'am. Well, I fly commercial Honolulu to Manila and Manila to Saigon, then I pick up a C-130 to Da Nang. Most likely after that I'll be sent to the front, being as I don't have any special skills."

"Then, you haven't been yet?" Kate asked.

"Been? Course I've been. I just finished spending my first R&R here in Honolulu. Me and my girlfriend, we were gonna meet here. I made the reservation over six months ago. She was supposed to fly in from Midland—Midland, Texas—that's where I'm from, see, but she, she and I . . . Well, I guess she had a change a plans."

Kate looked at him.

"I sure do appreciate the way you've been as kind as y'have. Thanks for lettin' me take your picture. You're real pretty, ma'am. Would you mind if I asked your name? I guess your sister's the moody kind," he said, scratching the side of his head with his thumbnail after she told him. "I don't think I said anything out a line over there by the candy machine, but I sure am sorry if I did. Y'all take care now, y'hear?"

"We'll do that," Kate said.

Annie was standing behind a plant with huge elephant-ear leaves, waiting for him to leave. She dropped onto the bench and kicked off her shoes.

"Forget about him, Annie. He's gone."

"What did you say he could do that for? What gives you the right to say who can take my picture? I don't want some fucking goon walking around with my picture in his wallet pretending I'm his girlfriend."

"He isn't going to pretend you're his girlfriend. We're both in it. He just wants a picture of us because we're American and because he thinks we're pretty. Maybe he thinks he's never going to see anyone like us again."

"What do you mean?"

"Annie, didn't you hear him say he was on his way back to Vietnam?"

"No—well, I don't care if he is because I know what he's going to do with that picture. He's going to lie inside some filthy sleeping bag out under some ugly fucking Vietnamese moon and he's going to jack off looking at my picture. That's what he's going to do with it."

"Annie, you'd better get out of the habit of talking that way."

As soon as she had buckled her seatbelt, Annie propped her rolled-up poncho into the window and leaned her head against it, pretending she wanted to sleep. For a while she tried thinking about Thompson, tried remembering the walk they'd taken the night before along the San Lorenzo, but nothing very much came back except the way the plum trees had looked, so big in the dark, and the way the pebbly sand had looked flaked with gold at the bottom of the stream they'd crossed. Whether she wanted to let him or not, the soldier in polyester and cowboy boots was slipping back into her mind.

How was she supposed to have known he was a GI? He wasn't wearing a uniform. Maybe if his hair had been longer and he'd been wearing blue jeans. Maybe they have to dress that way. As the plane taxied to the end of the runway, she kept seeing his blue eyes looking down at her, his hand stretched out, trying to help her up from the floor. Actually, when she thought about it, his hands were nice. They weren't thin like his body; they were strong looking. He just hasn't grown into them yet, she thought. She imagined him wearing army fatigues and a faded green cap and he looked much better. His face was browner and his eyes looked serious with the cap low over his brow. She'd been to Saigon. She knew what soldiers looked like.

She flew into Saigon almost every time she flew back to the States from Kuala Lumpur. Sometime during the summer of 1968 Annie had spent an hour or two walking around the Tan Son Nhat transit lounge. He was too young to have been there, but someone like him had been. Someone dressed in loose fatigues, sitting on a wooden bench painted a pale blue in a room lined with wooden benches like a church full of pews, crowded with men dressed just like him—rows and rows of young men with suntanned faces looking out from under caps or dark green helmets with eyes almost as young as hers. Their black hightop boots were propped on overstuffed army knapsacks. There'd been guns and ammunition belts and metal boxes like tackle boxes and bigger ones that she knew were footlockers.

She'd never had that many men looking at her all at once, and all she could think about was that she probably never would again. In a way it had felt good, but there was also something wrong with the way they looked back at her. Something too cautious, their faces tucked back, almost shy, as if they'd be breaking some kind of law if they smiled at her. They were complacent or they were intrigued, but a screen of unlikelihood blocked her from them. She'd let her purse that was hanging over her shoulder bang against her back as she walked down one aisle and up the next dressed in a khaki green paisley mini-skirt, brown sandals, and a green T-shirt. Her bangs were fashionably long and her body was good for a twelve-year-old. Why wouldn't anyone say anything to her?

She passed row after row of GIs looking for the handsomest one she could find. Then maybe she'd just stand in front of him and ask him what his name was. No, she wouldn't have to ask him that. It'd be printed right there on his pocket over his heart. But she could ask him where he was from. She could ask him what kind of music he liked. She could tell him she listened to Radio Saigon every night at her desk in KL while she did her homework. She could tell him about the way the large triangular shadow her pencil made across her paper made her imagine what it would be like to be blind because of the way it blocked most of the words on the page. She could ask him if that'd ever happened to him. She could tell him she lived in Kuala Lumpur because her father was a geologist there; then she could get his address and they could write each other letters. She was going to spend the summer with her sister in California, but she'd be back through before school started in September. Maybe they could meet each other then, or maybe he could come to KL on his leave. He got leave, didn't he? When she got back, maybe they could listen to Radio Saigon at the same time every night. Maybe he could dedicate a song to her and she'd hear their names said together over the air all the way in KL. Then she could tell everyone that she had an older boyfriend who was a soldier in Vietnam.

An older American soldier was sitting at the linoleum table in a corner. He was also dressed in fatigues, but something about his straight-backed posture and his concentration made her suspect he was a commander. He sat in his chair, his boots side by side on the floor, watching what seemed to be coffee slowly dripping from a small silver canister he was holding over a glass of ice that was already partially filled with a milky brown liquid. It wasn't the glass that looked off to Annie. They drank coffee that way in Malaysia; it was the ice. She thought it looked like a woman's drink with the milk and the small silver spoon. A voice over the intercom was announcing the departure of her flight. All she'd wanted was the chance to talk to one of them. Except for the men who worked in her father's office and the few boys at school, she hadn't seen an American male in a whole year. And if she didn't meet someone in California this summer, she'd have to wait another whole year. A stewardess was already leading the passengers who had decided to disembark while the plane was refueled back across the tarmac towards the plane. She stood looking at the roomful of faces, her hand in a fist holding the strap of her purse at her hip before she walked out onto the runway. They were so handsome. The stewardess was impatient. Annie could tell by the way she held her head, her hair blowing into her face above the collar of her navy blue suit. She motioned again with her fingers and Annie followed.

The 747 banked toward the lights of Waikiki for the

benefit of the passengers who were still awake. Annie felt her sister leaning over her shoulder to look, but she pretended to be asleep. She needed to understand why those soldiers had ignored her. She remembered she'd even regretted not bringing her flight bag into the transit lounge that day. If she'd had her camera with her, she could have taken a few snapshots of the best-looking guys. Then, if she hadn't been able to convince her friends that she had an older boyfriend who was a soldier in Vietnam, she would have at least had something to pin to her bulletin board.

Her sister had turned the reading light on. Annie opened her eyes just enough to look at her hands in her lap. She still wore the jade ring her father had given her when she was nine, and her right hand still looked wider across the palm than her left, but she wasn't the same person with the bangs in her eyes, hanging around a transit lounge needing to get picked up by a GI. Maybe she wasn't exactly a woman yet, but she had Thompson. That had to mean something. There had to be some reason a thirty-one-year-old man was interested in a girl who was only seventeen. She twisted the swivel attached to the piece of fishing line he'd tied to her wrist before she left, trying to imagine what that could be.

GLASSING THE HORIZON

I see myself slouched in the rearview mirror
of this '46 Willy's I've been lent for the weekend:
my hair is orange and gold and dark at the roots,
windtorn, pulled back and to the side in a green
    rubber band.
My legs are chalky and scratched,
my socks fallen down around scuffed white shoes.

You are glassing the horizon through the lowered window
of your state truck. It is November
and you're lean and dark in a beard and dark glasses.
We're not saying anything, just facing each other,
but the space of five winters closes
when your steel door opens and I see your legs straighten,
hear your boots crack through sand as hard as crusted snow
on this barren road to Naha.

There's a black wooden box
you're reaching for behind the rear window.
You're opening a padlock.
Then you're back behind the wheel and
I'm leaning my face through your lowered window,
watching you pull open your revolver.
I smell your hands as you open a canister in your lap,
smell the gold-butted silver bullets
you're pouring into your palm.
Turning them over and over in your hand
they sound like shells underwater washing across riffled sand
and I'm thinking I want to be underwater
breathing your hands.

A voice through static calls from your radio.
You lift the receiver, and without a compass,

without a map, without hesitation,
look past your sleeve to the white water, the horizon,
say: north-northwest—about nine miles—
there's an opening in the channel—
It is the sound of your voice,
the words you choose and the way you say them,
your eyes turned toward the rough water
while wind through beach grass beats sand against my legs,
pushes foam across the waterline
that tells me what you are.

I can see that you would rather I didn't stay when the police
begin to arrive in their Cherokees and their Scouts,
    and I don't,
but I leave my fingerprints on your rearview mirror
because I want you to remember later
that the last thing you did before I went away
was cover my fingers there with your hands.

GEOGRAPHERS

"How do they do it, the ones who make love without love?"
                                                    – Sharon Olds

They do it easily
after hours and hours and hours
have turned into the smell of rain.

And they do it without forethought.

Maybe she swims late into twilight
so her face will look flushed when he opens the door.
Maybe he sees the edge of the coast from the water
where he spends the afternoon prone on waxed glass
lifting, falling, wet
and, waiting for evening,
sees the way it has been cut by waves, rain, wind,
understands what he hasn't been able to articulate:
the link between to describe, to carve, and the earth
until dark.

Maybe when he has opened the door
and they are crossing the street
their hands touch,
or her fingers graze the hem of his shorts,
so that later, when she wants to know if he knows
      how to swing,
and he holds her hands in his to show her
and she becomes dizzy turning and falls to his bed
and he asks leaning over her if she is all right,
and she is able to take his hands from behind her
so he comes slowly close to her back
so that when their fingers
begin to seem to unravel

long in the expanse between wing and spine,

their touch roaming from shoulder to rib
from belly to hip,
becomes, they suppose,
what is called sex without love.

THE WOODEN STUDIO

The story is funereal. White or oxidized or both. It is like something found in a tomb laid waste. If I close my eyes, I see it like a perfectly preserved relic, a bone or copper ring, or perhaps a ceramic urn. In a museum it would be behind glass, recognizable and whole, a thing of remarkable beauty. But as it exists now, a story in need of excavation, I fear it may be irreparably fractured. Nevertheless, I am compelled by the child I am having to attempt even the most vain excavation. Although she is only four months past conception, I fear in the future she will have no access to this story. Too much lies buried. It is as if a temple once ordained by gods is now over-run by a decadent plant. The lives from which she proceeds are obscured.

It seems that the story may have begun when her father, a photographer, took a photograph of me lying out in the yard while a large female peafowl lay in the small of my back as if on a nest. As I remember, it was a truly lovely photograph and quite unexpected. The peafowl was full grown and intensely colored as if it were dipped in an Oriental dye bath after being minutely detailed in India ink, but certainly it must have been too beaked and clawed for such intimate contact. There is violence inherent at the sight of a peafowl which makes it seem impossible that a female stepped gently onto the small of my back, and that I did not jump up in fear. Yet I remember that I did not. I was familiar with this particular peafowl as it was one of several I kept in my yard. They were free to roam the property at will, and often I would come home to find one perched in the eaves of my house or on the roof. I had one cock and three females. It was one of the females that stepped onto the small of my back that afternoon, her whole weight devastating until she settled and alleviated the concentration of it from her terrible claws. She stayed there until she decided to leave. Somehow the photograph became famous and for a short time was reproduced in the form of postcards.

We lived in a former banana patch, and there were still many banana trees on the property. Ripe bananas did not fall to the ground like crescent moons as a sentimental poet may imagine. Rather the fruit, which followed the appearance of a large black flower hanging from the tree like the human heart hangs in the Egyptian Book of the Dead, was most often eaten green by rats. The only yellow bananas we saw were picked green and allowed to ripen in the kitchen. Primarily the banana trees yielded mosquitos, which bred in the water constantly trapped between the stalks which make up in layers the banana's trunk. We kept the mosquitos away from the house by always burning a poisonous punk.

The smell of the mosquito punk is for me the smell of sex. Yes, we made love often in that house. The baby, Isabel, may have been conceived there, and yet the association, no, I should say fusion, I have in my mind between the mosquito punk and the act of love happened earlier. As I search for the reasons, what comes to mind is not the men of whom I can remember little, but the architecture. Yes, my life seems at times tied only to the tiles and doors and walls of buildings. Events are ruinous in my memory. But to say that those walls, those tiles are the only memory is to lie. Other things do come back; it's just that they follow the architecture, which comes back first and with most intensity, with most importance.

Making love in the house in the bananas, or anywhere really, is always like dancing to the music from Mahler's *Kindertotenlieder*. I am always there. In that dance. And in a certain wooden studio.

I break out in a bath of sweat, my feet point automatically, as if by reflex, and I turn in my mind the turns of the whole body. I am always in the wooden studio where I first heard Mahler, where in the middle of an arabesque I knew that desire which has been with me ever since, indefatigable and identifiable only in the smell of the poisonous punk, in certain buildings, and in music.

I think I must have made my way to that dancing studio in silver street shoes. I know that it was a strange studio, sequestered between a Catholic priory and the foreign consulate of a small Oriental country. It was a neighborhood being dispossessed of its privacy, its affluence, as one by one old homes were stripped of hedges, made public, institutionalized.

In that immediate area the studio alone remained in private hands. It was entirely wooden, unpainted and graceful, with an Eastern appeal, as if it were a small misplaced portion of a Russian wooden palace. The hollow wooden steps at the entrance led down a corridor to a small courtyard where there was an old-fashioned swimming pool, empty of water. It was a deep pool set between two stone lions, and the tiles in the pool were loose and laid in a geometric design.

So you were able to find me, he says. Here, because the details escape my memory, I am embellishing. Sometimes I cannot really remember that man. So you were able to find me, he must have said, emerging from one of several wooden doorways. He is older, with silver hair and an angular Egyptian body. He wears the black tights of a dancer and a sweater. Although you do not have much training, you'll do, he says. He wants me to dance with him in a piece he has choreographed for a contest. I must have been introduced to him by my ballet teacher, Mrs. Ota.

The room we go to is bare and wooden and octagonal. It is the kind of secret, unexpected room you might find at the top of a spiral staircase. Bamboo blinds are drawn and eliminate all but enough sunlight to make the rosin on the floor light up like rough topaz. Put on your ballet slippers, he says. My only ornaments are a silver ring and the silver street shoes, which I take off. He asks me to tie my hair in a green scarf. The scarf is extremely long, and I wrap it around my head again and again. The dance will begin with you lying on me as if you are my child, he says. He turns on the music, and I hear for the first time the music of the *Kindertotenlieder*. We begin to be bitten by large mosquitos, and he lights a punk. The smoke from the smoldering punk fills the room, a poisonous incense.

My sister and I, as children, often centered our play around the tomb of a child prince. The tomb was near a grove of royal palms which, unlike other palms, have lovely smooth white trunks that grow tall and straight like white marble columns. For us they were always the columns of a large palace very much like an Islamic mosque, based on pictures of the Taj Mahal, onion-domed, and reflecting the order of God. The child prince lay in a tomb behind the most beautiful black wrought iron fence in the world, which was leafed in gold, the posts alternating a fleur-de-lis and a coronet. We were obsessed by Prince Albert, whom we believed to have grown just old enough in the other world to be our age. I believe it was the specter of Prince Albert beckoning to me in my dreams which made me into a child somnambulist. Although I do not remember my actual excursions, I distinctly remember mornings after his visits when I found myself in my own bed tightly rolled up in my white bed sheet, as if in a mummy cloth, barely able to breath and soaking in sweat. Of course I was too young to realize that the boy prince was probably an incubus; all I knew was that when I woke up I wasn't as awake as when I was sleeping. Only at the mosque of palms were my waking and sleeping worlds bridged.

Around that time I learned something from my sister, Lydia, which I will teach Isabel, the child in my womb, no matter what else. He chooses you at night because it is dark and your bed is nearer the door, my sister says, in daylight, in the real world, he would want me. I believed her utterly, suspecting then what I now know to be true, that ultimately it is the waking flesh with which we must reckon. And I was not beautiful. I did not become even vaguely beautiful for years and only after the decline of Lydia's beauty, which I doubt she would agree has been at all dimmed.

You see, she was born with the most lovely golden eyes and skin, and by the time she was five years old, she had the longest opulent orange hair I've ever seen. I can't say enough about her beauty. Her beauty gave her a personality which was magnetic. For instance, as a little girl, she could climb into the small tree where we had hung a bird feeder without scattering the birds from the seed. That is a picture I have of her. She's five, and she's sitting in a little tree that's flawlessly trimmed into a round shape. Surrounding her are five or more red cardinals like ripe fruit. It is a picture that resembles a medieval tapestry. It is a picture that illustrates the lesson I learned from her: beauty is imperative.

Lydia is now dead to our mother.

I was fifteen when I danced with the master. My steps were not childlike, or in any way caricatured; they were the steps of a child. The piece was of the avant garde and meant to display the emotional and technical virtuosity of the male dancer in an art created for women. Later, when I understood Mahler's *Kindertotenlieder*, I realized that my part was really that of a child ghost. The ghost of the dancer's daughter. But at fifteen, I was not a child nor was I acquainted with death. What I felt during the final *pas de deux*, when he lifted me into his arms and then laid me down on the ground, himself over me, was sexual desire played out fully in rehearsal but left latent during our performances at the University Theater. Perhaps he was not a master, but instead, a young student of choreography, who became famous only later. I know only his artistic seriousness and the complicity of our desire.

It was in the wooden studio that I was first singled out for myself alone. Where I did not suffer by comparison to Lydia. I guess what happened to me in the wooden studio couldn't actually have happened to her because she was indisposed by pregnancy, a condition that would change everything—change the course fate had chosen for her.

Her life, the one she should have had, is, for me, inexplicably tied to a certain dress. It was a black dress with large blue roses. Large dark and less dark blue roses that looked as if they had fallen onto her from out of the sky. She wore it often in her early pregnancy, before anyone knew what was to follow, during the time only she was singled out. She must have known she was pregnant but she manifested no particular concern. Nor did she ever, even much later. I remember the dress fit her like a glove.

Had Isabel's father been around then, there would have been a photograph of her in this dress. He would have seen the possibility in it. The vast possibility of her beauty. And in hindsight, I think the photograph would have revealed her condition. It would have shown how her breasts were too full for the slenderness of her body at that time. It would have objectified the situation.

We grew up two children in a house of many balconies, a bare drafty house with tall ceilings and stucco walls. Our mother was blind and so we were not supervised like other children. We were not kept from hiking in the water reserve forests where we encountered strange forgotten stone walls and the sudden appearances of large black moths. We were often allowed to walk the long walk to the mausoleum where we once found two black puppies which grew into large Dobermans that followed us everywhere, even to school where they stay outside our classrooms, aggravating the teachers, and growling when other children approached. And so our environment was benign to us and would have continued to be so, I believe, had we remained children.

Only when we left our little elementary school and had to catch the bus to the intermediate school, did we begin to experience the cruelties which would eventually lead to Lydia's transformation and to which our mother was truly blind. At the large city intermediate school, left without any protection, we were spit on, pinched and robbed, and pissed on for being white. It was an anticolonialist sentiment made personal.

I can only imagine how it happened, her pregnancy: we had often left school during the middle of the day and walked in the scorching sun up the long hill until we reached the mausoleum and the surrounding graveyards. Lydia must have gone there alone one day. Maybe it was when I had a cold. She must have walked by herself leaving in her wake only the aura of her beauty. She was growing more and more beautiful.

Some boys from the school must have followed her, a group of the older ones, the ones capable of being physically attracted to her while hating her whiteness. Their anger must have been building for months—how could the most beautiful girl in the school be white—so white that none of them could date her publicly? Harassing her had had no effect. She had taken their spit and cruelty. She had given them her bus money and walk-ed home. They must have hated her. They followed her and caught up with her somewhere in one of the graveyards. She never told me any of this, yet I know it must have happened. She was at the time almost fourteen and a half.

This is how it is: she's frightened. She knows they are behind her, laughing amongst themselves in order to reduce the tension created by what they are going to do. They light cigarettes and walk faster. The walk is interminable, and it is very hot. She walks along the trail of dirt and dead grass that is worn down by so many feet the way animal trails are worn. Are they three or five? She thinks maybe someone is at the mausoleum if she can make it that far. Sometimes there are guides to help tourists. But they are closing in on her. Suddenly she is struck between her shoulder blades by something wet, sweet and sticky, something that gets tangled in her hair. They are throwing rotten mangos and she knows there is no escape. It is a Wednesday. She leaves the path because she cannot bear that her humiliation be seen from the road. They reach her as she reaches the group of palms. One of them pushes her onto the ground that is oddly cool after her flight in the hot sun. They hope this attack will free them to look at the other girls who are dark and small and feminine. Girls who understand the price of being deemed beautiful.

I surprised myself by marrying the young photographer; I had always been more comfortable in the arms of an older man. But he was beautiful, slight in stature, with long sun-streaked hair and eyes indistinguishable in color, like those of a cat, distinct only in their luminosity. He provided well for me. Imagine our wooden house in the bananas, filled with many fine vases and urns.

The scenes in the wooden studio, enacted between myself and the dancing master, would probably have proved disappointing had they been filmed. They would have shown only a skinny child desperately trying to follow the instructions of an older adult. Yes, he must have been middle-aged. I say this because of the way he behaves after their encounters. During the music he dances with her, leading her through various combinations of steps, stark in their execution: lifting her over his head, asking her to stretch, to extend a leg, arch her back. When he sets her down on the wooden floor and lies on her, what she has begun to anticipate, barely conscious of it, is suddenly occurring, although she is at first uncertain whether this too is part of the dance. Only when he asks her to slip her leotard off her shoulders does she know for certain that he is seducing her. She feels as if she has been waiting for this her whole life, yet she feels strangely undefined. It is as if the weight of this man's body were resting on someone else, not herself. Still it is his weight which she enjoys, has always desired. When his lovemaking ends, he abruptly stands, wipes himself with a towel, and leaves the room. She sits up, herself again, skinny, naked, and alone in the middle of a bare room, a room bleached of color, shivering in her own perspiration, which has become very cold. He returns some time later, showered, fully dressed in trousers and a blue work shirt and tosses on the floor near her feet a thin turquoise-colored kimono. It is silk, and when she puts it on it sticks to her breasts which are wet with sweat and between her legs which are wet with semen. Where it is wet it becomes transparent.

He lights a cigarette with a small monogrammed lighter and says, you will have to work harder if I am to use you. For a while it is like this afterward—like nothing—it is a ritual. The ritual of denial.

You must remember Lydia's beautiful abundant mass of orange hair. Only if you remember it can you understand the power of the Destructor, his power to change, alter, nullify. She met him on a city bus in the midst of the business district on her way to see a doctor about her pregnancy. I don't know for sure, but I think the Destructor must have laughed at her condition. Laughed cruelly. I have seen him do this on other occasions, so I know he is capable of it. I guess his laugh must have mirrored something of Lydia's own view of herself. I think she felt she deserved to be laughed at, although this she kept hidden, and so when it finally happened, the sound of his laughter was the sound of something expected, familiar. It was an old friend.

Don't think he was immune to the power of her beauty. In fact, I am convinced that he was even more acutely attuned to it than were most others. Her beauty challenged his power. It awakened in him an avarice. He wanted to possess Lydia, swallow her, annex her to himself. And so, after he laughed, scorned her in public, he launched a campaign to acquire her. Oddly enough, he himself was unsure, until after it had been accomplished, just how fine a prospect she was for his kind of workmanship. Even he was surprised at the level of his own destruction. With Lydia he reached a new height. She was his masterpiece.

Lydia's relationship with the Destructor was like that of an addict to heroin. He affected her like heroin. At first there was the euphoria that came when he convinced her to sever the child from herself forever. It would be best, of course, if it died inside the womb, he said. What is next best is to market the child to people who will pay to take it off our hands, wealthy people who will pay black market prices for a white child. I will say that I am the father, and we will pass the child off as white.

When the baby was gone, Lydia changed in other ways, predictable ways really. She became very pale, her skin lost its goldenness. Dark purple rings appeared under her eyes. Yet it was in this state that she came to rely on the Destructor more completely. She gave herself to him. She allowed him to express his personal taste through her. He chose her clothes. He dressed beautiful Lydia in dark solids, particularly navy. He liked Lydia in wools and suedes. Fabrics that retain heat. He liked her to wear very wide belts, belts that were five or more inches wide and of genuine lizard, and earrings that were large plates of silver or gold. Finally she gave him her hair, her hair that by this time nearly reached the floor. He cut it off himself, the entire length of it, which he kept, I think, as a souvenir or trophy. He cut her hair so short that only one-half inch was left all over. She looked like a victim of an internment camp or of brain cancer. But really she was the victim of an addiction. He was heroin.

After Lydia's baby was born, our mother asked why she wanted to marry the Destructor. She said Lydia was too young, that she hardly knew him. Lydia answered that she owed him. Owed him for alleviating her terrible misery. You owe the person who saves you, she said. No one else has ever saved me. In spite of Lydia's claims, I think the Destructor enjoyed her pain, the labor and the hemorrhaging that came later. Close to death like that, there was no trace of the opulent girl on the bus, a girl so seemingly out of reach. In her pain, Lydia was made dependent on him, as on a drug.

I think the reason I surrendered to the man in the wooden studio was because he embodied the glamour of evil.

But the dancer was not the only older man. Later, when out of boredom I worked at the harbor, I met another. He was the man mainly responsible for my peafowl. Of course I had always wanted peafowl ever since I found out that the most beautiful of princesses had kept peafowl. That lovely princess, eternally pictured in her youth, with large serious eyes and lovely gowns with high necks and trains, had kept the rare white peafowl on the lawns of her house near the beach. Hers was a life of such beauty, a beauty inexplicably tied to her white peafowl. And it was my friend, Raven Lee, who helped me to possess peafowl of my own, particularly that peafowl that stepped gently onto the small of my back, with which I was photographed.

He was sixty-five. I remember because he retired from his job soon after I myself left the harbor, but that is not what's important. Nor is the age sixty-five important. He was no more sixty-five than he was fifty or sixty, or any other specific age. He was instead all ages. He was a man whose whole life was in his face, in the lines of his face, in his eyes. His previous years had not slipped away from him. All of sixty-four was still right there in his face, as was all of eighteen.

It was a hard face, the veteran of three wars. He was a hard man, hard to know, one who treated newcomers to the harbor with suspicion and prejudice. He was a man with many old friends and few new ones. Yet I found him supremely attractive. In my eyes he possessed everything. He had the ability to tell stories, to exemplify and explain all that was stored in the rich planes and lines of his face. Any woman fortunate enough to be loved by him would be immortalized. I divined this immediately. She would exist like a diamond in Raven's stories and later would glitter in the memories of all his friends, in those of anyone within the range of his voice.

Such was the case of his wife whom he loved and admired, I thought, above all else, and to whose value and clarity I aspired. She was a beautiful Oriental with fine black hair, and like all women from Asia who can afford it, had autonomy, in the form of a fabulous collection of jewels, emeralds, jades, and diamonds. She who possessed innumerable diamonds was herself the queen among them. She was a diamond of the kind discovered in ancient idols, named, legendary, powerful. She was immortal. She will always be known as a woman for whom the world relinquishes its treasures, bends its rules.

It's like this: at home he keeps many birds. Not exotic parrots or songbirds but game. He keeps cages and yards of large game birds which are never slaughtered: geese, chickens, fighting chickens, pheasant, turkey and peafowl. All my birds are so beautiful, he tells his wife at night, beautiful like the birds in dreams. For him quitting time at the harbor means going home to feed his birds. One afternoon he comes home to find that someone unknown has left unlatched the door to the cage of his peafowl. He finds all three outside their cage perched on its roof.

He walks back to his house for a mop. With it he beats the

first peafowl, a cock, off the tin roof and into his chickens. The peacock excites the chickens, but soon he is able to chase it back into its own cage. Then he beats the second off the roof. This one flutters a bit and lands in his outdoor Oriental bath, which his wife had recently filled for him with steaming hot water. Because the second is wet, Raven apprehends it easily and returns it to its cage. I keep my peafowl in cages, he tells me, so that my neighbors can't admire my beautiful birds. If they want to see such birds, they should get their own. About this he is unrelenting.

When he strikes the third peafowl, a hen, it manages to fly a fair distance. It escapes his yard entirely and flies in the direction of the stream which borders his property. He tracks the bird for a long time, until it is nearly dark, but can't find it.

My wife can't sleep, he says. At first she thinks that her jewelry isn't safe; she feels a sense of loss. She gets out of bed and reassures herself about it but still she can't sleep. Raven, she whispers to me, where do you think that bird is? That was such a beautiful bird. She lies in bed in the dark thinking about my missing bird, and it seems to her that that particular one had been the most beautiful. Its feathers were the finest if not the longest. Yes, the peahen now missing had been the most brilliant. My wife begins to dream that the feathers of the missing peahen are as shiny as emeralds and sapphires. Suddenly she wakes up and hears that it has begun to rain. She can endure it no longer, you see, that the most beautiful of my birds is missing, so she gets up, wraps herself in a robe, and finds a flashlight. She walks out into the dark rain alone, toward the stream. As soon as she reaches the stream itself, the missing peahen comes out of the foliage straight toward her. She kneels down and the peahen steps into her lap. Somehow she manages to lift it into her arms and carry it back to me. It came to me, she tells me when I meet her at the door. It just came to me. She amazes herself. This is how he described it to me the next day.

It's strange how in adult life we constantly seek to reenact the failed relationships of our younger selves. This was true for Raven. For him, I was a current substitute for a certain white girl who sat near him in school some fifty years earlier. For myself, I loved him because I could love him innocently. I needed to love an older man innocently, as one loves a deity, not a lover. I needed to replace the man of the wooden studio with someone innocent. I needed a love that could not be consummated. My love for Raven, I thought, could restore in me a state of grace.

Raven told me she was white, the first girl he loved. This is how I know. White with long yellow hair and large breasts which he used to stare at whenever he could and think about often. He was without the usual resentment of whites because he had grown up on a military base where his father ran a laundry, and where he learned well the status of whites from the constant laundering and starching of white dress uniforms which were ironed and lined up row after row in his father's laundry, as if at attention. It is an image which never leaves him. Sometimes when he closes his eyes in exhaustion, he sees on the inside of his eyelids rows of starched white uniforms. At the school he attended, there were enough whites to form a substantial minority. He felt no shame at noticing the breasts of a white girl, only admiration and desire.

Often Raven showed her that he noticed them, those breasts. He whispered to her during class. He made his friends laugh by making motions with his hands over his own chest until she got little tears in the corners of her eyes that she barely kept from spilling down her cheeks. To him her tears were indescribably attractive. Finally he asked her to meet him in one of the nearby cane fields where all the boys took girls to drink and make love. When she failed to arrive he never spoke to her again. He said he later took many other girls to the field to drink and make love, but he was faithful to none of them.

Of course when Raven told me this, he was referring to the cane fields as they were in the old days. Since, they have become the location of gangland executions. A boy from my intermediate school, Clayton T., was found recently, blindfolded, hands bound behind his back, a single bullet through the head. There was another man found dead beside him, but he was older, a hardened criminal. Someone who went to Clayton T.'s funeral told me that his mother wore a black lace dress, and that his father had looked angry, like he despised his own son.

★ ★ ★ ★

Although we eat lunch together everyday and meet for coffee in the mornings, in the evening I leave Raven and return to the house in the bananas. I walk to a bus stop to catch the bus home to the windward side of the island. The nearest stop is two blocks away from the harbor, and often I walk with dozens of office girls, stenographers, secretaries, and word processors. These are girls exquisitely dressed in silk and jersey dresses purchased from the big department store. They carry leather handbags and sometimes small white paper bags printed with orchids or gold letters, bags from the small boutiques popular during the lunch hour. They move down the many streets of the business section like schools of tropical fish, gentle, graceful, and varicolored. The business section is a world of glass buildings, window displays, and tiled sidewalks: an aquarium in which I feel a lack of air, near drowning.

It happened on several occasions. And at different locations, but the effect was always the same. Raven would save my dignity. I would be in a crowd of beautiful secretaries, the only one among them laden with huge cardboard boxes or brown paper bags, dripping with the booty ill gotten off of the barges and boats that daily pass in and out of the harbor. The fresh pineapple, raw sugar, salmon steaks, and the boxes of white lobster tails packed in ice were all for favors: prime dockage, waived demurrage fees, and others the details of which were not even whispered. Very often I would walk beside the secretaries weighted down like a stevedore. Hot and sweaty and often smelling like fish, I moved awkwardly through the business district. Then at a certain busy intersection, it was impossible to say in advance where or when,

Raven would save me.

He'd pass by in his car, slow down, and pause at the curb some feet ahead of me and the inevitable beauties. I love you, sweetheart, he'd call. I'd wait. Those around me would fluster and blush in embarrassment, each trying to ascertain whether she were the one to whom he was speaking. When each decided she was, I'd step forward and say, bye Raven, and walk on, because by now the intersection would be clear.

Several months before I quit working at the harbor, Raven gave me three peachicks in a cardboard box to raise at home. He had them shipped over from another island on a barge. They were worth twenty-five dollars apiece. They were worth everything.

I return to the house in the bananas; the house where Isabel was conceived, and where she was formed slightly misshapen in my womb, a baroque pearl. She was also born a pearl, small and silent, and very blue. I recognized her completely as my own. The fact of her death was unfathomable. Even silent, still and frozen in the fetal curvature, I recognized her completely and knew her for the daughter I had always foreseen.

Yet I received nine blue sympathy cards. It was remarkable how, when set side by side, they were all blue. One was lettered in blue script *In Your sorrow* . . . There was a blue rose, blue sea shell, blue scroll, blue paper fan, a blue landscape, a blue seascape, the blue clouds of heaven, and the blue praying hands of Jesus. To this world Isabel was dead. In the bananas, her passing was marked only by the shrieking of the peafowl.

Her father, the photographer, felt we must do something more. She must be commemorated by an obelisk, some kind of stone to signify our vast affection for her in memoriam, he said. This opposed my desire to take her home from the hospital, wrap her in banana leaves like a large fruit and bury her illegally in the back yard. It would have seemed less terrible to me to return a large fruit to the earth, more in line with the fruit's inevitable fate. But my young husband could not have accepted this even if we could have managed it.

And so began our quests, first for the proper grave site, and later for the stone. The grave site had to be of the older variety since we were also searching for a standing stone. In the older cemeteries where standing stones were still permitted, few plots were available. Much of the empty space had been previously sold in family parcels. We visited the parcels of the best families: the Dowsetts, Walkers, and Kahanamokus, to learn what was desirable. A plot surrounded by a marked foot path was of primary importance. No one must step on the site itself without proper reverence, we agreed. A tree seemed required to promote the proper atmosphere of peace and tranquility and shade. Evergreens and flowering trees were apparently most valued. And of course the site must be maintained regularly, preferably by very old Filipino gardeners in coolie hats who worked in quiet dignity with hand tools rather than motorized ones so as not to shatter the peace of the departed. Surprisingly, we found within a couple of days, a plot meeting all these requirements. The death of an infant invariably brings with it certain sympathies even among those for whom it is a steady business. We buried Isabel in an elegant plot without fanfare or ado, and with this I was satisfied.

My husband's search for the right stone, however, had barely begun. Gravestones are cut overseas, we were told. Our establishment merely engraves pre-cut stones with personal sentiments. No one hand carves headstones anymore. Well, no one we can think of. Certainly not figurines and the like. Isabel's grave remained unmarked for months, and it seemed, I'm sure, to an outside observer as if her death had little effect, as if a fruit had fallen to the earth and nothing more.

★　　★　　★　　★

Without Isabel, the stories I had been unearthing for her and formulating into a cohesive entity began to come apart. The story as a whole began to crack into individual pieces each unrelated to the others and each oddly devoid of significance. The pieces of my story remained in the palm of my hand, impotent and inert like a handful of golden scarabs all without the power to evoke the soul.

I was sterile. I had no job and spent my days cooking fabulous meals for a man for whom I felt little and who often left town. Regardless of his infrequent presence, I emptied the refrigerator daily of shrimp, vegetables, eggs, pears, and large white fish. In a copper skillet I sautéed the shrimp, in the oven baked the fish, basting it in white wine and butter. I marinated the vegetables and glazed the pears. The eggs I boiled and ate myself, plain.

I spend the rest of the morning X'ing out all the episodes in my memory which I feel no longer belong to me. The wooden house is often empty; the man I am married to travels.

It is while he is away that I formulate an obsession, lesbian in nature, with a certain French writer. In my empty wooden house, I stitch white French lace to all my white bedding. After dressing the bed, I lie in it and imagine French kissing, and the French woman who is at present nearly 70, often cranky, cruel even, and disdainful of me. I imagine her entire body, finely wrinkled all over, skin like a mosquito net, but utterly soft. It is terribly real and when I open my eyes after thinking of her like that, the walls of my bedroom seem distant and unreal.

Sometimes, in the middle of this obsession, she, my French writer, becomes confused. As if superimposed by a certain image of my mother, a weak image, but one which I cannot permanently X. It is of my mother as a piece of white twine. She is entwined with me. Wrapped around me like a knot, a fabulous example of macramé. She is weeping over the loss of her other daughter. You, she tells me, are my obedient child. She teaches without mouthing the words that in disobedience lies death. To my mother Lydia is dead.

I call Lydia and instead reach the Destructor. She doesn't want to talk to you, much less eat lunch with you, he says. He refuses to let me hear this from Lydia herself. Every time she sees you, she gets upset, he tells me. I won't let her be hurt like that, he says and hangs up.

One day I am able to reach her when he isn't home. She isn't sure whether she can meet me for lunch, but expresses a condolence as to the death of Isabel. I am pregnant again, I say. Right then she tells me that she has found, just that minute, the minute I spoke, one of only 5,000 promotional emeralds in her box of green laundry powder. I think this: You could call it fate or luck or God's will, but really this is what's left of the life she was meant for.

An emerald in a box of laundry soap, she repeats, imagine.

During those still nights of the second pregnancy, as I lay in bed with my eyes closed, everything took on an aquatic uncertainty. I felt I was floating, randomly and unceasingly over incandescent green waves. My insomnia was an ocean. Memories vividly emerged of the fear I had in my childhood of sudden tsunamis. I remembered a story I knew of some friends who, while playing hooky from school, drove their car along the coastal highway toward a favorite surf site and found to the dismay of all of them live fish flipping on the black top and the sea very far out. That is the nature of tsunamis. It is possible to sit on the sand on a perfectly calm day and for the calm expanse of blue water to suddenly begin to rush inland.

When I open my eyes in this state of insomnia, the walls of my bedroom seem to alternate between receding very far out and rapidly rushing forward; the walls advance and withdraw in erratic patterns like the water of tsunamis. I am in constant danger of being swept away by the walls of my bedroom.

Around this time my husband returns again from an extended trip, and together we find the tombstones. We make this discovery quite by accident while driving through the ratty streets of an area occupied by several hundred small businesses. The streets are narrow and winding and lined with warehouses, auto body shops, reupholstery operations, and the like. Merely by accident we notice a garage door open that until now had always been shut and seemingly unused. It is a rolling garage door, half drawn, and beyond it: multitudes of winged creatures.

We stop and together tentatively approach the strange opening. No one intervenes as we step inside. I must tell you we are shocked. The garage is old-fashioned with tall windows and everywhere we look are angels. Sunlight shines in eight of nine windows and lights the limestone angels so that they glitter and are shockingly white. Most are two or three feet high but some are taller than we. Beautifully carved, winged, of stern expression, and androgynous, each seems somehow unlike stone, as if without effort it might levitate. We are alone for some time, transfixed by a spectacle which seems to offer complete satisfaction, total satiation after a long thirst. Encountering this congregation of angels encased in this unlikely concrete garage was like unwittingly gaining entrance into a magnificent geode.

These were angels which embodied the concept of life everlasting. Their beauty countered the random disorder implied by Isabel's death, its futility, the coldness of her flesh. The maker of these angels before us seemed somehow to have reversed the laws of thermodynamics. For, as we waited, the blazing sunlight faded and in the ensuing gloom the limestone angels gained an even greater preternatural warmth.

I will give anything to own one of these, my husband says. His words are to me a deathly premonition and I become fearful of such a desire. The garage now seems to me to have acquired the sanctity of a church. The removal of one of these angels would be a desecration.

The owner was eerie. He emerged from out of a particularly dark corner of the garage, of that I am sure, but I cannot say how long he had been there, watching.

I can't help you. I no longer sell what you want, he said, I am the young master of an antiquated art.

But these here, my husband asks, can't I buy one of these here? There is an acute desperation in his voice. An anguish which I have only heard once or twice in the past. It is the voice of fear known only to those lovers who love obsessively. Perhaps love is the wrong word, lover the wrong word; I am referring to the fear of those infatuated, or of sexual deviants; the incestuous, necrophilic, pedophile. It is the fear generated by the impending inaccessibility of the object of lust. Or of separation by death.

Such fear I first encountered in the wooden studio, in the voice of my dancing master. Yet you must doubt this. You must have foreseen immediately the tragedy inherent in a relationship between a young child and a dancing master such as the one I have described, the man in the wooden studio. The sordid ending of this affair must have seemed evident to you at the start. It goes like this: the young girl is discarded like a tattered costume as soon as it becomes clear that the experience inflicted upon her has taken its toll, that it has somehow tarnished her. Such a man must ever seek virginity. He may resort to small doses of sadism which prolong the illusion of novelty, but this will not halt his eventual boredom. It is well known that such a man has no use for a full blown rose nor even for the spring bud in early summer. This is wisdom conventional in nature. Yet, it seems, I was never a rose.

I defied all predicted scenarios and was able to keep the attention of my dancing master because at age 15 I did not care about his affection and because at age 15 my nature seemed impermanent. He was unable to determine how to manipulate me because what I cared passionately for one day, I forgot the next. He could deprive me of nothing which he knew I wanted because I seldom wanted anything twice. I was like a dandelion turning from sun to moon, leaf to feather, a thing rooted to a thing floating. I multiplied in his presence into many selves, which were scattered around him everywhere. He was unable to focus on the character of any one. I was as hard to control as are dandelions.

★   ★   ★   ★

It ends on a whim. After our performance in the contest, I refuse to dance to any other melancholy dances. I refuse his discipline, the rituals of denial, my artistic seriousness. I refuse him. I say I am common, a dandelion.

He cannot accept it, my finale, my exit, the scattering of myself into the winds.

The last time I went to the wooden studio, he filled the ruined pool for me with deep cool water, which, as I lowered my body into it, lapped gently against the clawed feet of the stone lions *en gardant*. In my black bathing suit, I imagine now that I must have moved through the dark cool water in the pool like a seal, diving and surfacing without disturbing the tranquility of the water, which was nearly still and which seemed on the surface lacquered. This is a romantic vision of myself, I know, and yet, how else can I explain the dancing master's anguished voice as he called out to me that final time? As if by swimming in the pool, by moving smoothly through water, I had created the movement his choreography could not. As I think of it now, the music of Mahler's *Kindertoten-lieder* was best expressed by a solitary childish girl swimming in a ruined pool of still water as if unfamiliar with any solidity, with earth itself.

Lydia learned this lesson well: in disobedience is death. She learned as well to choose for whom she would die and for whom she would live. She was at once dead to our mother and living for the Destructor. When he instructed her not to speak to us, her own sister and mother, she chose even to avoid us at the market. If we were to meet accidentally, say near the meats and fish, she would return abruptly to the produce, setting the large purple heads of cabbage rolling chaotically in her cart as she rushed off. Sometimes we circled back as well and approached her again in the vegetables, forcing another frantic U-turn away from us. In this way my mother and I tortured Lydia with the expressed intent of making her see us. But she remained one of the walking dead, a reanimated corpse with no free thought, action, or will, a slave to the Destructor. Of course, because our mother is blind, I was the instigation of this particular practice, but she was, I thought at the time, in complete agreement.

On the baby dress my mother sent for Isabel, all the horses

were upside down. It had been hers. It was not really a baby dress but rather the dress of a young child three or four years of age. I believe her mother made it, one of the few things my mother remembers her mother giving her. It must have been during the War because the dress is made of feed sack. My mother remembers her mother keeping large chickens during the War. She tells of sitting on some back steps while feeding her mother's chickens from a sack of meal worms and corn too heavy for her to lift. At first these chickens frightened my mother, who was tiny for her age and sightless. They crowded around her, pecking at her arms, shoulders, and belly. Sometimes she was so afraid she dumped over the bag of feed and they fought among themselves. But after a while, she says, they got to know her. Sometimes if my mother, who has always loved music, made up one of her strange, whiny tunes, a large hen would roost on her lap.

My mother's mother must have made the dress out of empty feed sack during a year when the feed sack was printed with beautiful blue horses, horses that captured the imagination of my mother as a child. She loved the idea of them. In such a beautiful dress, I could play the violin, my mother remembers saying when the dress was finally finished. This upset my mother's mother who told her, music is not in the heart, it exists on a page, as lines of notes on a page.

About the chickens my mother fed, she has heard it said they were black and the plumpest in the area.

I understand now that my mother loved us best when we were in absentia. For instance, Lydia, now dead to my mother, is ever more beloved. Our mother has me put all of Lydia's childhood photographs in dark oval frames. Not for herself, who can't see them, but for others. She even asks my husband, a professional photographer, to touch up a large black and white studio portrait. She asks him to add tears to Lydia's lashes and cheeks. Upon seeing such a photograph, everyone will see Lydia as the personification of sorrow, she says. My mother has sacrificed her house to Lydia. Our mother's house has become Lydia's shrine. On the grand piano in my mother's living room, my mother plunks out one finger melodies to which she adds strange mournful words:

> Hey Lydia
> little girl
> why do you open
> that box of new stars?
> To lick and stick
> over all your body
> so you'll be flecked with gold?
> Hey Lydia
> little girl
> hold my hand
> once my precious starlet
> where are your gold stars now?

Her songs, such as this one, which I transcribe as accurately as I can, seem to reflect instances in our childhood which are nearly forgotten. Instances such as when Lydia stole a box of stars from a teacher at the elementary school. For months thereafter she liked to stick stars on her skin as a substitute for jewelry. My mother mythologizes Lydia's childhood.

Perhaps I should speak more directly concerning how the circumstances of my life have changed since meeting my young husband. At fifteen and sixteen, due to my relationship with the dancing master, my circle of friends consisted of artists—poets, sculptors, painters, and dancers. At first my dancing master accompanied me to the gatherings of these people, both glittering and sleazy, their parties, openings, and performances. I attended at his side, beautifully dressed and bejeweled. Profoundly silent. I could neither nod nor smile without his sanction, such was our agreement at that time about discipline. As I characterize it now, I see my early relationship with the dancing master as similar to that of a woman in a convent. Yet, oddly, I was accustomed to it. It was similar in substance to my childhood devotion to Prince Albert. Then, as the solitary priestess to the mosque of palms, and later in the wooden studio, my privation was really self-inflicted, controlled by some element of my imagination. The hours I spent on my knees worshipfully arranging stones in honor of the Prince, as well as readying myself with strings of leaves for his nocturnal visits, were feats of self-discipline. I denied myself all forms of childish pleasure, trips to the beach, rice candies, the joining of clubs, in order to maintain a single-mindedness of purpose. Yet such devotion was not a second nature. How else could I have so easily changed?

Consider the lack of external and internal discipline in my present life. I rise from bed whenever I want, morning or night; I eat whatever I want, eggs and flowers; I buy what I want. I have no obligations, no commitments. My peafowl are fed on no schedule. My life today stands in total opposition to my life in the wooden studio. Yet, had I remained with the master, wouldn't I have merely been attempting to seize a life not really mine? A life more in line with the one originally designed for Lydia? I cannot imagine myself without this present viscosity. Incoherence defines me.

This is something I remember from our childhood in the big empty house, the house of many balconies, a horror which our blind mother never believed. It was our own private *Walpurgisnacht*, not occurring reliably on the eve of May, but rather on a random night in High Summer. It is the Roach Mating Night. I do not profess to know the entomological details of the mating practices of the large roach of our island, nor do I deny the popular wisdom which has it that roaches mate unceasingly, inhabiting the average household by the thousands. But I do know from experience that on a certain hot night every summer, unpredictable to us, the roaches in our area make a festival of it. They crawl out of the cracks in sidewalks, up from the sewers, out of the closets, and together take flight. They swarm in clouds down the streets, beat up against the screens, enter houses by the dozens and bump into lamp shades, crawl between sofa cushions, hide in the folds of draperies, and in their frenzied flight they are nearly indestructible. We beat on them with the heels of shoes. On the chairs they are large and shiny, like candied dates. They do not die easily. Our mother cannot see them. She screams at us for beating the walls and furniture with the heels of our shoes, for puncturing the lampshades. She accuses us of tormenting her with false stories, of going on a mad rampage. In the morning, after a sleepless night, we sweep their crisp carcasses out of the house.

BARBARA

1.
Here is my evidence of Barbara:
a shot of her riding Tony bareback
the day she told me I'd never learn how,
the 1950's silver Siamese bracelet we picked out
together, a tape of her songs,
one nameless letter, and a gold chain dangling
a small black pearl I never saw her wear.

There was no help against her.
Her early delight in tying me up
with clothesline in the barn, pretending
she was an Indian, then dragging me whimpering
to the edge of the loft, where she threatened
to push me off if I wouldn't eat snowberries
she said were poison. Mother said you don't
have to play with her. Didn't I though?

About that time I read in the news
about a girl kept home from school
by her step-sister, step-mother,
who held her in bed, fed her garbage,
stubbed her with cigarette-tattoos.
When they found her, she was not tied up.
No one could understand why she hadn't
just run away. I was afraid
I could, and dreamed constantly
about that girl, about what would actually
have happened if she'd tried to tell, until
I finally could think what I would have done,
a detailed, working plan.

Barbara, stranger.

Where did she come from? No one knew.
Her papers were sealed.
Her adopted parents took her to bars,
or worse, went out by themselves once she was three
and left her to wake up alone.
When Aunt Lorraine found her, gave her a home and a room
with checked curtains, she needed a light on
all night. Over and over in dreams
she recognized someone from behind
and called a name, then froze
as the face turned. *Aunt Lorraine!*
Aunt Lorraine! Help! There it is again!

She had to invent herself,
past and future, taking it as a sign
whenever she felt drawn to something.
Indians, palomino horses, our family.
And much more seriously than the rest of us
she played ouija, card-fortunes, games of fate.
If I believed her, she was part Cree.
I said I believed her.
My sister she loved, but Joy seemed to love
everyone equally. Next best was controllable me.

What I did about Barbara was lie.
Linking arms with Diane and Phyllis I yelled
what I wished were true: My mother says
you're a terrible influence on me,
and I can't hang around with you.
It worked for two years.

2.
Red jacket days. Barbara and I
fifteen and fourteen, inseparable now,
on long rainwalks singing duets
of Johnny Ray's "Little White Cloud
That Cried" and getting the details straight
in our Myth of Sue, born unfortunately
to family who hoped to turn her
into a gleaming violin that would play
their kind of music. Lucky for her,
she had a friend.
Right and wrong for us that year
was a matter of how we wore our hair.
Now it was Mother who couldn't choose
not to play games with Barbara.

She was losing fast, never knew when
she could look in my bedroom and find me there.
But I was learning: every boy's car—make and year,
where to buy Mogen David, Lucky Strikes
underage, where the boardinghouses were,
how to really swear—thanks to Barbara.
I taught myself to use freckles as an alibi, even
with Barbara. My progress delighted her.

No break, just such a bad snarling
of ligaments Dr. Hambrecht said let's immobilize
that ankle to let it mend. Good medicine,
but I walked on the plaster before it could set.
For my impatience, a haunting weakness there.
Ever since my right ankle has warned me
before thunder, cold, and reminded me
of Barbara, the friend I didn't quite choose

who made me stand up. She wanted to go
somewhere. The whole thing tightens.

3.
When you heard about Joy's death you wanted to
    know
when? what time of day? Then consulted Joy's chart,
for God's sake, and wrote to me: *It may be hard
for us to understand, but it's clear from her stars
somehow Joy's death was a release.* You went on
about houses, trines, I forget. How
I hated that. Threw the letter out.

What could your own chart have told you
that long, last, horrible year?

Things had been going well. Husband
number three was tender, reliable, had "a gift
for the long haul." Just in time. First
you lost your foot on his cycle two blocks from home,
too shattered to sew back on. I pitied for once
your belief in fate, but it was larger than I thought.
You cracked jokes about the prosthesis, the pain
of adjustment, the awkward fit, the smell.
Then came hepatitis, mistaken so long
for flu you became translucent,
could only eat yams. When I called
on Easter Sunday, you said I'd laugh
if I could see the jumpsuits you had to wear
to accommodate fluid your liver couldn't clear.
Guessing no one would let you talk about dying,
I asked what you really thought, would you make it?
I told you honestly I bet you would. And if you did

get well, was there one thing you'd be sure to do?
With a flicker of energy you answered
I'll raise a cub, a wolf-baby.

Your last letter, wavery, unsigned.
I didn't know until that last year
that when you were young you were afraid
of horses, even your own. You didn't get
the chance to be a wise old woman, but on the phone
(the wolf cub conversation), you told me
you had love now, love was everything.

And you were right in a way.
Joy died because she wanted to.

A LETTER FROM WORPSWEDE
(Paula Modersohn-Becker)

Milly, if I had made three good paintings in my life,
I could die now. But I haven't made one.
In two days I'll be twenty-nine.
Dear sister, how good you are to believe in me,
or want to, even in this dull time
when I have no proof of any becoming,
except what the family calls my arrogance.
I avoid the studio now, eight years of oils
and sketches stacked against the walls.

Study the masters, Father said, meaning
you will never be one, meaning revere technique
to learn some humility. Otto tells me:
learn to draw. I want to say *Otto,
look at your hand. Do you see lines around it?*
If I have masters, they are not the great Germans
anymore. I'd go back to those ancient
anonymous makers of the unforgettable
dark eyes awaiting eternity. Or follow Cézanne
who alone sees that color is truth, and *that's*
what painters are for. Why, to be, must I be willing
to be unkind? Well I must be, and I am willing.

Oh Milly, I'll be all right. I get like this
in February when spring and Paris are too far off
and my brushes turn stiff while I sit
on the opposite end of the couch reading in French
and Otto makes entries in his notebook entitled "Ideals"
and has no idea yet of my travel plans. I want to be
equally unaware of the way he turns his pipe to the side
to see the page, how he turns out studies
day after day and will overpaint, not realizing

the studies themselves are lovelier than anything
that buys us food. If only the sun would come out,
I'd insist on a skating tour in the bright cold.
You see? It's only my old winter mood.

YOUNG GIRL WITH FLOWER VASES
(Painting by Paula Modersohn–Becker)

No one will tell this girl
to put others first
or give her words
to read in silence.
No one will cover her up
when her father enters the room.
(Remember when your daughter sat with
knees uncrossed in sensual virginity?
What happened then?)
Ribbons for the soul,
clothes for her will be merely
ceremonial.

This is no child to play with.
Consult her about grave things
she couldn't know: how long
you may have left and whether
your father ever will
acknowledge you. She'll respond
without turning in a yellow-petalled
whisper and can no more be wrong
than sun can on the roof
or some leaf we can't identify.

TO CLARA RILKE-WESTHOFF, FEBRUARY 1902

No painting today.
Sunday, and I'm roasting veal.
Even these dried yellow stars
of coltsfoot seem melancholy.
Clara, I want you here.
These days I see in your stone only Rodin
and hear Rilke, Rilke in your mouth and pen.
Have we really kept our names?

Rilke says friendship exists
to guard the other's solitude.
Clara, my friend, I don't need
such care from you. Marriage provides
abundant loneliness.
The house you build and build
away from Worpswede,
what does it stand on? *The world
I no longer look for outside,*
what does that mean?
With the forest so near
you break up furniture to heat your food.
I too am hungry.
Not for lack of wood.

MY BREATHING

I depend now on an iron lung I've nicknamed "Mom." But only at night, to sleep. When I told the doctor I wanted to be free during the day to move what can move, he looked at me skeptically. It's not that I can't breathe, but since the accident I have to remember to do it. At first I broke out in hives from the responsibility.

I took up smoking so I'd have a reminder to inhale (that's the crux of it, the exhale follows). I have become keenly aware of rhythms I can tune my breathing to. I've taken an assembly line job and volunteer for overtime. I've bought a rocking chair and an old Coors neon sign. When it flashes on, I breathe.

Some things are out of the question. I can't take cat-naps, scuba-dive, French kiss, because I'm afraid of passing out. Other than that, I'm free all day.

*   *   *   *

I've taken up my flute again. I had to oil it quite a lot just to put it together. When I was twelve, I thought it was the ordinariness of my instrument that limited my tone. Since then I've heard Galway on the penny-whistle.

At first I couldn't make a sound and thought I'd forgotten what little I knew. But it wasn't my technique, the flute was blocked. I used the cleaning stick and finally the obstacles came out—some hardened saliva, smell of Camels and Old Spice, Miss Frank's voice telling me I'd never finish anything.

I've quit my job to practice flute. The little book of etudes is coming along nicely now, and I'm beginning to think I have in me the vibrato I always used to fake. Best of all, I have discovered the bottom of breath, the tranquility there. I just mark the phrasing, then memorize the pieces, breaths and all.

GLORIA OLCHOWY ROZEBOOM

WHITENESS VISIBLE

At dawn, Adele turned all of the furniture in the kitchen and living room upside down. It wasn't easy, because she was a small woman and she had to be quiet. Technically speaking, the furniture was hers, not Evan's, so she needn't worry he'd complain about that part of it.

She wanted to turn over everything in the bathroom, too, especially the sink and the toilet bowl. Evan had trimmed his beard yesterday evening. Yellowish-brown hairs clung to the sink's white oval rim. He had not flushed the toilet twice when he had risen in the middle of the night. She had listened and counted. But the sink was fastened to the wall and the toilet was stuck to the floor. And both of the bedrooms were off limits because Evan was asleep in one and his instruments and plants were in the other.

Gulping cold coffee, Adele leaned against the kitchen counter and glanced around. The table's shiny steel legs look-ed ready to kick. The grey vinyl chairs crouched alongside. She tiptoed into the living room. The red-and-white striped hide-a-bed mattress stuck out like a tongue between the blue cushions. Beside it, the flat brown rectangle of the coffee table squashed TV guides, empty beer cans, guitar picks, cigarette butts, and apple stems, the only part of an apple Evan did not eat.

Particularly striking were the pictures hanging upside down. It wasn't the placement of lakes and fields that was disrupting, because the blue of water was about the same as the blue of sky, and the green land was still more or less in the middle. Seeing the sun at the bottom and the dirt at the top was what made Adele feel dizzy.

The television, unfortunately, looked about the same. It was a square of glass any way you turned it and, when off, it always featured a miniature reflection of the room. But at least now the room was different.

Back in the kitchen she squirted a bit of dishwashing liquid in her cup and scrubbed it muttering, "Out damned spot!" Then she rinsed and dried it and put it in the cupboard, and returned the Sunlight to its alphabetical place between the Mr. Clean and the Windex. She carefully folded and hung up the dishtowel, avoiding the dirty dishes. She decided to leave one more message.

She took the black clothes she had worn the day before and carefully arranged them on the floor by the door, bending the arms of the sweater and the legs of the jeans, plumping the front and widening the sides to round them. She added socks with holes in the toes.

Black, she thought, black like ink, black like Hamlet, black like dirt, black like the dresses my mother wears now, black like a shadow, my shadow on the floor by the door in a world that is white.

Adele slid into a booth, because she felt less conspicuous there with her down-filled sleeping bag beside her. The window on her left was half-covered with frost. The thick, opaque crust had been scratched from the inside by a customer wanting to see out. She wondered what had happened to the miniature jukeboxes. Once, she had wanted to play her favorite song, "Abraham, Martin, and John." "A waste of time and money," her mother had said.

A thin, sad-looking waitress shuffled up to the table.

"What would you like?" The woman's pen hovered an inch above the pad of newsprint. It reminded her of her mother's lists of groceries and prices, phone numbers and clothing, and furniture. Clear records. Lassoing everything with a rope of ink, she used to say.

"Ma'am?" The woman sounded impatient.

"Coffee, please."

Adele opened four packages of cream, and poured and stirred them in. One for each large glass of the "milk of human kindness" her mother had made them drink every day when they were kids.

Yesterday, after work, Adele had gone to visit her mother in her basement suite, made even darker by closed curtains.

Surrounded by stacks of open books, she'd been sitting at her kitchen table, not eating or drinking, but writing by the light of a small candle. Words, words, and more words, for another article or poem. She had looked so beautiful in her black dress as she sat there, smelling of ink and writing like crazy, in the darkness. Alone.

Adele swallowed more coffee. She wondered what Evan would think when he saw the upside-down furniture and the black clothing on the floor. He should not have asked to move in with her. He should not have moved in. She glanced at the watch her mother had given her long ago either for Christmas or for her birthday. It wasn't even eight yet. Evan would still be sleeping. By ten he'd be up, but by then she'd be off the bus and walking. For once she was glad he was not a morning person. He had not had a father to sing to him at five or five-thirty in the morning, as her father had sung to her and her brothers and sister.

Good morning to you! Good morning to you!
We're all in our places with sun-shiny faces.

Fortunately, Evan hadn't noticed anything, despite the signs. It wasn't that she had left clues on purpose or anything. She just ate yogurt as she always did when she was stressed, yogurt with apples, that is, and she did not run the dishwasher every second night or remind him to water his plants on Monday or do the laundry on Thursday night. She'd forgotten to make the bed one morning and to iron the dress she wore to work that day. She had been afraid he would suspect something after that. But he had not.

The Greyhound Bus pulled into Rosebush, a town named after the Wild Rose, the provincial flower for Alberta. Today, Whitefields would have been a better name.

Adele scratched a bit of the ice off her window to see the main street of the small prairie town. A few farmers, probably up since five or six o'clock to do chores, had parked their trucks in front of Totocychuk's Grocery Store and were ambling over to the Rosebush Cafe for coffee and conversation. Their wives were not with them because they were at home on the farm taking care of the kids and washing the floors, baking bread, ironing, or finishing up running the separator for the milk. One Saturday morning, years ago, the woman on the farm next to theirs had had a miscarriage at four months while carrying two heavy pails from the barn to the house. Adele remembered the blood in the snow. She peered at the farmers as they neared the Cafe, their faces hidden by white puffs of warm breath in the cold air.

The Greyhound Bus had always stopped at the Rosebush Cafe. Her father had taken the whole family there after church for ice cream cones. All the farm kids met their parents there after Christmas caroling in the town. And it was where they went after her father picked her up from her first-grade classroom the day President Kennedy was shot in the head.

Adele began to feel queasy. She did not recognize the farmers on the street. She hadn't been back to this town or to the farm since her parents' divorce and her father's death.

She turned away from the window and exited the bus behind a large-boned but slim Slavic woman, very upright, who reminded Adele of her mother—when her mother was still teaching, that is, since after she had stopped, she had gained weight and developed back problems. She had also started taking valium and ironing pillowcases.

The cold felt like a slap when she stepped off the bus. She thought of Evan, warm and naked and asleep in her bed, as she wound her scarf around her neck. As she entered the cafe, she kept her chin buried in it, because now that the farmers were sitting inside they looked more familiar. And they were staring at her the way small-town types always stare at strangers. She slipped quickly into the Ladies' Room.

It was the way the women who sang in the church choir had stared down from the balcony at her mother. These members of the Catholic Women's League started rumors about her mother when she refused to help make *pyrogis* for the dinner to honor the Archbishop, who came to conduct the Confirmation Mass. Her full-time teaching had been no excuse for these members, who believed women should stay at home to cook, clean, and raise their kids. Their husbands agreed and gave her father an earful about this at the Rosebush Cafe.

Adele got off the toilet and pulled up and zipped her jeans. She realized for the first time how loose they had become and how hollow her stomach looked. She flushed twice, washed her hands, and headed for the EXIT. The index finger of one farmer's huge hand, red and chapped, clasping a small mug of hot coffee, tapped on the white porcelain rim as if trying to trigger a memory.

After shopping at the Co-op, the only grocery store in town that was not family-run, Adele began the three-mile walk west across the snow-covered fields. She did not look at her old school or the Our Lady of Perpetual Help Church as she passed them on her way.

Yes, it was true, she thought, as she trudged through the knee-deep snow, it was true that her mother hadn't had time for cooking for the church or for breast-feeding or for playing card games like Old Maid with her daughters as the mothers of Adele's town friends had. It was also true that, in those early years, her mother had detested absolutely the cleaning she was later to become so fanatic about.

But as a small child Adele had loved it when her mother had worked at the kitchen table with her books and papers spread all around her and had taught Adele the alphabet— especially the big "A" for apple and her name—and when she had returned on the Greyhound Bus from the Teachers' Convention in Edmonton carrying shopping bags filled with books. Books that smelled of ink. Not books like the *Fun with Dick and Jane* texts Adele had to read in grade one or the Harlequin Romances with titles like *Fires of Destiny* that were sold at Smigorowsky's Drug Store and read by the town girls in high school, but novels about growing up on the Canadian prairies or, better yet, books about Pocomoto, an adventurous redskinned orphan who never put down roots anywhere as he journeyed across Canada. Books with lots of black words on every page.

Black, Adele thought, as she marched through the snow. Black ink, black clothes, black shadows. Black like words. Black like life.

Later, when her mother was in a heaven of valium, it was

Adele who taught Albert, Mary, and Cam the alphabet, their names, the fairy tales, and the nursery rhymes. For helping out so much, her father bought her a cloth-bodied baby doll with a plastic bottle for milk. That doll's round, ruddy face inspired Adele's name for it. Rosy. She still had it carefully packed in a box labeled "Doll" in the basement. She had turned the label of this box, in the row of the other labeled and alphabetically-arranged boxes, to the wall. Evan hadn't noticed this.

Not that he came down to the basement much. She hadn't either until he had moved in. Then she had moved her books and her desk next to the boxes and his stored furniture.

About two weeks ago, though, Evan had come downstairs, and for the first time she tried to explain why she majored in English, rather than Political Philosophy, which turned out to be her minor.

"I chose English because I like to label parts of speech and learn new words and name things, Evan. Because having those names makes me feel there is meaning. That I have some control. See?"

Adele tugged at a strand of her long hair. She glanced at Evan's furniture stacked in the far corner, at the boxes lined up beside her, and then at her books on the shelves above them, in order according to author. Her eyes settled on the large volume of *The Collected Works of Shakespeare* beside Sartre's *Being and Nothingness*.

"So that on white blanks I can put in black words. Even if the rest is silence and a quintessence of dust signifying nothing. See?" She thought of her dead father and her living mother.

Evan leaned on her desk, folded his arms, and looked into her eyes.

"That's Hamlet and Macbeth again," she said.

Evan picked up one of her black pens and a blank piece of paper.

"Mind?"

"No, go ahead." It was strange to see Evan with a pen instead of a guitar pick in his hand. He wrote one sentence. Before she could bend over to read it, he folded the piece of paper up like a letter.

"Here," he said, "Special Delivery."

Adele opened it and read,

Music and stories are the same color.

She smiled at him. He shrugged and grinned, took one of her hands, and led her upstairs to his room. At the piano, she saw the unfinished piece of music—the tiny black notes suddenly coming to a stop.

She sat down on the rug, and while Evan played and sang "The Rose," to her, she named all of his plants.

Her favorite was a bleeding heart she named "Vincent" for Vincent van Gogh because van Gogh needed lots of direct sunlight and he loved those "high yellow notes." Also, because he loved to paint sunflowers, which the farm children found so difficult to raise in northern Alberta with its short growing season. And because he shot himself in the heart.

Adele breathed in and felt the cold go down her throat into her chest and gut. Just over a mile to go. She wondered whether she should have walked on the plowed roads, even though cross-country was shorter. Despite her fast pace, her toes were numb and the white of the snow was starting to get to her.

White. Like blank paper. Like pillowcases. Like pills. Like dresses for Baptism and Confirmation and Communion. And Matrimony. White like the Our Lady of Perpetual Help Church. White like Mr. Krawchuk's tight collar. White like her father's dead flesh.

Just remember in the springtime,
far beneath the bitter snow,
lies a seed that with the sun's love
in the spring becomes a rose.

After Evan had finished singing, amongst all the newly named plants and beside his favorite guitar, they had made love. Then, their bodies still tangled together on the rug, Evan had murmured, "You are a waltz in a world with two left feet."

Adele shivered and squinted as she looked to the end of the field, the last she had to cross to get to what was once her home. The bright white light hurt her eyes. She started singing

"Silent Night," the carol her family had sung together every Christmas Eve for years,

All is calm, all is bright.
Round yon virgin, mother and child.

It was funny to think of that harmony now,

Sleep in heavenly peace.

Her lips numb and heavy from the cold, she stopped singing.

"Miles and miles to go before I sleep," she intoned slowly and clumsily. "Frost." A hell of a name to be born with.

She kept marching. White silence. White pain. White holes. White. The color of virginity and frigidity and celibacy and matrimony. The color of cold. Of fucking coldness.

And on all those Christmas Eves, "Silent Night" had been followed by "Happy Birthday to You" sung on her behalf because the twenty-fourth of December was her birthday. A bad time for a daughter to be born. The presents and songs for the birthday of the Son always got the attention.

"I do not dream of white Christmases," she said with heavy lips and white breath to the white space before her. "White is the color of nightmare. Of hell. And of death." She felt the rhythm of her steps.

White like blank paper and dresses and fucking death.

Adele stopped. There they were—the house with the rose bushes in front of it, the single willow tree, and the barely discernible rectangle that had once upon a time been a garden. She looked back across the field over which she had come— two long lines punctuated with bootprints stretched out of sight. She turned and went on through the deep white drifts, past the lone willow tree dressed in snow, to the old garden. She tugged off a mitten and grasped one of the dead sunflower stalks. It was dry and cold.

Numbness crept up the backs of her legs and her spine. Her forehead, cheeks, and chin felt dry and brittle, ready to crack if she changed expression. Her ears, too, were numb. She remembered how her father had frozen the tips of his off playing hockey when he was a kid. She shivered again, this time convulsively, and decided she had better start a fire.

She walked to the house and placed her sleeping bag and purse and the groceries by the basement window, which she knew was somewhere under the snow. She headed to the thick bush west of the house where she knew she'd find wood.

Carrying it, she tripped and fell flat, the pieces of wood scattering around her. She slowly raised her body and saw the shape impressed in the snow. She thought of white angels and of the black clothes left this morning on the floor.

Then she looked up and saw the side of the house behind the dormant branches of the one willow tree that had not been burnt in the fire. The building's silhouette in shadow was a triangle on top of a square. A black arrow against the white horizon.

She picked up the wood and went on. After scooping away the snow and prying open the window, she threw in her sleeping bag and the wood, and dropped in her purse and the bag of groceries. Then she went in feet first with no difficulty. Not at all like the window she had climbed through between the front seat and the back of Evan's truck, on their third date when they had gone to a drive-in movie. Allegedly. The truth made itself known after Evan spilled his popcorn.

"Shit." He scooped what he could find back into the carton.

"What I was trying to say, I mean, what I was going to suggest is that we watch it from the back." He lit a cigarette and breathed the smoke in and then out. He faced the front window. "It's—" He paused. "It's more comfortable back there."

Adele glanced back into the canopied part of the truck. She saw pillows and a blanket. Evan stubbed out his cigarette.

"Well, what do you think?" This time Evan did not stammer. He turned and looked right at her. His blue gaze was steady.

Adele remembered last night. How his beard felt on her face. And his tongue in her mouth. Beginning to explore inside.

"I guess it's okay." She reached for the door handle.

"Hey, wait. We'll crawl through this window here. That

way, we don't have to open up the back." He smiled. "More private."

Before she could say anything more, he slid the window open and maneuvered his long, lean body through it. She handed him the popcorn and drinks. Then she looked at the small, square opening and hesitated.

"Evan, I think my hips are too wide. What if I get stuck?"

"You won't. Come on. I'll help you."

It had been a tight squeeze but she had made it. She remembered that, and the steam from their breathing on the windows and the rhythm of their bodies. Most of all, the very distinct feel of Evan's hands. His fingertips, calloused from playing the guitar, touching her. An ever so slight roughness on her skin.

After squashing a few pages of the Sunday comics she had brought along, Adele arranged the wood and lit the corner of a "Blondie" cartoon. The yellow flame curled around the body of the woman who was always cooking and shopping, like the mothers of the girls who lived in town.

As the fire blazed higher, she felt the painful pricking of her face, hands, and feet thawing. Hundreds of tiny needles sticking the skin simultaneously. She smiled anyway. Building fires was one thing that she did well, other than reciting Shakespeare and teaching. It had been her job on their camping trips when she hadn't had to worry about cleaning or organizing or grading or ironing.

Evan had played his guitar and mouth organ as she made the fire and then again as they sat by and enjoyed it. The best times were when he played and sang Neil Young's "Helpless." He even changed a few words of the song especially for her. "Town" to "farm" and "Ontario" to "Alberta":

> There is a farm in North Alberta
> with dream comfort memory to spare.
> And in my mind
> I still need a place to go.
> All my changes were there.
> Blue, blue windows behind the stars.
> Yellow moon on the rise . . .

There was the pungent smell of burning wood and their glowing red cheeks. Afterward, in the dark tent, Evan's warm skin with its bristly hair beneath her felt the way the black earth with green grass on it felt on a sunny summer day. And she wanted to disappear forever in the bush of the beard on his face . . .

Early the next morning, after making a fire to boil water for coffee, she had awakened Evan by playing a clumsy rendition of "Here Comes the Sun" on his guitar.

"Hey, that's pretty good!" Evan rubbed his eyes and yawned. "How come you never told me you played?"

Adele shrugged and continued strumming softly.

"One year, Daddy came home with a guitar after working most of the winter up north. Some of the other lumberjacks gave it to him after he entertained them with his songs." She paused to sip her coffee. "You know, he could play all the instruments, even though he never had a music lesson in his life. And he taught us kids the basic chords. From A to G."

She stopped playing and put the guitar down. Evan crawled out of the sleeping bag and sat next to her. He placed the guitar pick she had dropped back in her hand. "Keep practicing. You're good."

She stared at the guitar lying on its back. Evan put his arm around her shoulders.

"How does apple juice and bacon and eggs, sunny-side up, sound?"

As she was carrying her last load of wood to the house, Adele saw the rusty seed drill by one of the lopsided granaries. She had walked up and down its horizontal wooden plank part many times, while rehearsing Shakespeare.

In grade ten, Antony's "Lend me your ears" funeral speech. Mr. Krawchuk had wanted her to do lines by Portia or Calpurnia. She had told him point blank that she was not interested in the "wife" parts.

Then, the following year, both Lady Macbeth's "Unsex me here" speech and the prophecies of one of the witches. She shocked everyone when playing the "witch" part not because of wearing a black dress but because of wearing a beard. "You should be women, and yet your beards forbid me to interpret that you are so," she quoted for her defense. Krawchuk had frowned and cautioned her about being too literal.

Finally, just before high school graduation, Ophelia's flower speech, because Adele understood madness after a father's death and being told "Get thee to a nunnery!" This time, Krawchuk reminded her that madness was not a desirable state.

"Had I three ears, I'd hear thee!" Adele shouted to the white fields. Then, reconsidering, she muttered, "No. I'd cut them all off instead."

She returned to the house and dropped the wood by the fireplace. "Lend me your ears," she whispered with white breath.

Adele grabbed a couple of apples and a container of yogurt from the kitchen counter. Not quite bacon and eggs or a campsite in the Rocky Mountains, she thought, as she ripped the foil off the yogurt and then glanced at the four mildewed walls around her. And no Evan either. She left the cold kitchen with its checkered blood-red and milk-white linoleum. She placed more wood and sticks on the fire and watched the free play of the curved orange tongues.

"Freedom" was the song by Richie Havens that Evan had sung over and over again after cleaning and polishing all of his instruments to commemorate the twentieth anniversary of Woodstock:

> *Sometimes I feel like a motherless child,*
> *sometimes I feel like a motherless child . . .*

Evan crooned for the third or fourth time,

> *Sometimes I feel like a mother —*

"Christ, that's enough already!" Adele came out of the kitchen where she had been sorting and lining up the cans of soup she had just bought. She glared at Evan. "Sing something else, okay? I'm sick of that one."

> *A long way from my home . . .*

Evan concluded. He cleared his throat and swallowed some beer.

Adele noticed the wet circle from the can on the brown

wood of her coffee table. The coasters she had placed in the center of the table had not been touched.

"Any requests?" Evan's face was flushed. His thick curly hair and his beard were still damp from the shower. He sat, a white towel tied on, looking like Jesus with a guitar.

"Yeah . . 'I Get by With a Little Help From my Friends' or something."

"Joe Cocker, eh?" Evan grinned and paused for more beer and smoke. The half-inch of ashes that had accumulated on his cigarette dropped to the floor. He returned the white butt to the black ashtray she had set on the coffee table. Then he began:

> What would you do if I sang out of tune?
> Would you stand up and walk out on me?
> Lend me your ears and I'll sing you a song.
> I will try not to sing out of key.

Adele threw the apple core into the fire. She did not eat it as Evan would have.

Stretched out in her sleeping bag, she glanced around the empty living room. It had been empty like this the first time her mother had moved out, taking the kitchen and living room furniture. Adele had cried but it hadn't helped. She had baked bread for the kids and her father, but it hadn't risen. She had cooked, cleaned, and ironed, too, but it hadn't made things better.

So, she started wearing black, like Hamlet. And writing black words. And earning A's in every course. Even in physics class. Even when she was the only girl and all the boys called her "Judas."

One week ago, she had begun wearing black again, after Evan had proposed marriage. Marriage. A happily ever after in inflexible slippers of glass. Or something. A whiteness. Invading her black world.

Saturday, after Evan's last piano student had left, she had heard the door close and Evan's footsteps returning to his room.

She placed the black pen she had been using back in the jar of other black pens. She gathered up all of the notes she had written and put them in the bottom right-hand drawer of her desk. The top drawer was for lists. A list of the things she owned. A list of the men before Evan. And a list of deaths. Those of assassinated politicians and suicidal artists. That of her father.

She locked both drawers and slipped the key under *The Stone Angel*. Then she placed the stack of blank paper in the middle of the desktop. For blackening tomorrow.

She climbed slowly up the stairs and went over to the kitchen sink to wash the ink off her hands. The dirty dishes on the counter and the full ashtray on the table she tried to ignore. Then she went to Evan's room. He was looking out the window, idly scratching at some ice on it with a guitar pick.

"Good lesson?"

"Yeah. Joanne's doing real well." He stopped picking at the ice and turned to her. "Adele—" he began and stopped. He walked over to the piano and got a cigarette from the box sitting on top. Soon blue clouds of smoke hovered over the green plants and brown instruments.

"Well? What?" Adele went over to Evan and put her arms around his waist and her head on his chest. She remembered last week in this room, her naming the plants and them on the rug. Evan reached over to the ashtray and put out his cigarette. Adele felt him take a deep breath. Then he lifted her chin with his slightly rough finger tips.

"Adele," he said, looking directly into her eyes, "I've been thinking . . . that we should get married. In the spring." He paused. "It's time, isn't it?"

Adele stopped breathing and stepped back.

"What?" Her lips felt hard.

"Let's get married." Evan reached for her to bring her close again, but she turned and said over her shoulder as she left his room, "I'll think about it." Her voice was brittle.

He should not have asked her. She did not want to answer and she had avoided answering all week by spending most of her time in the basement. Every night since then she had worn flannel pajamas to bed and kept to her side and pretended to be asleep when Evan came home from his gigs. He had said and done nothing.

Adele stared at her black sweater and jeans on the green parka. They looked like dirt on top of grass instead of under it. She turned away. They weren't necessary because the down-filled sleeping bag was good down to minus twenty-five below and the checkered red-and-white flannel lining was soft and warm.

The shirts her father had worn when he worked up north in the bush camps had been made out of flannel. They were the shirts her mother burned, along with any other dirty clothes of his she found on the floor, the autumn before she moved out for good. The fire had gotten out of control. The willows with their golden autumn leaves and the huge tongue-shaped orange flames curling around them had looked like giant birthday candles. The house had somehow survived. So had one tree.

The dark wall in front of Adele flickered with patterns of light and shadow. The wind howled and the windows rattled as she clutched the soft, warm, flannel lining. Her father had died in a shirt of flannel, about three years ago, under a tree that had crushed his chest. A couple of the other men found him about a half hour after it happened. In the snow with blood on the front of his jacket. Already cold. Already fucking cold.

Adele looked into the hot flames, and felt herself falling. She saw one of Vincent van Gogh's self-portraits, the one missing an ear, explode into a million stars at the bottom of the black hole in his heart. Then Lady Macbeth and Vincent fetched a plastic pail of milk and tumbled down a hill covered with sunflowers. Mr. Clean's bald head rolled after them on slippery ice. Then, a big bang and an orange explosion. Walking over a snow-covered hill were Abraham, Martin, and John. Albert, Mary, and Cameron followed. Each carried a wild rose. Over a garden of weeds, in a white dress and glass slippers, Lady Macbeth hung from a rope of black ink. The spilled milk mixed with Vincent's blood on the black earth . . .

Adele opened her eyes. The fire had burned itself out. Shivering, she pulled on the black sweater and the black jeans. She used what was left of the Sunday comics to clean up the ashes. She put on her coat, scarf, and mittens, rolled up her sleeping bag, grabbed her purse, and went out.

There was no milk and no blood and no black earth. No sunflowers or roses or weeds. No stars. No night. Only the white sky and the white fields, all calm and bright and cold. And she. The one warm spot. A lone flame.

"Out, out brief candle," she said, and started her three-mile trek east.

Black clothing still sprawled on the floor by the door—the abbreviated message, the body word.

But new notes had been added. Adele scratched more ice off the door's small window. She cupped her hands around her eyes and leaned on the glass to see more clearly.

On the socks, covering the holes, were Evan's houseshoes, and placed on the high rib-knit neckline of the sweater was an oval-shaped piece of paper, on which thick, curly, yellowish-brown hair had carefully been shaped.

MAVIS HARA

CARNIVAL QUEEN

My friend Terry and I both have boy's nicknames. But that's the only thing about us that is the same. Terry is beautiful. She is about 5'4" tall, which is tall enough to be a stewardess. I am only 5 feet tall, which is too short, so I should know.

My mother keeps asking me why Terry is my friend. This makes me nervous, because I really don't know. Ever since we had the first senior class officers' meeting at my house and my mother found the empty tampax container in our waste basket she has been really asking a lot of questions about Terry. Terry and I are the only girls who were elected to office. She's treasurer and I'm secretary. The president, the vice-president, and the sergeant-at-arms are all boys. I guess that's why Terry and I hang out together. Like when we have to go to class activities and meetings she picks me up. I never even knew her before we were elected. I don't know who she used to hang around with, but it sure wasn't with me and my friends. We're too Japanese girl, you know, plain. I mean, Terry has skin like a porcelain doll. She has cheekbones like Garbo, a body like Ann Margaret, she has legs like, well, like not any Japanese girl I've ever seen. Like I said, she's beautiful. She always dresses perfectly, too. She always wears an outfit; a dress with matching straw bag and colored leather shoes. Her hair is always set, combed, and sprayed; she even wears nylon stockings under her jeans, even on really hot days. Terry is the only girl I know who has her own Liberty House charge card. Not that she ever goes shopping by herself. Whenever she goes near a store, her mother goes with her.

Funny, Terry has this beautiful face, perfect body, and nobody hates her. We hate Valerie Rosecrest. Valerie is the only girl in our P.E. class who can come out of the girl's showers, wrap a towel around herself under her arms and have it stay up by itself. No hands. She always takes the longest time in the showers and walks back to her locker past the rest of us, who are already dry and fumbling with the one hook on the back of our bras. Valerie's bra has five hooks on the back of it and needs all of them to stay closed. I think she hangs that thing across the top of her locker door on purpose just so we can walk past it and be blinded by it shining in the afternoon sun. One time, my friend Tina got fed up and snatched Val's bra. She wore it on top of her head and ran around the locker room. I swear, she looked like an albino Mickey Mouse. Nobody did anything but laugh. Funny, it was Terry who took the bra away and put it back on Val's locker again.

I don't know why we're friends, but I wasn't surprised when we ended up together as contestants in the Carnival Queen contest. The Carnival Queen contest is a tradition at McKinley. They have pictures of every Carnival Queen ever chosen hanging in the Auditorium corridor right next to the pictures of the senators, governors, politicians, and million-aires who graduated from the school. This year there are already five portraits of queens up there. All the girls are wear-ing long ball gowns and the same rhinestone crown which is placed on their heads by Mr. Harano, the principal. They have elbow length white gloves and they're carrying baby's breath and roses. The thing is, all the girls are *hapa*. Every one.

Every year, it is the same tradition. A big bunch of girls gets nominated to run, but everybody knows from interme-diate school on which girl in the class is actually going to win. She has to be *hapa*.

"They had to nominate me," I try to tell Terry. "I'm a class officer, but you, you actually have a chance to be the only Japanese girl to win." Terry had just won the American Legion essay contest the week before. You would think that being fashionable and coordinated all the time would take all her energy and wear her out, but her mother wants her to be smart too. She looks at me with this sad face I don't understand.

"I doubt it," she says.

Our first orientation meeting for contestants is today in the library after school. I walk to the meeting actually glad to be there after class. The last after school meeting I went to was the one I was forced to attend. That one had no contestants. Just potential school dropouts. The first meeting, I didn't know anybody there. Nobody I know in the student government crowd is like me and has actually flunked chemistry. All the guys who were coming in the door were the ones who hang around the bathrooms that I'm too scared to use. Nobody ever threatened me though, and after a while, dropout class wasn't half bad, but I have to admit, I like this meeting better. I sit down and watch the other contestants come through the door. I know the first name of almost every girl who walks in. Terry, of course, who is wearing her blue suede jumper and silk blouse, navy stockings and navy patent leather shoes. My friend Trudye, who has a great figure for an Oriental girl but who wears braces and coke bottle glasses. My friend Linda, who has a beautiful face but a basic *musubi*-shaped body. The Yanagawa twins, who have beautiful *hapa* faces, but pretty tragic, they inherited their father's genes and have government-issue Japanese-girl legs. Songleaders, cheerleaders, ROTC sponsors, student government committee heads, I know them all. Krissie Clifford, who is small and blonde, comes running in late. Krissie looks like a young version of Beaver's mother on the TV show. She's always running like she just fell out of the screen, and if she moves fast enough, she can catch up with the TV world and jump back in. Then she walks in. Leilani Jones. As soon as she walks in the door, everybody in the room turns to look at her. Every body in the room knows that Leilani is the only girl who can possibly win.

Lani is *hapa*, Japanese-*haole*. She inherited the best features from everybody. She is tall and slim, with light brown hair and butter frosting skin. I don't even know what she is wearing. Leilani is so beautiful it doesn't matter what she is wearing. She is smooth, and gracefully quiet. Her smile is soft and shiny. It's like looking at a pearl. Lani is not only beautiful, when you look at her all you hear is silence, like the air around her is stunned. We all know it. This is the only girl who can possibly win.

As soon as Leilani walks in, Mrs. Takahara, the teacher advisor says, "Well, now, take your seats everyone. We can begin."

We each take a wooden chair on either side of two rows of long library tables. There is a make-up kit and mirror at each of the places. Some of Mrs. Takahara's friends who are teachers are also sitting in.

"This is Mrs. Chung, beauty consultant of Kamedo cosmetics," Mrs. Takahara says, "she will show us the proper routines of skin cleansing and make-up. The Carnival Queen contest is a very special event. All the girls who are contestants must be worthy representatives of McKinley High School. This means the proper make-up and attitude. Mrs. Chung . . ."

I have to admire the beauty consultant. Even though her makeup is obvious as scaffolding in front of a building, it is so well done, kind of like the men who dance the girls' parts in Kabuki shows, you look at it and actually believe that what you are seeing is her face.

"First, we start with proper cleansing," she says. We stare into our own separate mirrors.

"First, we pin our hair so that it no longer hangs in our faces." All of the girls dig in handbags and come up with bob-by pins. Hairstyles disappear as we pin our hair straight back. The teachers look funny, kind of young without their teased hair. Mrs. Chung walks around to each station. She squeezes a glop of pink liquid on a cotton ball for each of us.

"Clean all the skin well," she says. "Get all the dirt and impurities out." We scrub hard with that cotton ball, we all know that our skin is loaded with lots of stuff that is impure. My friend Trudye gets kind of carried away. She was scrub-bing so hard around her eyes that she scrubbed off her scotch tape. She hurries over to Mrs. Takahara's chair, mumbles something and excuses herself. I figure she'll be gone pretty long, the only bathroom that is safe for us to use is all the way over in the other building.

"Now we moisturize," Mrs. Chung is going on. "We use this step to correct defects in the tones of our skins." I look over at Terry. I can't see any defects in any of the tones of her skin.

"This mauve moisturizer corrects sallow undertones," Mrs. Chung says.

"What's shallow?" I whisper to Terry.

"SALLOW," she whispers back disgusted. "Yellow."

"Oh," I say and gratefully receive the large glop of purple stuff Mrs. Chung is squeezing on my new cotton ball. Mrs. Chung squeezes a little on Terry's cotton ball too. When she passes Lani, she smiles and squeezes white stuff out from a different tube.

I happily sponge the purple stuff on. Terry is sponging too but I notice she is beginning to look like she has the flu. "Next, foundation," says Mrs. Chung. She is walking around, narrowing her eyes at each of us and handing us each a tube that she is sure is the correct color to bring out the best in our skin. Mrs. Chung hands me a plastic tube of dark beige. She gives Terry a tube of lighter beige and gives Lani a different tube altogether.

"Just a little translucent creme," she smiles to Lani who smiles back rainbow bubbles and strands of pearls.

Trudye comes rushing back and Linda catches her up on all the steps she's missed. I got to admit, without her glasses and with all that running, she has really pretty cheekbones and nice colored skin. I notice she has new scotch tape on too, and is really concentrating on what Mrs. Chung is saying next.

"Now that we have the proper foundation, we concentrate on the eyes," She pulls out a rubber and chrome pincer machine. She stands in front of Linda with it. I become concerned.

"The eyelashes sometimes grow in the wrong direction," Mrs. Chung informs us. "They must be trained to bend correctly. We use the Eyelash Curler to do this." She hands the machine to Linda. I watch as Linda puts the metal pincer up to her eye and catches her straight, heavy black lashes between the rubber pincer blades.

"Must be sore if they do it wrong and squeeze the eyelid meat," I breathe to Terry. Terry says nothing. She looks upset, like she is trying not to bring up her lunch.

"Eyeshadow must be applied to give the illusion of depth," says Mrs. Chung. "Light on top of the lid, close to the lashes, luminescent color on the whole lid, a dot of white in the center of the iris, and brown below the browbone to accentuate the crease." Mrs. Chung is going pretty fast now. I wonder what the girls who have Oriental eyelids without a crease are going to do. I check out the room quickly, over the top of my make-up mirror. Sure enough, all the Oriental girls here have a nice crease in their lids. Those who don't are wearing scotch tape. Mrs. Chung is passing out "pearlescent" eyeshadow.

"It's made of fish scales," Terry says. I have eyelids that are all right, but eyeshadow, especially sparkling eyeshadow, makes me look like a gecko, you know, with protruding eye sockets that go in separate directions. Terry has beautiful deep-socketed eyes and browbones that don't need any help to look well defined. I put on the stuff in spite of my better judgment and spend the rest of the time trying not to move my eyeballs too much, just in case anybody notices. Lani is putting on all this makeup too. But in her case, it just increases the pearly glow that her skin is already producing.

"This ends the makeup session," Mrs. Chung is saying. "Now our eyes and skins have the proper preparation for our roles as contestants for Carnival Queen."

"Ma, I running in the Carnival Queen contest," I was saying last night. My mother got that exasperated look on her face.

"You think you get chance!"

"No, but the teachers put in the names of all the student council guys." My mother is beginning to look like she is suffering again.

"When you were small, everybody used to tell me you should run for Cherry Blossom contest. But that was before you got so dark like your father. I always tell you no go out in the sun or wear lotion like me when you go out but you never listen."

"Yeah, Ma, but we get modeling lessons, make-up, how to walk."

"Good, might make you stand up straight. I would get you a back brace, but when you were small, we paid so much money for your legs, to get special shoes connected to a bar. You only cried and never would wear them. That's why you still have crooked legs."

That was last night. Now I'm here and Mrs. Takahara is telling us about the walking and modeling lessons.

"Imagine a string coming out of the top of your skull and connected to the ceiling. Shorten the string and walk with your chin out and back erect. Float! Put one foot in front of the other, point your toes outward and glide forward on the balls of your feet. When you stop, place one foot slightly behind the other at a forty-five degree angle. Put your weight on the back foot . . ." I should have worn the stupid shoes when I was small. I'm bow-legged. Just like my father. Leilani is not bow-legged. She looks great putting one long straight tibia in front of the other. I look kind of like a crab. We walk in circles around and around the room. Terry is definitely not happy. She's walking pretty far away from me. Once, when I pass her, I could swear she is crying.

"Wow, long practice, yeah?" I say as we walk across the lawn heading toward the bus. Terry, Trudye, Linda, and I are still together. A black Buick pulls up to the curb. Terry's Mom has come to pick her up. Terry's Mom always picks her up. She must have just come back from the beauty shop. Her head is wrapped in a pink net wind bonnet. Kind of like the cake we always get at weddings that my mother keeps on top of the television and never lets anybody eat.

"I'll call you," Terry says.

"I'm so glad that you and Theresa do things together," Terry's mother says. "Theresa needs girlfriends like you, Sam." I'm looking at the pink net around her face. I wonder if Terry's father ever gets the urge to smash her hair down to feel the shape of her head. Terry looks really uncomfortable as they drive away.

I feel uncomfortable too. Trudye and Linda's make-up looks really weird in the afternoon sunlight. My eyeballs feel larger than tank turrets and they must be glittering brilliantly too. The Liliha-Puunui bus comes and we all get on. The long center aisle of the bus gives me an idea. I put one foot in front of the other and practice walking down. Good thing it is late and the guys we go to school with are not getting on.

"You think Leilani is going to win?" Trudye asks.

"What?" I say as I almost lose my teeth against the metal pole I'm holding on to. The driver has just started up, and standing with your feet at a forty-five degree angle doesn't work on public transportation.

"Lani is probably going to win, yeah?" Trudye says again. She can hide her eye make-up behind her glasses and looks pretty much OK. "I'm going to stay in for the experience. Plus, I'm going to the orthodontist and take my braces out, and I asked my mother if I could have contact lenses and she said OK." Trudye goes on, but I don't listen. I get a seat by the window and spend the whole trip looking out so nobody sees my fish scale eyes.

I am not surprised when I get home and the phone begins to ring.

"Sam, it's Terry. You stay in the contest. But I decided I'm not going to run."

"That's nuts, Terry," I am half screaming at her, "you are the only one of us besides Lani that has a chance to win. You could be the first Japanese Carnival Queen that McKinley ever has." I am going to argue this one.

"Do you know the real name of this contest?" Terry asks.

"I don't know, Carnival Queen. I've never thought about it I guess."

"It's the Carnival Queen Scholarship Contest."

"Oh, so?" I'm still interested in arguing that only someone with legs like Terry even has a chance.

"Why are you running? How did you get nominated?" Terry asks.

"I'm Senior Class secretary, they had to nominate me, but you . . ."

"And WHY are you secretary," she cuts me off before I get another running start about chances.

"I don't know, I guess because I used to write poems for English class and they always got in the paper of the yearbook. And probably because Miss Chuck made me write a column for the newspaper for one year to bring up my social studies grade."

"See . . . and why am I running?"

"OK, you're class officer, and sponsor, and you won the American Legion essay contest . . ."

"And Krissy?"

"She's editor of the yearbook, and a sponsor and the Yanagawa twins are songleaders and Trudye is prom committee chairman and Linda . . ." I am getting into it.

"And Lani," says Terry quietly.

"Well, she's a sponsor I think . . ." I've lost some momentum. I really don't know.

"I'm a sponsor, and I know she's not," Terry says.

"Student government? No . . . I don't think so . . . not cheering, her sister is the one in the honor society, not . . . hey, not, couldn't be . . ."

"That's right," Terry says, "the only reason she's running is because she's supposed to win." It couldn't be true. "That means the rest of us are all running for nothing. The best we can do is second place." My ears are getting sore with the sense of what she says. "We're running because of what we did. But we're going to lose because of what we look like. Look, it's still good experience and you can still run if you like."

"Nah . . ." I say still dazed by it. "But what about Mrs. Takahara, what about your mother?" Terry is quiet.

"I think I can handle Mrs. Takahara," Terry finally says.

"I'll say I'm not running, too. If it's two of us, it won't be so bad." I am actually kind of relieved that this is the last day I'll have to put gecko eye make-up all over my face.

"Thanks, Sam . . ." Terry says.

"Yeah . . . My mother will actually be relieved. Ever since I forgot the ending at my piano recital in fifth grade, she gets really nervous if I'm in front of any audience."

"You want me to pick you up for the carnival Saturday night?" Terry asks.

"I'll ask my Mom," I say. "See you then . . ."

"Yeah . . ."

I think, "We're going to lose because of what we look like." I need a shower, my eyes are itching anyway. I'm glad my mother isn't home yet. I think best in the shower and sometimes I'm in there an hour or more.

Soon, with the world a small square of warm steam and tile walls, it all starts going through my head. The teachers looked so young in the make-up demonstration with their hair pinned back—they looked kind of like us. But we are going to lose because of what we look like. I soap the layers of make-up off my face. I guess they're tired of looking like us; *musubi* bodies, *daikon* legs, *furoshiki*-shaped, home-made dresses, *bento* tins to be packed in the early mornings, mud and sweat everywhere. The water is splashing down on my face and hair. But Krissy doesn't look like us, and she is going to lose too. Krissy looks like the Red Cross society lady from intermediate school. She looks like Beaver's mother on the television show. Too *haole*. She's going to lose because of the way she looks. Lani doesn't look anything like anything from the past. She looks like something that could only have been born underwater where all motions are slow and all sounds are soft. I turn off the water and towel off. Showers always make me feel clean and secure. I guess I can't blame even the teachers, everyone wants to feel safe and secure.

My mother is sitting at the table peeling an orange. She does this almost every night and I already know what she's going to say.

"Eat this orange, good for you, lots of vitamin C."

"I don't want to eat orange now, Ma." I know it is useless, but I say it anyway. My mother is the kind of Japanese lady who will hunch down real small when she passes in front of you when you're watching TV. Makes you think she's quiet and easy going, but not on the subject of vitamin C.

"I peeled it already. Want it." Some people actually think that my mother is shy.

"I not running in the contest. Terry and I going quit."

"Why?" my mother asks, like she really doesn't need to know.

"Terry said that we running for nothing. Everybody already knows Lani going win." My mother looks like she just tasted some orange peel.

"That's not the real reason," she hands me the orange and starts washing the dishes.

There's lots of things I don't understand. Like why Terry

hangs out with me. Why my mother is always so curious about her and now why she doesn't think this is the real reason that Terry is quitting the contest.

"What did the mother say about Terry quitting the contest?" my mother asks without turning around.

"I donno, nothing I guess."

"Hmmmmmm . . . that's not the real reason. That girl is different. The way the mother treats her is different." Gee, having a baby and being a mother must be really hard and it must really change a person because all I know is that my mother is really different from me.

Terry picks me up Saturday night in her brother's white Mustang. It's been a really busy week. I haven't even seen her since we quit the contest. We had to build the Senior class Starch Throwing booth.

"Hi, Sam. We're working until ten o'clock on the first shift, OK?" Terry is wearing a triangle denim scarf in her hair, a workshirt and jeans. Her face is flushed from driving with the Mustang's top down and she looks really glamorous.

"Yeah, I thought we weren't going to finish the booth this afternoon. Lucky thing my Dad and Lenny's Dad helped us with the hammering and Valerie's committee got the cardboard painted in time. We kind of ran out of workers because most of the girls . . ." I don't have to finish. Most of the student council girls are getting dressed up for the contest.

"Mrs. Sato and the cafeteria ladies finished cooking the starch and Neal and his friends and some of the football guys are going to carry the big pots of starch over to the booth for us." Terry is in charge of the manpower because she knows everybody.

"Terry's mother is on the phone!" my mother is calling to us from the house. Terry runs in to answer the phone. Funny, her mother always calls my house when Terry is supposed to pick me up. My mother looks out at me from the door. The look on her face says, "Checking up." Terry runs past her and jumps back in the car.

"You're lucky, your mother is really nice," she says.

We go down Kuakini Street and turn onto Liliha. We pass

School Street and head down the freeway on-ramp. Terry turns on K-POI and I settle down in my seat. Terry drives faster than my father. We weave in and out of cars as she guns the Mustang down H-1. I know this is not very safe, but I like the feeling in my stomach. It's like going down hills. My hair is flying wild and I feel so clean and good. Like the first day of algebra class before the symbols get mixed up. Like the first day of chemistry before we have to learn molar solutions. I feel like it's going to be the first day forever and I can make the clean feeling last and last. The ride is too short. We turn off by the Board of Water Supply station and we head down by the Art Academy and turn down Pensacola past Mr. Feiterra's green gardens and into the parking lot of the school.

"I wish you were still in the contest tonight," I tell Terry as we walk out toward the Carnival grounds. "I mean you are so perfect for the Carnival Queen. You were the only Japanese girl that was perfect enough to win."

"I thought you were my friend," Terry starts mumbling. "You sound like my mother. You only like me because of what you think I should be." She starts walking faster and is leaving me behind.

"Wait! What? How come you getting so mad?" I'm running to keep up with her.

"Perfect, perfect. What if I'm NOT perfect. What if I'm not what people think I am? What if I can't be what people think I am?" She's not making any sense to me and she's crying. "Why can't you just like me? I thought you were different. I thought you just liked me. I thought you were my friend because you just liked ME." I'm following her and I feel like it's exam time in chemistry. I'm flunking again and I don't understand.

We get to the Senior booth and Terry disappears behind the cardboard. Valerie Rosecrest is there and hands me a lot of paper cupcake cups and a cafeteria juice ladle.

"Quick, we need at least a hundred of these filled, we're going to be open in ten minutes."

"Try wait, I got to find Terry." I look behind the cardboard back of the booth. Terry is not there. I run all around the booth. Terry is nowhere in sight. The Senior booth is under a tent in the midway with all the games. There are lots of lightbulbs strung like kernels of corn on wires inside the tent. There's lots of game booths and rows and rows of stuffed animal prizes on clothes lines above each booth. I can't find Terry and I want to look around more, but all of a sudden the merry-go-round music starts and all the lights come on. The senior booth with its handpainted signs, "Starch Throw—three script" looks alive all of a sudden in the warm Carnival light.

"Come on, Sam!" Valerie is calling me. "We're opening. I need you to help!" I go back to the booth. Pretty soon Terry comes back and I look at her kind of worried, but under the soft popcorn light, you cannot even tell she was crying.

"Terry, Mr. Miller said that you're supposed to watch the script can and take it to the cafeteria when it's full." Val's talking to her, blocking my view. Some teachers are arriving for first shift. They need to put on shower caps and stick their heads through holes in the cardboard so students can buy paper cupcake cups full of starch to throw to try to hit the teachers in the face. Terry goes in the back to help the teachers get ready. Lots of guys from my drop-out class are lining up in the front of the booth.

"Eh, Sam, come on take my money. Ogawa's back there. He gave me the F in math. Gimme the starch!" Business is getting better and better all night. Me, Val, and Terry are running around the booth, taking script, filling cupcake cups, and getting out of the way fast when the guys throw the starch. Pretty soon, the grass in the middle of the booth turns into a mess that looks like thrown-up starch, and we are trying not to slip as we run around trying to keep up with business.

"Ladies and gentlemen, McKinley High School is proud to present the 1966 Carnival Queen and her court." It comes over the loudspeaker. It must be the end of the contest, ten o'clock. All the guys stop buying starch and turn to look toward the tent. Pretty soon, everyone in the tent has cleared the center aisle. They clap as five girls in evening dresses walk our way.

"Oh, great," I think. "I have starch in my hair and I don't want to see them." The girls are all dressed in long gowns and are wearing white gloves. The first girl is Linda. She looks so pretty in a maroon velvet A-line gown. Cannot see her *musubi*-shaped body and her face is just glowing. The rhinestones in her tiara are sparkling under each of the hundreds of carnival lights. The ribbon on her chest says "Third Princess." It's neat! Just like my cousin Carolyn's wedding. My toes are tingling under their coating of starch. The next is Trudye. She's not wearing braces and she looks so pretty in her lavender gown. Some of the guys are going "Wow," under their breath as she walks by. The first Princesses pass next. The Yanagawa twins. They're wearing matching pink gowns and have pink baby roses in their hair, which is in ringlets. Their tiaras look like lace snowflakes on their heads as they pass by. And last. Even though I know who this is going to be I really want to see her. Sure enough, everybody in the crowd gets quiet as she passes by. Lani looks like her white dress is made of sugar crystals. As she passes, her crown sparkles tiny rainbows under the hundreds of lightbulbs from the tent and flashbulbs popping like little suns.

The court walks through the crowd and stops at the Senior booth. Mr. Harano, the principal, steps out.

"Your majesty," he's talking to Lani who is really glowing. "I will become a target in the Senior booth in your honor. Will you and your Princesses please take aim and do your best as royal representatives of our school?"

I look around at Terry. The principal is acting so stupid. I can't believe he really runs the whole school. Terry must be getting so sick. But I look at her and she's standing in front of Lani and smiling. This is weird. She's the one who said the contest was fixed. She's the one who said everyone knew who was supposed to win. She's smiling at Lani like my grandmother used to smile at me when I was five. Like I was a sweet *mochi* dumpling floating in red bean soup. I cannot stand it. I quit the contest so she wouldn't have to quit alone. And she yells at me and hasn't talked to me all night. All I wanted was for her to be standing there instead of Lani.

The Carnival Queen and four Princesses line up in front of the booth. Val, Terry, and I scramble around giving each of them three cupcake cups of starch. They get ready to throw.

The guys from the newspaper and the yearbook get ready to take their picture. I lean as far back into the wall as I can. I know Trudye didn't have time to get contacts yet and she's not wearing any glasses. I wonder where Val is and if she can flatten out enough against the wall to get out of the way. Suddenly, a hand reaches out and grabs my ankle. I look down, and Terry, who is sitting under the counter of the booth with Val, grabs my hand and pulls me down on the grass with them. The ground here is nice and clean. The Carnival Queen and Princesses and the rows of stuffed animals are behind and above us. The air is filled with pink cupcake cups and starch as they throw. Mr. Harano closes his eyes, the flashbulbs go off, but no one comes close to hitting his face. Up above us everyone is laughing and clapping. Down below, Terry, Val, and I are nice and clean.

"Lani looks so pretty, Sam," Terry is looking at me and smiling.

"Yeah, even though the contest was juice she looks really good. Like a storybook," I say, hoping it's not sounding too fake.

"Thanks for quitting with me." Terry's smile is like the water that comes out from between the rocks at Kunawai stream. I feel so clean in that smile.

"It would have been lonely if I had to quit by myself," Terry says, looking down at our starch-covered shoes. She looks up at me and smiles again. And even if I'm covered with starch, I suddenly know that to her, I am beautiful. Her smile tells me that we're friends because I went to drop-out class. It is a smile that can wash away all the F's that Mr. Low, my chemistry teacher, will ever give. I have been waiting all my life for my mother to give me that smile. I know it is a smile that Terry's mother has never smiled at her. I don't know where she learned it.

It's quiet now, the Carnival Queen and her Princesses have walked away. Terry stands up first as she and Val and I start to crawl out from our safe place under the counter of the booth. She gives me her hand to pull me up and I can see her out in the bright Carnival light. Maybe every girl looks like a queen at one time in her life.

BONSAI

Walking down Kensington Gardens, we stop to admire
the potted red-pine: tiny branches and needles
shaped into a see-through cloud of lace
with no loose stitches. As the roots neatly fit
the vessel and sap flows thick, no part of it is deformed,

or so they say. How can I not tell you now about my mother,
a miniature, with soft hands and point-filed nails?
She'd modulate her voice to early morning sounds
and, almost weaving it, elegantly arrange her hair.
When I was a child, I thought she'd bloom like that forever.

"I saw her last week," I say sparely
and hold back. China trembling between her finger tips,
she carried on about her clipped, well-trimmed past
dreams, all come true because they were her size,
while my eyes followed the cat at the window sill.

The tag tells us the pruned tree will live longer
than the artless one. We walk and I know
you think of times when, clumsy, I struggle up
the hill not far from our house and breathe in all I can.

SMALL ENDEARMENTS

Jei Lee stirred from her sleep and unwound herself from the chenille bedspread that had twisted around her waist and thighs during the night. She burrowed her neck and shoulders into a fresh, cool patch on the starched white sheets and then, suddenly remembering the sleeping form curved around her feet at the bottom of the bed, drew a deep breath and held her body taut. Only her eyes flickered, as they scanned the opposite wall and the dim shape of the open window that looked across the distant rooftops of the valley.

Across the casement, a half-completed chintz panel, which had been draped over the curtain rod, billowed and floated to the center of the room, suspended for an instant like a miniature parachute as the tradewinds swept across the attic stillness. The panel contorted and rippled forward, then drifted diagonally, landing in a crumpled mass near the baseboard. The breeze continued, a welcome counterpoint to the warmth of the sunrise that glowed through the boughs of the gnarled tree outside the window. The autumn light gradually tinged the bunched dark green leaves and seeped over the sill, painting the rough beams of the ceiling with a lucent wash of color. In less than two or three minutes the room would fill with the rising heat, until the other windows were thrown open and the rusted electric fan perched on the bureau was switched on to labor and wheeze in vain against the sunlight that would flood Pauoa valley.

Jei squinted instinctively and withdrew her legs from beneath the sleeping form of her cousin Helena who had sprawled at the foot of the bed several hours before the Thanksgiving dawn.

"What time is it?" groaned Helena, still curled into a half-moon shape. "You up already?"

Jei knelt down and pushed back Helena's dark bangs, which had fallen across her face, and smiled at how much they resembled each other, even as cousins. Helena was eighteen, a year older than Jei. They had grown up together in homes that shared a rectangular lot at the back of the valley. Only two months ago they had been separated for the first time when Helena enrolled in courses at Maui Technical. The first weeks of school had not been the same for Jei without Helena to gossip with each morning on the bus to Roosevelt High School, and to share the exasperations caused by their mothers, who were sisters and also just a year apart.

"Wait—did your mother hear me come in?" Helena bolted upright, her head knocking the bottom of Jei's chin.

"Owwwwwahhhh!" yelped Jei, falling backwards, rubbing her jaw in pain.

"Oh, sorry—well did she?"

"No!" Jei snapped back. "And if you'd have told your family you were coming back, we wouldn't be sneaking around in the middle of the night. I can't believe you came here before seeing your folks."

Helena rolled off the bed and stood motionless, listening for Jei's mother. "Just wait until you go off to college. Hooooee, being homesick is bad—I couldn't wait until the Christmas break. I used most of my semester's savings, borrowed the rest, and got a flight yesterday afternoon. And just in time, too, I see. Since when did you spend your nights at the sewing machine making curtains?"

Jei looked sourly at her, then they both stopped breathing as they heard steps approaching. Helena threw Jei a panicked look and dashed into the storage closet.

"Thanksgiving morning and you're still up here?" Myra Lee's voice was filled with exasperation as she climbed the steep steps to the attic. "I'm counting on you to start the stuffing while I pick up the flowers from Mr. Nakamoto."

This Thanksgiving morning of 1958 officially started the holiday season for the Lee family, which meant preparing for traditions that materialized right on schedule. "Holidays are just three days in the rainy season," declared Myra Lee to anyone who would listen. "I've learned to be organized—so can you," was her motto. To Jei her mother's obsession with details was as persistent as the mourning doves that cooed their sorrowful two notes from the neighboring lychee trees.

"Where did this come from?" Mrs. Lee strode into the room and picked the curtain panel off the floor. She eyed the yards of chintz that spilled out from the sewing machine, cascading in a heap beneath the chair. Myra Lee held the offending curtain panel at arm's length to examine it. "Taking time away from your homework for this, when I could have sewn you curtains in an afternoon."

The previous weekend, Jei had decided on an impulse to move from her bedroom on the ground floor into the attic and, in turn, to cover the windows with chintz cafe curtains and matching double rows of ruffled valances. Although controlling a sewing machine to produce square-turned corners and straight edges was more complicated than she had at first thought, she struggled on, and was nearly finished when Helena's late night appearance interrupted her project.

Mrs. Lee's mouth pursed as she brought the panel closer for a detailed inspection, taking in the uneven tension of the stitching and the corner seaming that resembled a tiny scallop, instead of a crisp 90-degree angle. "What's done is done, I suppose, but I'll at least hang the valances to salvage something."

Before Jei could respond, her mother arranged the unwieldy mass of material into an exact layout on the bed and left the room.

"Salvage something?" Jei repeated in a stunned voice. A piercing squeal came from the closet, and through the narrow door opening, Jei saw Helena sitting cross-legged, her hand clamped over her mouth, her shoulders heaving convulsively.

Myra Lee returned with a stepladder and a wooden carry-all kit containing a hand drill, woodscrews of varying sizes, pencil, chalk of three different colors, screwdrivers (Phillips and regular), tape measure, and a canvas work apron belonging to Jei's grandfather emblazoned with the advertisement:

CANEC
TERMITE PROOF STRUCTURAL
INSULATION BOARD
Manufactured by HAWAIIAN CANE PRODUCTS, LTD.
Hilo, Territory of Hawaii, U.S.A.

Myra Lee had the maddening ability of making any task look effortless—from cooking to repairs, schoolteaching to stamp collecting, sewing to gardening. She smiled serenely at Jei as she positioned the step ladder.

"Now hand me the top valance on the rod and I'll mark where we can place it." She tied the work apron around her waist and inserted the correct tools in the front pockets, waiting expectantly.

Jei didn't move or look toward her mother. The command hung in the air between them. A few seconds passed until Jei reluctantly pressed the rod into her mother's firm grasp.

"The valance has to be *on* the rod, Jei. Hurry up, I've got other things to do."

"NO!" Jei started forward. "I can hang it myself! I want to start something and finish it myself for once!"

Mrs. Lee cocked her head toward Jei and two furrows emerged between her sparse eyebrows. "It'll only take a second for me to do it—I'm up here anyway . . ."

"No!" Jei stood her ground and gripped the other curtain rod, slowly tapping it against her kneecap. "I'll do it, Mother. You have to see Mr. Nakamoto anyway. While you're gone, I'll start dinner and take care of this."

Mrs. Lee stared at her daughter and her voice deliberately dropped a level. "You'll get it wrong and I'll have to redo it. But I don't have time to argue now." She climbed down from the stepladder, allowing her full weight to fall on the treads as if to imprint this momentary impasse. She gathered her tools, once again smoothing the curtains into a perfect layout on the bed.

"There's papaya on the kitchen counter and I'll be back in an hour. We'll discuss this later." With a final look of reproach, she untied the work apron and folded it over her arm, then she disappeared.

Helena waited a few extra seconds after the sound of footsteps before she pushed open the closet door and whooped with laughter. "You really showed her, Jei!" She rushed to the bed and snatched the half-finished panel, mimicking her aunt's horrified look as she scrutinized the crooked stitching.

"If you're through, can you leave now before you're caught?" inquired Jei sarcastically. "It's a miracle she didn't hear you in the closet, and I've got things to do."

"Fine with me," Helena shrugged, then turned to Jei with a look of innocence. "But you wouldn't turn me out without my papaya, would you? Besides, I want to see if we're ready for Thanksgiving."

"Why not, why not?" Jei muttered, as they waited for Myra Lee's Studebaker to pull out of the driveway. "Okay, see for yourself."

They hesitated before heading into the kitchen. "My God, it never changes, does it?" murmured Helena reverently.

The dining table was set for their Thanksgiving meal that would begin at five o'clock on the dot. Not a speck of food was in sight, but the dinner plates lay face down on the ivory damask tablecloth, defying any dust that might dare to settle through the morning and afternoon hours. Large oval platters were ready, crisscrossed by gleaming silver serving spoons, which coexisted with butter dishes on which knives waited expectantly, running precisely from the ten o'clock to two o'clock position, and poised to the left of the gold-toned dessert forks and spoons.

Myra Lee's menu never changed: roast turkey, rich gravy with bits of sautéed liver, chestnut and bread stuffing, steamed rice, translucent wedges of Maui onions with a side dish of Hawaiian salt, *lup cheong*, cornbread with *poha* jam, creamed green beans, whole cranberry sauce, *mirin-zuke*, sweet potato casserole with mini marshmallows, and Apo Ching's famous lime green jello salad.

Helena whistled in appreciation. "Amazing. She even arranges the dishes according to the basic food chain, descending order."

The cousins thought simultaneously of the jello salad as they gazed at the polished copper dome-shaped mold. The recipe had been first tried in the early '50s by their maternal grandmother, who had spotted it in a Hawaiian Electric Company cooking class flier. The discovery became a tradition. The cousins recalled how they stifled snorts of laughter over the years when the copper mold was transported from the refrigerator to the table.

The green gelatin was blended and engorged with several half-pound packages of Philadelphia cream cheese and chunks of pineapple that filled its center and studded the outside. To a stranger it looked as if something alien had landed on the dining room table and was trying to hide unobtrusively among the other dishes.

"Do you think it's extraterrestrial?" Jei whispered to Helena last Thanksgiving.

"Or even more frightening, does it have a half life?"

"Can't say for sure," Jei replied shaking her head. "I've seen parts of it in our refrigerator as late as February. Not a dent in it."

As they gazed over the table once more, Jei blushed as she realized there was one less setting this year. Her father had moved out of the house nearly six months earlier and she blinked back a sudden rush of tears at the thought of him.

A favorite pastime of Jei's cousins was guessing why Franklin and Myra Lee were ever drawn to one another. Uncle Franklin had no interest in how their household should run or look, while his wife elevated domesticity to a rarely seen art form.

Franklin Lee had owned a small grocery store mauka of Nimitz Highway, serving the Kalihi neighborhood. When a large mainland-owned supermarket opened less than two miles away, Mr. Lee was secretly delighted at the prospect of closing the store and taking an early retirement. Within two months after his settling into his new routine at home, it became obvious that his increased presence alarmed his wife. He did not fit in with the running of her household. Shortly afterward, he rented the lower half of his younger brother's house on the windward side of Oahu. By early May, Myra Lee had eradicated all traces of him from their home.

Jei and Helena returned to the attic, carrying sliced papaya, lemon wedges, and buttered bread that was sneaked out of the designated stuffing ingredient pile. They sat on the floor, eating greedily and talking over each other's sentences, reliving the curtain confrontation.

"You weren't here the day your mother helped us with the

wallpaper for our family room," giggled Helena. "Auntie Myra volunteered to help paper the room and spent days reading half a dozen books on wallpapering. Only thing she hadn't counted on was my mother's doing the measuring."

"Auntie Myra stood at the top of the ladder with a notepad and demanded the measurements every few seconds while my mother read them off as quickly as she could. I bet that was the first time they ever worked together without a fight."

Helena squeezed more lemon juice on the fruit. "Well, it wasn't really a surprise when the cut pieces of wallpaper were held against the wall. My mother swore that there were 35 inches to a yard, and sure enough there was a one inch gap above all the baseboards."

"I've heard that all of Pauoa could hear my mother's shriek when the first piece was glued in place," Jei grimaced. "What's great about your mother is that she never admits a mistake—that's how the border idea came up."

"Yeah," rejoined Helena. "Now I sort of like those hana-fuda cards pasted there, end to end."

"So what about our year-end projects?" Helena turned mischievously to Jei.

For the past three years they had each proposed a personal project to complete in December, rather than a list of New Year's resolutions. "No broken promises for us," they had sworn solemnly, "or doing what's expected."

Helena jumped on Jei's bed and lounged against the wall. "My project is showing you how to drive those high school boys crazy."

Jei scrambled to the door out of habit. "Not! What have you been doing on Maui anyway?" The door lock clicked smoothly into place.

"Well, it's just a beginning, and I have been trying to study at times."

"God, I don't believe you can do that so well—show me again!" Jei breathed in awe. They sat facing each other across the bed and Helena demonstrated how she let a second-year student she met at a mixer get his hand into her sweater and explore the tops of her breasts.

"The trick is to be sure and wear one of your Pandora

cardigan sweaters like this so it buttons up the back—never wear something that has buttons running down the front. Things could get out of control. Now, let him undo the top buttons of your sweater and just when he reaches the fourth, the *fourth* one, you move back smoothly against the car seat and anchor your back for your life. And then . . ."

As Helena leaned toward her spellbound cousin, she pressed back against an imaginary car seat, threw her most alluring look, and slowly let her cardigan slide down her upper arms until it stopped, as if on command, so that the neck band snuggled against the top of her chest.

"Ohhhh—" sighed Jei, "the way you can let it glide . . ."

"And most important of all," Helena instructed, cutting her off briskly and bouncing her elbows up into a locked right angle position, "is to control the arms so there's only enough room for his fingers to go no lower than the upper half of your bra.

"It's all in technique," she concluded, enjoying Jei's gaze of admiration. "Now your turn. You've seen the start of my project. What are you doing?"

Jei moved off the bed. "I've something to show you. I found this when I moved up here last week."

She knelt down and tugged at a worn cardboard box hidden under the bed. There was a musty smell clinging to the lid and its contents. Helena wrinkled her nose. Jei lifted the lid and removed a bulky roll of cotton fabric. At the bottom of the box lay bundles of glossy embroidery thread bisected by black paper bands, stacked according to color, alongside a wooden quilting hoop.

"It's a baby quilt, with hand appliqued rosebuds, vines, and angels. Look at the detail in the faces!"

They gingerly spread the quilt between them. The idea that this was sewn for an infant was absurd. The fine cambric was traced with nearly invisible ivory stitches that flowed into raised waves running across the surface. Emerald satin piping curled among the quilted rows forming tendrils circling delicate flowerets of blush pink roses and deep purple blossoms that resembled the ola'a beauty planted along Myra Lee's walkway.

There was something far more striking, though, than the delicate artistry of the quilt. It was only half-finished. A scattering of rusted straight pins marred the fabric and the batting which was discolored with age. The quilting abruptly stopped near the center, leaving a plump cherub half-secured by its ragged wing.

"Who started this?" wondered Helena.

Jei drew a deep breath. "My mother. This might be the only thing she never finished on time. It doesn't matter why, I guess, but it's strange."

Jei grazed the quilt with her fingertips, following the satin piping around the rows of stitching. "In fifth grade we learned about colonial Americans. Women sewed quilts for their children, using bits of calico they saved to come together in a special pattern. Small endearments—that's what they called them."

"So what are you saying?" Helena drew back and studied Jei as she returned the quilt to its box. "When are you going to tell me about your project?"

Jei tapped the lid into place. "I don't know, okay? I've got other things to think about. Before you go, look."

Once again Jei reached under the bed. She withdrew a square straw container with a hinged top and thrust it toward Helena.

Inside was a jumble of odd-shaped, jagged pieces of colored plastic. Tucked around one of the larger pieces was a yellowed rectangle of paper. Helena glanced at Jei and uncurled the paper that had the familiar blocklettering across it:

GIVE BIRTH TO A BOY,
YOU WANT A GOOD ONE,
WHO'LL WEAR BLUE ROSES
AND A CAP OF AN OFFICIAL.
RAISE A GIRL,
AND YOU WANT A CLEVER SKILLFUL ONE,
LIKE A POMEGRANATE AND A PEONY.

On the back of the paper was a faded notation in pencil, "NORTHERN SHANSI MARRIAGE RHYME."

"What's this stuff?" demanded Helena. "I'm glad I came back—have you gone nuts?"

"The paper was in the corner of the quilt box," said Jei. "Do you think it inspired her?" Jei's voice dropped softly. "I wonder what she thought was ahead?"

Neither of them spoke. One of the worst-kept family secrets was Auntie Myra's difficult pregnancy with Jei, ending with her inability to have any more children. Helena broke the awkward silence.

"But what's this?" She incredulously scooped up several of the plastic pieces from the container. "These are from someone's records. How'd they get in here?"

"Don't you recognize them?" Jei tensed her shoulders as she spoke and snatched the pieces from Helena's hand. "'How High the Moon,' 'Ka'ena,' 'Uwe Ka Wao,' 'Vaya Con Dios' . . ."

"Your father's collection?" gasped Helena. "What happened?" It was the first time since early summer that Helena had mentioned her uncle and she winced after blurting out her question.

Ever since junior high school, Helena had come to see her cousin every evening, kissing her uncle on her way to Jei's bedroom. He would be sitting in his koa rocker in the sunroom, sometimes reading a news magazine, but more often staring out the picture window, scanning the neighboring heights and constellations. But he would always be rocking slowly in time to his favorite songs.

Franklin Lee's passion was his records. He had accumulated a collection of guitar recordings from nearly every era, but his favorites were his Les Paul and Mary Ford 45s and the Hawaiian ballads sung by Alfred Apaka. The most exciting day in Franklin Lee's life was not his marriage nor the birth of his only child, but the day Les Paul's "Lover" album sold a million copies.

"A few days after Dad walked out on us, I was in shock," replied Jei. "I know it's a big joke that my parents stayed together as long as they did, but they kept out of each other's way—what's wrong with that?" Her voice quavered and she self-consciously twisted her class ring on her finger.

"They once talked about a trial separation, but this was real. My mother was secretly pleased there was one less person to cook and clean for. She even said how nice it would be to get back to her hobbies again.

'And me? Dad overlooked several of his records propped side by side on the bookshelf where his record player had been. I spotted them one afternoon as I was going through the sunroom. Something broke in me that moment. Those yellow and red well-worn 45s and the newer shiny black ones. They looked like angry swollen eyes following me as I crossed the room.

"I scooped them up and brought them to my room. And then I put one after another under my foot and snapped the other half up as hard as I could. I went through them all and here they are."

"Auwe," moaned Helena. "We've got to talk right away, but I have to get home before anyone wakes up." She hugged Jei, who looked distraught and worn.

"Later. Save some room for the jello."

At 4 o'clock that afternoon, Myra Lee stopped basting her 20-pound turkey in mid-action as she gazed in astonishment out her kitchen window and saw her sister and niece approaching the back door, strolling arm in arm.

"Jei!" she exclaimed. "Helena's back and heading this way. What does this mean?"

Jei casually stopped stirring the stuffing and looked surprised. "That you don't have enough chairs and place settings, Mother?"

"Of course not. Well, yes, well . . . hurry and get the extra plates from the sideboard, they're here already!" Myra Lee hissed her instructions as she steadied the enormous browned bird in its simmering juices and returned the oversized roasting tray to the waiting oven as calmly as she could.

"Helena! Your mother didn't tell me you were flying back for Thanksgiving. You didn't say anything, did you?" Myra Lee flashed a sharp look at her sister.

"Aiyah! What am I to do with her! She nearly scared me to death by showing up without a warning." Helena's mother shook her head sternly, but there were tiny crinkles at the edges of her eyes and she could barely contain a grin, as she nudged her daughter forward.

Helena rolled her eyes and gave her aunt a hug. Then she and Jei fell into each others arms and hopped around the kitchen table in glee.

"Enough, you two," proclaimed Jei's mother. "There's not enough room here. Now out of my kitchen—the others will be here any minute. No, not you, Marjorie, your help I can use right now to get back on schedule."

Without a glance backward, Jei and Helena disappeared into the dining room, leaving the sisters to engage in a spirited and largely contradictory discussion of how to celebrate the perfect family holiday.

That evening, Helena and Jei spread a blanket on the front lawn and surveyed the city together from the hilly slope, not saying much and occasionally nudging the other if a shooting star or a new, murky shape within the full harvest moon was spotted.

"Just like an evening picnic," murmured Jei.

"Yeah, but who could eat after that meal?" rejoined Helena. "It's like old times again. And I'm here to help you feel better about your mom and dad. Whatever you want to say, it's okay with me."

Jei leaned over and lightly kissed Helena on the cheek. She then pulled back and stared into the distance, her eyes following the last bus making its way through the valley and approaching them. "Thanks, I know. You make me feel better already. You'll see—by your next visit, I'll have done something about it, for me."

There was no reply, but none was expected by either one of them. The silence crumbled as the last bus that had wound through the valley paused slightly before the house, shifted gears awkwardly, and continued on the final bend of the heights.

Three days later, Helena returned to Maui, crying and laughing intermittently with Jei on their way to the airport, checking her carry on bag several times to make sure she had packed her paper bags of rock salt plum and li hing mui, rearranging them at the last minute to make room for Auntie Myra's waxed-paper-wrapped frozen cornbread from the

Thanksgiving dinner.

"Only a few weeks and I'll be back," consoled Helena. "By then I'll have post grad lessons for you," she added with a wink.

Driving back, Jei thought about Helena's last words. There wasn't much time to decide on her own year-end project. Ideas drifted by, but several more days passed until it finally came to her.

A guest teacher joined the high school art department for the month of December. She was an instructor at the local artists' cooperative and word quickly spread through the school about her classes.

"Can I help you? My name is Audrey Keamo." A friendly voice rang out from behind a large wooden loom in the middle of the art studio and a slender woman came around to greet Jei.

Jei moved back a step and shook her head. "Just looking around—I'm on my way out, really."

"Feel free—if you're not signed up for a workshop, you can add your name to the list. And help yourself to any of the literature, too."

Jei glanced through the pamphlets on her way home as the bus jostled her against the window. She had taken one of everything, entranced by the illustrations scattered throughout the text. The examples of fibers and knots amazed her with their combinations of snips of dried bark, flowers, and seed pods. Another pamphlet described the development of Chinese folk art embroidery.

Later that evening, after she and her mother shared a dinner without exchanging more than a dozen words, she could hardly wait to return to her room. She pushed aside her homework to glance through the pamphlets again, and, before she knew it, it was nearly eleven o'clock.

"Good night, Mom." Jei brushed her cheek against her mother's.

"Don't startle me like that! I nearly lost my grip and could have damaged this stamp!" Mrs. Lee crossly adjusted her glasses and continued to squeeze the stamp tongs with her other hand. "It's a shame you never had the patience for stamp collecting. If you did, you'd know that the condition of the stamp determines its value. It's essential to handle each one carefully and only with tongs. It's so easy to mar the surface or enlarge one of the perforations." Her voice softened. "Look, Jei, isn't the detail on this extraordinary?"

Mrs. Lee specialized in collecting stamps from the People's Republic of China. She leaned excitedly over a dark pink rectangle with black and white piglets in its center. "It's called 'sty full of fat pigs.' Isn't it wonderful?"

"Sure." Jei turned away, but cast a look over her shoulder at her mother who was intently folding a translucent hinge into thirds, ready to affix it to the back of the stamp. "I'm glad you've found something to tend to, Mother. You're so good at it."

The rest of the month Jei confined herself to three locations: School, to finish out her final exams, the artists' cooperative, to buy threads, needles, and yarn, and her room, where she spent hours hunched over a tangle of materials and sketches. "The instinct to create a design while the needle is still in hand," she repeated to herself, recalling a sentence from one of the books Mrs. Keamo had loaned her.

As the nights passed, she became lost in her work, yet felt a powerful force around her, encouraging her to continue. Even though she would have to leave for school in a few hours, she yearned to steal more time for herself, her project.

"Hooo-ee, I'm back!"

It was Christmas Eve day, late morning. Jei felt a hand shaking her shoulder, someone leaning over her. "It's me— you've fallen asleep, right here."

Helena's face was etched with concern as she shook her cousin once more. Jei slowly lifted her head from the crook of her elbow that protected a welter of yarns, filaments, and fabric. She sat up with a start.

"Did you let yourself in? Is anyone else with you?" There was an edge of fear in her voice.

"I used the spare key. What's this?" Helena bent down and picked several stray lengths of twine from the rug and brushed a strand from Jei's hair.

"It's ready, Helena. Look at my project."

Jei cleared an area on her desk and slowly propped up a round, wooden form. Helena stared, her eyes widening.

Surrounding the hoop's edges was a network of half-hitch knots of juri and pina fibers, anchoring a lacy explosion of threads crisscrossing and doubling back upon themselves, filling the center of the space with a tracery of brilliant color.

"Do you know what this is?" Jei pointed to the center of the hoop. "It's a needlelace circle. Needlelace knotting is like a spider's web. I followed the book Mrs. Keamo lent me, but added my own touches, too. See?"

Helena let out a sharp cry. "Isn't that hoop the one from the baby quilt box—the quilting frame you showed me?"

Jei did not answer her.

"Oh my God, it is," gasped Helena. "What have you done?"

The once musty smelling frame was now looped through with knots of varying widths and thicknesses. Irregularly shaped pieces of faded cotton were lashed to the lattice of yarn and thread woven across the open circle, material that Helena recognized as part of the scraps from the quilt box. Across the cotton were sinews of golden stitchings, darting through the surfaces.

"This is the *ding* or nail stitch. The gold thread rests on top of the cloth, another thread attaches it to the material. I found this Egyptian cotton in the quilt box, feel how thin and silky it is! The thread is supposed to look like a gleaming snake." Her voice rose as she continued. "And here, look at this—the seed stitch. It's a knot stitched onto the fabric. I filled the surrounding area with a cluster of tighter knots."

Helena leaned closer to the hoop, then stopped. Entangled among the threads and the stitched cotton were several of Auntie Myra's postage stamps, filled with Chinese writing, tucked among the open spaces and supported by fine stitches along their edges. Alongside the stamps were the plastic shards of Uncle Franklin's records, red, yellow, black, wedged into the knotting. And in the center of the piece was the delicate scrap of paper, with the Northern Shansi marriage rhyme, pierced at each corner with a length of embroidery thread.

Jei reached out and clasped her cousin's hand in her own. "Merry Christmas, Helena. To the both of us, clever and skillful, pomegranate and peony. Happy New Year."

DARLAINE MAHEALANI MUILAN DUDOIT

SILK DRAGONS

Dragons crawl upon the silken cloth,
laid with care over the porcelain skin
so fragile, one could tear it
beyond repair with an injured nail.
Gold silk threads connect the darting tongue
with perfect concentric circles of clouds
that lie heavily upon the shriveled breast,
and tie themselves neatly into contending frogs
at the matriarch's neck.

The owner of the dragons
grips the handles of her wheelchair
as we approach with cups of tea.
The twisted feet, two ivory carvings,
have escaped the embroidered slippers
and hang stranded in mid-air
like the limbs of a hung bird.
The cool eyes pierce my lowered lids
as easily as the oars of a turtle boat
through the waters of the Yellow Sea.
Cruel lips, two sentinels,
guard the ancient faith
of the decaying womb.

Like a good Chinese daughter,
my head is bowed in reverence
to the male Buddha,
while my hand trembles with the urge
to toss the dark, burning liquid
upon the landscape of my ancestors.

A PORTRAIT OF WILLY

The story went:
an old Japanese man
wandered through the post-war streets,
baby bundled in his arms,
in search of the highest bidder.
My grandmother, a Hakka, took him for free,
as a brother for her only son,
as a masculine addition to her Confucian accounts.

In his childhood photos
he is placed like an afterthought,
sandwiched between younger siblings,
a stray from the neighbor's yard.
His slanted eyes are closed
to slits so small
that the world must turn sideways to enter.
The short body stands stiffly at attention,
fists pressed hard against his side.

There is a later photo:
Flanked by my grandfather's dark grin
and the moonface of my grandmother,
his eyes stare fearlessly into the camera.
The starched collar of his khaki uniform
lies crushed beneath a carnation lei,
the cap is tilted fashionably to one side.
We do not see him
swallowed up into the darkness of the plane.

He did not become a hero;
his name is not carved
upon the black marble of the Washington monument.
He did not come home after the war.

At Christmas he sends family portraits
in which his children spill out
beyond the borders of the frame.
After a while,
he ceases to appear,
crowded out by contesting elbows.

But no matter which way we tell it,
the story always ends the same:
the Japanese face faded from the print;
the edges curled into a ball and blew away.
Only a vague outline remains
captured squarely on the page.

H. MCMANIMIE

BITUEN

Picture parallel irrigation
ditches scratched diagonally along
flat hundreds of acres. And cross-hatched
against the ditches, silt-brown soil heaped and
pressed up into fences that define
ownership. A stained glass window of corn
and mung and rice held in their green and
yellow seasons by the leaden lines of
mounded dirt. And there, off-center left,
the *bituen*, faintly blue.
                        The star they called
it, old ones living on that other
island. The orange fireball that once burned down
the sky. The bright *bituen* that flamed and
fell into rice fields filled with water for
growing, reflecting back the blue sky
from which it traveled. And he remembers
the old ones telling him how his great
grandfather was burned, star-singed when a piece
of the *bituen* broke loose, set the house
on fire. He still sees great grandfather with
one side of his face star-marked, and he
tells of passing the tall cone-shaped earthstar
as they traveled out from Vintar to
great grandfather's farm, climbed up the *bituen*
finding grip in the same cracks as weeds
and small trees.
                        The old ones found direction
from their *bituen*. Used their daystar on earth
as in the nightsky, to mark the way
that they must go along their daily
lives.

Is it that these ocean islands
duplicate the patterns of the sky?
And does the *bituen*, traveler between,
hold us like great grandfather, star-struck
and stitched forever to that far sky?

LAVA WATCH

1.

The lava began to flow seven years ago and everyone talked about it. An appearance of Pele—her will, her power. No one thought to mention the danger to our village huddled under the green in the fragrances near the sea's edge; our village so old no one had heard when it began. Pele was—well, Pele: dictatorial, implacable. We listened to surf, not lava.

My whole body, however, quivered with that plume of smoke up the mountain and the red night flares. I smelt the lava seven years ago—a light sulfur odor mingling with faint fumes of burnt earth and burnt leaves. People said I was crazy. They said you couldn't smell those things so far down the mountain slope, and especially so near the sea.

Through the years the lava moved on with a leisurely insistence. It had a secret pace. Who could tell what was going to be: how far the molten rock would travel? Only Pele. Goddesses seldom reveal their thoughts. Their moods speak only at moments of action—unless they are in a prophetic mood. Pele was a goddess of action—a sudden appearance, clothed in fire.

On the mountain slope the lava has left a huge irregular trail of darkness, a trail of the burned and engulfed. People have moved from their burned homes hunting new lives wherever they can find them. Now the lava is at the village: relentlessly moving as if it had all the time in the world, its huge curling paws touching into flame everything in their way.

During those seven years, I passed my 70th birthday and two of my daughters left their husbands and moved back home. I reared a grandson who called my house home— whenever he was there. Samuel was a rascal boy, full of city ways. I wanted to give him the old country ways. He was always restless. He wouldn't stay. He was like a bird. The lava brought him back for a while, and he hiked through the woods to where he could see it, sometimes camping for several days. Of course he wasn't supposed to do that, but he was expert at escaping notice. I finally decided that I mustn't worry about him. Or even ask him where he went. I guess I can't blame him too much for his mercurial behavior. My parents thought I was that way when I was young. After all, I had disappeared into California for a while. I wish I could be that way now, flitting from place to place. But I'm stuck here sitting around with old age, with the girls, Piilani and Harriet. And the lava has almost reached my back door.

2.

Piilani was impatient with her mother's attitude toward the coming of the lava. Mom didn't want to do anything. Couldn't she see the inevitable? Couldn't she feel it in her bones? She simply drifted serenely from day to day, acting as if the lava moving down the mountain were a stream of water. She watched the houses burn. Afterwards she embraced her old friends, her neighbors, and cried with them; she even gave them shelter for a night or two. She was, however, tranquil and steadfast. And she wouldn't allow anyone to remove her things from the house. "The time has not come," she said. Yet the lava was almost up to the old stone wall great grandpa had built long ago. The pond in the back yard had turned brown and seemed almost to be boiling. The water heaved, mud churning up from the bottom.

Look, Mom, your pond is turning to lava," Piilani said. Red anger was in her face. "It's time. For god's sake, it's time!"

Keahi looked beyond her daughter at the stark lava softened by the green foliage of the plumeria and hau trees. At some moment the leaves and fronds would burst into torches. She was sure the trees knew by now. Just as her father and grandfather in their graves in the side yard knew. Grandfather always said: Pele gives and Pele takes away.

Harriet the younger daughter embraced her. "Mom, you're a little confused. I don't blame you. Why don't you let Pii and me take charge?"

Keahi returned the embrace, then broke away from Harriet's arms. She had her plans, very simple ones. But she wouldn't tell her children until the first paw of lava touched the house. Maybe not then, if she could manage.

"I'll go inside now if you want and look things over." She saw the brightening in her daughters' faces. It made her sad. "Some things I'll leave, the junk things."

In the living room she touched the pieces of old koa furniture. She laid her hands on the big table which had been polished by three generations. It was silky to the touch. She picked up one of the poi pounders from the shelf and saw, as she had so many times, her grandfather sitting in the back yard pounding poi on the big board. He had thin legs, a little pot belly and a head of thick white hair. She always thought it looked like seafoam. Long ago the board had disappeared. Now poi came from the market. She smiled slightly: change, change in everything—people, plants, even the shape of the mountain and the shore. Only the lava remained in its ancient ways, oozing or pouring from craters and vents as it made its slow passage, the trail of Pele down the mountain.

She went to the bedroom and lay down. These days she was often tired. Especially since the lava had come close. It was the unhurried pace of everything, the uncertainty; and she had to admit it, the anxiety. She hated anxiety. She knew exactly what would happen. When? That was what she asked as her heart beat irregularly and her breathing was heavy. She felt as if the lava were pulsing in her, a part of her. Sometimes she wanted to be part of it, treading slowly, stretching, breaking into red coals and flame: a moment of celebration. Afterwards, always a black collapse, a dark settling down.

"Hey, Mom, Mr. Lee is here." Tommy Lee was from Civil Defense. He had spindly legs like grandpa and teeth too big for his face. He was a good man. Very sympathetic, very tough, very fair. He walked into her room.

"Hello, Tommy, want something to drink?"

"No thanks. I came to see if you have made plans. I figure another 48 hours."

"You usually figure right."

"Thanks, Keahi. I ought to know. But then you can't always be sure."

"I'll get some boxes and start packing. The girls are pretty much packed. I think their friend is bringing a truck today."

"That's good. What about you?"

She laughed. "What about me? Well, what about me?"

"Your safety is my job."

He was a little pompous, she thought.

"Okay, save me." She flung out her arms.

He smiled and gently slapped her elbow.

3.

The truck has come, the house is full of people, confusion, noise. I'm out near the wall. The lava touches it in places. Intermittent snake tongues of flame reach out. Shrubs fire up and fill the air with smoke. The black paws seem reluctant to climb our small wall. They puff in redness, shoot out orange and blue, then collapse into darkness. The lava has its own voice—it crackles, even a roar that becomes a tinkling sound as momentary cooling begins. It is its own thing.

I remember the first time I smelled the lava. It was the 1935 flow up between the mountains. It was cold and the air pricked my nose. Still the lava smell was warm like sun on rock on a hot day. The fumes were sulfuric. The cold air muted everything. Down here by the sea the salty air mingles with the lava; strange odors, bitter and choking, filter through the air.

"Mom, where are you?" Harriet is bellowing. She's always had a raucous voice, deep as a man's. She's like a man, aggressive, demanding. At the same time she's beautiful in a large sort of way. Like her father, big eyes and glossy hair.

She knows perfectly well where I am. There's no place to hide. She likes to yell. That's all.

She is suddenly standing next to me. Her face is sweaty and her t-shirt stained with dust and grease. The outline of her breasts is round and strong. "Mom, where's your stuff? You haven't even started yet!"

"I'll get to it in my own time. Don't worry."

"The point is you have to follow the lava's time. It's going to burn us down."

"Hush, girl." I dread their rage, their resistance. Piilani's just the same. They can't accept what they can't control.

"Your time," she snorts. "We know what your time is. Well, it's your own problem."

She's back in the house and I'm alone again. It's good being alone. I like peacefulness. Before the lava came so close, I could lie down and have a nap. No one asked if I was okay. I could sit in a chair and rock, letting images of the past swarm before my eyes. I could even see the days in San Francisco before I gave up and returned to my village. For many years I never doubted my decision. Only in these last seven years I have. And I don't understand why. Could it be that I too hate the ravaging, uncontrollable lava, spoiling everything? All the changes, new plans for life; and just at a time when I want to settle down, sink a little into the green and the earth. Why should it happen? A simple technical answer. Tommy says we're in a rift zone. Sooner or later there would have to be lava. I chose village life with the possibility of a fire I had forgotten was living under that earth.

More than fifty years ago I walked up and down San Francisco streets with their hard cement, cold wind plastering my clothes to me and the shadow of tall stern buildings. In the afternoon the fog always came in. The fog helped a little, blurring the hard rectangular edges of things. I yearned for soft air, sea sound, the clatter of coconut fronds.

But more than that I yearned for people: the village people, taking things as they come, living in the moment, the day—not always looking to a future which would take place at an unknown time, maybe never. If they were angry they shouted. If they loved, they hugged each other. If they were hungry, they ate. Of course they didn't much like change. Or the strangers coming in and trying to take their land and imitate their ways. They suffered, on occasion, from a somber melancholy.

In San Francisco I was becoming somebody else. I decided she wasn't what I wanted to be. If I had stayed there I would be crisp, business-like, money-minded, looking to the future. It might have been a good thing. I had a first-rate job. Everyone wondered why I suddenly resigned and went home. Who can say why now? Exactly why? I did it and that's all. Now the village for which I yearned is being devoured. And I don't have that whole other life I never lived. And so I go round and round as I did all those years ago. There will have to be another life. What?

"Hey, Mom!" This time it was Pii. "You can't stay here until the fire strikes the house. You've got to get your stuff together."

"Look, Pii, the lava has almost reached the top of the wall over there by the hala tree. You remember, we buried poor old Brownie under that tree."

"You talk like you're pupule. What are we going to do about you?"

"Just let me be crazy."

"Don't you understand the danger? After all the burned houses?" she muttered impatiently. "You should have stayed in San Francisco."

I was startled. Had she read my mind? I couldn't stop the tears. She put her arms around me. "I'm sorry," she said.

"What you said is good. The way the lava is good. Bursting through old, forgotten blocks."

4.

It's dark. Tommy comes to tell me that only this night is left. Tomorrow is the deadline. He asks if I need help—he'd send some men. I tell him no and kiss him on the cheek.

I can hear the lava rustling and belching along the wall. In one place it has gone over and a fat finger reaches toward the house. Darkness flames at moments from burning gas or burning trees. I get up and put some clothes in a bag. I hunt in the dark along the shelf of artifacts for the small stone bowl, once a lamp, and the small adze with a sharp edge. I hunt for the calabash my grandmother gave me. She had patched it in the old way. That's all I want to take. The other bowls, the poi pounders, the books and old fishing weights can stay. The furniture can stay. The refrigerator and stove, the rugs. I want to give them all to the lava, to Pele. She wants the village. It's hers. It's always been hers.

I walk around the house trying to fix myself in it forever. I, Keahi, forever in this old wooden house buried in lava. Of course the house will burn. It won't be a house—just a place where a house was. But the poi pounders might remain. And the fishhooks made of bone. Most things are fragile. Like this mountain slope continuously changing, like this very island with fire in its belly. With Pele.

It is dawn. Samuel is standing by my bedside. I ask him where he comes from and he says Australia. I don't ask why he was in Australia.

"I heard our house was going to burn. I came to get you."

He pulls me from bed and puts my old robe around me. "Come on, Tutu, or Tommy will be after you."

We hurriedly eat some left-over poi and bits of cold fried fish. He makes steaming coffee.

He opens the kitchen door wide so we can watch the lava. It has reached the oldest plumeria tree. One paw stretches toward the garage.

"It's an octopus," I say.

"Eh, Tutu, you always make fancy talk. No need wash the dishes. The lava will."

Tommy Lee shouts from the front door. "Hurry up, you two."

Samuel takes my two small bags and ushers me toward the door. "You go ahead," I say.

He gives me a questioning look.

"I'll be coming. Don't worry."

I had remembered my kukui nut necklace. Papa made it for me. During his last years when the sadness settled on him and he drank all the time, he polished kukui nuts. One day he wrapped a strand of white kukui in a ti leaf and gave it to me. It wasn't for a birthday or a celebration. He just gave it to me and shuffled off to his little room in the shed. That night I wore it when we ate. He smiled. I was fourteen at the time. He died a year later.

Samuel shouts from the door. "I'm coming to get you."

"No need," I answer.

I take the kukui nuts from my drawer and join the two on the lanai. Samuel puts his arms around me. His pick-up truck is out there on the road. Tommy's van is there. No sign of the girls.

"I want to watch," I say.

"Okay, if you let Sam take care of you," Tommy says.

They don't trust me. They have wild fantasies. I'm a mad old woman. Oh no, I whisper. I'm just Keahi at the moment when my house begins to burn. And I'm still inside. I put myself there last night. I'm inside with all the others who have lived there. I'm inside with all the thoughts I had in San Francisco—and after I came home. My life, quiet, drifting, is there, each moment of it moving into every other moment in the fire.

I grip Samuel's arm. The house is incandescent with flame—only its dark skeleton shows. The roof is crashing, the fire shouts and roars. I'm glad I left all those old things for it to have. The lava can take them away.

Samuel helps me climb into the truck. "The girls didn't want to watch," he says. "But they knew you would want to."

The house is taking a long time to go. Heavy smoke lingers, shadowing everything. It smells like wood and rock and garbage burning. I can't feel anything, I'm empty. It's frightening. Only my eyes watch the end of the house. The rest of me is somewhere else.

I turn away and put a hand on Samuel's thigh. "Where are we going?"

"Like we planned. The girls are at Aunty's, waiting."

"I don't mean that!"

Samuel races the engine of his car and starts off with a lurch. "Yeah, where the hell is any of us going?"

CROSS-STITCHED

On the Mission House walls,
photos of dead women
speak pious platitudes
(like cross-stitched samplers)
in black and white.
Stiff backs, stiff necks
belie embroidered words;
these ladies are not meek.
Taut faces, stretched in frames,
savor silent martyrdom.
Long-suffering is their pride.
Doomed to serve in Paradise,
they suffer the little children,
suffer the savages, suffer the heat,
and teach the native women
all they know: to read,
to write, to cypher, and to sew.

THE 'OLOMATUA

Tia eased herself out from behind the steering wheel of her pickup truck. The back of her maternity top sticky with sweat, she waved it back and forth at the hem in a fanning motion. She would fold up her cumbersome ankle-length *lavalava* to knee-level except Tu, her mother-in-law, for whom she was waiting to drive home, might come out any minute now from the Filiola Law Office and condemn her for it. A *matai* (titled chief), and the only female in the village council, Tu was a noted orator who, though better known as the *'olomatua* (old lady), was, in Tia's regard, a brutal dictator. Although her children had protested, the dictator filed a complaint against Tolo who, like her, was a *matai* with a clan in the same *'aiga potopoto*. Tolo had registered the Silia title in his name without consulting anyone, and the dictator was in Filiola's office to retain him as her legal counsel in the case.

Going to the back of the truck, Tia stiffened as the baby's kicks churned her insides. Sione, her husband, who worked as a loan officer in the Bank of Hawaii, had asked her to wait there in the air-conditioning, but she'd preferred to be alone. Once perched on the pickup bed, she brought her legs up to ease the tension from the swelling.

A taxi backed out from the Black Ace Stand, sending up spurts of water from a puddle. The newly-built *fale fono* (legislative chambers) stood imposing against the blue of the Pacific Ocean behind and the green of Rainmaker Mountain across the bay. Its glass walls, through which people peeked for a glimpse into the much-rumored gambling and ribald activities of the law-makers, and known to serve as mirrors for passers-by, glistened dazzlingly in the mid-morning sun. To the left, the Amerika Samoa Bank bustled with customers going in and out. A few stragglers passing by the police station and along the *malae* (the village green) were either on their way east toward Scanlan's, Annesley's, and Burns Philp's or up the rise to the residential area.

Beyond the Amerika Samoa Bank and to the right a crowd waited as the *Salamasina*, on its weekly trips from the neighboring Western Samoa, glided in to dock. Watching the stern of the boat loom larger by the minute, Tia remembered her own trip across on it four years ago.

The daughter of the *faife'au* (pastor), she had become bored with having to watch her every move because, as her mother nagged, "the village was watching." Her teaching job in the village school didn't promise an exciting future either and marriage prospects were limited by her parents' strict censorship—a process that eliminated almost all males except theological students from Malua. Determined not to be sent to New Zealand like her older sister, Tia had secretly arranged for a permit to American Samoa through a girlfriend's sister who lived there and whose husband worked in the immigration office.

Upon arrival, Tia waitressed at a local bar which, because of her immigration status, paid her under the table. The owner, an elderly man, docked her paycheck. "I've rented a room at the hotel," he said. "Come with me and get the rest of your pay, plus a bonus." Dying to yank the gray hairs from the man's eyebrows and ears and stuff them in his nose, she stormed out. "I'd rather sleep with a dog!" she called from the safety of the outside. Leaving that job, she waitressed at another bar until the St. Francis School, to which she'd taken her teaching credentials, sponsored her.

It was a year after Tia's arrival that she met Sione. Having taught her to play tennis, he'd then registered them both in the exclusive Tafuna Tennis Club. He also introduced her to golf, and wined and dined her at Soli's Restaurant, Ramona Lee's, and at the Rainmaker Hotel. They married a year and a half later, at which time she got a teaching job in the public school system. Sione had a three-bedroom home on his family's land and, except for his occasional night out with the boys, life with him was quiet and satisfying. That is, until the dictator returned from Hawaii where she'd stayed with Sione's oldest sister. "Tu's like an army general," Tia was warned repeatedly. "She'll demand every ounce of you."

On the day she arrived, the dictator, short and plump and with the voice of a man, demanded that Tia know her place. The *matai* of the village had come for the welcome-back ritual and the exchange of gifts: they bearing sticks of dried kava-roots, she, money. Some were leaving while a few still sat around the *fale* posts talking when Tia, beside Sione at the back, found herself under the dictator's hard stare. "You should be in the *umu*!" barked the dictator pointing to the cooking *fale*. Broad shoulders slightly stooped, she sat at one of the front posts, her legs partly crossed and hands at her hips. "You should have seen to the food and now the clean up." Coughing up phlegm, she spat on the rock foundation outside. "If your mother didn't tell you, *I* will! You came to this family to burn your eyes out, not drape yourself around Sione all the time."

Tia held her breath. Surely Sione would defend her. But in the air was only the echo of the dictator's bellow. Aching to scream in his face, Tia swallowed, almost choking on the explosion stuck in her throat. And the events of the next two weeks were testimony that Sione couldn't be counted on when it came to his mother. In one argument with him, she butchered the Tu title (which literally means "to stand") with derogatory extensions.

"Her name should have been *Tu ma le fana!*" Tia shouted. "She's more deadly than a gun." In another, she extended the name to *Tu a le ai tae* "because," she berated him, "only a shit-eater can be so cruel." Tia also loathed being referred to as *le fafine* (the woman). "Do I have to carve my name on my forehead?" she would rave. Once in a while Sione was sympathetic, but mostly, he'd say, "You know that's how it usually is." Now, more than two years since first meeting the dictator, Tia, about ready to have the baby, found herself entertaining other possible lives: one away from the dictator. Perhaps even away from the three-bedroom home, the two-year-old car, and Sione, who was probably oblivious to how he'd redeemed himself the night before.

The two of them were having supper when the phone rang. Scooping another spoon of beef gravy into her mouth, Tia was still chewing when she picked up the receiver. "Hello."

"Aue," bellowed the dictator. "Didn't your parents teach you not to talk with your mouth full? I'll never know what my son saw in you."

My gorgeous body, the beautiful organ between my legs, and a nicer personality than yours! Tia wanted to shout. Instead she mumbled, "I'm sorry."

"I need to be at Filiola's Law Office tomorrow at 10:30," the dictator continued. "Pick me up at ten."

No! It'll be too hot and I can barely fit behind the wheel now and you can just go to hell! But again, she only said, "I'll be there."

Having hung up, Tia went outside. The pebbles dug into her bare feet, but if she were to get her slippers, Sione would see the tears. Clad only in the *lavalava* hitched under her arms—her dress code around the house now—she was easy prey for mosquitoes; but she eased herself onto the bench under the mango tree to indulge in the fragrance from the plumerias and gardenias in the garden. The quiet of the night also promised solace. A flying fox glided away from the breadfruit tree. A star fell in the sky. "My baby! My husband!" she wished fiercely.

Then Sione was coming to her. "I thought you'd be here. Remember, they say you can't be in the dark alone?" He sat beside her. "Who was that on the phone?"

Hitler! she wanted to reply, but protecting herself against a loyal defense of his mother, she answered in her most casual voice, "Your mother."

"And?"

She relayed the exchange in as few words as she could, leaving out the fury eating away at her. Breathing deeply to stifle her sobs, she was startled when he kissed her cheek.

"You're crying," he observed. "I'm sorry."

An arm around her shoulders, he moved closer, and though she stiffened at first, she eventually slumped against him. She wept softly now, from time to time undoing from above her right breast the flap of her *lavalava* to wipe her face. And it was several minutes before either of them moved.

"Thank you," he whispered.

"For what?"

"For putting up with my family, my mother especially."

"You're the reason I try."

Tightening his hold on her, he whispered, "The reason is the three of us."

"I . . . I guess," she'd whispered.

A slim girl in a black skirt and red silk blouse who, to Tia, had to be holding her breath so as not to bust her skin-tight clothes, was coming toward the truck now, the clippety-clop of her shoes grating irritatingly. She lived in Pago Pago, two villages from Sione's. "Talofa," she said flashing a toothy smile. "Filiola wants you to come inside, please. He wants you to explain something to the old lady."

Tia heard the dictator's rattling cough from outside the door. As she entered, Filiola rose to shake her hand before reporting on the progress of his son whom Tia had in her classroom the year before. Then he asked, partly in English and partly in Samoan, if she understood the concept of ethics. "I know what the word means," she answered in kind, "but I don't know what you're getting at."

"You see," he said, "Tulou, Tolo's wife, is my cousin so I can't be involved in the case. Tu doesn't understand that."

Filiola was the third lawyer the dictator had tried to hire and Tia didn't welcome the job of crushing her hopes. She turned to the dictator who, meanwhile, was watching intently.

"Tu," Tia started. "The legal profession doesn't allow . . ."

"He won't be my lawyer, will he?" the dictator interrupted.

"I'm afraid not," Tia answered.

"Then let's get out of here! These greedy lawyers are interested only in corporate cases." Too embarrassed to apologize, Tia followed her. The next morning, the dictator went to court without a lawyer. Sione and his sisters, in reinforcing their disagreement, went to work as usual, leaving Tia to once again drive their mother and wait to take her back home.

Tolo came toward Tia and the dictator as they stood in the corner of the courtroom lobby. In a white shirt tucked into a red *lavalava*, he walked in short quick steps. His sister, brother, and several cousins remained in the opposite corner. Tulou, his wife, was trying to pacify her whining baby. "So, Auntie," he said to the dictator. "We're going to face each other in court?"

Tia eased backward and sat on the rail. Pack of Winstons in hand, the dictator took out a cigarette, put it in her mouth and flicked a lighter.

"I said relatives don't face each other in court," persisted Tolo.

"Well, did you think that having gone to school in America gives you the right to the 'aiga's highest title without consulting it?"

Tolo said it would have required a meeting of all member clans, would have taken more than one meeting, wasted too much time, let in too many vaguely qualified people. "Being the direct heir," he announced, "I have fifty percent right through blood. I was only trying to save everyone a lot of trouble."

Anxious for everyone to be inside so she could go to the car, recline the seat, and relax, Tia bunned up her braided hair. Coughing, the dictator went to the side and spat the phlegm into the hibiscus hedge alongside the building. The back of her dress was damp with sweat and Tia knew she'd soon want the box of tissues in the bag she held. Then a clerk was summoning them inside.

The baby kicked. Standing up, Tia felt as if one of its limbs had been drawn up then extended into her right hip joint. Handing over the bag with the tissues and the extra cigarette pack, Tia wished the dictator luck. But the older woman invited her in. "Tolo almost has his entire clan here; you might as well come with me."

Tia sat on the bench behind the dictator at one side of the aisle. At the other, Tolo sat with Watson, his lawyer, in the front-most bench while his supporters sat behind him. A female clerk in a red and white floral *puletasi* announced the arrival of the judges. In black gowns, the men, four Samoans, and a *Palagi* sat themselves at the long table to the clerk's left, the American flanked on both sides by two of his counterparts. Below the *Palagi*'s gown, black leather shoes, dark brown socks, and the legs of gray pants showed. As for the Samoans, three wore brown leather slippers while one wore black ones.

"This is a preliminary hearing," the clerk announced. "The court asks if the two parties have tried to reach an agreement through the *fa'a-Samoa*." After the translation, the clerk looked at Tolo's side.

"My client suggested that to the plaintiff," said Watson. His Samoan was colloquial: not only unflowery, but also using *k* instead of the more official *t* and incorrectly interchanging the *ng* and *n* sounds in several places. As the translator spoke, all eyes turned to Tu who mopped her face lingeringly without a response. Wondering at the ever-vocal woman, Tia peered at her from the side. The *'olomatua* was sweating profusely, the back of her light blue dress now a shade darker than the rest of it.

Tia knew she was going to engage Sione in another bitter argument tonight: about why he was letting her become the family chauffeur, why didn't he spare her this and many other situations, why he wasn't here with his mother. She wished she could enjoy the *'olomatua*'s difficulty, but she didn't feel her usual anger. In its place was a painful awareness that the next few moments were crucial to what the *'olomatua* stood for, and to the future of Sione and his sisters.

The clerk asked the *'olomatua* if she would consider withdrawing her complaint. Tia repeated the question in a fierce whisper and when there was still no response, she moved up to the front bench.

"They're waiting for you to say something, Tu," she whispered intensely. "You have to defend yourself or the case will be dismissed."

"They're speaking English so fast I can't keep up," said the *'olomatua*.

"Tell them to slow down the proceedings, and concentrate on the Samoan translations."

Inhaling deeply, the *'olomatua* looked at Tia. "Please stand up for me," she said. "I get dizzy when everyone babbles in English. I'll tell you what to say."

Looking at the judges, Tia cursed her own lack of foresight: her not staying in the car. There was a commotion from Tolo's side. Interlocking her shaking fingers, she gripped them tight. Her throat was dry, yet her armpits were damp and felt like they might drip any minute now. Her right hip joint throbbed and her bra, cutting into her, felt as if it would bust when she next breathed out. But she stood up.

"My husband's mother," she said, "cannot speak for herself today. But she will help me tell you her wishes."

"This woman's an outsider!" protested Tolo. "She has no right speaking on family matters."

But the *'olomatua* was whispering her address of the court now. Straining to catch every word, Tia repeated, recognizing genealogies, yet not able to distinguish which was for whom of the four Samoan judges. At the *'olomatua's* next word, Tia gasped before she could repeat them.

"I," she said, "soon-to-be mother of an heir to the Silia title, am not such an outsider anymore." Stretching a hand toward the *'olomatua*, Tia continued, "She has granted me that!"

The *'olomatua's* coaching was getting louder. "The last one to hold the Silia title was Tolo's father," she said. "Now the title should be held by a member of another clan. As head of one clan in the *'aiga potopoto*, I have come to fight for the title. My great grandfather was the first holder of the title. Tolo has nothing to compare with my years in the *matai* council and the length of my service in the *'aiga*." She was rising now, and when she stood steady, Tia went back to her place on the second bench.

Breathing hard, the baby's kicks and the throbbing in her right hip not helping, Tia sat back rubbing both sides of her stomach. The *'olomatua* was still standing, her rhetoric ringing in the courtroom. Looking back at Tia, she asked, "Are you all right?" With a momentary smile, Tia nodded.

CHICKEN FEET, SISTER STEW

The women in my family drop things,
their firstborn to last husbands.
Unwed sisters boast, "We're rich.
You won't catch us touched
by sticky kids or love."
They hate old cars.

Abbi and Bea sit cramped on a patch
quilt older than my wagon, trying
to touch nothing. "You left home,
married, and married again.
Mom so mad she sold her rings,
travelled, and died. Now you
have nothing. Your bag's a shame!"
They drop my drawstring bag.
"No money."

Light lips, cheek caves,
nails like skis. They lash
bluegreen lids with black glue.
Concrete and creases, the sixties look
screams like grilled lizards.
It is seven years since mom died.

The door, slammed in the market lot,
rattle-hums, spitting paint and
rust like fighters' teeth. Sisters
rush on adjusting pearls, bangles,
and slips. I think of making soup.

Their voices part at cabbages
and leeks. "Get chuck," Abbi says.
"No fat, no bone, ten pounds."

A butcher pushes chicken feet,
like poised hands. Cold drips
on my toes from yellow trays.

Bea picks the feet out of my cart.
"Nonsense, or what? Nobody eats
that kind of stuff." She leaves
the feet in Cheerios. "Get
bread, soda, can lichee."

I have the feet bagged
while Bea and Abbi command two lines.
Coffee beans rock on the floor
by the Lion bins. They wave me out
mouthing, "Go cool the car."
Such long wrists.

At their home, my wagon behind
double doors, they give me sacks
to fold. "Family coming by six.
Vacuum, polish, keep busy." Mom loved
chicken feet soup. The bag leaks on
their new kitchen floor.

Their chopping is manic. Veggies fly.
I boil a pot of water, drop feet in.
Sisters talk fast and low, their backs
to me. I pare the turnips when Abbi yells,
"I need that board." She takes it.
Bea pushes by, yanks at the oven.
My kettle crashes and she storms.
"Get rid of it." I hold
greens and a blade.

Chicken feet boiling.
Pads, wrinkles, graceful
softening bones. The light is gone.
I stir the soup, simmering.
Dinner is done, turnips, carrots,
potatoes, and greens. Large pieces
from Abbi's chuck, and Bea's lichee.
Fleshy fingers dance in broth and steam.

MALL

His home was rent-free summers in Hawaii
ten years for this woman, his friend.
Now, back the first time since his death,
she's low and sandy on the phone.
"I'm taking you out while I'm here."

Our reunion is loud in a Toyota wagon.
Her lips, painted Chinese red to match
active nails, propel each word.
We speed through Waikiki. "Let's yak all night."
A thumb jabs my side. "You guys always went
to Pizza Hut with him. Why not?"
My daughter and husband sit behind, sharing a frown.
By Kahala, I want a bottle of wine. She is nonstop
opinions above the roar of her open window and mine.
The air-conditioner cannot dilute her heavy scent:
Tahitian Coconut Tanning Oil.

In the restaurant, she says, "You were nothing
to him." She talks through pizza steam.
"He called a list you weren't even on.
You were just to pass the time when he couldn't get
anybody else." Olives on her plate rim,
again she says, "I can't believe he had so much money!
Shoulda bought a house with him! Damn, it's too late.
Did you know he was loaded?" She pays the bill,
grinning. "He always said you guys were great cheap dates.
Where to now?"

Our daughter falls away into B Cool
with barely a good-bye smile. My husband
feigns interest as the woman calls
from Following Sea. "So, what do you get?"

she yells, prodding the weave of a scarf.
I hold his ashes in a paper cup
pulled from a pocket in my bag. Her face,
a fast retreat, brushes a wall hanging
of sticks and twine. She stands,
shoulders playing large windchimes.
"I don't wanna see that!
What are you, crazy?"

Last week I tucked a purple gloxinia
from one of his favorite plants
inside my letter to his sister in New York.
She called to say, "It's perfect, velvet
still so rich, here in my hand."

THE LAST GOOD WITCH IN NEW YORK

It was February, and Miss Mahler had just turned forty-two. As a birthday present, she treated herself to a hair rinse and a facial at Sally's Coiffures. There were only four or five gray strands showing through the natural strawberry blonde, but students always noticed such things, and she wanted to look her best on the first day of the spring semester. Walking into the room with the confidence of a pleasantly large woman, she slipped her coat over the chair behind her and sat down at the unlovely chromium desk. Then she opened her bag, and, despite the NO SMOKING sign behind her above the blackboard, removed a crumpled packet of *Lucky Strikes* and eyed the cockeyed cylinder of the half-smoked cigarette she'd hastily stabbed into an ashtray at 6:10 a.m. and then retrieved on second thought "for later," which was now. She contemplated the butt, and, with the part of her mind she reserved for niggling social details, wondered whether she was being typecast as a stingy old maid by a moustached man in a football jacket. With a hint of a shrug, she lit the butt and, closing her eyes with the pleasure and relief of it, inhaled. Miss Mahler loved to smoke; she didn't give a fig for cancer, not even enough to change to filters. She'd been smoking since she was fifteen with none of the unpleasant coughing, dizzy spells, or nausea she'd been warned about by the matron of the Chicago orphanage where she'd spent her indifferent adolescence. Without so much as water in her eye, the fifteen-year-old Miss Mahler had smartly snapped a match against the sandpaper strip of a packet advertising cheap hosiery, and puffed away at her *Lucky* as if she'd been born to smoke.

Miss Mahler also loved to eat well. Despite numerous intervals spent on the verge of poverty, succeeded by ratchety upswings like that occasioned by a small but welcome advance from an ex-lover's textbook firm in Illinois for her delicate book of essays on college writing, she ate more than her adjunct lecturer's check allowed of lobster and rare filet mignon and wild rice. Wild rice reminded her of Indians, and Indians reminded her of her earliest childhood in Minnesota. Just looking at the green Indian embossed on the box of expensive wild rice on a supermarket shelf made her nostalgic for plains she hardly remembered. Oncoming depressions could be stalled by boarding the IRT at the Clark Street station and heading uptown for dinner at the Manhattan Fish House. Two dry martinis with lemon slivers, a stuffed pound-and-a-half lobster with butter sauce and a side order of wild rice, and a quivering quarter moon of nesselrode pie with black coffee were all she needed to go on without killing herself. Sometimes writing could do it, or even correcting student papers through the night with Mozart's Jupiter Symphony playing softly in the background. Though alternately sloppy and obsessive about her appearance, Miss Mahler was always fastidious about her students' papers, about her students in general. She prided herself on her fairness.

On rare occasions she felt sorry for herself and drank too much sherry in the mornings before work. But more often, she would escape her self-pity by getting lost in a Fred Astaire re-run at the Bleecker Street Cinema, or by having an affair like the one she was in the middle of right now. It wasn't a very satisfying affair, and the *I Ching* had warned her of "trouble with a loved one" unless she acted quickly, but she had a weakness for educated, brooding alcoholics like Clancy Thomas, men given to occasional violent outbursts between long periods of poetry-reading and tender caresses. Lately, the violent outbursts were becoming more frequent, and her landlady had written her a warning letter. There was also, intermittently, her platonic relationship with Joe, an ex-jockey whose shared passion for horses she found appealing. But Joe was only five-foot-two to her five-foot-ten, and she did not enjoy over-whelming men in bed; so she continued meeting Joe at the Saint George Coffee Shop, where he sold bus transfers for a small profit and ritually offered racing tips to the silk-suited gamblers with hairy knuckles who gathered there.

Miss Mahler could not overcome what she considered a

genetic penchant for strays, male or female, animal or human. She'd once nearly lost her job as a lecturer on *The Icelandic Sagas* at Bryn Mawr when word got around that it had been none other than *their* Miss Mahler who'd been involved in the scandal about the crazy lady psychologist who'd killed herself the summer past by downing a bucket of swimming pool paint. The Philadelphia papers had made her appear sordid, a fortune hunter who'd ingratiated herself with the unfortunate psychologist in hope of inheriting her Main Line mansion and garnishing a little trust fund for herself. But that wasn't how it was at all. She'd only volunteered out of pity to become the personal secretary of a perfect stranger she'd met at one of the cocktail parties for famous writers she attended from time to time. Doctor Quarles was an ugly, rambling stick of a woman who, despite her near baldness and weak bladder, had reminded Miss Mahler of her own gentle, dead mother. When the scandal broke, Miss Mahler had been tempted to flee to Portugal and live out her life in the Algarve, eating nothing but crayfish, writing ghoul stories under the pseudonym E.E. Quarles, and making a baby with a handsome young fisherman. But the Dean of Faculty at Bryn Mawr had reacted decently and kept her on, and her scandal soon faded behind the juicier ones brought along with the newest poet-in-residence. That was the year Miss Mahler published her first novel—a witty, sad little book about a postmaster's daughter that one prestigious literary review credited with "bearing a haunting touch of George Eliot." Miss Mahler fancied herself more in the vein of Jane Austen, but who was she to quibble with George Eliot? Five hundred copies of her book were sold, and that summer she had recklessly rented a log cabin with an outhouse near a lake in Western Connecticut, where, for the first time in her life, she had used a chamberpot.

On returning to New York, she'd enrolled in a "fat ladies' course" to take off the pounds accumulated during her sedentary summer with the chamber pot. It was important not to be obese in order to attract men; like her cat Ahkneton, Miss Mahler favored seasonal coupling. Summers were reserved for being alone and writing, but, come fall or spring and the teaching season, she found herself ready to preen, stamp, and whinny. Sex, like food, was an important animal function, as she saw it. A color photo of mating zebras in a *National Geographic* in her gynecologist's office had been the trigger for her troubled affair with Clancy Thomas, in fact.

The prospect of a dramatic turn of events in her love life and an evening class offering "The Greek Experience" had brought Miss Mahler back to the city. Jean Dixon had promised a shift in the stars for Aquarians. Miss Mahler could feel it coming with the same thrill she experienced when the great planetarium robot lolled its awesome head to the left, taking the entire night sky to the East with one sweep into dawn. Life, she thought, as she lit her second *Lucky Strike* was a cosmic swindle. Must remember to write that one down.

She stood, smoking calmly, and examined the faces in her class. At home in her peeling sublet apartment on Pierrepont Street, the first forty pages of what she knew to be her best book yet lay in a tea-stained folder on a kitchen table covered with cat dander. The faces were mostly old, even those under thirty, a clutch of haggard, shopworn foreheads, and here and there a kindly pair of brown eyes, a humorous tic of the lip. They examined her, too, boring past her houndstooth suit (too loud for this group which would better appreciate browns and navies), wondering whether her rebellious smoking meant she was common and given to slangy talk instead of serious teaching. All she needed was to hold on to her job and pay the rent for the next three months while she was writing her novel. She knew she was an excellent teacher, and she no longer cared about protecting herself from rumors. Let the students report her for smoking if they wanted to.

"Good evening," she said, smiling her tight, teacher smile. "My name is Leona Mahler. This is course number 043.762 Alpha, 'The Greek Experience.' Will you please pass your course cards to the front. If you are in the wrong class, now is certainly the time to find out." She gave them a comforting chuckle to let them know she wouldn't be disturbed by a blunder; but no one smiled.

Hands shuffled cards, the greater arcana, the IBM trumps. A man in a nappy sweater smelling of camphor got up and handed her the pack without a word.

"Thank you," she said.

No reply but a half nod that she might have imagined at that. Miss Mahler felt very alone. She rolled the rubber band from her wrist and made a dumb show of placing it around the umber-colored deck of cards. "It might be easier if we get all the official things out of the way first," she said hoarsely, and fell into a fit of coughing. She riffled through her bag as if searching for a pencil to divert attention from the heavy wracking noise of her coughing. She needed to touch something familiar, a talisman, her course plan, a favorite Waterman pen. At last she found a lone, sticky coughdrop at the bottom of her bag and popped it into her mouth. After she had stubbed out her cigarette in the little tin ashtray she carried with her for such occasions, the coughing spell subsided. She passed out her syllabus and gave her little speech enumerating the texts, examinations, and term papers. The cough drop diminished to a dot.

"Plato's *Republic*, Homer's *Iliad*, Aristophanes' *Lysistrata*, and the anthology of *Greek Tragedies* are all available in paperback at reduced prices for students at the college bookstore," she said, watching the assortment of pens and pencils move in front of her with hypnotic efficiency. With an inadvertent shudder, she was reminded suddenly of the yarrow sticks of the *I Ching*, and her volatile affair with Clancy Thomas. Something in her perspective had altered while she'd gone off; a hand was now stuck up in the air to her left. Good, a response.

"Yes?"

The hand belonged to a young woman whose face she had missed in scanning the room before. Had someone come in while she was dreamily rummaging through her bag? Had the woman kept her face lowered the whole time? Had she been there at all? The long, slender mercurial face of a light-skinned black woman, the color of pollen in the rain, shaped like an African statue of polished bone, now appeared before her with startling clarity. The woman wore two stiff, long beads in her tiny, close-set ears; her black eyes were lined with Egyptian kohl.

"Your booklist is a sham," she said. "It has nothing to do

with life here and now."

Miss Mahler, who thought of herself as the last good witch left in New York and had as little to do with the "here and now" as she could manage, almost said, "Why me?" out loud. Restraining herself, she said, "Your name is . . .?"

"Joanna Bright," the woman answered in a low, choked voice that seemed to be coming from the wall at the back of the room rather than from inside her throat.

Miss Mahler flushed to the hairline and looked down at the neat, umber-colored IBM trumps. She deliberately went through them slowly in search of the name and did not look up until she had composed herself. When the fire had receded from her face, she said, "I can't find your card here. Are you sure you're in the right class? Your name isn't on my class list either."

"They transferred me to this section the last minute. I'm in the right class."

Miss Mahler grew frightened. It was not, however, the young woman and her strange outburst that frightened her, but the frozen immobility of the faces stuck like puppets in the rows in front of her. She momentarily entertained the thought of excusing herself and fleeing from the room, of spending the rest of her life in the Algarve. But the woman's face held her fast; all else now blurred before that dusky, pointed face floating in its halo of dim, aqueous light. Maybe a migraine was coming on. She felt her eyes focusing oddly.

"Fine," she said. "Now will you please re-state your question. I'm afraid I wandered off for a moment."

"I didn't ask a question. I told you simply that I, for one, cannot respond with any interest to your booklist. It's meaningless to my experience," said Joanna Bright.

Nothing like this had ever happened to Miss Mahler before. No student had ever questioned her syllabus in the past. No student had ever challenged her position at all. "Great art is universal," Miss Mahler said. Then she stopped herself, wishing she could have swallowed her words, for the woman's eyebrows were arching and furrowing toward the bridge of her magnificent nose. Miss Mahler was now transfixed.

"That's bull, and you know it. It's *your* great literature, *your* great art, not mine," said Joanna Bright, lowering her head and scribbling something on her notepad.

Miss Mahler wondered if she had just been written off. She was overcome by a fierce desire to step forward, pull the notepad out from under the woman's pen, and read what she'd written to the class in a loud voice. Instead, she said, "I'm sorry, but the course is listed as the *Greek Experience*, and I assure you that you don't have to be Greek to appreciate it." Getting no response, she added with fake cheeriness, "Is anyone in the class Greek?" All heads turned deskward.

"Never mind," muttered Joanna Bright, "You obviously have no idea of what I'm talking about."

"It was you who brought up the point," Miss Mahler said. "Let's take some time to clarify this."

"I said never mind. Just drop it," said Joanna Bright without looking up from her notepad.

Miss Mahler felt a shaft wing through her heart. She didn't want to lose this class; she didn't want to antagonize Joanna Bright or anyone else with her syllabus. She wanted to say something kind, placating, but she was cut off by the obscene snort of the buzzer announcing the end of the class hour. The faces, now attached to bodies, gathered books and bags and walked out of the room talking animatedly and with many gestures: alive, warm-blooded, not like puppets at all. Joanna Bright stood and crossed quickly to the door. She wore a long bright yellow and red printed sari under a purple cape. Without so much as an "excuse me," she swept through the crowd of students like a toucan dispersing street pigeons.

Miss Mahler saved the incident for her subway ride back to Brooklyn Heights. She liked to mull on subways, preferring her thoughts to books and newspapers on the twenty-minute trip between school and home. Subways were the perfect place for scrambling through mental notes, phrases for her new novel, and for thrashing out arguments with Clancy Thomas. She walked with swift, long strides through the darkening, tree-lined streets and distracted herself from thoughts of Joanna Bright by sniffing the cold city air and looking into the lighted brownstone windows at portraits, bookcases, and wainscoting along Washington Square. She thought about zebras, and pictured them mating. But that made her think about Africa, and Joanna Bright, and she wanted to save that for the subway. She went into an all-night gourmet shop and bought an overpriced apple. By the time she'd finished eating it, she found herself in the rumbling, steamy belly of an empty, Brooklyn-bound train. A minstrel playing an accordion got on with Miss Mahler and began singing circus tunes, her vacant eyes rolled up in their sockets and a hideous leer for a smile. Since there were only the two of them in the car, it was impossible to ignore the blind singer in her laceless men's sneakers, her Union Newspaper apron covering her raggedy black coat. The apron had oversized pockets to permit coins. Miss Mahler dropped in fifty cents. She was trying hard to reconstruct the classroom scenery. She needed only the sound of the subway wheels in order to draw the background against which to replay the scene with Joanna Bright. The blind minstrel was distracting her. Across her mind's eye, she painted seats, chromium desk, green blackboard, venetian blinds, and even her ashtray. Then she placed students in their seats: recalling a pair of cat's eye glasses with rhinestone-clustered frames, the moustached man in the football jacket, and the student in the camphory sweater. Stationed firmly against the pole directly in front of her, the blind minstrel now embarked on a furious medley of patriotic songs as though to chide Miss Mahler for her meager, un-American donation.

Miss Mahler felt the second confrontation of the evening coming on. She sat with her eyes glued on the bellowing bundle of rags, convinced now that the minstrel was not blind. When at last she reached her stop, she got off the train and looked back to see the minstrel adjust the accordion strap around her neck and shuffle toward the next car. They can do what they will with my body, thought Miss Mahler as she entered the urine-smelling elevator leading to the street, but they will never have my soul. Her heart pumped fiercely as she hurried home, with Joanna Bright's mocking eyes for company.

At midnight, she was sitting at her typewriter drinking

coffee when an outrageously drunk Clancy Thomas turned the key in the lock and let himself into her apartment. As she was pouring him a useless cup of black coffee, he burnt a cigarette hole in the sofa. Now she was really in for it; the furniture belonged to the landlady, and the old hag had been snooping around in the apartment with her passkey during the day. A note containing the first warning about the neighbors' complaints had been left under a magnet on the refrigerator door. It warned her of "Too much loud typewriting at all hours. Too much loud fighting. And there is an army of cockroaches climbing through your pipes to my apartment because you are the only tenant in the building who refuses to allow the exterminator entry."

The burn in the sofa was a large, mocha brown around the edges, an amoeba-shaped hole in the yellow peony pattern that matched the dusty window draperies. Miss Mahler resolved right there to be rid of Clancy Thomas once and for all: whatever the cost, the loneliness, even if it meant involving the law. Two divorces had inured her to the waiting, the endless haggling and re-stating of what had already been claimed by the contesting parties. Mr. Murdock, her second husband, had been reasonable at first, suggesting that they merely divide their books between them and call it a day. Mr. Murdock was a physicist with no interests in life beyond anti-matter. Then he'd gone and confided their upcoming parting to a quark man at a physics convention and come home querulous and paranoid. Miss Mahler had ended up having to pay him to remove himself from their New Mexico stucco ranch house. If not exactly a litigious person, she was thereafter very careful about the legal aspects of her relationships with men.

When, after burning the hole in the sofa and being escorted to the door, Clancy Thomas grew bellicose and refused to leave, Miss Mahler called the police and had him ejected, not so quietly as she would have hoped, given the landlady's warning. By two in the morning she was physically exhausted and spiritually drained; she fell asleep at the typewriter without having written a word. The next morning, convinced that the planets Mercury and Mars were in malevolent conjunction, she sent off a letter to her half sister, an astrologer in Washington, D.C., asking about "future trends on the work, travel, and relationship fronts." Hidden within the shadowy houses of her chart, Miss Mahler believed, was the possibility of motherhood—with or without Clancy Thomas. In the haze that comprised her intensely fortified mystical life lay the swindling cosmic unknown, a world peopled by demonic minstrels, drunken lovers, and ruled by the greater IBM trumps. Two weeks went by and the letter came back to her with: MOVED! NO FORWARDING ADDRESS! stamped across the front in hellish red.

Her ex-jockey friend, Joe, vanished; his friends at the Saint George Coffee Shop had no idea where he'd gone. Maybe he was dead. Clancy Thomas, despite a stay order, continued to torment her with telephone calls and letters of apology that lavishly quoted John Donne. He even went so far as to appear in a semi-sober state outside her classroom door to beg her forgiveness. Miss Mahler relented, permitting him to take her home and stay the night. They made love and she'd just begun to want to trust him again when she awoke the next morning to find that he'd gone, taking three hundred dollars of her advance money in cash and her typewriter with him. Miss Mahler did not cry; she hardly ever did—not even at deaths which had touched her deeply in the past. She had lived too long and too closely with a truth that most people she knew, because they were insulated by talk of inflation, drip percolators versus Meliors, and dinner parties for the boss, never really thought about. Miss Mahler was exquisitely aware that at the bottom of it all, one was truly alone in the universe, truly entrusted to work out the scheme of things solo. She therefore did not waste a tear, but sat instead for fifteen minutes with her hands folded on the kitchen table in the empty square indentation left by her absent typewriter, grateful that Clancy Thomas had at least left her her manuscript. Then she rang up a sympathetic lawyer, aptly named Christian, whom she'd met at a poetry reading, and told him about the theft. Mr. Christian, whose wife had been a follower of Gurdjieff in her youth, did not pooh-pooh Miss Mahler's mystical claims, her references to retrograde Mercury. They talked amiably for an hour, and he told her to leave both Clancy and her landlady to him.

The next day, a Wednesday, Miss Mahler went to a pawn shop on Atlantic Avenue which had advertised in the newspapers that they were prepared to extend "the fairest deal in all Brooklyn." Wanting to believe the claim, or at least to test it out, she followed the unused tram tracks down Atlantic Avenue for the fifteen blocks from her apartment to the shop. She arrived to find it barred halfway by a diamond-patterned shutter made of iron, the owner having opened for the day five minutes earlier.

"Good morning," she called into the darkened clutter.

A hand bearing a chunky signet ring on its forefinger pushed aside a curtain, and a man who looked like a much put upon ghoul emerged. "What can I do for you?" he said, eyeing her Italian handbag and moving his lips like a religious devotee at his rosary.

"I'd like to buy a typewriter," she said.

"We're not officially open yet, Miss ... but, come over here." He wagged his forefinger with its chunky ring at her, beckoning her to no particular place she could make out in the dark. Miss Mahler started to the right.

"No, here," he said, motioning now to the left of the curtain.

Miss Mahler made her way through the forlorn tin and detritus of pawned lives toward a shelf crammed with paperweights, dried glass inkwells, and dust-caked leather office castaways of no recognizable shape or function.

"At the moment we have only three in stock," said the ghoul. "One just came in yesterday, in fact—an Italian typewriter, an Olivetti in excellent condition. All it needs is a ribbon. A terrific buy; see for yourself. I'll let you have it for sixty dollars." His long, nervous fingers fluttered over the closed typewriter case. "Fellow who sold it to me said he was a starving writer, said he'd be back for it. But if you ask me, he looked more like an alky. Those writers, they're all nuts or lushes." The ghoul went on talking in a nasal voice that seemed to be coming from behind the plastic Halloween mask that was his face.

Miss Mahler looked closely at what she immediately recognized to be her typewriter. She saw the nick in the steel plate that bore the serial number, turned it over and examined the familiar bruised felt of the left pedestal; her own erasures clung, still fresh, to the spiky underside of the machine like a cluster of rubbery marsupials clinging to their parent. Clancy Thomas hadn't even had the decency to pawn it in the Bronx. She said nothing, and bought the machine at sixty dollars, more than it was worth, considering that it was almost fifteen years old. The ghoul watched her carefully as she counted out the cash, half of it in singles. When he was satisfied that he had it all in legitimate bills, he sighed and began wrapping the typewriter in coarse brown paper and tying it with twine.

"You never know these days. I tell you . . ."

"Never mind, you needn't wrap it. I'll carry it in the case," she said, pulling off the wrapping and balling up the twine and handing it back to him. The ghoul made a clucking noise and examined the one-dollar bills again before handing her the typewriter over the counter.

"Writers . . . lunatics," she heard him say as she eased her way out the door past the preventive grillwork and into the street. The sunlight was blinding. A good omen, coming out of the darkness with her own typewriter: she'd made it through the underworld. That meant a new beginning. The theft had been a warning, but getting her typewriter back was a good omen.

At the wrought iron stoop of her rooming house, she was met by a man with a pleasant smile, wearing a tweed topcoat that seemed too heavy for the weather. He was sweating.

"Leona Mahler?" he asked, smiling.

"Yes?"

"Summons." He tapped her lightly on the wrist with a long white envelope, and, after leaving it in her outstretched hand, turned quickly and dashed off toward a waiting car. Miss Mahler ran after him, still holding the typewriter and shouting, "Wait! I'm not Leona Mahler, I'm her half sister Mae . . ." But she was too late. The car, a 1978 brown Oldsmobile, pulled away from the curb with a screech. Miss Mahler stood staring at the vacant curb space. Across the street, a feral dog limped past on three legs.

At school she talked about the Greeks. The semester was now in its fourth week, and the class was hostile to Plato's ideal republic. Miss Mahler often found herself straining to make Plato likeable, democratic. She couldn't. A few spokesmen dared to challenge her; the student with the tic of the lip, the woman with the kind eyes, and the man in the camphory sweater engaged in a heated dialogue. But the rest remained silent, a neatly arranged row of puppets propped in their seats. Joanna Bright made it a custom to arrive fifteen minutes before the end of the hour. Without removing her purple cape and star-spangled beret, she sat in the overheated classroom and stared at Miss Mahler, never opening her book or taking notes. Knowing there were only four weeks left in the term, Miss Mahler coped.

Her lawyer, Mr. Christian, assured her that her landlady could not possibly evict her, burnt sofa or no; the mood at the courts was definitely in favor of tenants—so she continued to work on her book to the exclusion of all else. Clancy Thomas did not return; Joe seemed to be gone for good. The decks were cleared, she was sure, for the book, only the book. For the time being she would closet all romantic impulses, all stamping and whinnying. She dropped out of the fat ladies' course and, for the fee saved, resumed her once-a-week lobster dinners at the Manhattan Fish House. The night before she was to appear in court she took a walk. She was standing in front of the newsstand at Pierrepont and Montegue, browsing through the Astrological Calendar, when a fire started. Sirens and fire engines, ladder, boots, and picks all made their way past her, but she didn't notice that the fire was right across the street from where she stood until the storekeeper in the deli on the ground floor of the flaming building, followed by a trail of customers, ran out onto the sidewalk, coughing and screaming, and waving his arms. Barricades now appeared, pressing her and the group of escapees against the newsstand. A second convoy of fire engines converged, wailing, then came to a halt. Above the deli, a decaying single-room-occupancy well known for its faulty wiring, building department violations, and the landlord's payoffs to the inspectors, was cascading flames like a saffron waterfall. Above the crackling din, the fire chief shouted through a bullhorn for his men to aim the water hoses above, not at, the deli. A flood of water burst forth from a hose, nearly throwing two firemen down on their backs with the force. A police car radio crackled orders in a babble of disembodied voices nearby. Above it all, the ominous creaking of rafters, accompanied by human screams, pierced the blazing night.

The owner of the newsstand, a recently-arrived Lebanese wearing wire-rimmed glasses, came out of his kiosk and stood close by her eating a huge yellow apple, his face glazed in the lick of reflected flame. "Look! Up there . . . up there, lady! See?" he cried, nudging at her elbow and motioning upward with his chin, the hand with the apple still held close to his mouth.

"What? What is it?" Without raising her eyes, Miss Mahler already felt the woman standing at the top floor window. She felt her—faded, alone, dazed with sleep and terror—as if she were sitting on the inside of her spine. Miss Mahler felt the woman's flailing arms, her crazed thoughts of childhood, the sweat like needles prickling her forehead, the wet, secret damp of her armpits, the water running down her inner thighs. Then she felt the rush of smoky air as she pulled the window sash, the buckling knees, and the tiny spiteful tongue of flame at the hem of her dress. She held her hands to her ears, but that did not shut out the woman's hellish screams as she leapt. The deli owner stood with his chin on his chest staring at the ground, his purple magic marker sticking out from behind his ear like a pointer. No one in the little crowd behind the barricade said a word. Two firemen covered the woman where she lay gently with a woolen blanket. Then they hurried back to the hoses. Now the crowd started to buzz with rumors, news, speculation.

When the fire had been contained to a smolder, a policeman lifted the barricade and shooed them away. The small knot of onlookers dispersed, each picking separate ways home.

The landlady had left another, more harshly worded letter

on Miss Mahler's kitchen table. Feeling strangely exhilarated, with Ahkneton asleep on her feet, she sat at the typewriter and wrote through the night. At seven the next morning she brewed a pot of Darjeeling, and then sat smoking and looking out of the window. A yellow sanitation truck sprayed down the muffled, early morning streets with long jets of water, though it was raining hard. According to Mr. Christian's latest telephone message, she had to be in court by nine. After washing her face and changing into what she thought looked like an appropriate courtroom dress, a gray wool knit with a high white collar, she searched through her "Day-by-Day Horoscope." Dixon flashed an ambiguous warning about watching out for finances. Miss Mahler opened a tin of Liver and Kidney Buffet and set it down on the floor for the cat. Then, after carefully placing her night's work in its folder, she left for court.

Despite Mr. Christian's sympathetic ear and his Gurdjieff connections, Miss Mahler lost yet another three hundred dollars, this time to her landlady, for the "nuisance value" she had proven. The judge, a bulky woman with teased blonde hair, had been particularly unsympathetic to Miss Mahler after the landlady's attorney had presented four large color photographs of the burn in the sofa. Mr. Christian shook her hand in the corridor outside the courtroom, refused his fee, and hurried off looking hurt; as though she'd personally injured him by offering to pay for a lost cause. With time to spare before school, she crossed toward Canal Street and entered a dark bar filled with Chinese patrons. It was a steamy, quiet place, with only a revolving Pabst Blue Ribbon Beer clock for light. The dazed, wizened Chinese clientele sat drinking in silence. Miss Mahler selected a seat under the revolving beer clock and ordered a dry martini with lemon peel. The bartender, a swarthy Latin wearing a wraparound apron, gave her a slanted smile as he twisted the lemon peel into a bow tie and suggestively dropped it into her drink. Miss Mahler removed several term papers on the Greek Experience from her bag and graded them. An hour passed. She ordered another martini. Joanna Bright had written a one-page indictment of Western culture. Miss Mahler, a queasy feeling spreading up from her gall bladder, put aside Joanna Bright's paper and paid the bartender, without giving him a tip this time. He appeared to have lost interest in her, for she had stayed too long nursing one drink. Gathering her bag and papers, she made her way past an angry-faced tramp with three days' worth of beard who reminded her of Clancy Thomas. She almost tripped over an undersized wraith in a white felt hat as she walked out the door. The rain had diminished to a drizzle. It was cold. Spring had been diverted after all.

She crossed the Bowery and spent the rest of the afternoon dozing against the scratchy woolen seat of a Chinese movie theater. When she woke the lights had been switched on, and the guttural dialogue and panicky music of the feature had stopped. A purple curtain covered the screen, and, except for her, the theatre was empty. Miss Mahler rushed into the street and hailed the first passing taxi that would have her, urging the driver to hurry uptown with the promise of a big tip. She'd never been late to a class in her life, and she wasn't going to be now. The driver passed a red light and almost struck a pedestrian on Houston Street, but he got her to Washington Square in time for class. She gave him a two-dollar tip, leaving only three dollars in her purse for herself. Having missed the elevator, she raced upstairs, panting at each landing, all the way to the fifth floor. When she entered her classroom and flung her bag onto the desk, she was near faint. Someone who was about to go, or had been on a vacation, was trying to explain his absence to her, but Miss Mahler could not listen. She plopped into her chair and tried to regain her equilibrium. She was sweating; her pulse was rapping like a gavel in her solar plexus. She made some conciliatory gestures at the vacationing student, just enough to get him to sit down in his seat and leave her breathing space. Then she scanned the roll and began returning term papers. This was the part she hated most; she feared she'd been cheated, that the good ones were all plagiarized, and she was guilty about the hopeless ones, those whom she'd never reached. She mostly detested having to sit in judgment of their lives, evaluating their opinions from her teacher's perch—as she herself had been judged that very morning. The usual flurry and contained hysteria prevailed as the students studied her scrawls with unforgiving scowls. "I'll be willing to answer any questions about your papers during my office hour," she said, hoping to forestall the usual storm of complaints. She had written "Unacceptable. Rewrite." on Joanna Bright's paper without giving her a grade. The woman in rhinestone-framed glasses wanted to know whether Plato really wanted *all* poets thrown out of the Republic, and Miss Mahler assured her that those who would conform to Plato's standards could remain. Joanna Bright strode in at that moment, wearing an ink black velvet jumper and thick cord stockings under her purple cape. A pair of six-inch gold earrings jangled defiantly at each step. Miss Mahler could see Joanna's aura; it was blazing red. She only saw people's auras in moments of great stress, when she was feeling most cut off from life. Ever since the Greek Experience had begun, and with it, the ambiguous warnings from the *I Ching* and Jean Dixon, her intuition had been growing: deeply, morbidly, in a way she could hardly decipher, and did not want to confront. Synchronicities were occurring at rapid speeds, too rapid for her to handle. Mae and Joe, her "loyal familiars," had both disappeared. She was down to three dollars.

Joanna Bright sprang forward, took her paper out of Miss Mahler's grasp, and scuttled it over Miss Mahler's shoulder onto the floor without even bothering to look at it. With an air of ritual contempt, she drew up her magnificent head and stared into Miss Mahler's face. Miss Mahler was conscious only of her own legs dangling unglamorously from the chair. She felt foolish, as she had when the judge pronounced her guilty that morning.

"I don't need this," said Joanna Bright.

Miss Mahler looked at her and said nothing.

"Bitch."

Miss Mahler made a movement, an unconscious twitch in preparation for she knew not what. Defensive? Better to deal with this standing. She got up from her chair.

"Why don't you answer me?"

"What do you want me to say?" Miss Mahler's voice was cracked and dry.

"That's just it. You have nothing to say. You're finished

. . . a fossil. Why don't you just fold up your tent and die?"

Miss Mahler contemplated her next move. She saw her astral body float out and gather her books and papers. Just as the astral Miss Mahler buttoned her coat and was about to walk out the door, Joanna Bright slapped her across the face. Then, hissing an unintelligible curse, she fled from the room. The puppets sat transfixed in their rows. Miss Mahler could not look at them a moment longer. "Class dismissed," she said.

Her cheek continued to sting as she rode the elevator down to street level. It only stopped after she had walked around Washington Square Park with her coat open and her face exposed to the wind. It had stopped raining. She sat down on a bench and smoked a cigarette. The park was strangely vacant. Feeling the sudden yearning for a dessert, she walked West until she reached a boat-shaped diner, where she sat down and ordered coffee and apple pie ala mode. For three hours Miss Mahler sat and thought about nothing at all. At midnight the counterman flickered the yellow fluorescent lights to signal closing. She did not move until the counterman told her to leave.

The subway station, like an empty catacomb, echoed her mind's silence. Joanna Bright's slap had cut the chain of her thoughts. She could not mull over the scene on the train, could not even trace the classroom, the venetian blinds, the blackboard in her mind's eye. It was not until she opened the door to her apartment and saw the burn in the sofa that the mechanism, her mind, came unstuck and started ticking again. I've been brain dead, she thought. Now I've come back to life. I'm midway through a new course. That slap was a message. She'd read on the subway platform: "When is a person really dead? If you want to know what doctors are saying about this controversial question, just pick up your April *Reader's Digest*." She now knew what she had to do. First, roll page one-hundred-and-fifty-five of the novel out of the typewriter. Next, set it into its proper place in the tea-stained folder. After that, cross into the tiny kitchenette behind the louvered screen and lift Ahkneton out of his box.

The cat stretched in her hands; she felt his sleeping

warmth as she opened the door and carried him down the steps into the street. Giving her a puzzled glance, he let her set him down before stalking away. Back in her apartment, Miss Mahler locked the door and fastened the brass chain. Calmly, she lit a *Lucky*. Now her mind was moving in fast forward. She ordered the pages of what she knew to be her best work, then read the manuscript through. Place the end of the cigarette to the title page. The paper caught rapidly. Holding it like a torch, moving gracefully, like an ancient Greek dancer, Miss Mahler lit the moldy draperies, the troublesome sofa; then she swept the flame of purifying fire across the amoeba-shaped burn. Drop the almost consumed wedge onto the floor. Stand at the center of the room, work done, smoke your cigarette. Miss Mahler thought about people who did terrible things to their neighbors; she thought about spurned lovers who threw lye into their ex-girlfriends' faces; blind beggars who were not really blind. She thought about women with dungeon-sized passkeys who flagellated innocents, and judges who valued property more than human life. Beads of sweat trickled from her eyebrows into the crevices of her face, along her nose, and down to her chin. The clatter of beams roared in her ears, and through the astral glare, Miss Mahler could see Joanna Bright dancing around her in a frenzy. Sit down on the still intact portion of the troublesome sofa and listen to what your accuser has to say.

WINTER 1989

Where is the paper and pen
in the dark early morning
when my eyes lift open
and will not shut?

The clock with its glowing face
is alive.
The insects will not stop singing
in the tall grass outside.
Tortured thoughts go
round and round my head
like tired little men who want to stop
but cannot rest
until the General says
you may go home.

The heads of Europe stir uneasily
thinking of the word "peace."
The Berlin Wall is down
but what has come up in its place?
And the electrician from Gdansk—
what is he doing now?
I fold my arms across my chest
and let the foundry hammers
ring in my head.

THE CROSS

She went to the screen door and looked out. Clouds were gathering over the mountain, adding a further gloom to the darkening sky.

"I shouldn't have told him I'd wait," Machi thought. "Why is it always like this?" His indifference only deepened the loneliness she felt sometimes, like now, when the sun was setting.

But Alex would expect her to be there, if only so he wouldn't have to return to an empty house, and then she would go or stay according to his mood.

She bit her lip. Alex had remarked once to her that she never got angry—"It comes out in other ways, later." Machi had laughed. But at the same time his remark had disturbed her.

"I get angry," she said to herself. "Sometimes I get so angry a darkness comes over my life like a huge shadow."

The road was darkening, and beyond it, in the valley, trees were losing their individual shapes, merging into each other and into their background. In a little while it would be dark. He had said he would return by six. It was nearing seven, and there was no sign of him. Should she leave his dinner on the stove and go? What could be keeping him? Had he ended his class late? Was he looking over some papers at his office?

She unlatched the door and stepped out.

A man was leaning against the wall at the foot of the stairs. His attitude was one of waiting, his hands in his pockets. His back curved against the wood. Now he turned to her, slowly, the cap shadowing his eyes. It was as if he had been waiting for her and now, as though the sight of her reassured him, he smiled.

She felt suddenly afraid.

He took a step up the stairs. She backed up a step and found the screen door against her back. She watched, as in a dream—this is a dream, she told herself—as he came slowly up the stairs. That was the terrible part of it. He was so unhurried.

She stumbled into the kitchen, opened a drawer, then another, although she knew—had known—which drawer the knives were in. She pulled it out: the wedge-shaped knife used for cutting vegetables and fish.

She hadn't latched the door. Now he was at the door, opening it. She stepped out of the kitchen to meet him in the parlor. The kitchen was too small. She didn't want to be cornered there.

He hadn't shaved for several days. The shadows around his eyes were dark, as if he hadn't slept either. He looked like a seaman, with the rough outdoor smell of sweat and the ocean on him.

He grinned at her. Even when he saw the knife, he kept grinning. There was no fear in his eyes, only a kind of recognition. He stepped toward her.

The knife went into his stomach. It was she who cried out as it went in. It went in so easily. He kept looking at her, registering no surprise. It was a small wound. She was about to pull the knife out, but he put his large hands over hers and pushed the knife in. The whole of the wedge-shaped knife disappeared into his stomach.

He stood looking at her, like a man watching a woman's orgasm, she thought. The look was interested, disinterested, tender.

Then she put her hands to her mouth to scream, but no scream came out. He stumbled back until the couch touched his knees and he sat.

She pushed the screen door and went running out. Running. Where? Into the darkness. Now it was dark. It had gone in so easily. Like putting it into a fish belly. Or like putting the tip of the knife into the stomach lining of a fish to take the white parasites out. The streetlights cast shadows of flying tree branches.

★   ★   ★   ★

He kissed her breast, and then the nipple. It was like a cherry, hard, on top of a smooth and firm scoop of ice cream. Her skin was cool. It was cool and smooth under his hand.

She moaned, shifted, and then he was pressing her against him and she was pushing herself away. Tears were falling down her cheeks. He tasted them as he kissed her and then they shuddered together, clinging. He had known that women cried, but hers seemed tears of contrition, not ecstacy. He had tried to talk to her about it.

He tried again, when, dressed, they sat in the livingroom. She never seemed comfortable lingering in the bedroom, so they sat, rather formally, in the livingroom; she in the armchair, he on the sofa bed.

Made-up, she seemed distant, a political campaigner or IBM representative just stepping into the cool parlor for a few minutes of business. Her powder covered the traces of tears. Her lipstick made her lips look less vulnerable. Before making love, he noticed, she rarely wore lipstick.

In fact, when he had first met her at the museum, he had thought she was a high school student. She had that air of loneliness a young girl would have if, in high school, she was seriously interested in art.

"Machi, before you met me, was there someone who hurt you?"

She flinched, then a veil went down over her eyes.

"No. Why do you ask?"

Joseph shook his head. He leaned forward and kissed her. "When will I see you again?"

"I don't know." She looked uncomfortable, as she did when the conversation became too intimate. Joseph thought, she's either afraid of becoming too close, or afraid of being cast out.

"Tomorrow?"

"No. I—I have something to do."

"Wednesday night, then."

She nodded.

She hadn't told him what she did, so he had no way of knowing how she spent the day, or the nights when she wasn't with him.

Sex was only half the battle, he thought ruefully, although the modern age would have you believe a relationship lived or died on it. Sex, in fact, was the easy part of a relationship—the common meeting ground—and not, as it should have been, the most sanctified and cherished intimacy.

He thought of her lips, of her soft thigh against his hands, her breasts that fit his cupped hand so exactly. How could he be a moralist when his desire to reach her mind and soul was linked so intimately with her body.

"Who else do I have today?"

"Mr. Vourganas was the last patient, Dr. Chang," said Kathy, his receptionist.

Joseph nodded.

It was nice having the afternoon off. He pulled on his coat and left the office.

Because he was with people all day, he liked to spend the afternoons he had free alone, in the park, communicating with trees. He laughed at the thought. But it was true—plants gave him the energy he in turn gave to his patients. The quietness, breath, healing. Sunlight and filter. Drawing water into the roots. Rising from the fresh smell of dirt.

He walked along a different path today, was overtaken by joggers, saw women walking their babies in carriages, people running their dogs. Near the arboretum a group of children were gathered, waiting to go in. Waiting, thought Joseph with amusement, was the wrong word. They were talking and looking around, laughing, punching each other, dropping things and picking them up, looking into the brown bags they held, taking their jackets off and putting them on.

Two teachers stood at the head of the line. A little to one side was a little girl and a woman. The woman was crouched to the level of the girl, and on her face was a look of earnestness.

Joseph stopped by a boy at the end of the line.

"Who is that?"

The boy looked. "That's Miss Koizumi. She's my brother's teacher. My brother's in the second grade."

"Oh? And what are you?"

"First," he said between missing teeth. "This is my best friend, Tommy."

Joseph said hello to Tommy, touched the tops of both of their shiny heads, and walked toward Miss Koizumi.

Machi looked up at Joseph coolly, but did he imagine a flicker in her eyelids?

"Hello," she said.

"I thought you might need help."

Machi bit her lip. "As a matter of fact, I do. I was just wondering what to do. Sarah's not feeling well, and I think she may have a fever."

Joseph put his hand to the small girl's forehead.

He nodded. "There is a slight fever."

"I think I should take her back to school and the infirmary can call her parents, but we came on the bus. Do you—"

"Yes. It's parked just on the other side. I can drive both of you."

Machi went to talk to the other two teachers and returned.

"They can manage. They think it'll be wise to take Sarah back, too."

Joseph closed the snaps on the child's jacket and between them they walked the child to the car.

Joseph looked into Machi's face. Her eyes were closed. The perspiration on her upper lip and forehead looked like dew. He thought of how she had looked today with the child, her earnestness, gentleness, what a good mother she'd make.

Machi opened her eyes. She seemed dazed to see his eyes on her. Then she turned her head.

"Please, don't look at me like that."

"Like what?" Joseph asked, puzzled by the anguish in her voice.

"Like I—like you—" she started to cry.

★   ★   ★   ★

The question that haunted her was—whom had she stabbed? They said, as she had guessed, that he was a seaman, off the merchant vessel *Anchorage*; that he had had a history of unstableness, drunken bouts, fistfights, violent outpourings of what, frustration, rage? But he hadn't been drunk that day. He had been lucid when he had taken her hands and pushed the knife into him. And his eyes had told her something she did not want to believe. It's not me you're killing, they had said.

For in that moment when the knife had gone in deep, Machi imagined she was killing Alex. It was Alex's stomach that the thin blade was slicing so easily. Alex who never kept his promises to her and didn't care.

Later, when Alex found her at Professor Omori's house just down the street—after he had found the body and called the police—Machi had looked into his face and felt nothing. Had anything ever existed between them? She had started laughing, laughing. Out of the darkness a white hand came out and slapped her. There were whispered words of hysteria and shock. But her cheeks hardly stung. It had all been in her mind, and now there was nothing left.

She left with him, but he no longer existed. He held her against him and said words to comfort her against the memory of that moment when the knife had gone in—or the moment when she knew it would have to go in—but all she felt was the space between them. She had ached for three years for a sign of his affection. Suddenly it didn't matter anymore.

Why did he choose me, she thought. In that act he had isolated her from the rest of humanity. And the look on his face when the knife had gone in—not concern for himself, but a lover's concern for her.

"Was it—nice?" Sometimes she imagined she heard those words at night. "Was it nice for you?"

Why had he stamped her in that way? For her to carry on his rage against the world? For her to remember his existence as no one had remembered it during his lifetime? Or was he in his last act taking upon himself her rage and absolving her of it?

She felt like the Roman who had stabbed Jesus with the spear when he was on the cross. But no, no, she wasn't the criminal. Certainly, that man hadn't been Christ. Why then did she feel that people stared at her? How could she account for the shame she felt when Joseph looked at her with tenderness. Tears would flow each time she thought of it. He had made her a criminal when all she had been—had wanted to be—was a victim of circumstance.

SHEILA GARDINER

CHANGES OF BEING

Say, when Roethke wrote of a dark time,
was he ever terror-bound on a pavement of glass—
measuring the terribleness below with the retracing
of the same labyrinth above,
not missing a beat, ever?
No matter.
Once you know how to return to the source
you can give yourself to the winds of chance.
Rising slowly at first you cast no shadow
between the indifferent eye of the moon
and the sax-throb of earth's turn.
When you look down, there's your tiny mama
tending her radishes,
your deadly serious daddy,
changing a tire.
And before you can say "Bye Bye Blackbird"
or turn off a Hitler harangue on the wireless,
you're over a Moroccan bazaar with the smells
of hashish and musk mixing in the fly-heavy noontime heat.
Discreetly you stand waiting for your assignation
with a party unknown,
admiring, in the meantime, the Israeli oranges, those
perfect suns of delight.
The eggplant, grapes clustered there
are like sleeping children and too much to bear.
Camels dance a waltz of sorrow and you reach to wipe
   their tears.

PLAY IT WITH PATHOS, RUBY

I understand
someone purporting to be my father
made his entrance across these boards
wearing a wrinkled linen suit
(white of course),
panama hat,
a used-up song and dance man,
playing to an empty house.
Let me tell you right off
my father, thick-handed son
of Yorkshire farmers
would never wear a white suit
much less trust anyone who did.
Bound and blinded by righteousness,
and a man who got his
money's worth
with a death rattle for a laugh.
In front of a painted stage curtain
thatched cottage, hollyhocks,
bluebirds and such
(you know the kind)
the imposter waits for an audience
that never comes.
Strikes elegant poses, head tilted
just so.
Even in that darkened house
I see his shadow spring from wingtip shoes.
I keep trying to reach him.
Scenes shift, slip away with
doors opening into empty rooms.
Torn lace curtains rise and fall.
Soon I forget
what it is I have to tell him.

It doesn't matter. I am too busy
being Ruby Keeler,
wearing bowtied/blackpatent/tap shoes.
Singing "Beside a Waterfall,"
and all the time
searching past the houselights
for a panama hat,
white linen suit.

SUSAN NUNES

THE SCIENCE OF SYMMETRY—A LOVE STORY

For all the frittered days
That I have spent in shapeless ways,
Give me one perfect thing.

Hannah has a body thrown together from mismatched parts. Nothing fits. The hemispheres war with each other. To lie with her spoon fashion but not fitting is to feel the contradictions, her mystery. Hannah is all problem. In my work a problem is a beginning, the discovery that defies explanation. I pursue problems. That is probably why I pursued her.

The first time I saw Hannah was in the courtyard of the student center where I ate lunch most days. The women on this campus are beautiful, and, from my vantage point, I could observe a perfect female universe and feel like the fixed center around which everyone revolved. Then Hannah came barreling through the place like a meteor gone mad. I could have ignored her—science is selective, after all—but it isn't my style to set aside intrusions. Intrusions of one sort or another are my metier. Maybe it was her face, which was completely incongruous with everything from her neck on down. Maybe it was the way she made the place turn on HER movements, upending everything. Or maybe it was the image of white sneakers with green laces, imprinted on my mind like a profound equation.

She disappeared into the cafeteria, but a connection was made. In the final analysis, I am a theoretician; clumsy with tools, suspicious of anything that challenges my ideas, but drawn to them, too. In the days that followed, I found myself waiting for her. Maybe a week later, she appeared again.

In those moments it took her to pass through the courtyard, I studied her. Nothing is perfect, but she was all contradiction. Where one expected straight lines, angles prevailed. Curves turned in on themselves. Her right shoulder was raised almost to the level of her ear and thrust forward as if impatient to move ahead. In protest, her wrist bent back on itself, so that her hand, palm jutting out, acted like a brake. Her left side appeared to have given in to the pull of gravity, and the arm hung limply at her side.

But before she disappeared, I saw that her face was perfect. And she had black, black hair that did things in the sunlight I've never seen hair do.

I was pursuing a woman named Julia at the time, one of a long line of experiments that I imagined made me the envy of my colleagues. That night as Julia and I made love, my mind fixed on the apparition in the courtyard, and I wanted to do things I knew Julia wouldn't stand for. It shook me. I took refuge in the lab at two in the morning and worked until the cleaning woman came in to empty the wastebaskets. At least the patterns of electrons on the surface of copper were predictable.

My first contact with her outside the world of the court-yard showed me how far gone my behavior was. Normally, I like to be in control, prepared for all possibilities. Hannah caught me unawares. I was walking on the mall heading in the direction of the lab and my mind was on a research proposal, the design of an experiment, some new deadlines. I wasn't aware of her until she was right in front of me. She said, "Watch it," and pushed past. I caught the scent of her hair as her shoulder brushed my arm.

I turned and watched her step off the curb at the top of the walk and launch herself across the campus road. By the time she reached the other side I had begun to follow her. Pure impulse.

From behind I could see that her left leg seemed normal enough, but she had to keep it bent in order to accommodate the right one. This leg was considerably shorter and turned in at the knee and out again at the ankle, so that the inside of her foot brushed the ground with every step. She was wearing the same white shoes.

I kept her in sight as she negotiated the parking lot, her head bobbing above the cars. She paused under a shower tree near the stoplight and adjusted her backpack. I hung back, shielded by a pickup truck. When the light turned green, she veered across the street and then climbed into a handi-van parked at the end of the block. A moment later, it pulled into traffic. I waited at the street corner until it disappeared.

Later, thoroughly disgusted with myself for having invaded someone's space, I headed for the lab and nailed my eyes to the computer screen. The neat rows of figures contained the predictions of one of my theories. My idea, if it made sense was supposed to predict what would happen down the hall where my partner played with the equipment. Actually, you could reduce everything to a set of these symbols.

Not all my work is numbers. Sometimes, I cover ideas that have emotional appeal. The idea of symmetry, for instance, is mathematical. But I don't just give students the formula to memorize; they would never get the point. Instead, I start by saying that symmetry, however you define it, whether beauty, harmony, or balance, is an idea with which we try to create order and perfection. It's the norm from which we deviate. I turn on the slide projector and the torso of a young man fills the screen. Usually, someone in the back row starts to whistle and I have to wait a moment for the laughter to subside. When I hit the button again, the full figure comes on. It's a dramatic moment. I say, "Fourth Century, Greek," and give them a few moments for the full effect. It's a balanced figure, the face turned up and the arm held out in the pose of adoration, but it is not perfectly symmetrical. We discuss some of the deviations. The left foot, for example, is actually pointed a little forward with the weight resting on the right foot, which raises the right hip slightly. I want them to see that the features that wander from recognized principles of balance and proportion are the ones that need explanation.

It's the same in science, I tell them. The deviations interest us because they force changes in what we regard as law. At the same time, ours is still a search for balance and proportion. Yet again, as scientists we cannot be too confident in the rules of symmetry. Position, direction, left, right—these are relative concepts. It's all relative. The idea is so basic that we hold to it, even as we observe an organism's symmetry.

I keep the photograph on the screen and turn up the lights. For some students, the paradox works. For the rest, it matters little. I merely propose that the norm of perfection is life-defying.

Would my speculations about Hannah have amounted to anything? Probably not. At a distance, she was an interesting problem. She had no reality for me. I had no intention of putting flesh on that disordered frame. But she changed all that. And she did it on her terms, not mine, and on a day when the light did things to her hair.

I was in the courtyard as is my habit, calculating the odds of her transit, when she tilted through the gate, made a beeline for my table, and planted herself before me.

"I want you to stop!" she exclaimed.

Encumbered by a mouthful of sandwich, I couldn't say anything.

"I may be crippled," she continued, "but I'm not blind. I don't like being followed. Next time I'm calling the police!"

I tried to apologize, but she lowered her voice and hissed, "Just cut it out!" She watched me squirm for a moment, then turned to leave.

People sitting nearby were starting to notice. I stood up. "Wait," I said to her retreating figure. "I'm sorry. Please."

She paused. I plunged on, telling her I meant no harm, that she had to sit down, please, so I could explain. Her eyes widened, and she gave me a you've-got-to-be-kidding look. I told her I felt like a jerk, but she must please listen. I pulled out a chair.

She stared at it a moment, but finally she sat.

"Well?" she asked.

How, without sounded perverse, do you tell someone who looks like Hannah that she fascinates you? But it was true, and so I began at the beginning and finished with the day on the mall when I followed her. She watched my face through the ordeal, and when I finished, she leaned forward to take off her backpack. I started to help her but she shook her head. Her movements were practiced, but there were tiny beads of sweat on her upper lip.

Then she smiled. "Who are you, anyway?"

"Stephen Woods," I told her.

She held out her good hand and I took it. Her grip was firm. "I'm Hannah. Hannah Mei Lum. What do you do, Stephen, besides pursue the physically impaired?"

"I teach physics." She studied my face as I talked, her head tilted, her expression intent, almost as if she were hard of hearing. She had wheat-colored skin, dark eyes, and a full mouth. A cap of straight black hair, shiny as lacquer, framed her small face. She asked questions about my work and laughed good naturedly at my efforts to explain, without numbers or graphs, what it was I did. She said she was a graduate student in English and worked part time as an editor for a publishing company. She thought it great to be paid to read. Her voice had a musical quality and she delivered each sentence whole and complete. I lost track of time.

Finally, she held up her limp left arm with her good one, looked at her watch, and said it was time to go.

I told her to come by the lab sometime and I'd show her what we did there. After giving her directions during the complicated production of her departure, I watched her bumpy progress through the gate. After she disappeared it was like waking up from a dream. The courtyard was empty, chairs abandoned at odd angles as if everyone had followed in her wake.

I was preoccupied for days afterward. The nearest thing I can compare it to is the way my mind is when I'm really excited by a problem. It consumes me until I have an explanation. When I was with Julia I would be thinking what it would be like with Hannah. How would you negotiate that tangle of limbs? One night, staring at an equation on my screen, it struck me that Hannah's name was symmetrical, too.

We started meeting regularly in the courtyard. I thought she was remarkably open and easy to know. She was an only child—"the dream of aging loins"—she said merrily. Her parents were basically good people who couldn't look at her without guilt. A hundred years ago, they would have buried her in the fields. They compensated by denying her nothing. She was sent to the best schools, anything to keep her away. After college in the East and trying to live there on her own, the cold got to her and she came here.

There was no bitterness in her tone. She laughed without effort, and I found myself liking her very much indeed.

The first time she visited my laboratory I was immensely pleased. In the section where we keep the machines and electronic equipment, I explained that while my work consisted of thinking a lot and juggling mathematical symbols, here my co-worker actually measured things to test my ideas.

She said, "So you're the great predictor," and asked what my track record had been.

Not too bad, I told her. She stopped in front of one of the spectrometers and I said it was our agitator, that it riled up the atoms so we could see what happened. She peered at the specimen through the glass.

"Do your theories account for all the unexplained instances?" she asked.

I said that even successful theories often failed to predict what happened in new situations. The question was how to modify my ideas enough to restore harmony.

"I see," she said, backing off the machine and eyeing it warily.

I looked forward to these visits, came to miss her if she didn't show up. Soon we were meeting for coffee or lunch, then movies on the weekends. She took me to foreign films, and she endured my more plebeian tastes.

One day I told her she was extraordinary.

She rolled her eyes and dropped the subject. A few days later I brought it up again. "Did I say something wrong?" I asked.

"Don't look so wounded," she said gently. She held up her limp left arm. "There's no merit in contending with this . . . lumber. But it's all I know." She let her arm flop back on her lap. "What you call extraordinary is, to me, frightfully banal."

"I meant YOU were extraordinary," I insisted.

"No, I am very ordinary."

My passion to know her had kept me in a state of perpetual excitement. Now I wanted her. But I had no idea how to approach the problem. If she gave me an opening, how was I to negotiate her?

She was sitting in my office, insisting that science couldn't deal with surprises the way art could, and I told her that, to the contrary, good physicists were poets, only they made images with numbers. She thought about that for a moment, face solemn and hand twitching.

Finally she said, "These are your small victories, aren't they? A line of symbols, a little bit of order."

"Good, I finally win one."

"No," she said. "You just made your point. Mine is that art can create disorder, make us uncomfortable, lie even, so that we may see the truth."

She grasped the arm of the chair with her good hand and held out her foot somewhat in my direction. "Let me show you my small victories. My shoes, Professor: Observe closely. Here, the laces."

I edged my chair closer, held her foot gently, and pulled at the bright green laces.

"Notice anything?" she asked.

"Green?"

"Obvious. What else?"

"Elastic?" I ventured.

She nodded. I was on the right track, but I was thinking of how fragile her foot was.

"Pre-tied," she announced.

"Pre-tied?"

"Right."

"I don't get it."

"A small victory, Stephen. One of the banalities of being extraordinary."

She explained how she used to have an awful time with her shoes, but with these laces, she didn't have to tie them. She laughed and started to pull her foot away, but I held onto it. She opened her mouth to protest, but stopped when she looked at me. I ran my fingers on the ankle bone, feeling its angular deformity, the sharp turn it made from the expected path. I followed that meandering bone up her calf to the knee.

"Am I hurting you?"

She shook her head.

"Does what caused this have a name?"

"Yes, but it's not important. The bones have a mind of their own. That's what I tell children. Does the explanation satisfy you, Stephen?" She smiled ironically. "If it doesn't, there is a book in the library called *Skeletal Disorders* which describes it nicely."

A boundary had finally been crossed, and I knew I stood on the edge of discovery.

Later, after I placed her on my bed like a collapsed marionette and undressed her, I was confounded by the immensity of my desire. I saw all the contradictions, and somehow fit that tangled form. Then, to my surprise, Hannah took me, and I became a mindless participant in her rhythms. Only hours later did she release me. I carried her to my car and she let me arrange her body and limbs and strap her in. She asked me to drive with the top down and laughed as I wrapped her head in a silk scarf. On the way, her hair escaped its bonds, whipping against her face like a torrent.

I think about my work, how I spend my life chasing things that don't fit, to find the regularity beneath them all. With women, that same discovery drove me to new conquests. With Hannah, the knowledge made me want to know more. Everytime I caught a glimpse of her cutting a wide swath through ordinary people, the feeling was reaffirmed. Everything eventually danced to Hannah's music.

I guess we make an odd couple. People stare, and Julia thinks I've gone off the deep end. "Sick," she said when she returned my apartment keys, "sick, sick, sick," and made me spill coffee all over my work papers. Hannah still doesn't think of us as a couple. When I bring it up, entwined in her crooked arms, she says our lives are too separate, and then laughs at her joke. I'm finally getting to the point where I'm content with what we have, even if I can't figure it out. I'll be sitting at the computer terminal and find myself turned-on, and I won't know if it's the beauty of the equation or the thought of Hannah.

Science, I tell my students, is the denial of the world ruled by caprice. It rests on the proposition that nature is knowable and dependable, uniform and orderly. I'll write a formula on the blackboard, one of my theories, and tell them that it's a statement about a class of facts gleaned through observation. But I know it isn't so neat. I don't have anything like that for Hannah or what I feel, and sometimes that troubles my need for certainty.

"You know, Stephen," she said once, "Due to your insistence on order, you're miles removed from human experience. Relax and enjoy."

I want to say, "Hannah, you lurched into my life and personified all the incongruities that keep me on edge." But I know she'd laugh at the pomposity of language and my choice of words. I wonder whether she will leave me one day, careen into another experience, and upend that world the way she has done mine. The thought of this feeds my sense of disproportion.

"I am not a mystery," she says. We were in bed on a Sunday morning in a tangle of newspapers, sheets, and limbs. She located her limp arm and studied it for a moment, moving it every which way as if it were separate from her. "You're drawn to this because you don't understand the why of it. That's the problem with your science. You go after the detail that doesn't fit your principle. You adjust your principle to restore balance. And once you've done that you've got to move on to the next case."

I thought about the endless possibilities of my work and the incongruities of her form.

"Poor Stephen," she said, elbowing me. "Don't look so serious."

Yesterday, coming home in the late afternoon, I noticed some cartons stacked in the driveway for the refuse collectors. They looked ominously like the aftermath of a major move. My chest tightened and I thought, "Oh God, she's gone." But then I heard her calling, "Stephen, is that you?"

Relieved, I started up the walk. Then I noticed something hanging out of one of the boxes. It was a green shoelace. I stood there with a slew of images descending upon me, details of face, hair, eyes, lines of numbers, letters, symbols, an eddy of limbs, fragments searching for a center, for something to hold them long enough to be resolved. Something as simple as a shoelace pulled them into a whole.

I laughed at the merging, as if the point of a joke were made clear. "Perfect," I thought, "perfect." I put the lace into my pocket and walked confidently up the path to the front door.

SECRETS

"He knew your mother."

That's all I needed to know.
My shiny young face smiled up at his thin
long face with a scar and a missed tooth.
Anyone who had known my mother won my rapt attention.
I caught glimpses of her only through others.

He carried a small lumpy pack
and a battered wooden case.
His pants were patched
and I didn't much let his smell bother me even.

Grandma said "stay for supper."
And supper stretched out for weeks.

Evenings were different and magical
with Freeman in the house.
The violin came out of the old wooden case
and he played for his supper. (Grandma told me he played
classical music like "Humoresque" as well as fiddle.)

My crippled aunt was as amazing as Freeman.
She could play on the piano
anything he could on the violin
after she had heard it once.

I would go to bed out on the sloping back porch
while they still played.
There I could dream of Freeman
as the music reached out into the lilac perfumed night,
the soft curtain billowing in and out the window
with the rhythm of the spring breeze.

Many times sitting on a straight wooden chair in the kitchen
he would pat his knee and invite me to sit.
His hard, thin hand would gently lift my gingham dress
and stray to the elastic of my long black bloomers.

No one knew.
I didn't tell.

HIS EYE IS ON THE SPARROW

I wanted to wash it off.

Stamp the manure—cow dung we called it—from my shoes, sometimes my feet, cement over the path to the cow barn.

Rid the kitchen of the smell on their pants legs, the smell that permeated the place when they came in laced with sweat, these outdoor men, farmers and cowboys. Farm women too with cow dung sometimes clinging to the hems of their long skirts.

There you would stand, Mama (Grandma was always Mama to me), bent over the outdoor wash basin, scooping up water to wipe away the sweat that ran in little rivers down your face. "Wash up before you come in," you would remind us.

You carried the full bucket of rich warm milk down the cellar steps to be strained and run through the separator. Humming a favorite hymn as you went:

> *Oh for a thousand tongues to sing, our great redeemers praise*
> *The glories of my God and King, the wonders of his grace.*

Please God, let me be like Janie. Janie the banker's daughter. I could sink down in one of the real leather chairs in the living room and listen to the soft southern drawl of mother and daughter—the smell of freshly baked bread perfuming the house. Let me not have to fight the bedbugs and pretend we don't have them, turning the mattresses over and putting kerosene on. I denied it best I could and didn't ask friends to stay over.

Mama, were you so tired you didn't care anymore?

Sometimes I'd sneak off—it was easy, you didn't miss me much anyway. There was passion in the sweet smelling hay of the barn loft where *True Story* magazines were hidden and where young men with swollen trousers teased and tried. And then I would remember another of your hymns:

> *His eye is on the sparrow and I know he watches me.*
> *I know because . . .*

Could He really? Could God see me full of passion, pretending it wasn't there—under a blanket on a hay ride covered with silly girlish laughter, hiding the hot, the red hot aliveness, body stinging with waves from head to foot?

> *I know because I'm happy*
> *I know because I'm free*
> *His eye is on the sparrow and I know he watches me.*

God, if you can watch over the sparrow, can't you take this away? Keep me pure as I want to be. Please God make me pure and tears fell away on my cheeks and I cleaned my shoes and curled my hair and studied my lessons.

Your humming threaded through my thoughts as I supplied the words:

> *There is a fountain filled with blood*
> *Drawn from Immanuel's veins*

Mama, your small muffled sounds of sex at night with "papa" when you were old were sounds of both passion and pain. Your womb had already dropped painfully against the bladder. Yet you bore it and left musky smelling rags carelessly thrown into the closet. I'd smell them in disgust of your uncleanness, never realizing that the musk of sex got into my nostrils and I was drawn over and over to my discovery of the forbidden.

Did I learn passion from you somehow in spite of my disgust of your shrunken breasts or your swollen stomach with its permanent pregnant shelf?

> *There is a fountain filled with blood,*
> *Drawn from Immanuel's veins,*
> *And sinners plunged beneath that flood, lose all their guilty*
>   *stains*
> *Lose all their guilty stains,*

Lose all my guilty stains.

A WAILING WALL

I used the machete as my weapon,
the creeping branches in my rain forest yard were the target;
I slashed and piled the branches and wished
for oblivion or a wailing wall.

I grabbed for a ti plant, missed and went sliding
down the muddy hill.
The sharp blade of the machete dulled—
I grabbed the bow saw and sawed away
on the felled tough branch of a guava tree.

I lay on the damp grass out of breath,
my head against a warm stone.
—unbidden the image of her returned,
that last look after the doctor said, "It's over."

Her quiet face, still warm, framed by her graying hair.
My only daughter.
In her countenance, visages of family women
who had gone before her.

I looked up through the gnarled twisted branches
of the kukui tree with the pale green leaves
shaped like the maple leaves of my childhood.
Dappled light spread over the stone, the grass and my
      limp body.

The stone became my wailing wall.

LIGHT

The bulbul has flown into the house.
He clings panting to the window curtain,
black crest up and beak open,
his heart racing, black eyes bright.

There is a residue of light
upon his shining feathers.
He showers the air
with bright bird senses.

My house is dark.
Within it I beat as frantically as he,
and so I grasp him,
open my hand and
let the sky take him.

Light frees us both and puts us out.
For darkness does not want us.

DUSTING BOOKS

Three bearded brothers on a bench,
all in their sixties, now confront me
as I am dusting books.
This 1890 photograph was taken by
someone's knickered nephew trying his tripod.
After one hundred years, the picture taken,
their stares now rise to censure me.
Black business suits, stiff collars,
three gold watch chains swagged across three paunches,
three thumbs hooked in three watch pockets
ready to pull the time in
Boston, Brooklyn, or Connecticut.
They do not like my century.

Contemporaries often murmured—
"gentlemen they were, and all philanthropists.
They listened to the poor,
(if these should speak to them).
Oh yes, and they collected books."

Who would remember them except for books?
Their bookplates name them:
Joseph, Nathan, Alan.
Today, as glittering dust in shafts of sun,
they trail my reading eyes.
With turning of a page they sigh together.
The volumes with the broken spines
lean as on ghostly cheeks.
Dust fingers weave in all the spaces.
Where are the missing books
whose bodies travelled them
to far exotica or to themselves?
Those volumes left are sick with

pox and yellowing.

I dust and sneeze. I take the picture down.
My own watch ticks with modern certainty
that I will never read them.

SPEAKING TO KUAN YIN

Kuan, let me be
blue snow
holding
whole sky.

Kuan, why wasn't I home
when you left a paper bag
of smooth yellow star fruit
between door and screen?

I sewed in the panels
on your butterfly dress.
It's too bad, Kuan,
you made me rip out
those lumpy seams.

How is it, Kuan,
when I saw the weight
fall on your finger,
you're the one
who comforted me?

Kuan, I bolted away again
for fear a friend would leave first.
Lead me back
to my bugbear, success.

Kuan, be the stable bar,
raised higher and higher,
over which I can vault
for the joy of it.

When we sat on the lanai laughing,

an old lady stumped past: "Giddy young people!"
She never saw it was you, ancient Kuan,
whose wit set us off.

Will your pale ring,
loosed to dark space,
find me, Kuan,
after light years of tumble?

KUAN YIN, INVENTOR

Kuan Yin concocted the first piece of paper
of mulberry and fishnet.
Her silkworms were chewing, chewing
mulberry leaves,
while Kuan Yin in red silk
was whisked to the emperor.
He deigned to unwrap
this twenty-eighth concubine
on nights of no moon:
not caring
whether she conceived
auspiciously.
Kuan Yin
tore off mulberry bark
and pounded a paste,
flavor: chewed wood.
Imperial gardeners
found her silkworms had languished.

Since Kuan Yin could not enter his presence at will,
the first sheet of paper,
apparently blank,
was presented to the emperor
by a eunuch.
The emperor bowed.
He did not know what to do with the paper.

At night in the museum,
after the guards swing the iron gates,
Kuan Yin forages for empty cigarette packs,
smoothed open,
and with centuries-old ink,
found by the curators

slightly displaced,
she traces a character for mulberry,
a character for fishnet,
through which she imagines
carp rising.

CONTRIBUTORS

Nell Altizer's book *The Man Who Died En Route* received the 1988 Juniper Prize from the University of Massachusetts Press. She has published in numerous journals, among them *The Massachusetts Review, Prairie Schooner,* and *Shenandoah,* and teaches literature and creative writing at the University of Hawaii-Manoa.

Priscilla Atkins has poems published in *Bamboo Ridge, Chaminade Literary Review, Hawaii Review,* and an anthology *Rainbows and Rhapsodies: Poetry of the Eighties.*

Cristina Bacchilega was born in Verona, Italy and teaches in the English Department at UH-Manoa. Her mother Shanta is from Madras, India and her daughter Bruna was born in Honolulu, Hawaii.

Susan Barnett has published poems in *Lake Superior Review, Midwest Review, Blue Mesa Review, Chaminade Literary Review,* and *Rainbird.* Non-fiction articles have appeared in Stanford University's *Surviving.* Her fiction won grand prize in the 1988 National League of PEN Women (Hawaii Chapter) writing competition. She believes, like Levertov, that "poetry is a process of discovery, revealing inherent music."

Perle Besserman is the author of *The Way of Witches, Monsters, Oriental Mystics and Magicians* (all published by Doubleday); *Individuals All* (Macmillan); *The Private Labyrinth of Malcolm Lowry* (Holt, Rinehart, Winston); *Kabbalah: The Way of the Jewish Mystic* (Doubleday/Shambhala); and a forthcoming book *Crazy Clouds: Zen Radicals, Rebels, and Reformers* (Shambhala). Her fiction includes an autobiographical novel, *Pilgrimage* (Houghton Mifflin), stories published in *The Southern Humanities Review, Briarcliff Review,* and *Transatlantic Review.* She has written for publications as varied as *Mānoa, The Village Voice,* and *East/West.* Besserman teaches literature and writing at the

University of Hawaii.

Lyn Walters Buckley was born in Honolulu and educated in Hawaii's public schools. She lives in Nuuanu with her husband and 2-year-old son.

Meredith Carson has had poems published locally in *Hawaii Review, Chaminade Literary Review, Bamboo Ridge,* and *Poetry East-West.* She has self-published two small chapbooks and has taken many courses in poetry at the University of Hawaii since 1970 when she moved to Hawaii and decided to take up poetry seriously.

Sue Lin Chong would like to thank her family, friends, and especially the members of study group—the bearers of criticism and encouragement over the past several years.

Sue Cowing has lived in Honolulu thirty years. Her poems have appeared in *Bamboo Ridge, Chaminade Literary Review, Hawaii Review, Bloomsbury Review, Virginia Quarterly,* and *Wormwood Review.* She has collected a manuscript of poems entitled *The Photographer's Daughters* which includes a section of poems on turn-of-the-century artist Paula Modersohn-Becker.

Darlaine Mahealani Muilan Dudoit was born in Honolulu of a Chinese mother and a Hawaiian-Caucasian father. Her fiction has appeared in the *Chaminade Literary Review,* and in 1989 she won the Academy of Poets University and College Poetry Competition and the Ernest Hemingway Memorial Award for Poetry at the University of Hawaii-Manoa. She is currently working on her B.A. in English and Spanish at UH-Manoa.

Lisa Erb grew up in Hawaii. Her poems have appeared in *Mānoa, Chaminade Literary Review, Literary Arts Hawaii, Indiana Review, Sonora Review, Southern Poetry Review,* and *Suisun Valley Review.*

Audrey Forcier was born in Seoul, Korea in 1959. After attending Indiana University, she moved to the Big Island in 1981.

She is currently gallery director at the Volcano Art Center.

Epi Enari Fuaau was born in Western Samoa. In her late teens, she moved to American Samoa where she lived for eighteen years. She presently lives in Honolulu where she is studying for a Ph.D. in American Studies at the University of Hawaii-Manoa.

Sheila Gardiner first saw light of day somewhere in the wilderness of northern British Columbia and subsequently lived in Los Angeles, San Francisco, Seattle, New York City, and Sydney before settling in Hawaii in 1975. "I've been writing and taking workshops for eons, while single parenting three kids and surviving forty fascinating years of secretarial work."

Norma Wunderlich Gorst is a writer and editor who has lived in Hawaii for 21 years. She is grateful to *Bamboo Ridge Press* for many years of fine publishing and for this opportunity to appear again in one of their publications.

T. M. Goto has published poems in the continental United States *(Caprice, Genre)* as well as locally *(Bamboo Ridge, Brouhaha, Chaminade Literary Review, Hawai'i Review, Kaimana: Literary Arts Hawai'i, Pleiades, Rain Bird, Ramrod, Scrawling Wall, Voices)*. Since 1985 she has taught English at UH-Manoa, Leeward Community College, Kapiolani Community College, and Honolulu Community College, as well as Drama at Windward Community College. Currently completing her doctorate in Feminist Theatre, she is dedicated to reproductive rights.

Stella Jeng Guillory, born in Fujian Province, China, in 1942, did her undergraduate work in Taiwan and completed her graduate studies in Organic Chemistry at Cornell University in 1971. From 1971 to 1984 she worked as a researcher in the Department of Biochemistry and Biophysics at the University of Hawaii. She currently resides with her husband Richard and daughter Amber in Honolulu.

Jessica Hagedorn, born and raised in the Philippines and now living in New York, is the author of the novel *Dogeaters*, published by Pantheon Books in hardback and Viking/Penguin in paperback. *Dogeaters* was nominated for a National Book Award in 1990. She is presently at work on her second novel.

Marie Hara has published stories in *Bamboo Ridge, Chaminade Literary Review, Passages to the Dream Shore, Home to Stay,* and *The Best of Bamboo Ridge.* Her novel-in-progress *Lei* is about being *hapa* in Hawaii.

Mavis Hara would like to thank Priscilla Atkins, Juliet Lee, Cathy Davenport, and Jill Widner whose suggestions led to the present version of the story "Carnival Queen."

Lorna Hershinow teaches literature and writing at Windward Community College, and is HLAC's liaison for their People Who Write reading series. She is lately becoming a person who writes.

Diane Kahanu's role model was her brother Wayne. She was like a tail he grew. And while he experimented on her, and sometimes threw live lizards down the back of her dresses, he never cut her off or lost her.

Mahealani Kamauu is Executive Director of the Native Hawaiian Legal Corporation.

Faye Kicknosway, faculty at UH-Manoa, has published extensively in journals, magazines, and anthologies. She has received several awards for her work including in 1985 a National Endowment for the Arts Fellowship and a nomination for a Pulitzer Prize for her eighth collection of poetry, published by Viking Penguin, *Who Shall Know Them? All These Voices*, new and selected work, was published by Coffee House Press in 1986 and in 1989 a chapbook, *The Violence of Potatoes*, was published by Ridgeway Press.

Juliet S. Kono was born and raised in Hilo, Hawaii. She received her B.A. and M.A. from the University of Hawaii, Manoa. Her first book, *Hilo Rains*, was published by Bamboo Ridge Press in 1988. She teaches writing and lives with her husband in Honolulu.

Mari Kubo lives on the Big Island of Hawaii. She has always believed that truth is stranger than fiction, therefore perhaps out of truth we fashion our fiction.

Lynn Kuhns is a free-lance writer, owner of Communications, Ink, and lives on Oahu's Windward side. A graduate of the University of Wisconsin, she's written about shave ice, Dolly Parton, below-grade waterproofing, glider-riding, organic gardening, T-shirt art, and dolphins, among other things. She's currently working on a workbook for people who want to lose weight. While there's not much of a market for reflections about headless snapping turtles, she's glad to see a part of her Midwestern childhood in print.

Lee Kyselka is the mother of three, one of whom is the subject of a poem included in this anthology. After 30 years as a YMCA program director, she spent 10 years directing a summer science program at the University of Hawaii-Manoa. During the past decade, she has also worked with the Woman in Transition program at Windward and Leeward Community Colleges.

Cherylene Lee's plays have been performed by East West Players in Los Angeles, the Pan Asian Repertory Theatre in New York, the Asian American Theatre Company and the Chinese Cultural Center in San Francisco, Bay Area Playwrights Festival VII, and the Kumu Kahua Theatre in Honolulu. Her play *Yin Chin Bow* was co-winner of the 1990 "Best of Fest" for the Third Annual Spring Play Reading Series sponsored by the Third Step Theater in New York. She is currently a participant in the 1991 Mark Taper Mentor Playwrights Program in Los Angeles. Her poetry and short stories have been published by *The Southern California Anthology 1985, The International Examiner, Plexus, New Methods,* and she is particularly happy that her second appearance in *Bamboo Ridge* is in this volume by women.

Mary Lombard reads, swims, cooks and cleans, writes short stories and plays with her grandchildren in Lanikai where she lives with her husband and sons, Herman and Peter Mulder.

H. McManimie lives on the island of Kauai.

Mary Mitsuda was born in 1949 in Honolulu, works in all media, paints using six colors: red, blue, yellow, white, black and green.

Susan Nunes is the author of *A Small Obligation and Other Stories of Hilo* (Bamboo Ridge 1982) and three children's books, *Coyote Dreams* (Atheneum 1987), *Tiddalick* (Atheneum 1988), and *To Find the Way* (in press). Her short stories have been anthologized in several collections, most recently *Home to Stay* (Greenfield Review Press 1989) and *Stories from the American Mosaic* (Graywolf 1990). Ms. Nunes was born in Hilo and lived on Oahu for many years. She and her husband now make their home in Berkeley, California.

Joan Perkins received an A.B. from Vassar College, where she was awarded the school's Mark of Distinction (honors) for a creative thesis. Currently a graduate student in the Creative Writing Program at UH–Manoa, Perkins also teaches English literature at St. Andrew's Priory. She has previously published work in *Waluna*, a New York literary magazine.

Loretta Petrie is an administrator at Chaminade University and edits *Chaminade Literary Review*.

Kathy Phillips teaches English at the University of Hawaii. She has published a book entitled *Dying Gods in Twentieth Century Fiction* (Bucknell 1990).

Gloria Olchowy Rozeboom grew up on a small farm in north central Alberta in Canada. She has taught high school English for nine years and directed about forty plays. She is currently working on her M.A. in English at the University of Hawaii where her story won first place in the 1990-1991 Myrtle Clark Creative Writing Competition.

Marjorie Sinclair writes poetry, fiction, and biography. She lives and works in Honolulu.

Cathy Song is the author of *Picture Bride* (Yale), which won the Yale Series of Younger Poets Award and was nominated for the National Book Critics Circle Award, and *Frameless Windows, Squares of Light* (Norton). Her poetry has been widely anthologized in various collections including *The Morrow Anthology of Younger American Poets, The Heath Anthology of American Literature* and *The Norton Anthology of Modern Poetry*. She lives and teaches in Honolulu.

Susan Lee St. John lives in Kailua, Oahu with her husband Robert and their son Eliot. Her work has also appeared in *Pake: Writings by Chinese in Hawaii* and *The Forbidden Stitch: An Asian American Women's Anthology*. She currently teaches with the Poets-in-the-Schools.

Miyoko Sugano is associate professor of English at the University of Hawaii, Hilo. She is grateful to Cathy Song, Juliet Kono, Sue Cowing, and the other writers who gathered at the Volcano Arts Center Writing Workshop, Summer 1990 for the poems that emerged there.

M. Suzuki works as a freelance graphic designer while studying Glassblowing, Sculpture and English at the University of Hawaii at Manoa. Her poetry has been published in *Hawaii Review* and *Bamboo Ridge*.

Adrienne Tien: "I live in New York City's Chinatown, and although these streets have often been an inspiration, I look forward to moving to a quieter place with some green grass and trees in sight. Meanwhile, I am writing short stories, trying to get my third novel to come to life and working as a free-lance script supervisor in independent film production. I am also pleased to be recently married. My husband keeps looking over my shoulder and protesting that I haven't yet written a story about him."

Fuku Yokoyama Tsukiyama: "Although I was born on the Stanley Sherwood Ranch near the foothills of Salinas, California, Honolulu is my home, since I have lived here longer than I have anywhere else. I have lived and studied successively in the Salinas Valley schools; the Poston, Arizona concentration camp II; Philadelphia—RN state of Pennsylvania; Washington, D.C.; and the University of Hawaii (BA English). Interests: writing, tennis, reading Asian American literature, travel, drama, music."

Amy Uyematsu is a sansei from Los Angeles. She has been publishing poetry since 1983. Recent work can be seen in *Harbinger, Poetry/LA, West/Word 3,* and *Gidra 1990.*

Judith Vates is a nom de plume for Judith Dente-Matsuda. Vates is the Latin word for prophet. Sir Phillip Sidney and Thomas Hobbes acknowledged its use in reference to poets held in high esteem by the Greeks and Romans.

Jill Widner is living in Utah this year.

Tamara Wong-Morrison teaches poetry to elementary students as part of the Poets-in-the-Schools Program for the island of Hawaii. Her 15-year collection of poems, *Hawaii Voice: Bitter and Butterscotch* still awaits publication.

Holly Yamada lives in Honolulu.

Leona Yamada's work has been published in *Bamboo Ridge, Hawaii Review, Chaminade Literary Review,* and *Kentucky Poetry Review.* She has poems scheduled for publication in upcoming issues of *Blue Mesa Review* and *Contact II.*

Lois-Ann Yamanaka is originally from Hilo, Hawaii. She lives in

Kahaluu with her husband John and continues to write and write and write.

Chin Yung has been choreographing dances on the Big Island for the last fifteen years, drawing her inspiration from Pele and the volcano. She has also been actively creating, administering and teaching in educational programs which serve the arts, psychology, and women's issues and has received numerous grants and awards for this work. She would like to thank Cathy, Juliet, and *Bamboo Ridge* for nurturing her first publication.